ALSO BY C.J. RYAN

DEXTA
GLORIOUS TREASON

THE FIFTH
QUADRANT

C. J. RYAN

BANTAM BOOKS

THE FIFTH QUADRANT
A Bantam Spectra Book / October 2006

Published by
Bantam Dell
A Division of Random House, Inc.
New York, New York

Bantam Books, the rooster colophon, Spectra, and the portrayal of a
boxed "s" are trademarks of Random House, Inc.

ISBN-10: 0-553-58902-4
ISBN-13: 978-0-553-58902-3

Printed in the United States of America
Published simultaneously in Canada

www.bantamdell.com

OPM 10 9 8 7 6 5 4 3 2 1

THE FIFTH
QUADRANT

chapter 1

THE LIGHT OF THE TWO SUNS BEAT DOWN ON the baking streets of Cartago like a curse. One of them was small, blue, and hot; the other was fat, red, and less hot. They were separated in the sky by about the width of a fist held at arm's length, and Cartago whirled endlessly about a point somewhere between the two blazing orbs. In the streets they cast twin shadows, which angled away from one another slightly, as if reluctant to admit they knew each other.

Gloria VanDeen followed her host and his entourage through the swarming streets, enjoying the color and bustle and the singsong entreaties of the bazaar merchants. Exotic, fantailed phoenixbirds could be hers for only ten crowns, or perhaps even seven. Silken scarves and golden bangles and cotton caftans of the highest quality would only enhance her astonishing beauty, and at a price so low she would feel guilty for taking such advantage of the poor but honest merchants of Cartago; but the honor of being permitted to offer garments and jewelry to grace the famous form of

Gloria VanDeen would more than offset the financial loss. The most beautiful woman in all the Empire surely deserved no less than the finest craftsmanship and artistry in the entire Sector—nay, the entire Quadrant!

"I would buy you something as a souvenir," Praetor Ulmani said to her, "but that would surely cause a riot. The merchant whose wares you wore would become insufferable, and his competition, unable to bear their shame, would doubtless kill him."

"Then I suppose it's best that I wear nothing," Gloria said with a smile. "I wouldn't want to be responsible for a tragedy."

"Spirit forbid it!" Ulmani grinned at her. Since nothing—or very nearly nothing—was precisely what Gloria was wearing, the comment seemed apt. Her soft, flowing, nearly transparent garment rested lightly on her shoulders and descended in narrow vees of sheer white fabric, front and rear, shielding her from the suns but not from the hungry eyes that surrounded her.

Honestly, there were times when being Gloria VanDeen was just so damn much fun that it should have been illegal. Gloria smiled and waved happily to the throng in the streets, then let Ulmani take her elbow and usher her along.

The people of Cartago, like their Praetor, had many reasons to be grateful to Gloria VanDeen, and Gloria was aware that her beauty and sexual presence were prominent among them. Without those attributes, it was doubtful that she would have been able to fulfill the mission that had brought her here.

On this, the thirteenth day of January in the year 3218, Standard Calendar—just three days after her twenty-fifth birthday—Gloria VanDeen was the most famous, popular, and (quite possibly) important woman in an empire that spanned a sphere of space two thousand light-years in diameter and was home to some 3 trillion sentient beings. The fact that she was the former wife of the man who was now Emperor Charles V was of some importance, as was her position as head of the Office of Strategic Intervention—the newest action arm of the Department of Extraterrestrial Affairs, the sprawling bureaucracy that administered the Terran Empire. Alone, either one of those facts would have made her a woman of some consequence; together, they made her a potent force. But it was her beauty, brilliance, and courage that had won the hearts of the masses and made her, as was often said, the Sweetheart of the Empire.

At moments like this, Gloria was outrageously happy to be exactly who and what she was. She had just brought her mission on Cartago to a triumphant conclusion. And for a change, the intervention had been brief, bloodless, and relatively simple.

Cartago was a thirsty world, where a small population of some 5 million lived on the margins of a globe-girdling desert. Just 194 light-years from Earth, the planet had been settled some eight hundred years earlier in pre-Imperial days. In later years, it probably never would have been colonized at all, but in that first era of interstellar expansion, Earthmen were not very particular in their choice of new worlds. If a planet had oxygen in its atmosphere and a mean surface temperature somewhere between the freezing and boiling points of water, it was a candidate for settlement. Cartago qualified, if only just.

Over the centuries, the slowly growing population had splintered into what amounted to tribal groups, although the ethnic, cultural, and religious orientations of the three main tribes differed little. The only differences of real consequence concerned water and access to it. The Mountain Tribe controlled the flow of the precious liquid that trickled down to the dusty plains and the lands of the Eastern and Western Tribes. Accordingly, the Mountain Tribe had always selected the Praetor who headed the planetary government, such as it was. The coming of the Empire had remarkably little impact on Cartago, and generations of Imperial Governors and Dexta bureaucrats were content to let the natives work things out for themselves.

In recent years, however, the elders of the Eastern and Western Tribes had—for Spirit knew what bizarre reasons—taken to sending their brightest sons and daughters back to Earth to be educated in the law. Having nothing better to do when they returned to their homeworld, the young barristers began suing the other tribes over the only thing that mattered on their world— water. Thus, there had been angry protests, boycotts, insults, threats, and finally, the sequestration of water that had once flowed freely from the slopes of the central mountains. The Imperial Governor had been unable to persuade anyone to see the light of reason, and the tiny Dexta establishment on the planet had thrown up its arms in despair.

So Norman Mingus had sent Gloria to Cartago.

A year and a half earlier, before the creation of the OSI, Gloria—then a Level XIII Dexta bureaucrat—had used her wit and wiles to attract a thousand volunteers on the planet Pecos to help her avert a genocide on the backwater world of Mynjhino. Dexta Secretary Norman Mingus, taking note of her success, had recognized the extraordinary power she possessed and sought to employ it on a regular basis by appointing her to lead the new Office of Strategic Intervention. He had planned to use Gloria as his chessboard queen, dispatching her hither and yon throughout the Empire to hot spots where the existing bureaucratic machinery was failing to respond adequately to the challenges of the moment. In the year since the formation of the OSI, Gloria had only burnished her already gleaming reputation as the sexiest and most desirable woman in the Empire—and, in the process, had achieved some remarkable results for the benefit of Dexta and the Empire it served. She was wildly popular in every corner of the Empire—except, perhaps, for the Imperial Household itself, where Charles had yet to reconcile himself to the new role being played by the woman who had walked out on him nearly seven years earlier.

Cartago was the fifth intervention for Gloria and OSI, and by far, the easiest. Gloria hadn't even bothered to take along any staff; Cartago was just two days away from Earth via Flyer, and so help was relatively close at hand should any prove necessary.

None did. In less than two weeks on the planet, she had met with a handful of young lawyers, a clutch of tribal elders, and Praetor Ulmani, adroitly resolving their conflicts through a combination of judicious bribes and personal persuasion. The Dexta Comptroller would probably grumble about the bribes, small though they were, but Gloria had thoroughly enjoyed her sojourn on Cartago.

In fact, resolving the conflicts on Cartago had been so easy that Gloria seriously wondered if the whole mess had been cooked up by the young lawyers simply to lure her to their world. Probably not, she conceded; on a desert world, no one played games with water. Still, her fame and reputation had reached the point that she had to beware the Heisenberg Effect; her mere presence was enough to alter the terms of any equation.

At the moment, her presence in the streets of Cartago was altering the normal routine of the bazaar at searing midday, when energy levels and activity normally reached low ebb. Praetor Ulmani kept his grip on Gloria's elbow while his entourage of aides and security men plowed a path through the increasingly excited crowds. They could have taken an air-conditioned limo skimmer directly to the restaurant, but Ulmani had calculated that it could not hurt his popularity to be seen escorting Gloria through the teeming streets of his city. And Gloria didn't really mind being paraded as if she were one of Ulmani's hunting trophies; she was willing to let him get whatever political mileage he could out of the affair. He was a nice enough man and probably as good a leader as the planet needed. She was content to let him have his moment; all that really mattered to Gloria was that she had solved Cartago's problems and would soon be returning to Earth.

The outdoor restaurant was just ahead. Security men were already clearing a path while the maître d' stood before a large table in eager, fawning anticipation. Gloria impulsively decided to give everyone—not least of all Ulmani—one last reason to cheer. She turned to face Ulmani, pulled him close, and gave him an incendiary kiss. The cheers were deafening. Gloria released her hold on the astonished Praetor and grinned at him. "Your people adore you," she said.

"After this," Ulmani replied, "they may start worshipping me!"

They made their way through the wrought-iron gateway that delineated the restaurant, greeted the proprietor, and moved to the reserved table. One of Ulmani's aides pulled out a chair for her, and Gloria had just bent to be seated when the blue-green bolt of plasma crackled through the air just above her. The characteristic plasma thunderclap followed an instant later, as air rushed in to fill the ionized trail of the discharge. And just after that, Gloria heard the pained, startled moan from the aide standing behind her.

Before she could fully register what had happened, three security men were firing back, their plasma beams converging on a head and shoulders just visible on the rooftop across the street. The head and shoulders vanished in green fire, and the triple thunderclap echoed through the suddenly silent streets. As quickly as that, it was over.

Gloria was suddenly aware of the sharp smell of burned hair.

She looked around and saw Ulmani's aide slumping backwards against the white stucco wall of the building. Flames flickered along the torn sleeve of his garment and he stared in openmouthed wonder at the inch-in-diameter trench of blackened meat that now grooved his upper arm. Behind him, there was a smoldering hole in the wall.

Comprehension dawned, and Gloria slowly reached upward and ran her fingers through the singed tunnel that had scorched through her thick blond mane, just above her scalp.

I've been shot in the hair, she thought. *How very odd.*

chapter 2

GLORIA STOOD NAKED ON THE ALTAR BEFORE
fifty thousand entranced onlookers and an Empire-wide
vid audience that would eventually number a trillion or
more. As it was a Visitation Day, everyone else in the
cavernous Church of the Divine Spirit was naked, too,
including Archbishop Nesselrode, who stood next to her
as he droned on and on and on. What was there about
religion, she wondered, that turned so many people into
compulsive blabbermouths? Instead of standing in silent awe before their conception of the infinite, why did
people like the Archbishop feel the need to heap platitude upon platitude until the stack reached all the way
to the heavens above?

The Spirit Herself, at least, had been relatively con-
cise. Exactly eleven hundred and one years ago, to the
very hour—at this very spot—she had made her first
Visitation, in the middle of what was then a soccer stadium. She had spoken for just ten minutes, and, in her
six subsequent Visitations, never more than fifteen. It
made for a rather short gospel. In fact, the Book of the

Spirit was a remarkably slim volume for a document that had transformed human history.

After centuries of bloody conflicts, many of them inspired by religion, the Spirit had launched a new religion in the year 2117 that was now embraced by fully 70 percent of the Empire's population. It had been eleven centuries since the last religious war among humans, and no Spiritist had ever sponsored a pogrom, crusade, inquisition, jihad, or witch-hunt. The Spirit had made no miraculous claims nor offered magical spells and incantations; she demanded no extraordinary sacrifices and condemned only intolerance, greed, and stupidity. She threatened no hell and promised no heaven but the ones humans could make for themselves. Her gospel was gentle, worldly, even sensuous.

The Universal Church of the Spirit had grown in the wake of her Visitations and was now centered here, at the Mother Church in Rio de Janeiro. The church itself was one of the largest buildings on Earth, its main spire soaring nearly a kilometer above the rotating, circular altar where Gloria now stood, surrounded by legions of the faithful. She had come here today, in spite of many misgivings, to be honored for her life and her work—for her personification of the ideals and values espoused by the Spirit Herself.

It was ridiculous, of course. However, it also seemed unavoidable.

She had been putting off invitations from the UCS ever since her return from her mission to Sylvania, nearly six months ago. Events on that far-off world had been seized upon by devout Spiritists as living proof of the reality of the Spirit, and Gloria's role in those events had inspired their admiration. Gloria was all too aware of the underlying reality of those events but was hardly in a position to reveal the truth to the rest of the Empire. So here she was at last, very much against her will, being honored by people who would probably lynch her if only they knew the truth.

Some people even thought that Gloria resembled the Spirit. There was, perhaps, some truth in that assessment, if one ignored the fact that the Spirit's hair was raven while Gloria's was golden, and that Gloria was five-and-a-half feet tall to the Spirit's forty. But the Spirit's face, like Gloria's, was vaguely panracial in appearance, and her immense, nude body was every bit as attractive as Gloria's, although the Spirit's breasts were proportionately somewhat larger and her hips a bit broader.

But Gloria was real. The Spirit, according to the Cynics, was nothing more substantial than a clever holographic projection arranged by a band of maverick scientists, and her gospel nothing but a collection of slick catchphrases composed by advertising copywriters.

Gloria had always wanted to believe in the Spirit. Sometimes, she almost did. But after Sylvania, she now doubted that she ever really could. Sylvania had taught her how easy it was to create a fake deity and how eager people were to believe in one. Given the role that she had played in the fraud that was the Voice, Gloria could only assume that the Spirit had been a similar fraud.

Ironically, however, the Spiritists' enthusiastic acceptance of the Voice had probably forestalled an investigation that would undoubtedly have concluded with Gloria's spending the rest of her life on a prison world for high treason. It was therefore expedient for Gloria, finally, to accept the honors the Church wanted to bestow upon her. And in the long run, given her ambitions for her future at Dexta, it couldn't hurt to have close ties with the Spiritists. But still, it bothered her to be implicated so deeply in promoting the fraud of the Voice—and, presumably, the fraud of the Spirit.

But if the Spirit truly was a sham, it had been an incredibly effective and beneficial one—as had the Voice.

The Voice had helped save a planet from devastation, while the Spirit had probably kept the human race from destroying itself over a thousand years ago. Gloria found that she could not condemn a benevolent lie, any more than she could wholeheartedly embrace a destructive truth. People, in any case, would insist on believing whatever they wanted to believe. Today, they wanted to believe that Gloria VanDeen was an Avatar of the Spirit.

The Avatars of the Spirit (Gloria was about to become the 129th) were flesh-and-blood exemplars of the words and wisdom of the Spirit—in effect, they were saints for a religion that had no saints. Gloria didn't much care for the notion of becoming an Avatar of the Spirit, but the ceremony today would make her status official and eternal, as far as the Church was concerned.

During each of her Visitations, the Spirit had spoken of one of the Seven Seeds of Wisdom: Love, Compassion, Tolerance, Generosity, Knowledge, Joy, and Peace. Over the centuries, each of the Seeds had formed the core value of one of the Seven Septs of Spiritism. Members of the Church naturally gravitated to one or another of the Septs; doctors tended to embrace the Sept of Compassion, scholars belonged to the Sept of Knowledge, and so on. The Septs were not exactly separate denominations; they coexisted comfortably and compatibly under the broad tenets of Spiritist theology. The Sept of Joy was sponsoring Gloria's installation as an Avatar.

"Do not deny yourself Joy," the Spirit had counseled, "for it is a gift unto humankind and the wellspring of happiness." Theologians had generally taken "joy" to mean "sex," although the Spirit had never used precisely that word. The very fact that the Spirit had been nude argued that the human body was nothing to be ashamed of, and her warm endorsement of "joy" was taken as a sign that there was nothing sinful about sex. Indeed, some of the early Avatars of the Sept of Joy were courtesans, and one was an empress who earned a reputation rivaling that of Messalina. Gloria didn't think that she quite lived up to the standard set by her predecessors, and wasn't sure that she wanted to, but she could hardly deny that her sex life was as public and spectacular as anything the early thirty-third century had to offer.

Gloria had grown up at Court, under the reign of old Darius IV, when public nudity and sex were not only accepted but expected. Things had become more restrictive during the brief reign of grim, dour Gregory III; but now, under Charles, overripe decadence was once again the order of the day. That was fine with Gloria, who appreciated sex as much as anyone—more, in fact, since she possessed certain genetic enhancements that dramatically magnified her ability to give and receive pleasure. But she wasn't sure how she felt about her own sexuality being officially recognized and all but sanctified by the Church. Somehow, she felt, her volcanic orgasms ought to be a personal matter, if not necessarily a private one.

Archbishop Nesselrode reached his peroration, at long last, and Gloria leaned forward slightly as the Archbishop placed a gold chain necklace over her head. Depending from it was a ruby-red mustard seed, since the ruby was the designated gemstone of the Sept of Joy. With this symbolic act, Gloria was now confirmed as an Avatar of the Spirit.

Fifty thousand voices roared their approval. But Gloria could only stand there and smile wanly as the altar slowly rotated to let everyone view the Church's newest Avatar.

Holy shit, she thought.

FOLLOWING THE CEREMONY, GLORIA JOINED with Church officials and the media at a reception. She sipped wine and nibbled canapés while a procession of naked men and women shook her hand, offered their congratulations, and wished her continued Joy. Many, it was clear, wanted to share that Joy with her; a few seemed ready and willing to do it then and there. Gloria graciously declined.

She wondered if it was going to be this way from now on. She had mixed feelings about the public reputation she had acquired in the past year or so. At times she adored it, but there were others when she wished she could go back to being plain old Gloria VanDeen, anonymous Avatar of Nothing and Nobody's Sweetheart.

But no, that was ridiculous too. She was, after all, the former wife of the man who was now Emperor, and royals didn't wed anonymous nobodies. Gloria was a member of a wealthy and prominent family and her beauty had attracted boys and men ever since she first blossomed. She had a face that could probably launch about 990 ships, if not a thousand, and a body that could launch a thousand more. With a genetic heritage from six continents, she boasted a flowing blond mane, flawless skin the shade of coffee with a little cream, and arresting, exotically angled eyes the color of polished turquoise. Her lips were perhaps a little thin for perfection, but they curved upward slightly at the sides, in a hint of a permanent, bemused smile. Her body was slim and athletic, her breasts not large but firm, globular, and tipped by erect, cylindrical nipples. Her navel was artistically whorled; thanks to her genetic enhancements, it was—like her nipples—as erotically sensitive as the primary sexual features of any normal woman. She could achieve orgasms in mere seconds, if she chose, or drag them out endlessly until sheer exhaustion finally brought them to a halt. Sex with Gloria VanDeen was an experience no one ever forgot.

She was inescapably special, and knew it. But still . . . an Avatar of Joy?

Gloria sighed, shook her head slightly to clear away the reveries, and tried to focus on the next person who wanted to meet her. This one, anomalously, was wearing clothing, Visitation Day notwithstanding. And not just any clothing—he was decked out in the Imperial livery of the House of Hazar.

The young man leaned close and whispered in her ear. "Pardon the intrusion, Ms. VanDeen, but the Emperor would very much like to see you, at your earliest convenience."

Gloria had been afraid of this. The Emperor's main Residence was in Rio, and Charles was bound to have been aware that she was in the city.

"My earliest convenience? Tell him that would be in about five years, give or take."

The messenger, unsmiling, shook his head. "That won't do, ma'am. His Imperial Highness was quite clear that I was not to take no for an answer. There's a limo waiting just outside, and the Emperor instructed me to tell you that there will be absolutely no media present. You can come and go in complete privacy."

"There are media reps in this room right now," Gloria pointed out. "If they see me leaving with you . . ."

"They will report nothing, ma'am. The Household will see to that."

And, of course, the Household could. The Empire might have had nominal freedom of the press, but in some areas, that freedom was more theoretical than actual.

Gloria bowed to the inevitable. "Let me make my apologies to the Archbishop," she said.

THE LIMO DEPOSITED GLORIA AT THE ENTRANCE to the Imperial Horticultural Gardens on the grounds of the Residence. Here, exobotanists had assembled a unique collection of plant species from all over the

Empire, and had somehow gotten them to grow in harmony without annihilating either each other or the native species of Earth. The result, one critic had noted, looked as if Salvador Dali had taken up gardening.

Gloria wandered through the gateway, past a bright blue hedge, and under the drooping boughs of a quaking willow from DeSantos IV; when she brushed against its fronds, they drew back as if in fright. She spotted Charles strolling along a pathway between a fragrant, carnivorous gluetree from somewhere in the Pleiades Cluster and a pygmy sequoia that was all of four feet tall from a high-gravity world. The Emperor smiled and nodded at the sight of her, and casually walked onward in her direction.

"What's this?" he asked, pointing at her. "Clothing? On a Visitation Day? I would have expected better from an Avatar of Joy."

"It may be a Visitation Day, and this may be Rio," Gloria replied, "but back home in Manhattan, it's still January."

"Indeed. Tell me, have you had any snow there yet? The Imperial Climatologist tells me we'll see it in our lifetime."

"Not that I've noticed. But I hear they had a little up in Poughkeepsie last year."

"Something to look forward to, then. What fun, waiting for an ice age." Charles stopped in front of Gloria and held out both hands to her. She hesitated a moment, then took them in hers. They held each other and stared in silence for what felt like a long time.

Charles, at twenty-eight, was looking more like an Emperor with each passing year. His medium-length dirty blond hair was artlessly tousled over the tops of his ears, and his closely trimmed beard emphasized rather than concealed the arrogant thrust of his chin. His nose was characteristic of the Hazar Dynasty, being rather long and bony, and his watery blue eyes seemed to radiate condescension. He was still slim and fit, and was tall enough to look down on most people with lofty nonchalance.

It had been nearly a year since Gloria had seen him face-to-face. Upon her return from Mynjhino, Charles had seen fit to award her a Distinguished Service Medal; having been embarrassed and frustrated by her performance during that episode, he had concluded that the only way to deal with it was to reward her. On the other hand, her service on Sylvania had inspired no award, only icy silence.

Charles finally released his grip on her hands and gave her an appraising once-over with his eyes. She was clothed now, true, but only minimally, in a pale blue wrap dress that was loosely fastened at the waist, exposing far more than it covered.

"You've done something to your hair," he said at last.

"Oh . . . yes, something was done to it," Gloria admitted. Her hairdresser in Manhattan had performed some creative first aid on her damaged 'do following her return from Cartago, and her long, Dura-styled mane now flowed halfway down her back in apparent good health.

"So I heard," Charles said. "Dammit, Glory, if Mingus keeps sending you to these two-crown shit holes, sooner or later you are going to get seriously hurt. And for what? So a bunch of provincials can water their fucking lawns?"

"People live on those shit holes, Charles," Gloria responded. "They have rights and needs, the same as anyone else in the Empire. Dexta does what it can to see that they receive the respect and attention they are due."

"Spoken like the career bureaucrat you've become," Charles snorted.

"Thank you." Gloria smiled. "That's the nicest thing you've said to me in years."

Charles shook his head in evident disgust. "I cannot fathom why you are at Dexta. I never could. It's a barbaric environment, as I'm sure even you would admit, considering everything that was done to you when you started out there. And now you've become Mingus's Girl Friday, which I find appalling."

"I'm sure *you* would."

"He's a hundred and thirty years old!"

"A hundred and thirty one," Gloria corrected. "Why, Charles, are you *jealous*?"

"Please, don't be disgusting. If you are fucking the old coot, I'd rather not know about it."

"Actually," said Gloria, "I'm not. By his choice, not mine, I hasten to point out."

"Wise of him," Charles said. "He's too old to handle an Avatar of Joy." Charles looked upward toward the treetops and the sky and shook his head. "An Avatar of Joy, Spirit save us! You know, don't you, that if it weren't for the damned Spiritists, you'd probably be spending the rest of your life on a prison world for what you did on Sylvania?"

"Me?" Gloria asked innocently. "What did *I* do?"

"You know damned well what you did! You ruined a quadrillion crowns' worth of Fergusite. Only I can't touch you for it, because of the fucking Voice and the idiot Spiritists who think the whole thing was divine intervention, instead of a plot—a goddamn conspiracy—by you and Mingus! Don't deny it, Glory. I don't know how you managed that business with the Voice, but—"

"Oh, ye of little faith!" Gloria laughed.

Charles seemed about to respond, but stopped himself abruptly and reeled in his rage. He walked down the path a few paces and pointed at a large, gnarled tree a few meters away. "Know what that is?" he asked.

"Beats me."

"It's a glashpadoza tree. The native species on Belonna V believe that the glashpadoza absorbs all of the sins of the clan that grows it. That's why it's so hellishly ugly." He turned to look at her. "Would you care for a cutting?"

"Are you suggesting that I need my own glashpadoza tree?"

"Don't you?"

Gloria considered the question seriously. She had committed many sins on Sylvania, and the business with the Voice and the Fergusite was far from the most serious. A spaceship with five evil men in it had never reached its destination, and only Gloria knew the reason.

She looked again at the tree. "I might have a good spot to grow one of those at my place on Long Island," she said finally.

"I thought you might," Charles said. "I'll have the Imperial Gardener see to it."

Charles went over to her, stared into her face for a moment, then carefully put his arm around her shoulders and drew her closer. She didn't resist.

"I know more about what happened on Sylvania than you think I do," he said softly. "I'm not saying you were wrong. If it had been me, I'd have done the same—or worse, probably. But tell me, Glory, are you planning to make a habit of that sort of thing?"

She looked up into his eyes. "What if I am?" she asked.

"Then don't just play at it," he said. "Don't think you can go around dispensing justice and righteousness, ad hoc, on behalf of Dexta, because you can't. Sooner or later it will catch up with you, and not even Norman Mingus—not even *I*—will be able to save you from the consequences. If you're going to do it, do it right."

"What do you mean?"

"Don't do it as a Dexta drone, Glory. Or even as an Avatar of Joy. Do it as Empress!"

• • •

GLORIA WAS TAKEN ABACK BY CHARLES'S PRO-
posal. A year and a half ago, just before she left for
Mynjhino, he had made it clear that he wanted her back;
but she had long since chosen another path and had no
intention of retreating into Charles's waiting arms.

They had married young and divorced young. At the
time, Charles was seventh in line to the throne, then
sixth after old Darius finally died, and seemed unlikely
ever to be Emperor. He seemed unlikely, in fact, ever to
be much of anything other than a wealthy, privileged
wastrel. He had persuaded her to suspend her educa-
tion, and together they had spent much of their marriage gadding about the Empire in his luxurious yacht.
But in her travels, Gloria had become fascinated with
exosociology: the study of the lives and cultures of the
Empire's many denizens, human and otherwise. When
she decided to return to school and continue her studies, Charles had absolutely forbidden it. So she had left
him and never looked back.

More than two years later, after Gloria had completed her studies and joined Dexta, a botched coup
known as the Fifth of October Plot had killed Gregory,
his two sons, and three of his nephews, leaving the
Imperial throne to Charles. Gloria had sighed in relief at
her narrow escape from having become Empress. The
last thing she wanted was to be a useless, ineffectual ornament to the reign of Charles V. She drew immense
satisfaction from her work at Dexta, and would have
been miserable if condemned to spend her life in ceremonial playacting.

She broke away from Charles and began walking
down one of the pathways at a brisk pace. Charles followed behind, apparently content to give her some
space.

Empress! Spirit, why did he think she would want

to be Empress? She had more real power now, as head of the Office of Strategic Intervention, than most Empresses ever dreamed of possessing. There had been an unbroken line of forty-seven male Emperors, dating back to Hazar the Great in 2522, 696 years ago. Unlike the kings and potentates of antiquity, producing male offspring was no hit-or-miss proposition for the Emperors of the Terran Empire. Empresses were simply the wives of Emperors, and not rulers in their own right.

Oh, five or six of them had obtained considerable power, being married to weak or dim-witted men, but they were the exceptions rather than the rule. And some Emperors had done without Empresses altogether, preferring to sire their offspring with a series of Imperial Consorts.

"I know what you're thinking," Charles said from behind her. "But this would be different. I'd give you real power, Glory."

Gloria stopped so abruptly that she skidded forward a bit on the crushed stone of the pathway. She whirled around and faced Charles.

"And what is that supposed to mean?" she demanded.

"Just what I said. Real power. We'll work out the provisions in detail, put it in writing, sign it, and publish it. I wouldn't be able to back out even if I wanted to."

She stared at him, took a couple of steps toward him, then stopped and stared at him some more, her eyes narrowing in suspicion. "What are you up to, Chuckles?"

He grinned at her. "No good, I assure you. No good at all. But since you insist, I shall reveal to you the details of my nefarious plot." Charles closed the distance between them and put his hands on her shoulders. "What I intend," he said, "is to wed and bed the most beautiful and popular woman in the Empire so that we can fuck each other like crazed minks whenever we want. And what's more, I want that woman to give me the benefit of her very great intelligence, creativity, and courage in ruling an Empire of three trillion sentient beings, every one of whom would be thrilled and delighted to have her for their Empress. There, you see? An evil plot, if ever there was one."

"You're serious, aren't you?"

"Entirely. You'd be, if you like, my coruler. I would retain primacy, of course—the laws would require that in any event. But you would have full authority in virtually any area that you prefer. Spirit, Glory, I have no interest in doing half the things I'm required to do, anyway! Believe me, I'd *welcome* sharing the load with you. And the people would love it. Together, we'd be the best rulers this old Empire has ever seen!"

"And . . . ?" Gloria prodded. She wasn't ready to buy into this fantasy just yet.

Charles removed his hands from her shoulders and stepped back. He nodded and said, "And . . . I'm under increasing pressure these days to produce an heir, one way or another. I could find an acceptable Consort easily enough, but I'd much prefer to do it with you. Hostmother, of course, so you needn't trouble yourself with a pregnancy. And it really is necessary, Gloria. I mean, you know who's next in line of succession at the moment, don't you? Cousin Larry. And I know what you think of *him*."

"Larry?" Gloria groaned. "Lord Brockinbrough the Detestable?"

"The very one. How did you describe him that time? Old enough to be my father, unscrupulous enough to be my brother, and immature enough to be my son? Wonderful line, that. Even Larry appreciated it. Anyway, I really need to cook up a more appropriate heir, and there is no DNA I'd rather entwine with mine than thine."

Gloria frowned, looked at the ground, chewed her lower lip for a moment, then looked back up at Charles. "And . . . ?"

"And," Charles said with a laugh, "your approval numbers in the polls are better than mine. I don't want to spend the next century competing with you, Glory. I'd rather pool our resources. And there's one more *and.*"

"Which is?"

Charles wrapped his arms around her, pulled her to him, and kissed her with Imperial urgency. She responded with urgency of her own. Time and turmoil dissolved, disappointments and frustrations faded away; whatever had gone wrong between them, some things remained as right and inevitable as they had been in the beginning. He tightened his hold on her, and she made no attempt to resist. Moments later they lay sprawled in the grass beneath the gnarled limbs of the glashpadoza tree.

chapter 3

IN MIDAFTERNOON, GLORIA TRANSITED BACK to Dexta Headquarters in Manhattan, after spending two hours rolling in the grass beneath the glashpadoza tree with the Emperor. Charles had genetic enhancements of his own, and despite his essentially selfish nature, he was a marvelous lover. Whatever regrets Gloria had about their marriage, they didn't include sex.

She walked along the main concourse, feeling every eye on her, as if people somehow knew she had just been humping the Emperor. But what an afternoon . . .

Empress! Spirit!

She had made no commitment, but she hadn't said no, either. That, in itself, surprised her. It was an offer that could not be dismissed casually, if at all. Certainly, it would be a life-changing decision. Charles understood that and didn't press the issue; they had agreed that both of them would give the matter more thought.

Gloria got into an elevator with several people she didn't know and said, "Forty," where the OSI had its offices. She heard two women standing behind her giggling to each other and resisted an urge to turn and look.

Another woman said, "Congratulations, Ms. VanDeen." Gloria's eyebrows shot upward. How could she have known?

Sensing Gloria's confusion, the woman added, "About being selected as an Avatar of the Spirit, I mean. That's quite an honor."

"Oh, yes, of course. Thank you."

"It reflects well on Dexta," the woman said. "We're all very proud of you." There were more giggles from behind her. The car reached the fortieth floor and Gloria smiled good-bye and stepped out, feeling relieved. Between Charles and the Church, Gloria was feeling strangely vulnerable and conspicuous today.

She entered the outer office of the OSI and stood just inside the door for a few seconds, like a queen bee surveying her hive. After a slow and uncertain start, the Office of Strategic Intervention was now a going concern, vibrant and humming with activity and purpose. They had handled five interventions, which had required Gloria's personal presence on the affected worlds, and were now ratcheting up their operations to include a host of lesser matters that could benefit from the OSI's attentions. Gloria had soon realized that she couldn't go everywhere and do everything herself, and there was really no need. She had assembled a crackerjack staff, and her people relished their assignments.

She smiled to her troops as she made her way to her own office and accepted their congratulations. Guarding the door to her inner sanctum, as usual, was her Executive Assistant and best friend, Petra Nash.

"Good afternoon, Your Avatarness," Petra said. "How does it feel to be a holy-holy?"

"Just fine," Gloria answered. "Anything happening that I need to know about?"

"A couple of messages on your console, nothing

real urgent. Grant Enright is still in Bombay with the GalaxCo people, and Althea is off to Luna for a long weekend with someone whose name I'm not supposed to mention, so I can't tell you that it's the Duke of Glastonbury. Jill Clymer says she'll have a report on some potential mess in Sector 19 for you tomorrow, and, let's see, Phil Benz wanted me to remind you that he's got Naval Reserve duty coming up next week. And if you have a few minutes, Pug and I need to talk with you."

"Certainly. Just come on in."

"Will do. Give me a minute to find the Pugnacious One."

Gloria smiled and watched for a moment as Petra got up from her desk and went off in search of Pug Ellison, her assistant, roommate, and lover. Petra was positively glowing these days, and Gloria could only marvel at the way her friend had blossomed with new-found self-confidence over the past six months. At Gloria's urging and with Pug's ardent approval, Petra was trying to be less of a Dog and more of a Tiger, and seemed to be managing the transition with style and enthusiasm. Today, she was showing her Tiger stripes in a gray miniskirt that barely concealed her shapely bottom and a matching jacket buttoned only at the waist to show off the subtle curves of her small, pert breasts.

In the metaphorical (but quite real) menagerie of Dexta, there were Lions, Tigers, Dogs, Moles, and Sheep. The Lions, mostly male, were the natural leaders, relying on strength and force of personality to secure their positions. Tigers, mostly female, were sleek and beautiful, using sex the way Lions used strength. Dogs came in two breeds: Pack Dogs, who roamed the lower levels of the bureaucracy as feral predators, savaging the weak and unprotected, and Lap Dogs, whose loyalty won them the patronage and protection of a willing superior. Moles were sneaky bureaucratic infighters, and the numerous Sheep were the anonymous, workaday backbone of the system.

The species had evolved over the centuries because Dexta was, by design, a Darwinian jungle where only the strong and smart could hope to survive and flourish. Each year, a hundred thousand new Level XV staffers joined Dexta, and fully 20 percent of them failed to survive the first twelve months. The Fifteens—and, indeed, everyone else, to one degree or another—were subjected to every imaginable form of social, psychological, physical, and sexual abuse in the brutal environment of Dexta. The point of it all was to weed out the weaklings and assure that those who remained functioned at peak efficiency all the time. The system was cruel and often downright sadistic, but it worked, and that was all that really mattered.

Both Gloria and Petra had almost failed to survive that first dreadful year. Gloria managed by becoming a Tiger—predator rather than prey—and Petra had become her faithful assistant and Lap Dog. Gloria was, with her background, breeding, and beauty, a natural Tiger in any case, while Petra—a diminutive, clever, but insecure refugee from an impoverished home in nearby Weehawken—had taken a while to work out for herself just who and what she was and wanted to be. But she seemed to have hit her stride finally, and Gloria was happy for her.

Gloria sat down at her desk, checked her console for a few moments, then looked up as Petra arrived with Pug in tow. Pug—Palmer, formally—was a good-looking young man with brown hair, blue-gray eyes, and open, friendly features. He was a bit under medium height, which left him a good seven or eight inches taller than Petra. And, at twenty-four, nearly three years younger. He was a Level XIV to Petra's Level XIII, but didn't seem to mind being her assistant. He was, in fact, extravagantly grateful to Gloria for bringing him aboard as a permanent member of the OSI team.

She had originally recruited him for the mission to Sylvania the previous spring, when OSI needed a band of independently wealthy, big-bucks bureaucrats who could stand up to the get-rich-itch that seemed to infect everyone who came to that brawling boomworld. Pug, a Level XV at the time, had been eager to prove that he was more than just a member of a fabulously wealthy family from New Cambridge, and his work had impressed Gloria. He and Petra had caught each other's eyes, and eventually they wound up in each other's arms.

Back in Manhattan, Gloria had used her clout as the Level X head of OSI—and her personal wealth—to secure a sumptuous apartment for Petra and Pug in the same midtown building as her own glamorous penthouse, three blocks from Dexta HQ. Normally, Thirteens and Fourteens resided in designated Dexta quarters in Brooklyn, but Gloria felt she owed Petra something better after their perilous and painful mission on Sylvania. For Petra, who'd grown up in dire poverty, the apartment seemed like a palace; for Gloria, who'd grown up in an actual palace, the apartment seemed a pittance. Gloria still felt guilty about what had happened on Sylvania, even though Petra, blessedly, had no coherent memories of the rape and assault that had nearly killed her.

Gloria got up from her desk and went over to the couch, beckoning Pug and Petra to join her there. Pug first got them coffee and tea, while Petra leaned close and inspected Gloria's new ruby mustard seed. "That's gotta be the smallest gem I've ever seen you wear," she said. "Usually they're about the size of softballs."

"We Avatars are a modest lot," Gloria explained. "So, what did you want to see me about?"

"Cartago," said Pug as he handed her a cup of coffee, then sat next to Petra on the couch. "We've gotten the initial report back from IntSec, and it's a little troubling. The Bugs have also turned up some additional information that—well, I'll let you characterize it for yourself. But it's a bit strange."

"Make that a *lot* strange," Petra amplified.

"Oh? Let's hear it."

"Well, first of all, the shooter on Cartago," said Pug. "There wasn't a lot left of him, and the DNA trace was inconclusive. That's not too surprising in itself. I mean, there are three trillion people in the Empire, and we don't have definitive genotypes on all of them. But the analysts do say, with a ninety-five percent confidence level, that the shooter was not a native of Cartago. And in light of what we've learned about the weapon . . . Well, as I said, it's troubling."

"What about the weapon?"

"It was a Mark IV plasma rifle."

"A Mark *IV*?" Gloria asked. "I thought those were obsolete."

"Not obsolete, exactly," Pug said. "I mean, they still work. But they've been outdated for about thirty or forty years. But this particular weapon is of special interest. You see, according to the serial number, it was a part of a shipment to Savoy at the beginning of the war with the Ch'gnth."

"Savoy? You're kidding!"

Pug shook his head. "The numbers check out. According to the records, that particular weapon was manufactured on Ostwelt in June of 3163, and shipped to Savoy that September, just a week before the Ch'gnth attack."

"Savoy!" Gloria exclaimed, impressed by the very mention of the name. To a denizen of the early-thirty-third-century Empire, saying that the rifle had come from Savoy was like saying it had come from Waterloo or Gettysburg. The Empire's last great war, against the Ch'gnth Confederacy, from 3163 to 3174, had been a desperate struggle, and it had all turned on the outcome of the first crucial battle for Savoy, in September 3163. The Empire's garrison on Savoy—and the entire population of the colony—had been wiped out by the Ch'gnth, but their last-ditch resistance had bought crucial time that allowed the Imperial Navy to assemble a fleet. It had struck back at Savoy in one of the most decisive naval engagements in history. Military historians compared it with Salamis and Midway. It had turned the tide of the war and led to the eventual Imperial victory.

"So," Gloria said, "we have a shooter who's not from Cartago using a weapon that should have been destroyed fifty-odd years ago. And for some reason, he wanted me dead."

"Initially," Pug said, "the Bugs figured that he may have been connected to PAIN or PHAP, but he could just as easily have been working a zamitat contract, or just some freelance nutcase." PAIN—the People's Anti-Imperialist Nexus—was an anarchist terrorist organization of marginal efficiency, and PHAP—the Pan-Human Alliance for Purity—was a racist fringe group of doubtful sanity. The zamitat was an Empire-wide criminal network, with ancestral ties leading back to the Mafia, the Yakuza, and similar organizations on other worlds. Gloria couldn't imagine why any of them would have targeted her.

"I can't see PHAP," Gloria said. "No aliens on Cartago. PAIN, you can never tell about, but they don't usually go in for solo assassinations. And I don't think the zamies have anything against me."

"Maybe not," Pug said, "but there's something else."

"This is the troubling part," Petra said.

"Which is . . . ?"

"This," said Pug, "is the second Mark IV plasma rifle from the Savoy shipment that has turned up in the past week."

"Last night," Petra said, "we received a report from

Watami III, in Sector 23. Six days ago, there was a terrorist attack on the Dexta offices there. They killed seven of our people, including the Imperial Secretary, along with three civilians who happened to be in the office. The complete list of victims is in your console."

"Spirit!" Gloria said, genuinely shocked by the news. "What happened?"

"Details are still a bit sketchy," Pug told her, "but it seems that three people burst into the office and opened up with plasma rifles. An Internal Security man killed one of them, but the other two made a clean getaway. Apparently they just fired at random, killing anyone they could. An hour later, PAIN released a statement on Watami, claiming credit for the attack."

"And then," Petra said, "this morning we got a report of another attack, four days ago on Kyushu Prime in Sector 20. Same sort of thing—three attackers with plasma rifles shooting up the Dexta office. Only four dead in this one—two Dexta, two civilian. And all of the attackers got away. Again, PAIN claimed it as their work."

Gloria leaned back on the couch, a deep frown creasing her features. "What the hell is going on?"

"IntSec is still putting it all together," said Pug. "Volkonski says he'll have a report for you in a couple of hours. But here's the thing that Petra and I are worried about. The terrorist who was killed on Watami was also using a Mark IV plasma rifle. And that rifle was also part of that Savoy shipment of 3163."

Gloria silently stared at Petra and Pug for several seconds.

"When Arkady gave us the initial report from Internal Security," Petra said, "he was very insistent about scheduling a meeting to set up coverage for you." Arkady Volkonski, head of the OSI's IntSec section, took it as his life's mission to see to it that nothing bad ever happened to Gloria or anyone else in OSI. He was, in Gloria's view, a trifle overzealous about it.

"He thinks," Pug said, "and we agree, that PAIN was also behind the attack on you on Cartago. From their point of view, it would make sense. They hate Dexta and the Empire, and you are a prominent symbol of both."

"Yes, but—" Gloria started to protest, then broke off. She didn't want to accept the notion that PAIN had specifically targeted her, but the evidence was staring her in the face. "The weapon," she said with glum resignation.

Pug nodded. "The Bugs don't have a clue how those weapons suddenly turned up, but they clearly connect Cartago with the other two attacks. Volkonski says you need protection, and Petra and I agree."

"I'll see him tomorrow," Gloria said, hoping she could find a reason between now and then to avoid it. She didn't like the fact that the crazies in PAIN wanted her dead, but she was also not about to submit to the round-the-clock attentions of the Bugs.

"Gloria?" Pug leaned around Petra to look at her.

"What?"

"Your safety is our primary concern, of course," he said. "But there's also a larger issue here."

"The weapons," Gloria said.

"Exactly. How in hell are weapons that were supposedly lost more than fifty years ago on Savoy popping up now? How did PAIN get their hands on them? And what happened to those weapons in the first place, back in 3163? We're going to need to do some serious historical research, and not all of the records we need are on Earth."

"Where are they?"

"Well," Pug said, "you know that things used to be organized a little differently. I mean, back before the war, before Secretary Mingus took over and reorganized the Department. Quadrant Administration used to be out in the field, not here in Manhattan. Savoy is in Quadrant 4—and both attacks on Dexta offices were also in Quadrant 4—so we'd need to go to the actual site of the old Quad Administration offices to get at the original records."

Gloria frowned. "I asked a simple question," she said. "For some reason, I'm not getting a simple answer. Just where is the actual site of the old Quad Administration offices?"

"Well . . ."

"On New Cambridge, Gloria," Petra broke in, rescuing Pug from further circumlocutions.

"Aha," Gloria said.

Pug smiled in embarrassment. "I was afraid you might think . . ."

"That you wanted an excuse for a little working vacation on your homeworld?"

"Um, well . . ."

"We'll have none of that in *my* office," Gloria declared firmly. "If it is necessary to send someone to New Cambridge to investigate this matter, they will go there to *work*. Is that understood?"

"Yes, ma'am."

"Good. Now, I think this does deserve further investigation, and I think it makes sense to send someone who is already familiar with New Cambridge and has connections there. I suppose that means you, Pug, but I'm reluctant to send a Fourteen off on an important field assignment without proper supervision. I think you need at least a Thirteen along to make sure you keep your nose to the grindstone and don't fritter away your time on family reunions and sightseeing tours and romantic getaways. Petra, I suppose I can rely on you to see to all of that?"

"Absolutely!"

"I knew I could count on you. Now, it occurs to me that this year's Quadrant Meeting is in Quad 4, and it's scheduled for New Cambridge in a few weeks. I wanted to get to that, myself. Ever been to a Quadrant Meeting?"

Both Pug and Petra shook their heads. "I went to one three years ago," Gloria said, smiling at the memory. "Quite a show."

Each year, on a rotating basis, one of the Quadrants hosted a grand gathering of the tribes. In an empire where communications took days or weeks, it was important for Dexta people to have a chance to make personal contact with their far-flung coworkers. Conflicts and controversies could be resolved face-to-face at the Quadrant Meetings, and they gave the Dexta brass an opportunity to assess the mood and morale of their troops. The formal agenda at the meetings always included a stupefying round of panels, committees, speeches, and seminars. Informally, much else happened.

"It's like going to the circus," Gloria said. "Anyway, I think the two of you should leave as soon as possible in order to have some results to report by the time I get there. I'll get a Flyer for you. Can you leave, say, the day after tomorrow?"

Pug and Petra grinned at her. "Anything you say, Gloria," Pug said.

"Uh . . . there is one thing, though," Petra added. "If we're going to be digging around in official Dexta records for the Quadrant—I mean, when we aren't frittering away our time with family reunions, sightseeing tours, and romantic getaways—we really ought to get authorization from the Quadrant Administrator."

"Good idea," Gloria said. "And while we're at it, another thought occurs to me. You said Jill Clymer has something brewing in Sector 19? That's Quad 4, too. Get her in here, then get me an appointment for this afternoon, if possible, with Cornell DuBray."

"Wow," said Petra. "The Quad Admin himself? Level Four?"

"We Avatars of the Spirit," Gloria said grandly, "don't bother with mere underlings. Anyway, I've been looking for an excuse to get acquainted with the upper-level Eagles, and this will do." She got to her feet and walked to her desk.

"Uh, Gloria . . . ?"

"What, Petra?"

"I think you ought to change before you go see DuBray."

"Why? What's the matter with what I've got on?"

Petra walked over to Gloria and reached for her back. She plucked something off it and held it up for Gloria to see. It was a blade of grass.

"And there are some grass stains, too."

Gloria rolled her eyes. No wonder people had been staring and giggling behind her back all afternoon! And that bastard Charles hadn't said a word . . .

"Life's just one big roll in the grass for you Avatars, huh?" Petra grinned impishly at her boss.

"Do not deny yourself joy," Gloria intoned dryly.

"Don't worry, we won't. And thanks, Gloria!"

GLORIA ENTERED THE OFFICE OF QUADRANT 4 Administrator Cornell DuBray dressed, she felt, like a proper Avatar of Joy. She had changed to a white lace band skirt—just a hoop of all-but-transparent fabric four inches wide—slung low on her hips. Her breasts were similarly covered, but not at all concealed, by a narrower hoop of the same fabric. She didn't normally come so close to outright nudity in the office, but it was, after all, a Visitation Day. And, in any case, she wanted to make a strong first impression on DuBray.

Far above the lowly Lions, Tigers, and Dogs in the Dexta pecking order were the Eagles—Level VII's and above—who actually ran the organization. Normally, a Level X like Gloria would never have any contact with a

Level IV like DuBray. But the Charter of the Office of Strategic Intervention, written by Norman Mingus himself, gave Gloria broadly defined powers and responsibilities and virtually unlimited access to Dexta personnel and records.

She had checked DuBray's file before coming to his office to gain a little more insight into a man who was already something of a Dexta legend. Cornell DuBray—ninety-seven years old and still as handsome and vigorous as a man half his chronological age—had been Quad 4 Admin for nearly forty-two years. For purposes of comparison, Gloria noted that DuBray's fellow Quadrant Administrators had been at their respective posts for twenty-three, nine, and six years. He had taken over the slot from Norman Mingus in 3176, when Mingus became the Dexta Secretary. He was the odds-on favorite to succeed Mingus as Secretary when Mingus finally retired or died—assuming he ever did.

During his tenure in Quad 4, DuBray had built a reputation as a tireless, ruthless, and sometimes tyrannical Administrator who never forgot a friend or a foe, and whose rewards for the former and punishments for the latter were equally lavish. There was nothing about it in the files, but it was said around Dexta that some of DuBray's early opponents had wound up on high-gravity prison worlds; there were, apparently, no recent opponents. DuBray's loyalty to Norman Mingus was unshakeable, and it was reciprocated by the Dexta Secretary.

He greeted Gloria at the door and ushered her into his palatial 110th-floor office. DuBray was just over six feet tall, beefy but not fat, and had long, pompadoured silvery locks and a thin mustache to match. His nose suggested Hazar blood, and his full lips looked supple and feminine. He had been married four times—leaving him one wife shy of Norman Mingus—and was said to pursue a sex life that the Sept of Joy might have noted with approval. He clasped Gloria's hands in his and stared at her, head to toe, with undisguised appreciation.

"Ms. VanDeen," he said, "it is a true pleasure to meet you at last. I suspected and hoped that our paths would cross eventually. Norman speaks of you often, and holds you in the highest regard. And I believe congratulations are in order today, are they not? I don't know that Dexta has ever had its own Avatar of the Spirit."

"Actually, there have been three," said Gloria, who had checked, "although it's been two hundred years since the last one. But thank you, Mr. DuBray. I've been looking forward to meeting you, as well. I had hoped to make the rounds of all the Quadrant Administrators long before now, but OSI has kept me pretty busy."

"So I gather," said DuBray. "Can I get you something to drink? Some wine, perhaps?"

"That would be lovely," Gloria said. She took a seat on a divan facing the windows, giving her a magnificent view of the January sunset over New Jersey. DuBray joined her on the divan a moment later, gave her a goblet of red wine, and clinked glasses with her.

"To Dexta," he said. "And to our mutual friend and patron, Norman Mingus."

"Long may he wave," Gloria said. She took a sip of the wine and found it excellent.

"A cabernet from the vineyards of Sonoma III, vintage 3196. The finest wine in my Quadrant and, for my money, the entire Empire."

"It's marvelous," Gloria agreed, taking another sip.

"I'm glad you think so. I'll have a case of it sent to you."

"Oh, please, don't trouble yourself."

"It's no trouble at all, I assure you," DuBray said, smiling wolfishly. "I didn't say I'd deliver it myself. Although I would be happy to do just that. You truly are a remarkably beautiful woman, Ms. VanDeen. I've seen the vids, of course, but having you here—in the flesh, as it were—adds an entirely new dimension to my appreciation of your charms."

"That's very nice of you to say, Mr. DuBray. And please, call me Gloria."

"Very well, I shall. Now tell me, Gloria, what good fortune brings you to me today? What can I do for you?"

"Well, as I said, I had hoped to make your acquaintance in any event, but I do have the excuse of some business matters. I wanted to let you know the OSI is going to be doing some work in Quadrant 4."

"That's very thoughtful of you. And what desperate shortcoming in my Quadrant, might I ask, requires your strategic intervention?" DuBray's eyes had narrowed slightly, and the look on his face was not entirely pleasant. This was a reaction Gloria had seen before from planetary and Sector authorities. If an OSI intervention was necessary, it could only mean that there was a malfunction somewhere in the existing Dexta bureaucracy. No one was happy to hear that.

"Oh, nothing desperate, I assure you," Gloria said as lightly as she could. "But it does look as if there have been some financial irregularities in Sector 19. One of my people is preparing a full report, and I'll send you a copy tomorrow. It only came to my attention this afternoon, so I'm afraid I don't have many details yet. But, in general, it seems that there has been some double- and perhaps even triple-flagging of various freighters. If the records are accurate, some freighters have apparently been showing up in two or more ports at the same time. We aren't sure exactly what's going on, but of course there are tax implications and the possibility of hijackings and phantom loads."

DuBray nodded. "I see," he said, and took a swallow of the excellent wine. "And what does Sector Administration have to say about all of this?"

"Nothing, yet," said Gloria. "Since we aren't sure

just who or what is involved here, we thought we'd hold off on notifying Sector. Under the circumstances, we felt it might be best to go directly to Quadrant."

"And swoop down on the malefactors from above, without warning?"

"If necessary. Of course, at the moment we still don't even know if there *are* any malefactors. It could all turn out to be accounting errors, or something similar. But to be safe, it made sense to handle it through Quadrant, initially."

"Indeed." DuBray pursed his lips, crossed his legs, and stared beyond the slums of New Jersey toward the setting sun. "And you will be going to Sector 19 yourself?"

Gloria shook her head. "An OSI team has already been dispatched, but I have no immediate plans to get personally involved. There is, however, another matter . . ."

"More happy news regarding my Quadrant? My cup runneth over."

Gloria shrugged. "Sorry, but part of my job is to tell people things they'd rather not hear."

DuBray looked at her again. "And you dress this way to soften the blow?"

"If it has that effect," Gloria said, "then so much the better. But the truth is, I dress this way because I enjoy it, and I've noticed that other people generally enjoy it, as well. You certainly have."

DuBray offered her a smile. "Point taken," he said. "Very well, then. Proceed."

Gloria took a deep breath, then launched into it. "Mr. DuBray," she said, "I'm sure you've already heard about the two PAIN attacks in your Quadrant."

DuBray nodded. "Ugly," he said. "Very ugly. But Internal Security is already dealing with it. What is OSI's interest in this?"

"One of the terrorists employed an old Mark IV

plasma rifle," Gloria said. "And last week on Cartago, another Mark IV was used in an attempt on my life. Both of those rifles were part of a shipment to Savoy in September 3163, just before the start of the war with the Ch'gnth."

DuBray gave her a sharp, probing stare, then abruptly got to his feet. He gazed at the glow on the horizon for a moment, drained the rest of his glass in one long pull, then went over to a sideboard to take the bottle and refill his glass. "Interesting," he said finally, after taking another sip of the wine.

"We need to get at the original records from 3163," Gloria continued, "when the Quadrant Administrator's office was on New Cambridge. Two of our people will be leaving for there in a couple of days. Of course, the OSI Charter gives them all necessary powers, but things might go a little easier for them on New Cambridge if they could take along an authorization from you."

DuBray took another swallow of wine and turned to look at her. "There were those of us," he said, "who warned Norman that this Office of Strategic Intervention was a spectacularly bad idea. Dexta already has an Inspector General's Office and a Comptroller, after all, and they have managed to keep the gears and cams reasonably free of grit down through the centuries, without any 'strategic interventions.' Some of us, in fact, told him to his face that his obvious infatuation with a certain young woman was leading him to make a potentially disastrous decision. But, of course, he ignored our advice—as was his privilege."

Gloria got to her feet and faced DuBray. "I see," she said.

"I doubt it. Come over here, if you would, Gloria." After locking eyes with him for a few seconds, Gloria walked around the divan and approached DuBray. He regarded her frostily for a moment, then put his glass down and, with no preamble, unknotted her top and pulled it away from her. Then he looked down at her bare breasts and smiled crookedly.

"What do you think you're doing?" she demanded.

"Isn't that obvious? I suppose you could say I'm performing a little strategic intervention of my own. If you want to play your games in *my* backyard, little girl, you'll play by my rules, or you won't play at all."

"We'll see about *that*," Gloria replied with some heat. "I'm not some bloody Fifteen anymore, and I don't have to put up with this bullshit from you or anyone else now! I'm head of the OSI and a Ten!"

"Yes, and I'm a Four," DuBray said blithely. "You see where that leaves you, don't you? Honestly, Gloria, did you really believe that things were any different at the upper levels of Dexta than at the lower ones? We just play the game with a little more finesse and style up here. When you were a Fifteen, you saved your job by letting the Pack Dogs fuck you on the floor of the restrooms, didn't you?"

Gloria could only stare at him in smoldering silence. She wondered how in hell he had heard about *that*.

"Well," DuBray went on, "I have a very comfortable bed in the next room. If you expect to strategically intervene in my Quadrant, you'll join me on it."

The idea of having sex with a superior at Dexta to preserve or promote her career was hardly novel to Gloria. That had always been part of the game, and by becoming a Tiger she had committed herself to playing it. But after Mynjhino and her appointment to head the OSI, she had come to realize that her success at Dexta depended on the quality of her work more than on her sexual stratagems. And there was no one at Dexta—not even Norman Mingus—that she *had* to screw. So she was annoyed by DuBray's arrogance and presumption.

Gloria smiled sweetly at him. "I'm afraid I'll have to decline your very kind invitation, Mr. DuBray. You might have had a shot at me if you actually had half the finesse you think you have. But you see, I'm allergic to assholes."

Gloria pivoted smartly and marched out of the office, leaving DuBray standing there holding the scrap of cloth in his hand.

"You're making a mistake," he said over her shoulder, but Gloria just slammed the door on him.

chapter **4**

"THAT MOTHERFUCKING BASTARD! THAT IN-credible son of a bitch!"

Gloria swept into Petra's apartment like a thunderstorm, raging almost incoherently as she paced around in little circles, her thin lips drawn tight and her eyes blazing. Petra didn't think she'd ever seen her so overwrought. Wearing nothing but a tinier-than-usual band skirt, her ruby mustard seed bouncing around between her breasts in her agitation, Gloria seemed to be on the verge of doing physical violence to someone. She usually reserved language like this for Charles—but somehow, Petra didn't think it was directed at him this time.

"Which motherfucking bastard?" Petra ventured to inquire.

"DuBray! Cornell Fucking DuBray, that arrogant asshole! Who the hell does he think he is, treating me like a goddamn Fifteen?"

"What happened?" Pug asked.

"Nothing happened! Nothing at all, because I didn't *let* it happen! I'm a *Ten* now, dammit, not some frightened, brainless Fifteen! How *dare* he treat me that way? How *dare* he? 'If you want to play games in *my* backyard, little girl, you'll play by *my* rules!' Can you imagine? He actually said that! *Little girl?* Why, that arrogant, motherfucking—"

Gloria stopped short when she finally realized that she, Petra, and Pug were not the only people in the room. Petra's mother stood at the doorway to the kitchen, gazing at Gloria with more than her usual degree of disapproval.

"Uh . . . Mrs. Nash!" Gloria stammered. "I didn't see you. Uh . . . hello. How are you? I'm sorry, I didn't . . . uh, I apologize . . ."

"Mom," Petra quickly broke in, "Gloria's had a tough day at the office."

"Yes, I can see that," said Mrs. Nash. "Perhaps she should have stayed there until she recovered some semblance of civility."

Petra sighed. Her mother had never approved of Gloria, or her daughter's association with such a person. Oh, she didn't mind the perks that went with knowing Gloria, like the invitations to fancy parties in Gloria's penthouse, or the free family vacation Gloria had sprung for last year; but she had always found Gloria herself to be too wild and disrespectful of propriety. In particular, she disapproved of Gloria's repeated public contretemps with the Emperor. In Mrs. Nash's view, the Emperor—any Emperor—ought to have been treated with the utmost deference and respect. Of course, Mrs. Nash had never even met an Emperor, let alone been married to one.

The only man Mrs. Nash had ever been married to in her sixty-three years was Mr. Nash, Petra's father, who had fled some twenty years ago, when Petra was six. In consequence, she distrusted men in general—much as she distrusted women who consorted with them. She tolerated Pug, principally because he was from a wealthy family, but somehow always managed to convey the impression that she considered him to be beneath her daughter. Her mother, Petra realized, was a galaxy-class snob, probably because she had been poor all her life. Now that her daughter was moving up in the world, it gave her new opportunities to express her disapproval of and disappointment in virtually everything and everyone, including Petra.

"Gloria," Petra said, "Mom's going to be minding the apartment while Pug and I are on New Cambridge. Uh . . . we're still going, aren't we?"

"Damn right you are . . . I mean, yes, of course. You won't have DuBray's seal of approval, which may mean that you'll have to do without any cooperation from the Dexta staff on New Cambridge. But you've got full authority under the OSI Charter, so don't put up with any bullsh—uh, don't—"

"We won't," Petra said. "Can I get you a drink or something?"

"No, no, I just wanted to let off some steam on my way upstairs." Gloria turned to face Mrs. Nash and said, "I do apologize for my unseemly outburst, Mrs. Nash."

"That's quite all right, Gloria," Mrs. Nash said loftily, now that she had attained the moral high ground. "Tell me, though, do you usually dress like this at work? From the way my daughter dresses these days, it wouldn't surprise me, but I confess, I didn't think you went around the office *completely* naked."

"Well," Gloria tried to explain, "it's been kind of an unusual day, Mrs. Nash. You see . . ."

"It's a Visitation Day, Mom," Petra put in. But that didn't impress Mrs. Nash, who had sampled and discarded Spiritism years ago.

"Yes," she said, "I believe I heard something about that vulgar . . . *ceremony*. I gather you are now some sort of Avatar? I suppose that means you can go around naked all the time, if you want?"

"Well, as a matter of fact, it does," Gloria said. "But to tell you the truth—"

"That's quite all right, Gloria," Mrs. Nash cut in. "You owe me no explanations. I don't pretend to understand you young people in any case. However, I can tell you that when I was your age, we showed a little more respect for—"

"Bullshit, Mom!" Petra had heard about as much as she could take. "When you were our age, old Darius was on the throne and people acted a lot wilder than anyone does today. So spare us your laments for the Good Old Days, okay? Gloria, I'm sorry."

"No, I'm the one who's sorry. I just needed to vent. See you at the office tomorrow. Good night, Pug . . . and Mrs. Nash." Gloria made a hasty exit.

When Gloria was gone, Petra, fists on hips, confronted her mother. "After all Gloria's done for us," she said, "you'd think you could make at least a little effort to be nice to her!"

"After what *she's* done?" Mrs. Nash said in frank astonishment. "You mean, after all *you've* done for her! Why, that woman could hardly function without you. And after what happened to you on Sylvania—"

"I've told you before, that wasn't Gloria's fault."

"No, of course not. All she did was force you to work as a prostitute. And if a prostitute gets assaulted, why, it hardly matters, does it?"

"Dammit, Mom, you know perfectly well I was working undercover as a bar girl, *not* a prostitute!"

"Well, I suppose the distinction escapes me. I tell you, that woman has corrupted you, Petra. Yes, that's it, she's *corrupted* you! Just look at the way you're dressed right now."

"Yeah," Pug said, grinning.

"You keep out of this, young man. I know where *you* stand in all of this. People like you and Gloria just seem to think you can *buy* whatever—and whomever—you want."

"Right," said Petra. "Like Gloria bought us this apartment."

"Gloria? I was under the impression that your young man paid the rent."

"Pug pays the rent, but Gloria got us the lease. It would have taken years to get a place half this good without her help."

"Well, that was very nice of her, then, I suppose," Mrs. Nash allowed. "Of course, the way she works you, you barely get a chance to spend any time here, as it is. Fortunately, you have a mother who is willing to drop everything at a moment's notice and take care of your precious apartment for you."

"Drop what?" Petra wondered. "Tuesday night bingo in Weehawken? The two-crown window at Paramus Raceway?"

Mrs. Nash tossed her nose into the air and sniffed, "I don't have to stand here and be insulted." With that, she swiftly retreated into her guest bedroom.

"Good," Petra said loudly enough for her to hear, "then I won't have to stand here and insult you!" Petra shook her head and turned to face Pug. "Mothers," she cried.

Pug grinned at her. "Wait till you meet mine."

GLORIA FOUND A CASE OF SONOMA III CABER-net, vintage 3196, waiting at her front door when she reached her penthouse. She briefly debated whether to dump it all down the garbage chute but decided that would be a waste of outrage—and good wine. Instead, she took the case inside, opened a bottle, drank a glass-ful as she fixed herself a salad, and then another as she ate it. DuBray might have been an asshole, but he knew his wine.

She supposed she should have expected it. DuBray certainly had the reputation. Still, it had been more than two years since the last time a superior at Dexta had insisted that she have sex with him. Somehow, she had simply assumed that she was beyond all of that now. As a notorious Tiger, she had established a reputation of her own, and even before Mynjhino and her promotion, the Twelves and Tens she had dealt with on a daily basis had shown her a wary respect. If Gloria had sex with anyone at Dexta, it was by her choice and on her terms. Until now . . .

Gloria felt like smashing something. But she returned her salad plate to the kitchen intact and poured another glass of wine instead. Rather than smashing something, she decided, she would *get* smashed. After a day like today, she figured, she had earned it.

She was so pissed off about DuBray, she had hardly even thought about Charles and his offer. Empress— with real power! That suddenly had great appeal; as Empress, she might have DuBray flayed alive, inch by inch. There were, she knew, catacombs deep beneath the Residence in Rio where such things had actually happened—centuries ago, supposedly. She doubted that Charles had ordered any tortures himself, although he was such a bastard at times that she wouldn't rule out the possibility.

Gloria took the bottle and glass and curled up on a comfortable sofa. "Music," she said. "File C, random." A moment later, the penthouse reverberated with the raw rhythms of Early Blues. Bessie Smith, Muddy Waters, Etta James, B. B. King—Gloria knew and loved them all, and when she'd had a little more wine, she began to sing along.

A little more wine found her dancing as well as singing. Just like a good little Avatar of Joy.

Her mother would be thrilled when she heard the news. Gloria's parents were fabulously wealthy, truly wonderful people, and if they couldn't quite understand why their daughter should want to hold down an actual job—much less one at Dexta—they at least tolerated her attempts to make herself a useful and productive member of society. They had apparently never felt the need to be anything but what they were—a yachtsman of Empire-wide renown and his devoted mate. Currently, they were six hundred light-years away on some watery world for a round-the-planet regatta. Dad knew everything there was to be known about the sea, and used to tell her stories about Nelson and Magellan and Cook. And Mom was loving, smart, and sexy; she would be so proud when she heard that Gloria was an Avatar of the Spirit. She'd be even prouder if Gloria accepted Charles's offer and became Empress. In her own way, Gloria's mother was just as much of a snob as Petra's.

Fred and Georgia VanDeen were such good people; Gloria missed them desperately at times. Petra's mother might have been a pain, but at least she was handy. Sometimes Gloria wanted to cry when she thought about how far away Mom was, and how long it had been since she had been able to crawl into that warm, loving lap and tell her all her troubles . . . like . . . like how people were trying to *kill* her, and how they'd missed by *that* much! How she could still smell the burned hair . . .

Ray Charles was crooning about how Georgia was on his mind . . . and Mom—Georgia—was on Gloria's mind, too, and she wanted to be able to tell her about . . . about . . . *the burned hair*!

Spirit! If she'd bent to take her seat a tenth of a second later . . .

And suddenly, Gloria was sobbing and shaking. She couldn't stop. She tried to pour some more wine, but just couldn't manage it. Couldn't stop shaking.

Mom, they're trying to kill me!

First there was Mynjhino, when she'd had more narrow escapes than she could count. And then

Sylvania, where no one had actually tried to kill her, but Grunfeld's thugs had tried to rape her . . . and then, all the burned and ruined bodies at Pizen Flats . . . Ted, Gus, all of them. Burned the way she would have been burned on Cartago if she'd been just a fraction of a second later . . .

Gloria sank to the carpet and curled herself into a ball, but still she could not stop shaking. It all over-whelmed her now—all the close calls, the people who depended on her to do her job, the faith of Norman Mingus, the trust and love of Petra, the confidence of her staff, and Charles, yes, Chuckles himself, back in her life suddenly, and he still wanted her, and that bas-tard DuBray wanted her, too, an Avatar of the Spirit now, and all of it, all of it, pressing down upon her, and Georgia on her mind and so far away . . . *and the smell of burned hair!*

THE LIMO SKIMMER MADE ITS WAY UPTOWN, toward Harlem. For centuries, Harlem had been the home of the city's African community, and to the extent that there was still such a thing as an African community in Manhattan, it was still in Harlem. But after more than a millennium of Transit technology and global culture, distinct ethnic communities were getting hard to find on Earth. For anything resembling ethnic purity, it was necessary to travel to the colonies, where physical isola-tion and (in some cases) intentional segregation had preserved a degree of cultural and genetic distinctive-ness. In Manhattan, it was easier to find Chinese restau-rants in Chinatown than Chinese people. Gloria's own six-continent genetic blend was, perhaps, an extreme case, but not really unusual.

Gloria sat in the rear of the skimmer, smoking a jigli cigarette. Jigli was probably the strongest natural aphro-disiac in the Empire. She had discovered the herb on

Mynjhino and still had a substantial hoard of an especially potent, refined version of it. This was her second jigli cigarette of the evening, and it was enough to get the shakes more or less under control. In addition to igniting a fire in her groin and producing an all-over tingling sensation in her skin, the jigli had a calming influence on her. At least, it allowed her to concentrate all her thoughts on one thing—sex—and avoid thinking of other things, like the smell of burned hair.

But the jigli was not enough. Not on this night. Not after this day.

Tonight, she needed something more.

The limo driver found the correct side street and halted in front of a subtle sign that marked the entrance to a subterranean establishment that went by the name of Club Twelve Twenty-Nine. In blue neon, the glowing outline of a clockface perpetually registered the time—12:29. Gloria got out of the limo and braved the brisk January air on her mostly bare body for the few seconds it took her to reach the door of the club.

She had been here a few times before during her years in Manhattan—usually with friends but also alone a couple of times. It was the kind of place that well-to-do young New Yorkers knew about from word of mouth, and could frequent in relative privacy and security. As Gloria entered, one of the massive bouncers, who could be counted on to keep media reps and imagers out, nodded to her and said, "Good evening, Ms. VanDeen. Nice to see you here again." Gloria gave the bouncer a smile, paused for a few moments to let her eyes adjust to the dim, half-light in the club, then headed for the bar.

Arnold was on duty behind the bar. Gloria knew him a little, the way one knew bartenders and waiters around town a little—not really as people, but as reliable fixtures. Arnold was a good-looking young man with somewhat dusky skin, very short, dark hair, and a worldly gleam in his eyes.

"Evening, Gloria," Arnold said. "You know, I had a feeling you might just show up tonight. Avatar of Joy, huh?"

"That's me," Gloria admitted. "How have you been, Arnold?"

"About the same," he said. "Altairian brandy still your drink?"

Gloria nodded, and Arnold went to fetch a bottle. The men on either side of her at the bar were staring at her breasts with obvious interest.

Arnold returned with the brandy bottle and a snifter. "Pour one for yourself, Arnold," Gloria told him. "On me."

"Don't mind if I do," he said. He produced another snifter and poured the amber liquid into it. They clinked glasses and sipped a little. He grinned at her. "Smooth," he said. It ought to have been; Altairian brandy was allegedly one of the best and certainly one of the most expensive liquors in the Empire.

At the back of the room, a few people were dancing to a small instrumental combo. They were playing twenty-seventh-century Syntho, which Gloria had always thought of as blues by and for computers. In the vast diversity of the modern Empire, and with fourteen or fifteen centuries worth of popular culture to draw on, there was no longer any dominant theme in music, art, or literature. Gloria's preference for twentieth-century blues was hardly unique, and around town one could find clubs that specialized in everything from nineteenth-century waltzes to the depressing, lugubrious ballads of the twenty-fourth century, to the minimalist syncopations favored by musicians of Gloria's own generation. Syntho was not at the top of her list of favorites, but she didn't mind it.

Gloria took another sip of the expensive brandy, then leaned forward to talk quietly to Arnold. "I think maybe lemon-lime tonight," she said.

Arnold nodded. "Whatever you want, Gloria," he said. "But have you tried the new wild cherry?"

Gloria shook her head. "I think I'll stick with the lemon-lime. I'm just a creature of habit, I guess."

"Pretty soon," Arnold said, giving her a conspiratorial wink, "you may want to change your habits."

"Oh?"

"Twenty-nine's divine," he said, "but Forty-eight'll be great."

"You have it?"

Arnold frowned. "Not yet," he said. "But the word is that it's being tested on half a dozen of the Core Colonies, and it ought to be available here in a few months. In the meantime, lemon-lime we got."

The bartender gestured like a stage magician and suddenly he was holding a small white lozenge between his thumb and forefinger. Gloria took his hand in hers, and when she pulled away again, Arnold's hand was empty.

It was called Orgastria-29. If jigli was the most powerful natural erotogenic substance in the Empire, Orgastria-29 was its bioengineered equivalent. Unlike jigli, which simply aroused erotic sensations, Orgastria-29 intensified them. It was one of a class of intensifiers, which flooded the brain with a carefully designed suite of neuroreceptors. Intensifiers could magnify, deepen, and enhance virtually any human emotional state. There were intensifiers such as "sobbers," which created an exaggerated sense of melancholy and produced a cathartic effect that was considered useful in some forms of psychological therapy and as a mood builder at certain concerts and poetry readings. And "laffers," which made almost anything seem hilarious. Orgastria-29—or Twenty-nine as it was known—intensified sexual sensations to the point of producing physical seizures at the moment of orgasm.

Twenty-nine, in fact, was so good at what it did that

it was illegal. Orgastria-17 was a safe, legal, and very popular product. Twenty-nine could kill.

It didn't kill very often, but often enough for it to be registered as a controlled substance in the *Imperial Pharmacoepia*. Twenty-nine was generally taken in the form of flavored lozenges the user sucked on, getting small but steady doses of intensified sexual sensations. With her already-enhanced genetic equipment, and with the addition of jigli, Gloria was capable of sustained, continuing orgasmic episodes lasting more than an hour when she was under the influence of Twenty-nine. Most people got by with less than that, but a few wanted even more. They crunched down.

Crunching down simply meant grinding the Orgastria lozenge to powder between the molars. It produced an almost instant deluge of intensifying receptors that caused the brain to go into something similar to an epileptic seizure—a cerebral electrical storm. Most of the time the seizure was harmless and produced only an overload of ecstatic sensation that subsided after a few minutes. But sometimes, for some people, the seizure overwhelmed and shut down normal brain function. If a neutralizing agent could be administered quickly enough, brain function could be restored before permanent damage or death resulted. Clubs like Twelve Twenty-Nine generally kept a supply of the neutralizer on hand, thus avoiding the public embarrassment and legal difficulties of having people die on their premises. Nevertheless, people did die from Twenty-nine.

And so, people who wanted Twenty-nine had to get it from people like Arnold, in places like Club Twelve Twenty-Nine.

"Tell me about Forty-eight," Gloria said to Arnold.

"From what I've been told, it's like a whole new level," Arnold said. "Like crunching down on Twenty-nine, but it's sustained and you don't pass out. You just go to the top of the mountain and stay there an hour or so."

"Is it safe?"

Arnold shrugged. "I guess that's what they're testing. I don't think you'd want to crunch down on it, anyway. The zamies aren't idiots. They don't want to kill the clients, you know. By the time it's widely available, I'm sure it'll be as safe as Twenty-nine."

"Sounds good," Gloria said. "In the meantime, do you have a null-room free for tonight?"

"For an Avatar of Joy? Of course we do! I'll just extend our regrets to another party and set you up in Number Three."

"Thanks, Arnold. I really appreciate it."

"My pleasure, ma'am. I might even drop in on my break, just to make sure everything is going smoothly." Arnold smiled at her. Gloria smiled back.

Arnold held up a pad, and Gloria tapped it lightly with her left index finger, not bothering to read the numbers. The pad registered her fingerprint and did a first-order DNA scan, then charged the total to her account. The purchase of the Twenty-nine would be hidden by the expense of the brandy and the rental of the null-room.

"See you later, Arnold," Gloria said. She backed away from the bar and snaked her way through the crowd until she reached Null-Room Number Three. She tapped the entrance plate for another DNA scan, changed the Preferences indicator from Private to Open, then went into the room as the door slid open. She kicked off her shoes, slipped out of the scrap of band skirt, then dived forward.

She started to fall, but was quickly grabbed by the null field, and floated comfortably for several seconds until she arrived at the dead center of the room, equidistant from walls, floor, and ceiling. Gloria, who paid little attention to technical matters, was vaguely aware that this was not actual antigravity, but merely a convenient approximation of it created by an array of mass-repulsion units similar to the ones in skimmers.

In some ways, Gloria preferred null-rooms like this to the zero-gravity facilities that were available in some orbital installations. The absence of gravity was simply that, and you just bounced around like a Ping-Pong ball, which could be annoying. But in a null-room, it felt as if the air itself had thickened to the point where you could swim through it, which you couldn't do in zero G. The mass-repulsion fields pressed against you gently from all sides, like a ghostly massage, and merely floating there by yourself was sensuous and sexy.

But Gloria was not alone for long. People in the bar had seen her enter the room and noticed that she had designated it as Open. An engraved invitation could not have been more to the point. Half a dozen men and women quickly floated in after her, and Gloria slipped the lemon-lime lozenge into her mouth.

They came at her from every angle, every direction, and Gloria sighed in contentment. The tension and frustration and fear drained away from her, and she gave no further thought to Charles or DuBray or the Universal Church of the Spirit or to what had nearly happened to her on distant worlds. All that mattered was what was happening to her here and now in Harlem, in Club Twelve Twenty-Nine, in Null-Room Three. She felt the familiar jigli tingle and the sudden surge of intensity as she sucked on the lozenge, and surrendered herself to the rippling, roaring orgasmic ride that began within seconds of the first penetration of her golden, electric body.

It went on and on, and finally, when everything was just right, Gloria crunched down.

chapter 5

GLORIA WENT FLYING THROUGH THE AIR AND landed, very abruptly, ass first on the padding. She was stunned for a moment, not so much by the impact as by the fact that it had happened at all. Petra had actually thrown her.

Across the small gymnasium, Petra stood staring back at Gloria, a half smile on her face, almost as if she were embarrassed by what she had just done. Gloria shook her head and pushed herself up to her feet. "Got me," she said.

"First time."

Gloria nodded in acknowledgment. She had been trying to train Petra in the art of Qatsima for nearly six months, ever since their return from Sylvania. Three mornings each week, they reserved this small padded room in the Dexta Rec Center and Gloria attempted to indoctrinate Petra in the subtle, methodical, and wonderfully effective discipline of Qatsima. Part martial art, part acrobatics, part ballet, Qatsima had been developed centuries earlier by humans and the native species on the planet of Songchai. Gloria had taken it up after leaving Charles, principally as a way of keeping her body toned, but also as a means of self-defense; once away from Charles and his omnipresent security guards, she wanted to be able to take care of herself. She had developed a real flair for the art, and was now ranked as a Master—although she was well aware that the *true* Qatsima Masters could have wiped the floor with her.

Yet this morning, even Petra had sent her flying. Of course, after last night at the Club Twelve Twenty-Nine, Gloria was short on sleep and hungover on wine, brandy, jigli, Orgastria-29, and a nightlong explosion of sex. She figured she was operating at no better than about 70 percent efficiency. Still, Petra had honestly bested her, and that had never happened before.

"You're getting good at this, kiddo," Gloria said. Actually, Petra was still pretty awful at it, and Gloria doubted that she would ever become truly skilled. But mastery of just a few moves, and the element of surprise, might save her in the future from what had happened to her on Sylvania.

Sylvania had changed their relationship as much as Mynjhino. Before Mynjhino, Petra had simply been her cute little assistant—flighty, smart-mouthed, and devoted. They had become best friends after Mynjhino, but Sylvania had somehow altered the balance between them. Petra, who was two years older than Gloria, no longer seemed like a little sister; on Sylvania, Petra had even asserted herself once and told Gloria to stop behaving like a self-pitying jerk. There was now a growing equality in their relationship that belied their relative positions in the Dexta hierarchy.

Gloria wearily assumed a crouch and spread her arms. "More?"

Petra shook her head. "That was one to quit on," she said. "Anyway, it'll give you something to think about the next few weeks while I'm away on New Cambridge."

"And give you time to gloat. Enjoy it while you can." Gloria picked up a towel and mopped away some of the sweat.

Petra picked up her own towel. "I'm going to practice on Pug," she said as she walked toward the door.

"Does he know that?" Gloria asked.

"Not yet," Petra cackled. "Hit the showers?"

Gloria shook her head. "I've got the room for another twenty minutes," she said. "And after the way you just humiliated me, I think I'm going to stay here a while and work on a few things. And maybe sweat off some recent excesses."

"Why are your excesses always so much more excessive than my excesses?" Petra wondered.

"Probably because you're smarter than I am. Go get your shower . . . before I decide to bounce you off the ceiling."

"Sore loser," Petra called over her shoulder as she left the room.

Gloria concentrated on some stretching exercises and leg raises, trying to ease some of the tightness she felt in her muscles. Twenty-nine tended to make the muscles spasm, and the day after a session could sometimes feel like the day after a triathlon. She had begun doing sit-ups when the door opened and a very large man entered the gym. He was at least a foot taller and a hundred pounds heavier than Gloria, with short, spiky blond hair and a thick neck. He removed the warm-ups he was wearing, leaving him in nothing but a breechclout and his rippling muscles.

Gloria got to her feet and said, "Excuse me, but I have the room for another fifteen minutes."

"Is that so?" the man asked. "Well, I think you're wrong. In fact, I know you are. This room is mine."

"If you'll just check the—"

"I don't have to check anything. The room is mine."

Gloria was becoming annoyed; more than that, a

tickle of fear and suspicion began to play at the edges of her mind.

"You're Gloria VanDeen," the man said. "A Ten."

"That's right."

"I'm Erik Manko," he said. "Also a Ten."

"Level doesn't matter. I signed up for this gym, and—"

"Level matters a great deal," Manko contradicted. "In fact, in this case, it's the only thing that matters. As you know, Dexta has a time-honored method of resolving disputes between those of equal level."

"*What?*" Gloria was aghast. "You can't be serious!"

"I'm perfectly serious," Manko said. "Let me show you how serious I am." With that, Manko calmly stepped toward her, balled his fist, and swung at her. Gloria saw it coming and just managed to duck, so that instead of breaking her jaw, his fist merely glanced off the side of her skull, stunning her and sending her spinning to the padded floor.

Gloria was dazed for a moment, but realized that she was in grave danger. As a coequal Ten, Manko could all but kill her if he wanted. The *Dexta Code* forbade superiors from striking their inferiors, or subordinates striking their superiors, but it allowed those of equal level to work out their differences by physical force, if necessary. It was a fairly common occurrence at the lower levels, usually among Fifteens—just another aspect of the brutal Dexta routine. Gloria had been involved in such conflicts twice before. Once, as a Fifteen, another Fifteen had thought that he would teach her a lesson, and was, instead, taught a quick and painful Qatsima lesson by Gloria; then, on Mynjhino, she had literally kicked the ass of a traitorous fellow Thirteen. But a fight between Tens? Over whose gym it was? Gloria couldn't quite believe it, but had no time to ponder the meaning of it all. Manko was moving toward her, so Gloria instinctively assumed the Qatsima posture known as the Wounded Bird. Manko was in for a surprise . . .

Except that it was Gloria who was surprised. Manko countered with a Dancing Cobra that not only neutralized Gloria's Wounded Bird, but used it against her to get a grip on both of her ankles. *He knows Qatsima,* Gloria thought as Manko whirled her around and threw her against one of the padded walls. She slammed into it with her back and shoulders, then sank to the floor.

Before she could recover her breath, Manko was on her again. She tried to claw at his eyes and knee his groin, but he was too fast and too big and simply overpowered her. Qatsima moves could defeat sheer size sometimes, but they had little hope of prevailing against both size *and* Qatsima. Manko punched her hard in the belly, doubling her over, then picked her up and threw her against another wall. Then did it again.

Gloria began to lose track of what was happening. Somehow, she found herself stretched out across his knee, and he spanked her with the flat of his hand, the impact so hard that it sounded like the crack of a whip. Then he picked her up, whirled her around again, and threw her against another wall.

As she lay crumpled against the wall, her legs splayed, Manko approached her again, smiling slightly. "Don't worry," he said, "I'm not going to rape you. That would be against the *Code*, wouldn't it?" Instead, he simply gave her a powerful, barefooted kick in her groin. And another.

"Why?" Gloria gasped. "Why are you doing this?"

Manko leaned over her and smiled in her face. "Administrator DuBray will be contacting you in a few days," he said, "after you've had a chance to heal. Don't disappoint him, Gloria. I'd hate to have to do this again."

He straightened up and started to turn to go, but stopped and looked back down at her. "No, that's not true," he said. "I'd enjoy doing it again." Then he left.

Gloria tried to get to her feet, but couldn't. The pain overwhelmed her, and she sank back to the floor and passed out. The person who had signed up for the gymnasium next found her there ten minutes later, bleeding and unconscious.

"NORMAN? IT'S GLORIA. I NEED TO SEE YOU." Gloria stood in the access booth at the Dexta VIP Transit and waited for Norman Mingus to respond to her audio signal. A few moments later, an overhead light turned green, and Gloria stepped through the Transit ring.

She stepped out into Idaho. The guard at the Transit booth nodded to her, quickly ran a detector over her body, then nodded again. "Welcome, Ms. VanDeen," he said. "Just go into the house and up to the third-floor observation deck. I believe you'll find Secretary Mingus there."

Gloria thanked him, then walked along the heated sidewalk, across a broad courtyard hip deep in snow, to the front porch of the home of Norman Mingus. Snow might have been scarce in New York these many centuries, but there was still plenty of it in the northern Rockies. The house looked like it might have been built by a nineteenth-century robber baron, with its gables and cornices, gingerbread and Victorian flourishes. In fact, Gloria knew, Mingus had built it barely ten years ago. With access via personal Transit—something available only to the very rich or very powerful—there weren't even any roads connecting the house with the rest of the world; it was completely isolated, two miles above sea level and twenty miles from the nearest town. As she stepped onto the porch, Gloria paused and looked around Mingus's aerie, seeing the snow-covered mountains and valleys as they must have appeared to the

Crow and Blackfeet whose land this had been fifteen centuries ago.

An aide met Gloria inside the front door and led her up two flights of stairs to the third floor. He pointed toward the observation deck and departed. Gloria opened the outer door and stepped out onto an open-air platform with a sweeping view of the mountains marching off to the south. Mass-repulsion units preserved a bubble of warm air over the deck, but Norman Mingus sat in a comfortable-looking chair under a layer or two of thick blankets. He looked up at Gloria's arrival but didn't attempt to rise.

"Gloria," he said, "I'm sorry I haven't been available at the office the last few days. My doctors decided I needed a new pancreas, so they took one out of cold storage and plugged it in. I should be fine in a couple of—Spirit! What the hell happened to you?"

Gloria smiled lamely. "I had a little . . . confrontation . . . a couple of days ago," she said. "But it's nothing to worry about. I'll be fine." The doctors at Dexta had administered Quik-Knit to her three broken ribs and nanomeds that were already repairing her bruises and lacerations, cell by cell. In two or three days, no one would be able to tell that she had recently been beaten and bloodied. In the meantime, her entire body ached.

Mingus started to rise, but Gloria gestured him back down. "No, don't get up. In fact, I think I'll pull up a chair and join you. Looks pretty comfy." Gloria, in tight jeans and a tighter cashmere turtleneck, moved another chair next to Mingus's and sat down, sighing a little at the still-sharp pain in her ribs as she moved.

"Well?" Mingus asked, arching his eyebrows. Norman Mingus, at 131 years of age, had a face that was pink and almost unlined, with sharply etched aristocratic features and an unruly shock of thinning white hair. Gloria always thought he looked like a retired schoolteacher, or maybe a country parson. But there was nothing mild or passive in his blue-gray eyes; they accurately reflected forty years of experience in running a galactic empire.

Gloria scrunched around in the chair, trying to find a comfortable and pain-free position. "I ran into another Ten named Erik Manko," she said. "He pounded on me for a while."

Mingus nodded and sighed heavily. "So," he said, "you've finally run afoul of Cornell DuBray. I've been expecting it, but it honestly surprises me that he would resort to such means. Manko is his personal Hammer, you know."

"I didn't think there were any Hammers left in Dexta," Gloria said. "I mean, I've heard about them, but I thought they were . . ."

"History?" Mingus shook his head. "Not quite, although I did try. That was one of the reforms I introduced, years ago. Hammers used to be quite common around Dexta. Some Sector and Quadrant Administrators damn near had their own private armies. I tried to put an end to all that, but there are still a few individuals like Manko around. If you check his record, though, I'll wager you'll find that he was either promoted or demoted to a Ten the day before you encountered him."

"I did check," said Gloria. "You're right, he was demoted from a Nine. It seems he's been bouncing back and forth between Eight and Twelve for the last ten years."

"As required by DuBray. Tell me, what did you do to set all of this in motion?"

"I went to see DuBray about some routine business. Nothing more."

"That would be enough. I suppose I should have warned you. Cornell was steadfastly and vociferously opposed to the creation of OSI. Like a lot of the older hands around Dexta, he didn't see the need for it and resented the potential intrusion into his domain. But it surprises me that he would unleash Manko on you."

"Well," said Gloria, "there was a little more to it than that. DuBray insisted on having sex with me, then and there. Norman, he treated me like a Fifteen!"

"I see," said Mingus. "And of course, you resented that."

"Damn right, I did! I don't have to put up with that shit anymore. I'm a Ten now—"

"And he's a Four."

Gloria turned in her chair to look at Mingus. "That's what *he* said. Are you telling me that it's okay? That he can get away with that?"

"Of course he can get away with that. Gloria, the man is a Four and has held his present position for over forty years! You've been a Ten for what, about a year?"

"About that," Gloria said sullenly. She didn't like the turn this conversation was taking.

"Gloria," Mingus said, a trace of impatience in his voice, "I bumped you from a Thirteen to a Ten. In case you didn't realize it, that was all but unprecedented in the history of Dexta. And I gave you powers and responsibilities at OSI that were far beyond those normally entrusted to a Ten. I suppose it's natural that all of that should have gone to your head. But let me remind you that as a Ten, you are just one of some six thousand Tens within Dexta. You are a midlevel bureaucrat, nothing more."

"Norman," Gloria said, "how many Tens come visit you here at your home?"

Mingus stared at her for a long moment, then smiled. "All right, then," he conceded, "perhaps you are something more than a mere Ten. In my eyes, at least— but not in DuBray's. And that's all that is truly relevant here. I'm sorry about what happened to you, Gloria. I regret it more than I can say, and I intend to have words about it with DuBray. Nevertheless, you cannot come running to me every time one of your superiors gives you a hard time. You will have to find your own way of coping with the Cornell DuBrays of this organization. I can't and won't intervene on your behalf."

Gloria felt appropriately abashed. "I understand, Norman," she said. "And I didn't really come here just to complain about the way DuBray treated me. There's something else. You know, don't you, that someone took a shot at me on Cartago?"

"Yes, I did hear about that. Very disturbing. Have there been developments I should know about?"

"I think so," Gloria said. "In fact, I need to ask you some questions, Norman. Questions that go back more than fifty years, to when you were the Quadrant 4 Administrator."

"Oh?"

"The weapon that was used in the attack on me on Cartago was originally part of a shipment of arms that was sent to Savoy in September of 3163, just before the Ch'gnth attack."

Mingus suddenly leaned back in his chair and seemed to focus his gaze on a distant mountaintop. He was silent for several moments, then breathed, "Savoy."

"And there's more. Another weapon from that same shipment was involved in one of the terrorist attacks in Quadrant 4 last week. It would seem that PAIN has somehow gotten its hands on weapons that were supposedly destroyed fifty-five years ago."

Mingus turned to look into her eyes. Then he looked once more at the distant snow-covered peaks and seemed lost in private thoughts or, perhaps, memories.

"Lewis and Clark returned from the Pacific through that pass," Mingus said at last, pointing to a notch in the mountains some thirty miles to the south. "Or, at any rate, Lewis did. They had split up by that point; then they joined up again down on the Missouri."

"Fascinating," said Gloria.

"I always wanted to follow the old Lewis and Clark Trail," Mingus said. "Never did, of course, and it's too late now. I'm too old, and most of it's gone, anyway. One more regret in a life that's full of them."

Mingus closed his eyes for a moment and sighed heavily. "You can't imagine what it was like, Gloria," he said. "Wartime, I mean. It was a truly desperate time. The Ch'gnth would have exterminated us if they could. In the end, we damn near exterminated them. But it didn't have to turn out that way. It could just as easily have gone against us. Believe me, I know—most of that damned war was fought in my Quadrant."

"I know. You're in all the history books. You'd have been remembered, Norman, even if you had never become Dexta Secretary."

"History books!" Mingus snorted. He took a sip of tea. "Let me tell you something, Gloria. If you live long enough to read about yourself in a history book, you'll never again trust anything you read in *any* history book. Alexander, Washington, Napoleon, Churchill, Hazar— nowadays, I'm not even sure any of 'em really existed. Maybe it was *all* lies."

"Did the history books lie about you?" Gloria asked him.

Mingus gave a short, bitter laugh. "Well, I'll just say that lies were told, and let it go at that."

He took another sip of tea and turned to look at Gloria. "I'm very concerned about this, Gloria. I'd always tended to dismiss PAIN as inconsequential idiots. Raving anarchist ideologues, the kind of people who used to throw bombs into the Tsar's carriage. But these recent attacks are clearly well coordinated, and now it would seem that you were one of their targets."

"A symbolic one, at best." Gloria shrugged.

"Those are usually the most important ones," Mingus pointed out. "You, my dear, are perhaps the most visible symbol of Dexta and the Empire these days.

In the warped view of the anarchists, killing you would represent a considerable triumph. I am going to order additional security for you, and you will accept it without complaint. Is that clear?"

"Yessir," Gloria answered obediently. Mingus stared at her for several seconds, as if trying to assure himself that she had meant what she said.

"The question I really want to answer, though," Gloria told him, "is how PAIN came by those weapons from the Savoy shipment. They seem to have enough of them to carry out several nearly simultaneous, widely separated attacks. What can you tell me about that shipment, Norman?"

Mingus shook his head wearily. "It was a long time ago," he said.

"But Savoy was a pretty significant event," Gloria pointed out.

"They were *all* significant events! You simply have no idea, Gloria—none! In those days, the very fate of the human race hung in the balance. We could have lost it all—the Empire, even our very existence as a species. In those weeks leading up to the onset of hostilities, I found myself making decisions on a daily basis that might affect the course of events for the next millennium. That final shipment to Savoy . . . it was just one more. Spirit knows what finally became of it."

"I see," said Gloria. "And you don't remember any details about it?"

"Not really," he said.

"Well, I'm sending an OSI team to New Cambridge to dig around in the original records. Maybe if we can find out what really happened to that shipment, we can figure out how PAIN got their hands on it."

Mingus looked back toward the distant peaks. "Perhaps so," he said. "In the meantime, be very careful, Gloria."

Gloria sensed that she was being dismissed. She still

had many more questions, but decided that this was not the time to ask them. Still, there was one thing more that she needed to say.

"Norman? I think you should know about this. Charles wants me back. He wants me to be Empress, and he's offered me real and meaningful power."

Mingus raised an eyebrow. "Has he, now?"

"He says we should pool our resources instead of competing. He says that together, we could be the best leaders the Empire has ever had."

"He might just be right about that," Mingus said, nodding thoughtfully. "On the other hand, between the two of you, the Empire might just find itself plunged into an all-out civil war. What did you tell him?"

"I said I needed time to think about it. There's a lot to consider. I never wanted to be Empress and felt lucky to have divorced him when I did. But to have real power . . . I just don't know. I can't deny that it has an appeal."

"Of course it does. Somebody once said that power is the ultimate aphrodisiac. I won't say that power is better than sex, but it's at least as good. Seems that way at my age, at any rate."

"But I have some power at Dexta, too," Gloria said. "And I've *earned* that. In time, maybe I'll earn more."

"How much more?" Mingus gave her a long, probing stare. "Just what are your ambitions, Gloria? What do you hope to achieve at Dexta?"

"Norman," she said, "I intend to be your successor. I intend to run Dexta someday."

Mingus took a moment or two to react, then shook his head. "*My* successor? My successor's successor, perhaps . . . but mine? Gloria, the youngest Secretary in Dexta's history was, I believe, fifty-seven. You are twenty-five, and I am a hundred and thirty-one. Just how long do you expect me to live, anyway?"

Gloria smiled at him. "Forever, I hope." She leaned

over and gave him an affectionate peck on his cheek. "People live to be nearly two hundred, you know."

"And I have no intention of becoming one of them. After a hundred and fifty, it's just not worth it. A hundred and thirty is no day at the beach, either, I can tell you. I will say this much, though. I'll never resign my position. I've been employed by Dexta for one hundred and seven years; it's the only paycheck I've ever drawn. I'd die without Dexta, so I might just as well die within Dexta."

"I'd take it as a personal favor," Gloria said, "if you put it off for another twenty or thirty years. That might be enough to give me a shot at being the next Secretary."

"It might, at that," Mingus conceded. "But you must realize that if I drop dead tomorrow—and my doctors refuse to promise me that I won't, new pancreas or no— my obvious successor would be Cornell DuBray. He would have the Dexta vote locked up, and he has more than enough influence with Parliament. He'd probably get the Emperor's vote as well, if it came to that."

Dexta Secretaries were chosen democratically, but the electorate was limited and elite. Parliament, senior Dexta personnel (Sevens and above), and the Emperor each had one vote. Two votes were necessary for a candidate to achieve office, and the appointment was effectively for life, since all three votes were necessary for removal from office. Mingus had been nominated by Darius IV in 3176, and had been confirmed with three votes. Charles might have liked to remove him and install a younger, more pliable Secretary, and there were those in Parliament who thought that he had been in power far too long; but his support among upper-level Dexta people was unquestioned. If both the Emperor and Parliament turned against Mingus, his support within Dexta would probably erode in time, but it would have taken a major scandal to dump him. Practically speaking, the office was his for as long as he wanted it.

"Gloria," Mingus said, smiling, "it seems you have a rather extraordinary choice to make. You can achieve immediate and certain, if limited, power by becoming Empress. Or you can spend decades working to earn a deeper and more meaningful power by attempting to become Dexta Secretary. I doubt that anyone in the history of the Empire—or the human race, for that matter—has ever faced such a choice, or such an opportunity. Choose wisely, my dear."

chapter 6

THE NEXT MORNING GLORIA MET WITH SOME
of her senior staff in a small conference room. Gath-
ered around the table, sharing coffee and bagels, were
OSI Administrator Grant Enright, Level X; Deputy
Administrator Jillian Clymer, Level XI; OSI Internal
Security Coordinator Arkady Volkonski, Level XII; and
Elaine Murakami, Level XIV, subbing for Petra as
Gloria's assistant and gatekeeper.

Enright was a conventionally handsome, fortyish
Lion who had been Gloria's boss back in Sector 8. He
was happily married—a rarity in Dexta, where marriage
by lower-level personnel was actively discouraged—and
enjoyed the distinction of being one of the few human
males who had ever said no to Gloria. He had little patience with the sexual stratagems so often employed in
Dexta and had become Gloria's friend rather than her
lover. Enright was efficient, friendly, and soft-spoken,
and seemed to have been born to be an administrator.
He kept OSI functioning with brisk efficiency during
Gloria's frequent absences.

Yet for all his abilities, Gloria had lately come to realize that Enright lacked the inner creative spark that distinguished true leaders. Given everything that had happened or almost happened to her in the past year, Gloria had inevitably been driven to give some thought to a possible successor for herself at OSI, and she doubted that Enright was the best person for the job. A better candidate, it seemed to her, was Jillian Clymer, who had been recruited for the Sylvania mission and had then accepted Gloria's invitation to join OSI on a permanent basis.

Jillian was a curvy, apple-cheeked blond from a small agricultural world in Sector 2, whose radiant smile, enthusiasm, and positive attitude had made her a welcome addition to the OSI staff. She had inherited a modest fortune and, like Gloria, had married young and divorced young before joining Dexta. In the Dexta bestiary she would have been classified as a Lion, but, like most women in OSI, she had begun to take on some Tigerish traits under Gloria's influence. Today, she wore a standard, Dexta-gray skirt and a matching V-necked sweater with, very obviously, nothing under it. Arkady Volkonski had apparently taken note.

Volkonski, a dark, glowering Cossack—distinguished by his ingrained sense of irony and a single, unpunctuated eyebrow—professed unlimited devotion to Gloria. But he was no Lap Dog; he was more of a Rottweiler. He took any assault on Gloria—from outside Dexta or from within—as a personal affront.

Enright led off the meeting by bringing Gloria up to speed on various administrative matters. Elaine Murakami nibbled at the edges of a bagel while taking notes on her pad. She had worked for Gloria back in Sector 8, before the creation of OSI. A thin, attractive, would-be Tiger, she was energetic and loyal, but had somehow failed to impress Gloria with any deeper qualities. And Gloria found her hero-worship frankly annoying. She was not comfortable with the notion of being anyone's role model, no matter what the Spiritists said about her.

When Enright had concluded his presentation, Gloria turned to Jill Clymer. "Where do we stand on the double-flagging in Sector 19?" she asked.

"Nothing new to report," Jill said. "As you know, I sent a team from Finance out to Staghorn last week, but it's five-hundred-and-some-odd light-years. Their Cruiser should have arrived yesterday, which means we could get an initial report via messenger in a few days." Messengers were reusable automated spacecraft that traveled at a rate of about 150 light-years per day; they were the standard means of disseminating information within the Empire. For more urgent communications, courier spacecraft could do two hundred light-years in a day, which meant that Earth was no more than five days away from the frontiers of the Empire. However, couriers were expensive, since they carried no fuel for deceleration and could, therefore, be used only once.

"And the initial report was filed by the Imperial Secretary on Staghorn?" Enright asked.

Jill nodded. "She seemed to regard it as something of a hot potato. One of her Finance people came to her with what looked like some suspicious data, and she took one look and sent it off to us. Seems she didn't want to have to deal with some of the big names involved."

"Big names?" Gloria asked.

"Big locally, at any rate," Jill explained. "The evidence, such as it is, points toward an outfit called Wendover Freight and Storage, which is based on Staghorn and is the major local transport company in the Sector. It also does business in Sectors 20 and 21."

"Big Twelve connections?" Gloria wondered.

"None, as far as we can tell," Jill said. "Of course, it's not always easy to sort out corporate connections. I've got someone checking out their history; Wendover has been in business nearly a century, so you would expect at least some Big Twelve affiliations. But nothing has turned up yet."

"That in itself seems a bit odd," Gloria opined.

Jill shrugged. "There are a few genuine independents left, and Wendover may be one of them. Still, if they are engaged in a large-scale double-flagging operation, it would make sense for them to have some ties to one or more of the Big Twelve."

"Or not," Gloria suggested. "Maybe the lack of a profitable connection to the big boys is what's driving them into the double-flagging scam. Just how good is this evidence? And what about the Dexta office on Staghorn? You said the ImpSec was nervous about dealing with this. Could there be Dexta involvement?"

"Your guess is as good as mine," Jill said. "But to tell you the truth, it wouldn't surprise me. A good double-flagging scam takes inside help. I've checked out a dozen or so examples of this kind of thing over the past five or six centuries, and every one of them involved someone in Dexta. And I'll bet the ImpSec on Staghorn thinks so, too—which is why she sent this to us instead of the Comptroller. Gloria? Are we going to get any help on this from Quadrant?"

"No," Gloria answered flatly. "Probably just the reverse."

"I see," Jill said. "DuBray's determined to be an asshole?"

"It's what he does best," Gloria said.

"Speaking of DuBray," Volkonski put in, "I still say you should let me deal with this Manko character."

Gloria reluctantly shook her head. "You know I can't do that, Arkady," she told him.

"Then just look the other way and let me handle it in some unofficial, unobtrusive way. Like maybe kneecapping the son of a bitch in some dark alley."

Gloria smiled, then reached out and ran her index

finger along the underside of Volkonski's chin. "You're such a sweet, sensitive man, Arkady," she said. "But I can't let you risk your career over this. It's my problem; I'll deal with it myself."

"Then promote me to a Ten," urged Volkonski, "and let me be *your* Hammer."

"Not possible," Gloria reminded him. "Anyway, I'm not sure you could take him in a fair fight."

"Who said anything about a fair fight?" he asked. "You forget, I'm a Bug."

But it had to be Gloria's own fight, she knew, fair or not. When she was a Fifteen, she had endured worse than anything DuBray had done so far. If she had survived that, she could survive this. And, she asked herself, if she couldn't find a way to handle DuBray, did she really deserve to be Dexta Secretary? Dealing with reptiles like DuBray, after all, was part of the job.

"And speaking of Bugs," said Enright, "what is Internal Security doing about PAIN?"

The previous day, Internal Security had convened an upper-level staff conference to address the terrorist problem. Despite his relatively low rank in the Dexta hierarchy, Volkonski had been invited to the meeting in recognition of his role at OSI and the fact that Gloria had been targeted.

"There are things that I can't discuss with you," Volkonski said, looking a little guilty about it.

"We understand that, Arkady," Gloria said. Internal Security was notoriously stingy with information, even within the ranks of Dexta. "Just tell us what you can."

"Well, as you might imagine, the three attacks on Dexta personnel have caused something of a stir in IntSec. The assumption is that the PAIN faction responsible is based in Quadrant 4, since two of the attacks were there—although Cartago is in Quad 2. Anyway, measures are being taken. One might usefully surmise that said measures would include rousting every known or suspected radical in the Quadrant and shaking them until their teeth rattle. Perhaps something worthwhile will emerge."

"And that's it?" Jill asked.

"What would you have us do, Jillian?" Volkonski asked sadly. "There are a limited number of us, after all. Even working night and day, there are only so many citizens whose civil rights we can violate. Anyway, the real problem is that PAIN is, paradoxically, an organization of anarchists. In other words, it's no 'organization' at all—just a voluntary, free-form convergence of like-minded morons. Supposedly, there are only Indians, no chiefs."

"Still," Enright insisted, "*somebody* must be calling the shots. Three nearly simultaneous attacks spread across two Quadrants couldn't be a coincidence."

Volkonski scowled and thought for a moment. "One might presume," he went on, "that an organization such as Internal Security, when confronted with a threat such as PAIN, might attempt to infiltrate the opposition and glean information from the inside. Such information might even now be winging its way toward Earth. If such were the case, then an organization such as Internal Security might be weighing options and preparing possible responses in anticipation of the receipt of such information."

Jillian gave him a cool, level stare. "You don't have a clue, do you?"

Volkonski shook his head.

That afternoon, as Gloria was trying to catch a few surreptitious winks at her desk, a pinging sounded and the face of Elaine Murakami appeared on her console. "Gloria? Can you take a meeting with Eli Opatnu? He's the—"

"I know who he is," Gloria said. She had never met him, but he was well-known within Dexta and was considered to be something of a rising star. Not yet forty, he was already a Level VII, the Administrator of Sector 19. "When does he want to see me?"

"Right now," said Elaine. "He's here."

"Okay," Gloria said, "give me a minute, then send him in." Gloria got to her feet, tried to rub some of the sleep out of her eyes, then gave her head a good shake to signal her long, flowing mane to restore itself to Dura-styled order. She took a quick glance in the closet mirror and was reasonably satisfied with what she saw. Her pale yellow minidress was relatively modest—perhaps too modest, it occurred to her when she thought of the images she had seen of Eli Opatnu. She pressed a hidden contact in a seam and the smart fabric of the dress retracted. She pressed another contact, adjusted the opacity of the fabric to 40 percent, then declared herself ready to meet Opatnu.

The Sector 19 Administrator entered her office a moment later. Elaine closed the door behind him and Gloria extended her hand. "Hi," she said, smiling broadly, "I'm Gloria VanDeen. Very pleased to meet you, Mr. Opatnu."

"It's Eli," he said, taking her hand. He grasped it firmly in his own and held it while he slowly surveyed every inch of her face and body—and Gloria did the same with his. Opatnu was the product of the same sort of genetic stewpot that had created Gloria, and his face seemed to bear traces of the Andes, Himalayas, and Alps. He had longish, jet-black hair with a hint of a wave in it, a strong, European nose, vividly green eyes, and skin that reminded Gloria of the color of an old saddle. He was tall and lean, but there was nothing fragile about him. His hand in hers was warm and forthright, with long, almost delicate fingers.

Gloria tried to catch her breath. *Why don't we skip the preliminaries,* she wondered, *and just start screwing here and now?* From the look in his eyes, she figured that Opatnu was probably thinking the same thing.

They finally released their grip on one another. "I'm glad you dropped by," Gloria said. "I was planning to pay you a visit in a couple of days. Please, have a seat."

She sat next to him on the couch, and they spent a few more seconds silently smiling at each other. She could almost see the waves of heat rising between them. Gloria was never shy or reticent where sex was concerned, but she couldn't recall the last time she had been so thoroughly overwhelmed by a man's sexual presence. Charles, maybe, long ago, when she was young and easily impressed. But not many since. Eli Opatnu was downright breathtaking.

"Thank you for seeing me on such short notice," Opatnu said at last.

"My pleasure," Gloria said.

"Mine too," he said, breaking into a grin. His teeth were so white that it almost hurt to look at them.

Gloria started to reach for him, almost reflexively, but managed to divert her motion in another direction, and wound up standing up again, even though she had just sat down.

"Uh . . . can I get you something to drink . . . Eli?"

"No thank you . . . Gloria. I'm fine."

"Yes, I can see that. I mean, uh, it's a pleasure to finally meet you. I've heard a lot of good things about the work you've done in Sector 19."

"I have a full squad of creative publicists at work night and day," he explained. "Oddly enough, I don't think I've ever heard *anything* about you."

"I'm the shy, retiring type," Gloria said. "And may I ask, what brings you here today?"

"I think you know," Opatnu said.

Gloria nodded, then sat down next to him again.

"You've started an investigation in my Sector," he said. "I hoped you could give me an explanation."

"Perhaps," Gloria said. "But first, I'd appreciate it

if you could tell me how you heard about the investigation."

"Oh," he said vaguely, "I have my sources."

"I'm sure you do," Gloria agreed. "And I'd like to know who those sources are. An OSI investigation is supposed to be secret, at least at this point in the process. Sector Administration has not yet been officially notified."

"I understand that, Gloria," Opatnu said. "However, I'm sure you must understand that I can't reveal my sources. Let's just say that I keep an ear to the ground."

"I don't want to get off on the wrong foot with you . . . Eli," Gloria said, meaning every word. "But I'm very concerned about this lapse in OSI security. By any chance, did you hear something about this from anyone in Quadrant?"

Opatnu shrugged. "If I did—and I'm not confirming or denying anything—I certainly wouldn't be at liberty to tell you. Let it go, Gloria. Pursuing this isn't going to get either one of us anything."

"It's not something I can ignore, Eli. If someone from this office—or elsewhere in Dexta—is leaking restricted information, I need to know about it. I cannot have OSI operations compromised, or my people endangered, by lax security and loose lips."

"I seriously doubt that anyone is being endangered," Opatnu said. He sat up a little straighter on the couch and his gaze was no longer as open and friendly as it had been. Neither was Gloria's.

"I have a team on Staghorn," she said. "If someone has already sent word of their mission via messenger or courier, it's possible that they could be in some jeopardy. This is not simply some bureaucratic turf battle, Eli. I need to know how you found out about the investigation."

"I can't help you," Opatnu said. He got to his feet and she got to hers.

"Then I can't help you, either. You'll be informed about the investigation in due course, through proper channels. And if you or any of your people in Sector get in the way, the OSI will come down on you so hard, you'll wonder what hit you."

Opatnu nodded. "All right," he said, "if that's the way you want to play it." He took a step toward the door, then pivoted sharply, grabbed Gloria by her shoulders, pulled her to him, and gave her a long, smoldering kiss that she found herself returning with full intensity. It was at least a minute before they broke.

"That doesn't make any difference," Gloria told him.

"I know," he said, and left.

But it did.

chapter 7

THE COLONY ON NEW CAMBRIDGE, 362 LIGHT-years from Earth, was founded in the year 2367 by a party of young emigrants who had recently graduated from Harvard and the Massachusetts Institute of Technology. Wishing to make it clear that the Cambridge they were honoring was the one in New, rather than Old, England, they assigned the major settlements on the planet's two continents place names that came from the ancient American city they had left. Thus, on the west coast of the western continent stood the great city of Brattle, complemented on the east coast of the eastern continent by the metropolis of Kendall. Between the two lay the planet's greatest city, Central. It was situated on the east coast of the western continent, facing the Dardanelles-like, thirty-mile-wide strait that separated the two landmasses.

In the eight-and-a-half centuries since the colony's founding, the population of New Cambridge had swollen to over 10 billion, and it had become the most important and prosperous world in all of Quadrant 4.

Indeed, in the entire Empire, only Earth and two or three other planets could rival it. Pug Ellison's ancestors had been among the founders, and his family had done its part in promoting the colony's growth. They had profited accordingly, as Petra fully realized for the first time when the limo skimmer brought them to the gates of the Ellison Compound north of Central, high on a shelf of the cliff overlooking the straits.

"Your front yard is bigger than Weehawken," Petra noted.

"Yes, but we don't have a backyard at all, thanks to the cliff face."

"No backyard? Driver, take me back to the port! I'll be damned if I'm going to stay with some lowlife no-account who doesn't even have a backyard."

"Would it help if I told you that I have a bed that's also bigger than Weehawken?"

"Suitable for team sports, no doubt?"

"I prefer one-on-one, myself. But if you'd like, we could call in the staff and choose up sides."

"Hmm," Petra hummed. "We'll save that for later, I think . . . in case I get bored in this cheap dump of yours. Spirit, Pug, just how rich *are* you, anyhow?"

"So rich," he said, "that numbers really have no meaning. Seriously, I couldn't tell you the family's net worth within the nearest trillion crowns."

They debarked from the limo at a side entrance to the immense edifice that Pug called home. The building reminded Petra of an ancient European cathedral. It appeared to have been hacked out of the same rocks as the cliff face that soared behind it, looming a thousand feet above in the crisp, blue sky. She had never seen a house with flying buttresses.

The inside was cavernous and as intimidating as the exterior. The entrance anteroom—Petra thought of it as a mudroom—was larger than the apartment she had grown up in. Pug led her onward through columned corridors and nameless rooms hung with vast, ornate tapestries. Their footsteps echoed on the polished marble floor.

"Where are the gargoyles?" Petra wondered. "There ought to be gargoyles."

"You mean my parents?" Pug asked with a smirk. "Right this way, I think."

Sure enough, the next room they entered contained an immense hearth with a blazing fire, complex chandeliers hanging from a high, vaulted ceiling, plush furniture of mahogany and gold satin, and sitting on it, Pug's parents. They got to their feet and greeted their son with smiles that seemed cool but genuine. Pug didn't quite hug his mother, but gave her an affectionate kiss on her cheek, then turned to his father and shook hands as if closing a business agreement.

"Mother, Father," he said, "you're both looking well. It's wonderful to see you again."

"It's been more than a year, dear," his mother said. "Far too long. And who is this delightful creature?"

"This," Pug said proudly, "is Petra."

Petra stepped forward and extended her hand to Mrs. Ellison, who offered her own in return. It was cool and limp. Mr. Ellison's grip was strong and confident, and he gazed at Petra with evident appreciation. Pug's parents, she knew, were both in their eighties but, thanks to antigerontologicals, looked half that. His mother was slim and fair-haired, with frosty blue eyes and an arctic smile. His father had the same friendly, open face as his son, but with a hint of gray in his hair and crinkly, skeptical eyes.

"So pleased to meet you at last, dear," said Mrs. Ellison. "Palmer has mentioned you, of course, but it's so difficult to truly know someone based on sketchy descriptions."

"But accurate, it would seem," added Mr. Ellison. "I

recall words such as 'beautiful' and 'wonderful' and 'charming.' "

Petra found herself on the verge of a blush. She had dressed for this grand meeting in a modest but slightly saucy blue dress, with a neckline deep enough to have attracted Mr. Ellison's attention. This was the first time she had ever really gone through this particular ritual—Meeting Your Man's Family—and she wasn't entirely sure how to approach the event. The fact that it was taking place in a room the size of a Transit station complicated matters; what should have been an intimate gathering seemed more like a state occasion. She felt like an ambassador presenting her credentials to some lofty monarchs.

"It's wonderful to meet you both," Petra said, smiling. She looked around her. "Nice little place you have here."

"It serves," Mr. Ellison said modestly. "But any home can always stand to be brightened by the presence of a beautiful and charming young woman."

"Indeed," said Mrs. Ellison. She took Petra by the hand and led her to a divan. "Now, dear, sit down and tell us all about yourself."

"I WAS BORN IN NEW JERSEY, AND I'VE WORKED for Dexta two-and-a-half years." Petra slapped herself in the forehead and flopped over backward onto the bed-the-size-of-Weehawken. "Spirit! I sounded like I was applying for a job. I sounded like an idiot!"

"Most everyone does when they first meet my parents," Pug said. "Ordinary people tend to get tongue-tied in the presence of overblown opulence. But you'll get over it."

"Will they? I mean, first impressions are supposed to be important, aren't they? By now, your parents have probably concluded that their son is infatuated with some brainless peasant girl."

Pug smiled. "They'd have thought that no matter what you said. Relax, they'll get over it and so will you. They're just people, Petra."

"Yes," Petra protested, "but I can tell that they were expecting . . . more, somehow. I mean, you told them I was beautiful. *Gloria's* beautiful! I'm just . . . cute. Cute and little."

"You look beautiful to me," Pug said, staring at her naked body. "And as for your size, I think we fit just fine." Pug crawled on top of her and started to demonstrate, but Petra twisted over and tried to crawl away from him.

"Race you to the other side," she challenged.

Pug grabbed her leg and held her in place. "Too dangerous," he said. "You might get lost under the sheets. Even worse, you might run into some of my old girlfriends under there."

That got Petra's attention. She reached back and grabbed Pug by the nose. "Old girlfriends?" she demanded. "You told me they were all dead, or in convents."

"Well, they are, with one or two exceptions . . . *oww!*"

"And what about those exceptions, huh?"

"Well," Pug said, trying to extract his nose from Petra's grip, "you might meet some of them at the party next week. I wouldn't worry about it if I were you. I mean, you can see how big this bed is . . . *yowww!*"

"That's a Qatsima grip Gloria taught me. Would you like to see some more?"

"Not just now, thank you." Pug managed to free himself.

Petra stretched out on her back and stared upward, trying to make out the details of some preposterous mural on the ceiling. Pug lay next to her and amused himself by playing with her small, round breasts. He toyed with her nipples until they were fully erect, then leaned over and kissed them. Petra squirmed for a bit, then sighed contentedly.

"Are those billygoats or satyrs up there?"

"What kind of parents would put satyrs on their son's ceiling? They're goats, and those are cows, and pigs, and chickens . . . the Ellisons started out here as farmers, you see. That section of the mural commemorates our agricultural roots. Over there, you can see the industrial era, and off in that corner you see commerce, science, and philanthropy."

"And what kind of parents would put the family history on their son's ceiling?" Petra wondered.

Pug shrugged. "Ambitious ones?"

"How do they feel about their only son being at Dexta?"

"They aren't thrilled about it," Pug conceded.

Petra propped herself up on one elbow and looked into Pug's face. "And how do they feel about your being my assistant?"

"That," Pug said with a rueful nod, "does bother them a bit. Understand, it's not simply that *you* outrank me. It's that *anyone* outranks me. They think I ought to have Mingus's job. Well, in a year or two, anyway."

"Can't have it," Petra told him. "That job's reserved for Gloria. And when she gets it, I'll be her gatekeeper . . . which will make *me* the most powerful woman in the Empire!"

"Be sure to mention that to my parents. *That* would impress them."

"I'll make a note of it." She put her arms around his neck and pulled him on top of her. "Now, about those old girlfriends. Did any of them ever do *this*?"

"Is that some kind of Qatsima move?" Pug managed to grunt.

"Nope. That's a *Petra* move."

"Better yet," Pug gasped.

GLORIA MARCHED THROUGH THE OUTER OFFICE of Quadrant 4 Administrator Cornell DuBray and into his inner sanctum, feeling a mixture of resentment and trepidation. He had summoned her and she had come, but she still had no clear idea of how she would handle the situation. Her indecision was even reflected in her clothing—a relatively modest dark miniskirt, and a light blue, nearly transparent blouse which she had finally decided to leave unbuttoned to the waist. She was determined not to be intimidated by DuBray; on the other hand, Eric Manko intimidated the hell out of her.

She found DuBray waiting for her in his inner office, flanked by the three other Quadrant Administrators. They were standing next to one another, like a firing squad. Gloria stared at them in silence for several moments. No one offered her a chair.

One of them, Manton Grigsby from Quadrant 2, Gloria already knew slightly from her days in Sector 8. He was a small, dapper, efficient man, and had held his present position for just six years, which made him the junior Quad Admin. Next to him, on DuBray's left, stood Mustafa Algeciras, a swarthy, somewhat portly man from a colony world in Quadrant 3. He was the highest-ranking nonterrestrial in Dexta, making him highly visible and politically indispensable.

Standing to DuBray's right was Elsinore Chandra, a woman Gloria had admired from afar for years. She had been the Quadrant 1 Administrator for nearly as long as Gloria had been alive, and was a certified Dexta legend. Chandra was over a hundred now, but still looked slinky and seductive, with a long woven braid of dark hair thrown casually over her left shoulder and descending nearly to the floor. Her features were sharp and distinct, with large brown eyes that appraised Gloria with professional interest. Chandra had been the Gloria VanDeen of her day, Dexta's most prominent Tiger of the mid-thirty-second century. Whenever Gloria found herself wondering if it was really possible to succeed as a Dexta Tiger, she would think of Chandra and know that it was.

"Thank you for coming," DuBray said with a perfunctory but oily smile. "Mr. Grigsby, Mr. Algeciras, and Ms. Chandra and I thought it might be useful for you to meet with us and get a few things straight. We probably should have done this sooner, but we wanted to see how you and your Office of Strategic Intervention performed. Frankly, some of us didn't expect you—or it—to last very long."

"I'm still here," Gloria said. She nodded toward Grigsby. "It's nice to see you again, Mr. Grigsby."

"And you, Ms. VanDeen," Grigsby said, smiling a little. Gloria stepped toward him and shook his hand.

Then she offered her hand to Algeciras, who took it in both of his own hands, kissed it, and looked into her eyes. "A pleasure to meet you at last, Ms. VanDeen. I look forward to getting to know you much better, but for now, it seems we must tend to business." He released her hand as if letting a captive bird fly away.

She didn't bother to greet DuBray, but turned to Chandra and offered her a warm smile as they clasped hands. "Ms. Chandra," she said, "it's an honor to meet you. I've been an admirer of yours for a long time."

"And I have taken note of you, as well, Ms. VanDeen. You play the game rather nicely, I think. You are off to an excellent start at Dexta. But it would be a shame to see such a promising career derailed."

"Derailed?"

"It's not really your fault," Chandra said. "I blame Norman Mingus entirely. I told that old goat what a monumentally bad idea this Office of Strategic Intervention of his was. But he hasn't listened to me since I kicked him out of my bedroom, twenty years ago. I gather that you aren't fucking him, though, are you? Is that your choice, or his?"

"I don't think that's really any of your business," Gloria replied.

"No," Chandra said, "I suppose it's not. No more than it's any of my business that Cornell sicced his pet psychopath on you for not putting out." She gave DuBray a not-very-friendly glance.

"I seem to recall a time," DuBray said, smirking at Chandra, "when you had a virtual platoon of handsome young Hammers at your disposal, Elsie."

"Maybe I did," Chandra sniffed, "but at least I never had to have anyone beaten up to get him to go to bed with me." She looked back at Gloria. "I admire your grit, Ms. VanDeen, if not your good sense. You must realize that if you intend to remain in Dexta, the day will eventually come when you find yourself having sex with Cornell DuBray. It's not really as awful as you might imagine. I lived through it, dear, and so will you."

"Thank you, Elsie, for that ringing endorsement. But leaving personal matters to one side for the moment, the purpose of this meeting, Ms. VanDeen, is to acquaint you with some realities. The four of us are presenting what you might call a United Front against the Office of Strategic Intervention, and we wanted you— and Norman—to understand that we mean business."

"It's true, you see," said Algeciras, spreading his arms a little, as if in apology. "The OSI has no logical place in the structure of Dexta. Its sudden growth is like that of a malignancy in an otherwise healthy body. And like a malignancy, it must be excised."

"Putting it a little less colorfully," Grigsby said, "we see OSI as counterproductive and contrary to the best interests of Dexta. Its charter infringes on the inherent powers of Quadrant, and even Sector, Administrators. The very existence of OSI implies the incompetence of the normal bureaucracy. Dexta is perfectly capable of functioning without the aid of highly public 'strategic interventions.' "

"What he means, dear," said Chandra, "is that you make us look bad. The public loves it, of course, but it's bad for morale among Dexta people. If you're the good guy in these little dramas, that makes the rest of Dexta look like bad guys. And we're not"—she paused and eyed DuBray for a moment, then continued—"or most of us aren't, at any rate."

"We've discussed all of this with Norman," DuBray said, "but he refuses to accept reality. I wonder sometimes if he's really up to the demands of the job anymore. In any case, he intends to continue his little experiment, regardless of the consequences. Of course, the consequences for Norman won't be nearly as painful as they are for you."

Grigsby frowned and said, "That's not really necessary, DuBray." He turned to Gloria and said, "While I may not agree with my colleague's methods, I am in complete agreement concerning his goals. We all are. Norman Mingus doesn't run Dexta, Ms. VanDeen—*we* do. You should keep that in mind."

"Whatever the OSI Charter may say," Algeciras told her, "as a practical matter, you will need our cooperation in order to function. And that you will not get."

"What's more," said Chandra, "most of the Sector Administrators support our position. Wherever OSI attempts to operate, you will find not only no cooperation, but determined opposition. I realize that the OSI Charter gives you certain peremptory powers, and Norman will certainly give you as much leeway as the *Dexta Code* allows. Nevertheless, within Dexta the OSI will be treated as a pariah. Think about what that would mean—for your office, and for you personally, dear."

Gloria had stood there listening in silence, all the while feeling a rising tide of emotion within her. Most of it was anger, along with outrage and defiance. But there was fear there, too. The most powerful people in Dexta had just declared war on her and OSI.

She took a deep breath. "Norman Mingus created the OSI and appointed me to lead it. If he should decide that he made a mistake and wants to remove me or dissolve the office, that would be entirely up to him. Not you—him. Until that happens, I intend to do my job to the best of my ability, come what may. If you expect me to quit, you'd better think again."

DuBray shook his head. "No, we don't expect you to quit," he said. "You have become very famous and popular with the masses, and we have no intention of letting ourselves be drawn into some unseemly public pissing match. As a matter of fact, we earnestly hope that you will continue in your present position. The OSI does have its uses, and its glamorous leader is certainly an asset to Dexta."

"Then what do you want?" Gloria demanded. DuBray started to answer, but Gloria cut him off. "No, not *you*. I know what *you* want. What about the rest of you?"

"We simply want your cooperation," said Grigsby. "In fact, we insist on it. Regardless of what the OSI Charter may say, all future OSI operations must receive prior approval from the appropriate Quadrant Administrator."

"You can't just come charging onto our turf like an avenging angel," said Chandra. "We will decide when a 'strategic intervention' is necessary and appropriate and when it is not. If you think you see a need for an intervention, come to us. If Norman assigns you to an intervention, come to us. If we agree that it is necessary, you can then proceed with our blessing and support. If we disagree, then there will be no intervention."

"What if Secretary Mingus orders me to proceed?"

"Leave Mingus to us," DuBray said.

"And what if I decide to ignore you and do what I think is best?" Gloria locked eyes with each of the Quadrant Administrators in turn.

"That would be foolish, dear," said Chandra, shaking her head. "You are young and idealistic, and Spirit knows we can use some of that around here. But don't imagine for a moment that your beauty and charm and courage somehow outweigh our institutional power. And while I can personally promise you fair and decent treatment, I'm afraid that I don't speak for everyone on that point."

DuBray smiled innocently. "Power exists to be used," he said. "You've already seen one aspect of the power at my disposal. If you continue to defy me, you'll see it again."

"Okay, this is where I get off." Manton Grigsby shot DuBray a dirty look, then walked past Gloria and out the door.

"And I, as well," said Chandra. She stepped forward and stopped in front of Gloria. "Although, I must say that there was a time when I would have stayed. You are remarkably attractive, although I think I could have given you a run for your money when I was in my prime." Chandra leaned forward and quickly whispered in Gloria's ear, "Fight dirty, dear. It's your only hope." She gave Gloria another smile, then left the room.

Gloria looked toward Algeciras and DuBray. Each man returned her gaze with a malicious half smile, like wolves contemplating their prey.

"I'll be going now, too," Gloria said. "I'll think about what you've said." She turned smartly and walked to the door, relieved to be making a quick exit. Her relief died stillborn. Waiting for her in the outer office stood a huge and grinning Erik Manko.

• • •

GLORIA STAYED IN HER OFFICE LATE THAT
night, brooding. Her ribs still ached, but this time
Manko had not beaten her badly, possibly in deference
to DuBray's office furniture. He had merely punched
her and thrown her a couple of times, enough to make
his point. Then he had methodically stripped her,
picked her up, and delivered her to DuBray and
Algeciras in the inner office. Gloria was too frightened
to try to fight Manko, and was discouraged by Chandra's
words about the inevitability of it. Amid a wave of disgust and anger, she submitted to the Fours, as she had
once submitted to the Fifteens. For her job. For Dexta.

"Fuck Dexta!" Gloria abruptly said aloud to the
empty office. She had seen Dexta at its worst today, both
personally and professionally. Four entrenched bureaucrats were waging a turf war against Norman Mingus,
and Gloria and the OSI were simply pawns in their
game. The fact that OSI had been doing good and necessary work did not enter into their consideration. The
bureaucracy operated according to its own imperatives,
and could not tolerate a maverick in its midst. It all
made such perfect sense that Gloria even found herself
agreeing in principle. The Quadrant Administrators had
every right to feel affronted by the existence of OSI. Of
course they would attempt to fight back.

More than that, Gloria realized that each of the four
Quad Admins had reason to see her as a personal threat.
Power within Dexta was a finite commodity; the more of
it Gloria gained, the less would be shared by DuBray,
Chandra, Algeciras, and Grigsby. If the OSI was a bu-
reaucratic annoyance, its sexy and charismatic leader
represented a potential rival for the ear of Norman
Mingus and the opinion of Parliament and the public.
So there was really no choice about it: The Quad
Admins *had* to oppose her.

But they didn't have to be such fucking pigs about
it! Gloria wondered what it said about an organization

when 50 percent of its upper management personnel were sadistic swine. Was that a requirement for the position, or was it something they learned on the job?

And yet, it was a job Gloria wanted. She wanted it so badly, it now seemed that she was willing to let smarmy jerks like DuBray and Algeciras have their way with her in order to preserve her position at Dexta. And why? So she could move onward and upward at Dexta until she became just like them?

"Fuck Dexta!" she said again, louder. "I don't have to do this, you know," she said to the silent walls, "I could be Empress."

Empress.

Coruler, more or less, of 3 trillion beings and a sphere of space two thousand light-years in diameter. An empire of 2653 worlds and counting. Empress.

Empress, as opposed to sexual plaything for depraved bureaucrats.

Algeciras had oozed over her like a bloated amoeba, dripping good intentions and romantic bile. He seemed to believe he was offering himself as a gift to her, and didn't understand why she would fail to accept it joyously.

DuBray had been less subtle. His choice of point of entry didn't surprise her, and she had simply leaned across his desk and accepted his pile-driving, battering-ram attentions without comment. From the sound of the muffled, urgent grunts he made as he went about his business behind her, she got the impression that DuBray really wasn't enjoying himself very much, either. This wasn't about sex. It was about domination.

"Fuck Dexta!" Gloria shouted it out.

Empress wouldn't be so bad, maybe. Gloria VanDeen-Hazar, Empress and Avatar of Joy.

Except that Empress was not the job she really wanted. Abruptly, she laughed out loud at her own audacity. It wasn't enough that she wanted to run the Empire—she insisted on running it on *her* terms. Empress wasn't good enough; only Secretary of Dexta would do.

A sharp rapping at her office door was followed by the appearance of Arkady Volkonski. He stuck his head into the office and looked around. "I thought I heard a profanity directed against Dexta," he said.

"Stick around and you may hear it again," Gloria told him.

"I'd have to report you to someone," Volkonski informed her. "Disloyalty and seditious speech are to be discouraged."

"That's what I like about you, Arkady. I know I can always count on you to be a fascist."

"I wish you'd let me be one with Manko," Volkonski said.

"No!" Gloria barked. "I mean it, Arkady, I don't want you even thinking about Manko. I will not allow you to risk your career over this."

Volkonski frowned, but nodded. "Very well. But what *are* you going to do about him?"

"I'm going to take the advice someone gave me today," Gloria told him. "Arkady, do you know how to get to Harlem?"

Volkonski shrugged. "Take the A Train?"

"YOU CAN'T COME IN WITH ME, ARKADY," Gloria told him as the skimmer hovered outside the entrance to Club Twelve Twenty-Nine. "I'll be perfectly safe in there, but you can keep a watch on the door if it makes you feel better."

"It would make me feel better if you didn't go in at all."

"It's just a club," Gloria assured him.

"Yes, and don't think I don't know what kind of club. Your personal life is your business, Gloria, but it bothers me—professionally and personally—to see you taking risks."

"Lately," said Gloria, "I've been taking a risk just getting out of bed in the morning. Relax, Arkady, I'll be fine. But I may be a while."

Gloria got out of the skimmer before Volkonski could raise any more objections. The bouncers welcomed her. Arnold was not behind the bar, but the woman on duty there directed her to a room to one side of the bar. She went in and found Arnold and a couple of other club employees lounging in some comfortable chairs, drinking beer, and watching a vid display of one of the null-rooms.

"Good evening, Arnold," Gloria said. "Do you suppose you and I could have a word in private?"

Arnold looked at the other workers and they dutifully exited. Gloria sat down in a chair next to Arnold. "You look better than ever tonight, Gloria," Arnold said. He reached for her and gave her upper thigh an affectionate squeeze. "What can I do for you?"

"I need a favor," she said. "I need to talk to a zamie."

Arnold leaned back in the chair and stared at her, clearly surprised. After a moment or two he nodded and said, "I can arrange that. Did you have anyone particular in mind?"

"I don't know from zamies," she said. "But I need to talk to someone as high up in the organization as you can manage."

"And would this conversation be of an official nature?"

"Call it semiofficial. It involves me personally, but there would be some Dexta interest. In any case, it would be off the record."

"Can I say what this is about?"

Gloria shook her head. "Only that it's a matter of some importance. I'd rather not say any more just now."

"All right," Arnold said. "I'll see what I can do. I assume I can reach you at Dexta?"

"Anytime."

"It may be a couple of days," he said. "I mean, I know some people, and they know some people . . . you know? Meantime, is there anything I can do for you tonight?"

"I was wondering if you have any Forty-eight yet?"

"Soon, they tell me. For now, all we have is Twenty-nine."

"In that case," Gloria said with a smile, "I think I'd like to try that wild cherry."

chapter 8

GLORIA TOOK THE NEXT MORNING OFF AND went to Rio. She wanted to talk to Charles. The Emperor, however, had ceremonial duties to attend to and would not be available for an hour or two. Gloria decided to kill the time with a walk in the Imperial Gardens.

She enjoyed the sights and smells of the botanical phantasmagoria, but was struck again by the symbolism of the place. Here, Terrans had deposited and nourished little bits and pieces of their Empire, green trophies of their triumphs. It seemed to Gloria that these biological oddities were really statements about the wealth and power of the Empire. We go where we want, and take what we want. Make careful note, O Faithful Subjects! We collected your plants, but we could just as easily have collected *you*!

Terran rule was not, by and large, cruel or oppressive. A few intransigent species had been wiped out during the course of mankind's expansion into the galaxy, but most had accepted the coming of the Earthers with varying degrees of acquiescence. Down through the centuries, the Empire had fought plenty of wars, large and small, and on some worlds there were still resistance movements and die-hard bands of guerrillas. But in the four decades since the defeat of the Ch'gnth, the Empire had mainly been at peace with itself, its subjects, and its neighbors. The era of peace was likely to continue indefinitely, since long-range probes had revealed no potential challenger to Terran hegemony within a thousand light-years of the Frontiers.

Contained within the Empire was a dazzling diversity of species, societies, and systems. Even leaving aside the alien civilizations, the human worlds of the Empire offered a cornucopia of cultures. Under the overarching rule of the Emperor, Parliament, and Dexta, individual worlds and small confederations had been free to work out their own systems of government and social organization. As long as they respected basic sentients' rights (at least in the abstract) and didn't overtly challenge Imperial rule or Dexta's ursine embrace, such worlds were welcome to develop as they would. Over 60 percent of human-inhabited planets operated under some form of democratic rule, but the others featured everything from feudal kingdoms and ancestral satrapies to communist collectives and fascist dictatorships. Seventy percent of the Empire's residents called themselves Spiritists, yet there were also enclaves where strict Muslims, Hindus, and Christians held sway. The Jews had worlds of their own. So did the French.

All things considered, it was a rather relaxed empire—the only kind possible, really, given the distances and numbers involved. It was a strategy that had worked well—the Terran Empire had already lasted longer than those of Rome, Britain, or America. The Empire didn't try too hard to impose its will as long as its subjects didn't try too hard to resist it. People like the anarchists of PAIN objected to the very principle of empire, but there was no simmering cauldron of discontent for them to tap into. The O'Neill Dictum—"all politics is local"—applied even on a galactic scale. The issues that bothered people in Quadrant 1 were unlikely to concern those a thousand light-years away in Quadrant 3. Ruling the Empire, it seemed to Gloria, was mainly a matter of preserving the natural equipoise and inertia that governed any such immense entity.

Ruling the Empire! She could do it, or half do it, with a single word to Charles. She *could* . . .

And yet, ruling the Empire was not quite the same thing as *running* it. Charles ruled the Empire, but Norman Mingus had more tangible power at his fingertips than did Charles, or any Emperor since Hazar the Great.

But what had Grigsby said? Mingus doesn't run Dexta, *we* do? As Charles ruled the Empire, Mingus ruled Dexta, but the Quad Admins actually ran it. Operational, day-to-day power within Dexta was concentrated in the grimy hands of DuBray, Chandra, Algeciras, and Grigsby. And that was not likely to change. What would that mean for the OSI?

Running the OSI was fun. It gave her the opportunity to dash all over the Empire and solve problems that didn't really matter very much in the grand scheme of things but deeply affected the lives of those involved. The dispute on Cartago had been barely a notch above trivial, and yet the people of that barren world were probably going to lead at least slightly better lives because of what Gloria had done. That was something to be proud of, and she was. And aside from the fact that now and then people tried to kill her, Gloria enjoyed her OSI missions.

There was an intense, almost sexual thrill about it all, like an extended ride on Orgastria-29. It was like screwing on a roller coaster, in full view of 3 trillion people.

Gloria smiled at the thought and found herself singing one of the old twentieth-century ditties she enjoyed: "And I'll have fun, fun, fun, till my daddy takes my T-Bird away!" She wasn't too clear on what a T-Bird was, but she liked the concept.

And she could go on having that kind of fun—until the Quad Admins took her T-Bird away. Gloria kicked at a pebble on the walkway and sent it flying. OSI was now all but officially under siege by the Quad Admins. She could hang on by her fingernails and try to keep the OSI independent and alive—but it was a battle that promised to be grim and costly.

Or, she could become Empress.

She held out her hands, palms up, and mentally weighed her options. In her left hand she put the advantages of being Empress. Immense power. A huge responsibility along with it, true, but still . . .

There were the perks. Having been wealthy all her life, Gloria seldom thought about money, but she did appreciate the luxuries it could buy. As Empress, she could have every luxury imaginable, and then some. Her left hand sagged a bit lower from the weight of the thought.

But would it really be . . . *fun, fun, fun*? Surrounded by Imperial Security, hounded incessantly by the media, some sort of living goddess to the adoring but demanding masses? All of that had a certain appeal to her, she had to admit, but it might become tiresome after the first twenty or thirty years.

In her right hand, she put Dexta. Dexta, *dexter;* Empress, *sinister.* Had she meant something by that?

Dexta . . . all the *fun, fun, fun* a girl could ask for. Like being terrorized by the Pack Dogs and her superiors when she was a Fifteen. Like having people try to kill her. Like being butt-fucked by Cornell DuBray. Like having to face the ugly little realities of life in the glorious Empire—attempted genocide on Mynjhino, and the smell of the fires in the park, where the Jhino troops were cremating the bodies of thousands of Myn. Or the camp at Pizen Flats on Sylvania, strewn with the remains of people who had been her friends.

But in the end, she had been able to redress the balance on those two worlds, though not without cost. She had made a difference. The Empire was a marginally better place than it would have been without her. That counted for something.

On the other hand, consider how much more she could do as Empress. And as Empress, she would have no Quad Admins standing in her way. She would not have to deal with Cornell DuBray. Only Charles . . .

She stared at her hands for a few moments, then threw them up in the air in defeat. She was damned if she knew *which* hand Charles should go in.

She had been young and stupid when she married him. Was she still young enough and stupid enough to marry him again? Spirit, hadn't she learned anything? Of course, it was different now. Back then, Charles had not been Emperor and was unlikely ever to be; she was simply his wife. And being his wife had not been all bad, in honesty. Charles, who had the male version of the enhanced genes Gloria boasted, was probably the best bedmate she'd ever had. And in spite of being an essentially selfish bastard, there were times when he had shown some dim signs of intelligence, compassion, and generosity.

Could she rule the Empire at his side? Have a son with him?

Gloria found herself standing in front of the gnarled glashpadoza tree, the one that absorbed the sins of its owner. An appropriate item for an emperor to have. And what, she wondered, would Dexta's glashpadoza tree be like? How big, how ugly would *that* one be?

At least she didn't have to decide between them at once. No, she could brood about it for weeks and let it eat up her life, instead.

Fun, fun, fun, she thought.

GLORIA'S ROUTE TO THE RESIDENCE TOOK HER past the swimming pool, where she found an unpleasant surprise. Laurence, Lord Brockinbrough—Charles's detestable cousin and heir—was camped out poolside, shielded from the fierce Rio sun by a purple robe and a broad-brimmed straw hat. He raised a hand to her and waved it idly. "Gloria," he called. "Grand to see you again, milady. Or should I say, my Empress?"

Gritting her teeth, Gloria managed a smile and a cool, "Hello, Larry."

It had been seven or eight years since she had seen him. He had put on weight. There had always been something snakelike about him, Gloria thought, but now he more closely resembled one of those plump lizards that lie around on rocks and wait for a meal to walk by. He was in his fifties and could have looked thirty, but the additional weight had pushed him into some nebulous zone of indeterminate middle age. His cheeks were full and round, his lips fleshy, his eyes still dark and impenetrable.

"I intend to be best man again," Larry told her, smiling impishly.

"Don't get your hopes up, Larry," Gloria replied. "Nothing has been decided."

"Playing the reluctant virgin, are we? I have to say, the role ill becomes you. I know you better than that, after all."

He knew her entirely too well. She and Charles had spent much of their marriage roaming the Empire in his luxurious yacht, and on some of those jaunts, they had been joined by Cousin Larry. Joined, even in bed. Charles enjoyed experimentation.

In those days, Charles had been nothing but a callow and superfluous member of a fecund dynastic clan, far from power or the prospect of it, and Larry an older and even more superfluous embarrassment to the Hazars. Somehow, they had latched on to each other and become what they described, in drunken giggles, as coconspirators in a Plot Against the Empire. They both affected a pose of being cynical young rebels, contemptuous of the dynasty that imprisoned them, although Larry was already getting a little old to be credible in the part. Charles had seemed to be studying his cousin, picking up pointers for what promised to be a life of idle merriment and utter uselessness.

A loud splash from the pool drew Gloria's attention. She saw a naked young man cavorting there with two equally naked young women.

"You remember my son, Gareth, of course," said Larry.

"That's Gareth?" Gloria asked in genuine surprise. She remembered him as a ten-year-old brat. He was the product of Larry's union with his first wife. The wife he had beaten to death in a drunken rage.

Such things happened, of course, even in the best of families. It was the media's *scandal du jour* for a time, but then Larry was packed off to a Rehabilitation Clinic for a year, and no more was said about it. And nothing at all was said about the second woman he killed, an anonymous nobody on some distant outworld. A little more rehabilitation, a little less booze, and Larry was once again fit to be seen in public.

"I wouldn't have recognized him," Gloria said, looking toward young Gareth in the pool.

"He had a rapid and successful puberty," Larry said. "He's eighteen now. Smart as a whip, too."

"Just a chip off the old block, huh?"

Larry smiled. "I'd like to think he's better than that."

"He'd almost have to be, wouldn't he?"

Lord Brockinbrough gave a minimal shrug. He must have been well aware that Gloria despised him; most people who knew him did. He simply refused to let that bother him.

"Gareth!" Larry called. "Come on over here and say hello to Gloria."

The young man dutifully swam over to the side of the pool, hauled himself out of it, and stood before Gloria, naked and dripping water from various appendages. He was tall, slim, and well formed, with the same serpentine eyes as his father. "Hi, Gloria," he said happily. "Been a long time." His eyes made a slow and deliberate inventory of everything revealed by Gloria's flimsy wrap dress, which was nearly all of her.

"Hello, Gareth. You've grown up, I see."

He glanced down at himself, then looked into Gloria's eyes and grinned. "Yes, I have," he said. "You might even like me now. Are you going to marry Charles again?"

"That remains to be determined," Gloria said formally, wondering if everyone in the Household was aware of Charles's proposition.

"Well," Gareth said, "if you don't, *I'm* available." He winked at her.

"I'll make a note of that," Gloria told him.

"No, really," Gareth persisted. "If marriage is out, maybe we could just fuck sometime. I mean, I know you did it with my dad, and I'm better than him. Isn't that right, girls?" he called to the young women in the pool. "I'm better than my dad, aren't I?" The girls grinned and nodded enthusiastically.

Gloria glanced at Lord Brockinbrough. "Is there a gene for narcissism?" she wondered aloud.

"Back in the pool, son. You're embarrassing Gloria,

who is a woman of refined sensibilities and lofty pretensions. Anyway, you're getting a hard-on, staring at her like that."

Gareth laughed. "Seeya later, Gloria!" He dived into the pool and porpoised his way back to the girls.

"All the grace and charm we've come to expect from the Brockinbroughs," Gloria observed.

"He still has a few rough edges," Larry admitted, "but I'm proud of him, I truly am. He may yet redeem the family name that I so thoughtlessly besmirched. I have great hopes for him."

"Hope is a wonderful thing," Gloria agreed.

"Charles has high hopes, too," Larry said. "Don't disappoint him, Gloria. Marry him. Give him a son. As things stand now, *I'm* his heir. I don't like that any more than the rest of the House of Hazar does. We would all be thrilled and gratified if you were to become Empress and relieve me of the burden and embarrassment of being next in the line of succession."

"I honestly haven't made up my mind, Larry," Gloria said.

"He needs you, Gloria. More than he realizes. He was devastated when you left him."

Gloria responded to that with a loud horselaugh.

"Well, he was," Larry insisted. "He may not have shown it, but he was deeply hurt."

"I seem to recall," Gloria said, "that after I left him, the two of you went off on an inspection tour of all the bordellos in Quadrant 3."

"It was merely a way of coping with his grief. Charles is deeper than you ever gave him credit for. He's an intelligent and caring man, but given his upbringing, he's always felt that he had to hide his inner self. Growing up as a Hazar is more of a burden than you can fully comprehend, Gloria. I never managed to overcome it, but Charles has, and will only improve with age— with you at his side."

Gloria didn't say anything in response. But she wondered if he could be right.

CHARLES WAS FREE, AND GLORIA WAS SENT into his private chambers. There, she found him changing out of his Imperial garb and into a tee shirt and a pair of old, faded jeans.

"Where does an Emperor get worn-out jeans?" she asked him.

"He simply keeps the same pair for ten years and threatens the catacombs for anyone who dares to mend, repair, or refurbish them. I had these jeans when we were together, Glory. I can still fit into them, too, thank you very much."

"One way, at least, that you don't take after Cousin Larry."

"Saw him, did you?"

"That misfortune was mine, yes."

"He's not as bad as you think he is."

"He said precisely the same thing about you."

"Really? Well, there, you see, that proves it's true for both of us. Now, what can I do for you? The Emperor is entirely at your disposal."

"Will I talk about myself in the third person, too, if I become Empress?"

"Probably," Charles said after a moment's thought. "There are times when I think of the Emperor as some other guy, some distinct entity, different from *me*."

"So, you take off your robes and garters and whatnot, get into your jeans, and suddenly you're no longer the Emperor? Is it as easy as that?"

Charles shook his head. "*Nothing* is easy for an emperor. But you get used to it. I did, and so will you."

"Maybe." Gloria sat down on the edge of the bed next to Charles as he put on a pair of sneakers. "What will it be like?" she asked him. "For us, I mean?"

"As husband and wife? Or as Emperor and Empress?"

"Both. You weren't exactly an ideal husband the first time around."

"I suppose we can take that as a given. Perhaps we can also assume that I learned something from the experience, and that I won't be quite as much of a cad in the future as I have been in the past. I expect that we would both retain a certain degree of freedom, however, if that's what's on your mind. Far be it from me to cramp the style of an Avatar of Joy."

Gloria nodded. She had to admit that marital fidelity was not a concept that worked well for either one of them. She had tried to be faithful to Charles after they were first married, but when it became obvious that he had no intention of cleaving only unto her, she had sown a few wild oats of her own. Well, more than a few, actually. And Cousin Larry was hardly the only person to have shared a bed with both of them.

"Mind you," Charles added, "I don't think it would be appropriate for the Empress to start humping beggars in the streets. But short of that, I think you'd probably be able to have as active a social life as you desire. No more trips to the Club Twelve Twenty-Nine, though. But I've set up a null-room here in the Residence, and as for drugs—"

"Dammit, Charles, you're having me followed!"

"Let's just say that I'm keeping tabs on you. For instance, I know that Cornell DuBray is giving you a hard time. And that Manko hominid . . . say the word, Glory, and I'll make him disappear."

"I can handle Manko myself," she insisted. "And DuBray, too."

"But why should you have to?" Charles asked in honest bafflement. "That's the part I just don't understand. Never have. What the hell are you trying to prove? You're rich, beautiful, and privileged—you always have been and you always will be. Why the pretensions of being just another working girl, carrying her lunch in a brown paper bag?"

Gloria snickered. "I'm hardly *that*."

"No, but you seem to want people to think that you are—when you aren't busy being an Avatar of Joy. It seems to me that you're trying to have things both ways, Gloria. You want to be an honest, dedicated bureaucrat, a true servant of the people, but at the same time you want to go on enjoying all the advantages of your wealth and position."

"I don't see why I can't do both. Being the glamorous Gloria VanDeen—you know, sometimes I think of *her* in the third person—gives me a certain power, both inside and outside Dexta. I use that power to do my job. You may not like some of the things I've done, but you can't deny that I've been pretty effective."

"But think how much more effective you could be as Empress." Charles seized her left hand and squeezed it. "Think of all the good you could do for humanity!"

Gloria abruptly pulled her hand away from him. "Oh, please," she groaned.

Charles grimaced. "Okay," he said, "I suppose that one doesn't work very well, coming from me. We both know that I care more about the well-being of my dogs than I do about the general run of humanity. As long as they aren't rioting in the streets for bread, I'm not too concerned about their happiness. Spirit, Gloria, there are *three trillion* of them. My job is to be concerned about the welfare of the anthill, not the ants. But if you *do* care about them—and I believe that you sincerely do—then here's your chance to do something for them."

"Like what?"

"Entertain them, for one. They need that, you know, almost as much as they need the bread. Bread and circuses, like in Rome. The plebs haven't changed in three thousand years, Gloria. They still want sex and spectacle, and who better to provide that than you?"

"I give them that already," Gloria pointed out. "What more would I be able to do if I were Empress? You talked about real power, Charles. What, exactly, are you offering?"

Charles got to his feet and wandered out onto a balcony. Gloria followed him and took in the green opulence of Rio and the looming bulk of Sugar Loaf. The central spire of the Spiritist Mother Church impaled the nearby sky. Far below them, she noticed the swimming pool, where Cousin Larry and son Gareth seemed to be busy having sex with the two young women she had seen.

"Sex and spectacle," she mused. "But what about power?"

"Within reason," Charles said at last, "I can see giving you authority over virtually anything you want, with the exception of the military and the economy."

"Those are pretty big exceptions, Chuckles."

"And necessary ones. The military can have only one commander-in-chief, and that must be the Emperor. Surely, you can see that. As for the economy, in a general sense, it runs itself. In a more specific sense, policies such as taxation, money supply, and resource development all involve a complex set of relationships among the Household, Parliament, and the Big Twelve. It wouldn't do to have you meddling in that miasma. You would find it stupefyingly boring, in any case."

"So what's left?"

"Social welfare, in all its many guises. Food for the starving, clothes for the needy, books for the ignorant. You could play an important role in seeing to it that the Empire is not populated exclusively by hungry, naked morons."

"If you control the economy," Gloria pointed out, "that would leave me distributing crumbs."

"What you get would depend on how well you play the game. It's nice to pretend that as Emperor I can just snap my fingers and get what I want, but that's not the way it works. I still have to fight for the programs and policies I favor, and I don't always get my way. Neither would you. But as Empress, you would carry considerable weight with the public and, therefore, with Parliament. What you ultimately achieved would be determined by your own abilities."

"What if some of my social welfare issues overlapped with your domain?"

"Such as?"

"The Big Twelve dominate some worlds in ways that go far beyond mere business. In some places, they are virtual feudal overlords."

"Aren't they just?" Charles said with a snort. "And you think you can do something about it?"

"I'd like to try," Gloria said.

Charles thought about it for a moment. "A ticklish area," he said at last. "But it strikes me that it might be useful if we could double-team them. 'Sorry, GalaxCo, I'd love to help you out, but it would upset the Empress.' That sort of thing. Together, we'd have some leverage with them." He turned to her and grinned. "It might even be fun."

"There are some other things," Gloria said. She pointed toward the sky. "There's still slavery out there."

Charles nodded. "I know," he said.

"Back on Mynjhino, Randall Sweet talked about selling me to the royal family on Shandrach. What if I wanted to do something about those bastards?"

"You'd have my cautious support. I'm not Lincoln, and I have no intention of having an Antietam or a Gettysburg on my watch. But I don't much care for the slavers, and I wouldn't mind if the history books called me Charles the Emancipator. Sounds pretty good, don't you think?"

"So what does 'cautious support' mean, exactly?"

Charles sighed. "I guess it means that I'd be with you in principle, but that there are limits to how far I'd be willing to go in practice. I'm not going to let you drag me—and the Empire—into a crusade or a civil war over the issue. One thing you'll understand as Empress, Glory, is that you have to take the long view. Some problems may take decades to solve. Others may take centuries. Still others may have no solution at all. You have to be able to tell the difference and act on that understanding."

"I appreciate what you're saying, Charles, and I don't expect miracles. But you've been pretty vague about all of this."

"You want specifics? Very well, I'll consult with the appropriate people on my staff and draw up some sort of document laying out the details of our joint rule. You'll object to it, of course, and propose changes. We'll change the changes, and you'll change the changes to your changes. Eventually, we'll come to an agreement. Then we'll have something to wave in each other's face after we've violated the agreement."

"All right. Put your people to work on it."

Charles turned to face her and put his hands on her shoulders. "We're really going to do this, then?" he asked.

"We might," Gloria said airily, as if they were discussing having lunch. "I mentioned this to Mingus. He said we might do a great job together as Emperor and Empress."

Charles's eyebrows rose. "Norman said *that*? Well, then . . . what better endorsement could you want?"

"He also said that we might wind up leading the Empire into a civil war."

Charles laughed. "The Charlesists versus the

Glorianos? What fun! If I end up chopping off your head, I promise you I'll have it preserved and tastefully displayed in the Imperial Museum."

"And I," Gloria assured him, "will do the same with whatever part of you *I* chop off."

chapter 9

GLORIA STOOD ON THE SIDEWALK AT THE MAIN
entrance to the immense Dexta complex, which took up
twelve city blocks' worth of ground space in midtown
Manhattan. The day was raw and drizzly, and she wore a
buff-colored trench coat over her navy miniskirt and
jacket. People walking by stopped and stared at her
briefly, then continued on their way; Manhattanites had
always been accustomed to celebrities in their midst.

A long black limo pulled over to the curb and hovered there. A door popped open and Gloria stepped in.
She sat down next to a man in an expensive overcoat as
the door closed behind her and the skimmer pulled
away from the Dexta complex. Without bothering to
look, Gloria knew that behind the limo, another skimmer filled with Bugs was following at a discreet interval;
she had told Volkonski to keep his distance today.

"Ms. VanDeen?" the man said. "I'm Ed Smith.
Pleased to make your acquaintance." Gloria nodded politely and shook his hand. He was a prosperous-looking

man of about sixty, she guessed, a little overweight but with a healthy, ruddy look to his face.

"Smith?" Gloria couldn't help asking.

The man shrugged. "Okay, so I'm not Ed Smith. But you have to call me something, so it might just as well be Ed Smith, right?"

"Fair enough," Gloria said. "Thank you for agreeing to see me."

"It wasn't exactly a hardship," Smith said, grinning. "When I got the request, it took me about a nanosecond to clear my calendar. I've seen you in person before—here and there, around town—but I never really expected to have the pleasure of taking you to lunch. By the way, we'll be going to a little French restaurant we own over on the East Side. There's a private room, so we won't be seen or disturbed."

"French?" Gloria asked. "I have to confess, I was expecting Italian."

"Or maybe Russian? Or Japanese? Stereotypes die hard, I suppose. The fact is, I don't have a drop of Sicilian blood in me. The organization of which I am a part is—how shall I put this?—ecumenical."

"And if I could ask, just how did you become a part of it?"

"Believe it or not, I was recruited out of college," Smith said with a slightly embarrassed smile. "I ran the football and basketball betting pools at my fraternity. I was good at it, and pretty soon I was handling the sports book for every frat on campus. And when I graduated, instead of going with GalaxCo or Imperium, I accepted an offer from the zamitat. And I've never regretted it."

They arrived at the restaurant; Gloria mentioned that she had eaten there several times. "You do business with us every day, Gloria, whether you realize it or not," Smith told her as they got settled at a table in a private room. Since he seemed to know the place so well, Gloria let Smith order wine and their meal.

"This restaurant and places like the Club Twelve Twenty-Nine are only the tip of the iceberg," Smith explained. "We like to think of ourselves as the thirteenth of the Big Twelve. We have long-term relationships with each of them, as well as with Dexta, Parliament, and the Imperial Household itself. The zamitat provides important services that people want and need and are not otherwise available. We are a necessary social lubricant."

"I see," said Gloria. She knew little about the zamitat and was interested to learn how they viewed themselves.

"Governments," said Smith, "have sometimes felt it necessary—or politically expedient—to outlaw things like prostitution, gambling, drugs, alcohol, tobacco . . . whatever. But the demand for them never goes away. Organizations like the zamitat and its predecessors bridge the gap between what is politically desirable and what is socially necessary."

"Last year," Gloria said, "I found myself running a bordello on Sylvania. All perfectly legal, of course, but if it had been illegal, I don't think that would have made the slightest difference to our operation."

"Of course not. People want what they want, and other people have always found a way to provide it for them. As I said, we offer a necessary social service—no less than Dexta."

"Speaking of Dexta . . ."

Smith shook his head. "If you are not already aware of the nature of the links between the zamitat and Dexta, I am certainly not going to be the one to tell you. Given your position as head of the Office of Strategic Intervention, you might conceivably feel compelled to take action on such knowledge if you had it."

"Just a thought." Gloria shrugged. "Anyway, I didn't want to see you about that. It's something else entirely."

Smith smiled at her pleasantly. "How may we be of service?" he asked.

Gloria locked eyes with him. "Someone is trying to kill me," she said.

"That business recently on Cartago? Yes, I heard about that."

"There are reasons to think that PAIN was responsible. The attack on me seems to tie in with two terrorist episodes in Quadrant 4. Our security people are concentrating on that possibility. But I wonder if there might be other possibilities."

"Such as?"

"I've annoyed and frustrated a lot of people in my work at OSI. Including some of the Big Twelve."

Smith nodded. "And you think one of them might have taken out a contract on you?"

"That's one of the 'necessary services' the zamitat provides, isn't it?"

Smith stroked his chin for a moment, then took a sip of wine. "Interesting notion," he said. "But I can tell you that I've heard nothing about any such contract."

"And would you know, if one existed?" Gloria asked him.

"Not necessarily," Smith conceded after a moment's thought.

"Could I ask, just what is your position in the organization? I mean, how high up are you?"

Smith smiled a little. "I suppose," he said, "you could think of me as a vice president, of sorts. But that's really somewhat misleading. You see, the Big Twelve corporates are all vertically integrated and organized. There are distinct boxes on the organizational chart, leading upward to a well-defined hierarchy of leadership positions. With the zamitat, the organization and integration are more horizontal. We are, in effect, a cartel—a voluntary association of semiautonomous groups, which we refer to as divisions. Historically, they were known as 'families,' although blood ties and ethnic identity now have little or nothing to do with it in most cases.

The divisions are distinct entities, but they cooperate with one another rather than competing. When disputes arise, they are resolved by a sort of upper-level advisory board that has real but strictly limited powers. We have nothing comparable to a corporation's board of directors, and no chief executives."

"So what you're saying," Gloria attempted to summarize, "is that if some other division of your organization had agreed to a contract on me, you might not be aware of it."

Smith nodded. "Still," he said, "I would think that such a contract would be unlikely. I don't think any of our divisions would want to be involved in an attack on the most famous and popular woman in the Empire. There would have to be some motivation beyond mere money. Have you done anything that would seriously annoy any of our people?"

"Not that I know of," Gloria said. "Can you tell me, would the zamitat accept a contract from PAIN?"

"We've had dealings with them in the past," he said with a slight shrug, "but I'm not aware of anything like what you're suggesting. On the face of it, that seems unlikely to me. That assassin on Cartago was killed, wasn't he?"

"Instantly," said Gloria.

"Well, there you are. If it had been one of our people, he would not have let himself be killed, and you and I would not be enjoying each other's company today. What the zamitat offers, Gloria, is professionalism, in everything we do. The attack on you was clearly the work of an amateur."

Their meals arrived, and they dined in thoughtful silence for a while. At length, Gloria decided to explore another angle.

"There's something else," she said. "The attempt on my life, and at least one of the two terrorist attacks, involved the use of old Mark IV plasma rifles. And each of those rifles was part of a shipment to Savoy in 3163, just before the start of the war with the Ch'gnth."

Smith's eyebrows rose slightly. "You don't say?"

"Would the zamitat know anything about that?"

Smith pursed his lips, then said, "Before my time, I'm afraid."

"Mine too," said Gloria. "But those weapons should have been destroyed in the attack on Savoy in 3163. Yet, suddenly, here they are. It occurred to me that perhaps some of the weapons earmarked for the Savoy shipment were . . . shall we say, diverted. That's the kind of thing the zamitat does, isn't it?"

Smith drummed his fingers on the tablecloth for a moment, then nodded. "Such things have been known to happen," he admitted. "If I remember my history correctly, the Savoy colony was pretty much wiped out, wasn't it?"

"That's right."

"Then those weapons either never made it to Savoy or were somehow salvaged from the wreckage. I don't have any personal knowledge of this, but either way, zamitat involvement would not be improbable. I know the organization turned a substantial profit in the immediate postwar years simply by salvaging and reselling leftover ordnance. And, of course, we've always had substantial involvement in shipping and . . . um . . . diversions. But, again, I simply don't know."

"I understand," Gloria said. "But could you find out?"

Smith moved his head in an ambiguous side-to-side, up-and-down motion. "I could ask around. Some of our senior people might know. But remember the way we are organized, Gloria. Earth's involvement in some enterprise out in Quadrant 4, fifty or sixty years ago, may well have been pretty minimal. And even if there was some zamitat involvement in the Savoy business, it doesn't mean that there is any involvement in the current matter."

"I understand," Gloria said. "But at this point, *any* additional information would be welcome."

"Your people have no leads? That surprises me. The Bugs are usually pretty efficient."

"It's an odd case," Gloria pointed out. "They don't get many that have roots going back half a century."

"Neither do we," Smith said. "But I'll see what I can find out for you. I assume you can be reached at Dexta?"

"For now," Gloria said. "But next week, I take off for the Quadrant Meeting on New Cambridge."

"No problem," Smith said with a grin. "We'll be there, too."

Gloria ate in silence for a while. Zamitat help with the Savoy weapons might turn out to be useful, although it was something of a long shot. But that wasn't the real reason she had wanted to see Smith.

To this point, the contact had been clean and professional—chaste, in a way. But the next step, if she took it, might put her on a road from which there could be no turning back. She would be establishing a relationship. And it wouldn't be free.

Smith seemed to sense her discomfort. "Is there something else we can do for you, Gloria?" he asked.

A necessary service, she thought.

"Yes," she said at last. "I need a favor."

GLORIA WAS CURLED UP ON A COUCH IN HER penthouse, munching carrot sticks and reading a history of the war with the Ch'gnth when the text on her pad was overridden by a vid image from the downstairs desk. "There's an Eli Opatnu here for you, Ms. VanDeen," the guard at the desk informed her.

"Send him up," Gloria said. The news both surprised and pleased her. She put the carrot sticks away in the kitchen, then went to the front door. She was wearing only a very thin, blue silk robe, knotted at the waist.

After a moment's hesitation, she loosened the knot and pulled the fabric farther apart.

Opatnu gave her a toothy grin at the door and held up a bottle of wine. "A peace offering," he said.

"Everyone keeps giving me wine lately," Gloria said, ushering him in. "Tell you what. Hold off on the wine for a bit, and I'll fix us something better. Go on into the living room and make yourself comfortable."

"Whatever you say." Gloria watched him as he walked, taking note of his long, lean form and the graceful, unhurried rhythm of his movements. Plus, he had a great ass.

She popped a porcelain kettle into the 'wave and nuked it for a few seconds, then poured the contents into two big mugs. A moment later she arrived in the living room, handed one mug to Opatnu, then sat next to him on the couch. She raised the steaming mug, clinked it against his, and took a sip. He did the same.

"What's this? Some kind of tea?"

"Sort of," Gloria said. "It's from Mynjhino. I think you'll like it. Maybe you can open the wine a little later." Gloria drew her legs up and scrunched around on the couch. The movement was enough to cause the loose robe to fall away to the sides, uncovering her breasts. Opatnu took note, and Gloria noted his note-taking. Her skin was already tingling, and she didn't think it was just the jigli tea. She wondered if Eli might have some genetic enhancements of his own; some people had the ability to pump out pheromones on demand. Whatever the cause, she was suddenly feeling exceptionally randy.

"I thought I should apologize for what happened in your office," Opatnu said. "I just marched in there and expected you to tell me everything I wanted to know. It didn't occur to me that you had imperatives of your own. I hope my thoughtlessness hasn't irreparably damaged our relationship."

Gloria smiled slyly. "Oh," she said, "I have a feeling it will recover."

Opatnu grinned and stared at her bare breasts for a moment. "Oddly enough," he said, "I have that same feeling." He looked down at his steaming mug. "Say, what exactly is this, anyway?"

"You like it? It's called jigli. It is reputed to be the most powerful natural aphrodisiac in the Empire."

"Really? Funny, I've never heard of it."

"Almost no one has. You see, the Myn don't grow it for commercial use or export—that would violate their religious scruples. But I just happened to acquire some while I was on their planet."

"Interesting," he said, and took another sip. "Very interesting . . . where was I?"

"You were making a totally unnecessary apology," Gloria reminded him. "You had every right to be curious about an OSI intervention in your sector. I was going to brief you soon anyway, so I shouldn't have been so persnickety about those mysterious sources of yours. I'd still like to find out who they are, of course, but I won't press you on it. Not tonight, anyway."

"Thank you, Gloria. I appreciate that."

"As for our investigation, it concerns what is known, historically, as a double-flagging operation."

Opatnu nodded. "Freighters with multiple identities, that sort of thing?"

"Exactly," Gloria affirmed. "It works a couple of different ways. In one, you get yourself two identical freighters and give them the same name and duplicate sets of registration papers. The two freighters work in different places simultaneously, and pay whatever local tariffs apply, but only one of them pays the Imperial taxes. In another version, you get two or three sets of papers for a single freighter, then change its identity as appropriate to evade local taxation."

"Uh-huh," Opatnu nodded. "And you think this is happening in my sector?"

"We've received some preliminary indications of it," Gloria said. "I have a Financial team on Staghorn at the moment, checking to see if there's any substance to the charges. Of course, you must realize that in order for a scheme like this to work—"

"There would have to be Dexta involvement. You think I'm running a corrupt sector?"

"I don't think any such thing," Gloria insisted. "But corruption does happen. We don't care if people are cheating on their taxes, but if they are doing it with help from someone in Dexta, that makes it an OSI matter."

"I suppose so," Opatnu said with an air of glum resignation. "Look, Gloria, I like to think that I run a pretty clean shop, but you know as well as I do that there's corruption of one sort or another in all twenty-four sectors. But there are some things you need to understand about *my* sector."

"Like what?"

"Sector 19," Opatnu began, "has the second-lowest population density of any sector. About forty percent of our territory was Ch'gnth space, before the war. Expansion and settlement were blocked for centuries. In consequence, we only have eighty-six colonies in the sector—far below average. But in the decades since the war, all that territory has opened up for us."

"And you now have the highest growth rate of any sector," Gloria put in.

"Right. Something to be proud of, but it also presents problems that are unique to Sector 19. Because of our low population density, the Big Twelve have never been very interested in doing business in the sector. Too much empty space, too low a rate of return. Postwar expansion has attracted them, of course, but mainly to the Frontier region. The older, occupied sections of the sector are still underserved by the big corporates. And so, a lot of the sector's transport and commerce is in the hands of smaller local and regional concerns."

"Like Wendover Freight and Storage?" Gloria ventured.

"Wendover?" Opatnu gave her a sharp gaze. "You think Wendover is doing the double-flagging?"

"Possibly," Gloria said.

"Well," Opatnu said, "I suppose they'd be the logical candidate. They've been the major shipper in the sector for a century or more. And it may be that they decided they need to cut some corners in order to stay in business these days, given the unique circumstances in the sector. We've got a pretty good boom going on in the outer regions, which are dominated by the Big Twelve, and at the same time, we've got long-term stagnation in the rest of the sector, where Wendover does its business. But Gloria, if Wendover is guilty of something like this, and you take them out, that could turn stagnation into outright recession, or worse. I'm not defending anyone's criminal activity, understand, but I hope you'll keep the big picture in mind as you pursue this."

"Well," Gloria said, "I suppose I'll just have to rely on you to keep reminding me of the big picture." She leaned close to him and took his face in her hands. They locked eyes for a second, then plunged into a jigli-fired kiss that quickly evolved into eager groping.

Opatnu untied Gloria's robe and stared for a moment at her smooth, cocoa-colored flesh, the dark prominences of her straining nipples, and the honey-blond curls of her pubic mound. Meanwhile, she unbuttoned his shirt and ran her hands over the taut, almost hairless expanse of his chest. Then her hands descended to his belt, unfastened it, and opened up his trousers.

"Speaking of the big picture . . . !" she exclaimed.

"Like I said," Opatnu told her, "my sector is noted for its rapid expansion."

Opatnu thrust himself into her, and Gloria cried out

in delight. He was, she decided on the spot, as skilled and impressive a lover as Charles. She spasmed in electric rapture, and only in the very back of her mind did it occur to her that the moment would have been even better if she had a little Twenty-nine.

chapter 10

"I JUST WANTED TO LET YOU KNOW THAT I'LL BE leaving tomorrow for New Cambridge and the Quadrant Meeting. I suppose I'll see you there."

Gloria stood in front of Cornell DuBray in his plush office, wearing a nearly transparent shirtdress, minimally buttoned. She wanted to give him a good look at her body—the body he would never again touch.

"I guess Erik Manko won't be making the trip with you, will he?" Gloria added.

"What do you know about that?" DuBray snapped at her.

Gloria shrugged innocently. "Only that he was attacked and badly beaten. Right here on the streets of Manhattan. Shocking, isn't it, that such things still happen? But I'm sure he'll recover, in time."

"A month," DuBray snarled.

"Well, I hope he'll be more careful from now on. It would be terrible if something like that happened to him again."

"You've gone over the line, VanDeen," DuBray growled.

"Which line would that be?"

"You went outside of Dexta to settle a personal matter. You couldn't handle Manko yourself, so you hired some muscle to do the job for you. I've half a mind to have Internal Security look into this."

"Look into what? Manko's misfortune happened out on the city streets. It's a matter for the New York City Police Department, not IntSec. They have no jurisdiction."

"They do if I tell them they do. Don't get too clever with me, VanDeen. You'd regret it."

"More threats and bullying, DuBray? Where's all that upper-level finesse you're so proud of?"

"I can break you, VanDeen. Anytime I want."

"Would you like to try it here and now?"

DuBray offered her a thin, cold smile. "We are of unequal levels, as you are well aware. Don't think you can provoke me into physicality. I have other means at my disposal."

"You might give a little thought to some of the means at *my* disposal," Gloria suggested. "I'm not some anonymous Ten cowering before the awful power of a Four. The public adores me, Norman Mingus has faith in me, and I have powerful friends and relations—and *ex*-relations."

That gave DuBray pause, as Gloria had intended it should. This was the first time in her Dexta career that she had so directly referred to her Imperial connections. She had always been determined to succeed at Dexta without any help from Charles and without trading on her link to him. But DuBray, with or without the services of Erik Manko, was the most powerful obstacle she had encountered, and she had finally accepted the fact that she couldn't fight him with one hand tied behind her back. *Fight dirty,* Chandra had told her.

"OSI has work to do in Quadrant 4," Gloria told him. "We'll be doing it on New Cambridge, during the Quad Meeting. Don't get in our way, DuBray."

DuBray considered her words in silence for a few moments, then nodded slightly. "Very well, then," he said. "You've decided on war."

"Call it what you want. I'm fighting back."

"You're being stupid, VanDeen. I'm not alone in this, you know. All four Quadrant Administrators will be aligned against you."

"From now on," Gloria said, "you should think of OSI as the Fifth Quadrant."

"THE FIFTH QUADRANT? BUT THAT DOESN'T EVEN make sense," Grant Enright protested. "You can only have four quadrants."

"You have no poetry in your soul, Grant," Gloria replied. "I kind of like it. And it exactly describes what OSI must become. In order to survive at all, we have to make ourselves as strong and independent as the Quadrants themselves, and their Administrators."

"Especially the Administrators," said Enright, frowning a little.

"It's not simply personal, Grant. I mean—yes, it's personal, but it's much more than that. The Quad Admins mean to destroy or neuter the OSI. They intend to make life as difficult as possible for everyone in this office." Gloria looked around the room, where the entire OSI staff had gathered. Some were sitting at the big conference table, and more were standing along the walls. All of them were staring at Gloria.

"We are at war for our survival, people," she said. "It's as simple as that. I think OSI is worth saving, and I'm going to fight for it." For a brief moment, Gloria thought she might be able to get away with turning this into a rah-rah, pep-rally speech, stirring the troops' blood and getting them into a fighting mood. But she thought better of it, and went in another direction instead.

"It's going to get nasty, and it's possible that sticking with OSI may not be good for the long-term health of your Dexta career. If anyone wants out, I'll arrange for your transfer immediately. I won't blame anyone who wants to make the sane, safe choice. You have a lot invested in being at Dexta, and I won't force you to risk it for my sake."

"Oh, Gloria, darling," Althea Dante interrupted, "don't be so melodramatic about it. Of *course* we'll stay and help you fight the evil Quad Admins! I think it will be delicious."

Althea was probably telling the truth, Gloria reflected. Althea had some strange notions about what was fun, but Gloria was grateful to her for the strategic support. After Althea had spoken, no one else could think of anything they wanted to say. Gloria let the silence go on for only a few seconds before swiftly moving to change the subject.

"Elaine and I are off for New Cambridge in a Flyer tomorrow. But I really want to show the OSI flag at this meeting, so I'm sending a Cruiser, too. Jill, Althea, Brent, Darren, plus Arkady, and four or five of our Bugs. Our mission will be to assist Petra and Pug in their investigation on New Cambridge. Our *real* mission will be to sell OSI to everyone at the Quad Meeting. We are going to work that meeting like a local politician working a town fair or a funeral. Althea, when you get there, I want you to plan an OSI reception and dinner some night. Spare no expense, and forget about the entertainment budget. Bill me, if necessary. Just make certain it is the one event that everyone will want to attend."

"Gloria, darling," Althea gushed, "I do believe this is the best assignment I've ever received at Dexta! I promise you, it will be a party to remember." .

"Jill, Brent, and Darren," Gloria continued, "will join me at as many of the other receptions and parties as we can manage, and we'll haunt the committee meetings, general sessions, and the hotels, corridors, and restrooms. We are out to win friends for OSI, so we have to be friendly."

"Just how friendly?" Jill warily asked.

"I've never asked anyone in this office to screw someone for the sake of the job, and I never will. Anyway, we *can't* screw everyone, so it's probably just as well if we don't screw anyone. We don't want to make any of them angry because they were left out."

"Gloria, I hope you are not trying to tell me that I shouldn't screw anyone on New Cambridge," Althea complained.

"As the Spirit moves you, Althea, as the Spirit moves you—as always. I'm just saying that it's not official OSI policy."

Gloria turned to look at Enright, the OSI Administrator. "Grant," she said, "I couldn't help noticing that it's crowded in here."

Enright shrugged. "It's the biggest conference room we have," he said.

"Get a bigger one," Gloria told him. "If we are going to be the Fifth Quadrant, we need to look the part. When I get back from New Cambridge, I expect OSI to have twice the office space it does now. Beg, barter, or bully, as necessary, but get it done."

"Yes, ma'am."

"And once we have all that new office space, we're going to need bodies to fill it. I want you to get us a dozen new Fifteens. Bring them in straight out of training and we'll raise 'em up right. Also, review all the transfer requests—I know we have a lot of them. See if you can snag half a dozen good Fourteens and maybe a couple of Thirteens."

"How are we going to pay for all those people? There's nothing in our budget for anything like that."

"Initially, we can pay them out of contingency funds. But you're right; we'll have to start submitting Resource Allocation Amendments. I know you've got friends in the Comptroller's Office. Wine and dine them, call in old favors, renew old threats. Whatever it takes."

Gloria turned from Enright and looked around the room at the rest of her people. "What I want," she said, "is for all of you to analyze the overall structure of Dexta. Look into some of the more obscure and neglected corners of the organization. Office of Weights and Measures, the Bureau of Reclamation, the Exo-Technology Review. Did you know that there is such a thing as the Dexta Ornithological Survey? I want you to identify all the bureaucratic orphans you can find and invite them to join the OSI family. We'll absorb some of their functions, promise to support them in their core missions, and offer them an ally in the never-ending battle against the tyranny of the Quadrants. There are a lot of offices in Dexta that are not under Quadrant jurisdiction. Consequently, they have little power in intramural squabbles and get rolled by the Quads at budget time. They're used to that and most of them don't even bother to fight back. But if we can get them organized and aligned with us and each other, they'll gain a lot of clout—at least, that's going to be our sales pitch."

"Hey, Gloria?" someone at the back of the room said. "It might help a lot if we could promise all these people some . . . uh . . . personal attention from the head of OSI."

"Good idea. Start scheduling lunches for after my return from New Cambridge. In fact, I think I'll throw a party at my penthouse and invite all our new allies and recruits. Drop some hints about that. Be sure to mention my deep, *personal* gratitude to everyone who helps us. And it wouldn't hurt to remind them that I'm an

Avatar of Joy now." She grinned at her troops. "Never can tell *what* might happen with an Avatar of Joy!"

Grant Enright smiled along with everyone else, but shook his head. "I'm with you on this, Gloria," he said, "but I hope you realize what you're getting us into. This is nothing less than an attempt at an internal coup. A power play."

"Grant," Gloria said, "we don't have any choice. It's a fight we have to make. OSI either grows, or it dies. Think of it as our manifest destiny."

"Manifest destiny," Enright mused. "All right, then, manifest destiny it is. When do we invade Mexico?"

THE DEXTA OFFICE COMPLEX ON NEW CAMBRIDGE was a dark, massive structure built out of native rock. It dominated the skyline in downtown Central so thoroughly that the residents referred to it as "Gibraltar"—complete with a colony of baboons inhabiting it. The baboons, Petra and Pug discovered, were not friendly.

After a day of settling in and sightseeing, they approached the Dexta offices with a sense of eager anticipation. They reported to the Regional Office Administrator, or tried to, but soon found that no one was available to see them. It took them most of the morning to track down someone who could officially, if reluctantly, acknowledge their presence on New Cambridge.

"We want to examine old Quadrant records from fifty or sixty years ago," Petra explained to the administrator.

"Is that so?" said the administrator.

"Yes. Where can we work?"

"You'll have to find a spot."

"Can you recommend something?"

The administrator blandly shook his head. "Not really."

"Well, who can?" Pug asked.

"You'd need to talk to someone in Building Management."

But no one in Building Management seemed to want to talk to them. Another hour went by before someone's assistant deputy provided them with the necessary forms to be filled out. Forms completed, Petra and Pug waited expectantly to be assigned office space. They waited more than two hours. Finally, the assistant deputy's assistant told them to come back the next day.

The following day, after more hours of frustration, they were at last assigned an office. On closer inspection, the office turned out to be a utility closet. It was equipped with two desks, but no chairs, windows, or computers. Getting the computers took the rest of the day. They couldn't do anything about windows, but they did manage to steal two chairs.

On the third day they arrived early, ready to plunge into their assignment. It was a short plunge. They found that their computers could not access the necessary records. No explanation was immediately forthcoming. They spent most of the day finding someone who could (and would) speak to them on the subject.

"You want records from 3163?" asked a bored administrative coordinator.

"Yes!" cried Petra.

"Don't have 'em."

"What the hell do you mean you don't have them?" Pug exploded. "How could you not have them? The Quadrant Administration offices were right here in this building for over four hundred years. How could those records not exist?"

"Didn't say they didn't exist," the administrative coordinator responded. "Said we ain't got 'em."

"Well, who does?"

"Lessee . . . 3163, you say?"

"Yes."

"That would be over in the Archives Section.

Everything up to 3180 is there. That's when Mingus moved Quad Administration back to Earth, you know."

"So the records would be in the Archives Section's computers?" said Petra. "How do we tap into them?"

"You don't. Not from this building, anyway. Archives Section is a whole separate deal. Just down the block from here, in the Old Annex. Can't miss it."

Three days later, Petra and Pug at last settled in to begin their research in another utility closet in the Old Annex. They had uniformly been treated with opaque courtesy and bland indifference by the local Dexta staff, who regarded them not as plague-carriers, perhaps, but certainly as people who carried an unpleasant odor about them. For the first time, Petra understood at a visceral level why so many people throughout the Empire passionately hated Dexta.

She wanted to believe that Dexta got it right most of the time, and most of the time, it probably did. For all its flaws, shortcomings, overreaching, and outright idiocy, Dexta had somehow managed to keep the Empire humming for nearly seven hundred years. Dexta was the most successful bureaucracy in history, so it had to have been doing something right.

But successful or not, it was nevertheless still a bureaucracy, and dealing with it could be a nightmare for the citizens of the Empire. One way in which Dexta served the Empire was by functioning as a lightning rod for all the many resentments of the scattered masses, which would otherwise have focused on the Emperor. Whatever was wrong, it was Dexta's fault, not the Emperor's, who stood above the hurly-burly bureaucracy and thought only of what was best for his people. It was generally understood that Dexta thought only of what was best for Dexta.

The radicals of PAIN sought to exploit the popular displeasure with Dexta, but with little success, mainly owing to their anarchist agenda. Their ideological blinders seemed to prevent them from seeing that most people had little interest in overthrowing the established order. What they *really* wanted was simply a validated tax stamp or an export waiver, processed and delivered with minimum fuss and bother. PAIN's recent campaign of attacks on Dexta facilities throughout Quad 4 (there had been two more incidents in the past week) had inspired no mass uprisings, only cries for better security.

Still, whatever their political shortcomings, PAIN operatives had at least succeeded in laying their hands on a trove of plasma rifles that had supposedly been destroyed fifty-five years earlier. Now that they finally had access to the Archive Section's computers (not to mention desks and chairs), Petra and Pug went to work with a will. Petra began tracking the rifles from their point of orgin in the munitions factories on Ostwelt, while Pug pored over the records of shippers, warehouses, and port facilities.

It soon became apparent that the Quadrant's data storage system had been designed for the convenience of contemporary bureaucrats, not for historical researchers in some nebulous future. Finding what they needed was neither quick nor easy. The computer could call up specific documents, but only by their titles and dates, which Petra and Pug didn't know. They could zero in on a general place, date, or bureaucratic cubbyhole, but after that they mainly had to inspect every document in a file to see if it was what they were looking for. Eventually, they accumulated enough information to give the computer more specific instructions, and things began to go faster.

The Mark IV plasma rifles, twenty-four thousand of them, were manufactured on Ostwelt by Thor's Forge, Inc., a division of Imperium Ltd. The shipment earmarked for Savoy was lifted to the Ostwelt Orbital Station on June 22, 3163, loaded aboard a Trans-Empire freighter, and departed for New Cambridge on June 25. The freighter arrived at New Cambridge Orbital Station on August 2 and unloaded the rifles in an orbital warehouse owned by Stavros & Sons, Inc. On August 24, the rifles were loaded aboard another freighter as part of a larger shipment of military supplies, and departed for Savoy on August 27. Since no records were available from Savoy, it was unknown whether the shipment ever actually arrived there. The freighter should have reached Savoy on September 4. The Ch'gnth attacked on September 8. The freighter was not heard from again and was presumed to have been lost in the Ch'gnth attack. An insurance claim for the missing freighter was filed by its owner, B & Q Shipping, Inc., in March 3165, and the claim was paid in full by Centron Assurance, Ltd., a subsidiary of Servitor, in December 3167.

"So we don't know for sure that the rifles ever reached Savoy," Pug pointed out that evening as they sat before a blazing fire in one of the industrial-sized stone hearths that populated the Ellison family home. "Maybe they didn't."

"Which would make sense," said Petra as she scrunched around a bit to get comfortable in Pug's embrace. "Presumably, if they reached Savoy, they would have been destroyed, along with everything else."

"But the freighter never came back," Pug said. "If it didn't go to Savoy, where *did* it go, and why didn't it return?"

"There was a lot of other stuff in that shipment. Maybe if we knew what it was and where it came from, that might tell us something."

Pug nodded. "We'll need to check records from the warehouse, and lading bills from the shipper. So we'll have to track down B & Q Shipping and Stavros & Sons and go through their records."

"Also," Petra said, "we should get the Dexta documentation dealing with this shipment. Who put the shipment together, who authorized it, who accepted it at New Cambridge, who cleared transfer to Savoy? Fifty-five years isn't such a long time—some of the people who were involved with that shipment might still be around."

They fell silent for a while and listened to the crackling of the fire. Then Pug said, "I'll tell you what worries me about all of this."

"Me too."

"Me too, what?" Pug wanted to know.

"What worries you," said Petra. "Me too. It worries me too."

"But you don't even know what I was going to say."

Petra twisted around to get a better look at Pug. "Sure I do," she said.

"You mean it's gotten to the point where you can read my thoughts?"

Petra cackled like a villainess.

"Okay, Ms. Know-It-All, tell me what I was thinking."

"You were thinking that you were worried about the fact that there were twenty-four thousand rifles in that shipment, plus all that other stuff."

"Yeah," Pug said, "that was it, all right. If PAIN has some of the rifles, then maybe it has all of them. And the other stuff. They could have enough military hardware to equip a couple of infantry divisions. *That's* what worries me."

"Me too," said Petra.

chapter 11

GLORIA EMERGED FROM DEXTA HQ ONTO THE
teeming streets of Manhattan. It had rained earlier in
the day, and the streets and sidewalks were still wet, but
a fresh breeze from the north had blown the clouds
away and the late-afternoon sky was a deep, clean blue.
Shoppers and workers on their way home competed for
navigation rights on the jammed sidewalks, and the
high-pitched whine of a thousand skimmers contributed
an air of urgency to the scene. Gloria sensed but
scarcely noticed the ripple of attention that accompanied her as she made her way through the throng. Even
in her raincoat and rain hat, pulled low over her brow,
people recognized her. She was used to it; on a typical
day, the three-block walk to her home might produce
half a dozen requests for autographs, plus a smattering
of smiles and friendly calls of "Hi, Gloria!"

She was well accustomed to the burdens of her
celebrityhood by now and simply accepted the attention
as a fact of life. On some days, she actively embraced it
and paused to chat and pose for pictures with starstruck

tourists. Today, however, she was preoccupied with more practical matters, like packing for her trip to New Cambridge and making certain that she had accomplished every chore that needed to be done before her departure. With Petra gone, she felt oddly vulnerable and disorganized.

She had walked less than a block when a young woman abruptly stepped in front of her. Gloria stopped short and stared at her. She was wearing a long black leather coat and had very short, spiky black hair and intense green eyes.

"Gloria VanDeen!" the woman cried.

Before Gloria could respond, the woman raised her right arm and extended it toward her. Clutched in her hand was a plasma pistol.

"Gloria VanDeen," she repeated. "In the name of the Peoples Anti-Imperialist Nexus, I hereby—"

Her speech was cut short by a swarm of Bugs. One of them stepped between Gloria and the woman, blocking Gloria's view. She didn't see exactly what happened, but a second later the woman was facedown on the pavement, with three Internal Security men piled on top of her. The plasma pistol skittered away from her.

Gloria instinctively stepped back, as did everyone else on the crowded sidewalk. The woman twisted and squirmed beneath the Bugs and tried to bite one of them on the finger. "Pigs!" she cried. "Fascist swine!"

The Bug who had stepped between them bent down and collected the weapon. He turned and looked at Gloria. "You all right, ma'am?" he asked shyly.

Gloria managed to nod.

The Bug was a very young man, fresh-faced and fuzzy-cheeked, with short blond hair and innocent blue eyes. Gloria remembered his name. "Thank you, Reynolds," she said.

Reynolds nodded, almost as if he were embarrassed. It occurred to Gloria that stepping between her and the woman with the pistol had been nothing less than an act of suicidal self-sacrifice, yet Reynolds had acted instinctively in a split second. Gloria also realized that, at such close range, a plasma burst would have burned straight through Reynolds and killed her, standing behind him. Reynolds must have known that. So his action had been purely symbolic; but that didn't make Gloria appreciate it any less. She was going to have to stop taking her retinue of Bugs for granted.

The three other Bugs manhandled the young woman to her feet. She spat at them, but missed.

"Better get back to HQ, ma'am," Reynolds said.

"I guess so," Gloria agreed.

SHE INSISTED THAT HER NAME WAS KRUPSKAYA, but her DNA said that it was actually Eloise Howell, of Greenwich, Connecticut. She was twenty years old, and she couldn't shut up.

"It doesn't matter that I failed. Others will succeed! VanDeen and all the rest of the Imperial oppressors will fall, like autumn leaves before the hurricane of justice! History demands it! The masses demand it, three trillion of them! PAIN is the revolutionary vanguard, and our sacrifice, our example, will inspire the masses to storm the ramparts of Imperial arrogance and bring down the fascist overlords and their running-dog lackeys. That means *you*, Bug! Nothing you do can prevent it. Liberation is inevitable!"

"Pretty blabby, for an assassin," Arkady Volkonski observed. He and Gloria had been sitting before a viewscreen in an observation room for an hour, watching and listening as Eloise Howell declaimed.

"Lucky for me," Gloria said. "If she had just pulled the trigger instead of stopping to make a speech . . ."

"I think the speech is what mattered most to her," Volkonski said. "Radicals live on rhetoric. What else have they got? It's more real to them than action. It is to her, anyway."

The Bugs had quickly hauled Eloise Howell back to Dexta HQ and turned her over to Counterintelligence. Three CI agents shared the small interrogation room with her and had taken turns browbeating, threatening, and tempting her with offers of leniency in exchange for information. That was purely routine. Eloise liked to talk, so they had let her talk. Eventually, she would run down and begin to realize that all the revolutionary rhetoric in the galaxy would not help her. At that point, they would begin administering the drugs that would wring her dry and extract every secret she knew, every name, every plan, every dream.

"What will happen to her?" Gloria asked.

Volkonski shrugged. "Dicenzo Four," he said. Gloria nodded. Dicenzo Four was where the Empire deposited its political prisoners, a world of high gravity and low expectations. Eloise Howell, late of Greenwich, Connecticut, would spend the rest of her life there.

"I almost feel sorry for her."

"Don't," counseled Volkonski.

"I know. But she's just a kid."

Volkonski raised his single, unpunctuated eyebrow. "How many middle-aged assassins have you seen? Booth was twenty-six, Oswald twenty-four, and Tancredi was only nineteen. Young, stupid, and idealistic."

"Lots of us were young, stupid, and idealistic once," Gloria pointed out. "But most of us didn't turn into assassins. Why did Eloise?"

"By the time our friends in CI finish with her, we'll know the answer to that. I'll see to it that you receive a summary. But don't expect anything profound. Her father probably forgot her birthday when she was eight, and that turned her to a life of radical activism. Or radical rhetoric, anyway. You want to know why Eloise stopped to make her speech? It's because she wasn't able to pull that trigger. She *wanted* to be stopped. This way, she gets to make more speeches."

"Why would PAIN have chosen someone like her?"

"She probably chose herself. Or drew the short straw. My gut tells me that Eloise probably isn't connected to what happened on Cartago or the other terrorist attacks. She and her little cell of would-be terrorists probably heard about the other incidents and revved themselves up to strike their own blow for galactic liberation."

"You really think so?"

"Can't be sure at this stage," Volkonski said, "but I'd bet on it. For one thing, her pistol is a recent model, the kind you can get anywhere. No connection to the Savoy shipment. No reason to think this was part of some grand conspiracy. I doubt that we'll get anything useful from her."

"That's disappointing."

"It's typical. PAIN is not some sophisticated subversive cabal, Gloria. Until lately, they've never been more than a loud but minor irritant. People with a gripe against the Empire gravitate to it, but their anarchist ideology is self-limiting. How do you organize a bunch of people who reject the very concept of authority?" Volkonski shook his head. "PAIN has never posed a real threat to the Empire."

"But if they have the Savoy shipment . . . ?"

Volkonski sighed heavily. "That," he said, "would require a reevaluation of the threat level. Somewhere, somebody a hell of a lot smarter and more dangerous than Eloise Howell must be calling the shots."

"Today's pig, tomorrow's bacon!" cried Eloise Howell.

Volkonski smiled slightly. "Oink," he said.

• • •

MRS. ELLISON HAD INVITED PETRA TO TEA.
Petra equated "tea" with "coffee," and, therefore, with
relaxed informality. Mrs. Ellison seemed to equate it
with something entirely different. Petra sat next to her
on the gold satin couch in what she assumed was the Tea
Room, feeling uneasy about her jeans and tee shirt. Mrs.
Ellison, as always, looked as if she were about to chair a
meeting of the Well-Dressed Ladies Society.

They engaged in idle chitchat for a while. Mrs.
Ellison was much better at it, since Petra had nothing to
talk about except Dexta and Pug, and Mrs. Ellison's eyes
tended to glaze over whenever Dexta was mentioned.
That left Pug as their only point of common interest,
and Petra sensed that Mrs. Ellison would not be pleased
to hear about what a wonderful lover her son was.

Eventually, Mrs. Ellison's supply of idle chitchat was
exhausted, and she fixed Petra with a cold, level gaze.
"Ms. Nash, forgive me for being blunt, but may I ask,
just what are your intentions regarding my son?"

"Intentions?" Petra asked, playing for time. "How
do you mean?"

"Your intentions. Surely, that must be clear."

"I intend to stay with him, if that's what you mean."

"And if he were to leave Dexta and return here to
assist my husband?"

"I don't know," Petra replied. "But I do know that
Pug doesn't want to do that. He told me so, himself. He
likes Dexta, and he's proud of what he's accomplished
there. It's the first thing he's ever done on his *own*. Do
you know how much that means to him?"

"Better than you, my dear. I'm not unmindful
of Palmer's desire for independence. Within limits, it's
a healthy thing and I quite approve of it. Just as I approve of his relationship with you, in case you were
wondering—also within limits."

"And those limits would be . . . ?"

Mrs. Ellison frowned silently for a moment, as if deep in thought. Then she said, "Don't expect too much, Ms. Nash. You seem like a fine young woman, and I can understand my son's attachment to you. But his home and family are here—just as his future is here. If you expect to be part of that future, you must accept that fact. And you must learn what it means to be an Ellison."

"It means dressing for tea," Petra said. "I've learned that much."

Mrs. Ellison barely smiled. "That's a start," she said.

ELI OPATNU SAUNTERED INTO CORNELL DUBRAY'S office and found the Quadrant Administrator staring at the console on his desk. A million lights twinkled through the windows behind him. You could see a long way from the 110th floor.

"Someday I'm going to have an office like this," Opatnu said. "Maybe even *this* office."

DuBray looked up and regarded the young Sector Administrator for a moment. "Everyone is in such a *hurry* these days," he said with a hint of bemusement.

"Weren't you?" Opatnu asked.

DuBray leaned back in his chair. "As a matter of fact," he said, "no, I wasn't."

"Oh?"

"Fix us a couple of drinks," DuBray said, gesturing toward the bar to the left of his desk. "My usual." Opatnu did as he was instructed. DuBray got to his feet and stretched.

"When I was your age," DuBray told Opatnu, "we were in the middle of the war with the Ch'gnth. And the truth is that after those first, awful months, I had the time of my life. There I was, still a young man, paticipating in decisions that affected the fate of billions. It was heady stuff. I was almost sorry to see the war end. And, of course, I knew that when Norman moved up to Dexta Secretary—and the war guaranteed that he would—I'd take over Quadrant from him. So I really wasn't in a hurry. I didn't have to worry about my future."

Opatnu handed DuBray his drink, then took a sip of his own. "Must have been nice," he said, "not having to worry."

"But I get the impression that you *are* worried."

"Not worried, exactly. Just say that I'm concerned. This Wendover business could still blow up in our faces."

"I doubt it," DuBray said with unforced confidence. "In-house investigations can always be controlled, one way or another. It doesn't matter whether it's the Comptroller or Internal Security, or even the newly minted Office of Strategic Intervention. It's simply a matter of knowing how to play the game."

Opatnu shook his head. "Maybe. But VanDeen won't be easy to control."

"I was under the impression that you had already accomplished that."

"One quick fuck isn't going to be enough. Not with Gloria."

"What's this? Are your powers slipping, my friend?"

Opatnu shook his head. "I have my enhancements; Gloria has hers. For Gloria, sex is *always* great. She doesn't need me to find fulfillment."

DuBray considered this as he swirled the ice cubes around in his glass for a moment. "Perhaps so," he said. "But VanDeen is not the only woman in OSI."

"True," said Opatnu. "I've already got my eye on someone else who could be useful. But Gloria's people are remarkably dedicated. This isn't going to be easy."

"Easy or not, it must be done. You know what's at stake here."

"You mean, aside from my career—and yours?"

DuBray went to the bar and began fixing himself another drink. "My career," he said, "is perfectly secure. And yours, as well, if you don't take counsel from your fears. You're still young, Opatnu, so you lack a long-term perspective. Do you know how many investigations I've quashed over the years? Usually, all I have to do is rear up on my hind legs, let out a growl or two, and the problem is solved. VanDeen, I admit, presents an unusual challenge, but hardly an insurmountable one. If she continues to defy me and resist your persuasion, stronger means are available. I doubt that they will be necessary, but the option is always there."

"I heard that your 'stronger means' wound up in the hospital," Opatnu said with a slight smirk.

DuBray didn't quite snort. "Manko is useful, but he's hardly essential. I'm not talking about mere muscle here, or even sex. The purely physical is the lowest level of control. We use it because it's easy and it generally works. When it doesn't, we can turn to other methods. I can crush VanDeen anytime I want. I'd prefer to avoid that, but if she makes it necessary, I won't hesitate."

"I know," said Opatnu. "But sometimes, I wonder . . ." Opatnu trailed off and stared at the million glittering lights.

"What?"

Opatnu turned to look at DuBray. "If it's worth it," he said.

"It is," DuBray assured him. "But if you're having second thoughts about the choices you've made, I suggest that you get over it. When you finally get this office—and you will, when I move up to replace Mingus—remember that power is simply a tool, like a hammer. A carpenter doesn't sit around staring at his hammer, pondering its existential significance. He uses it to drive nails."

"I know," Opatnu said. He took a big swig of his drink. "And don't worry, I can handle VanDeen and OSI."

"Our friends expect no less," DuBray reminded him.

"Our friends," Opatnu said, "won't be disappointed."

chapter 12

THE DEXTA FLYER MANEUVERED AWAY FROM the dock at Earthport, accelerated smoothly for a few hours, then turned on its Ferguson Distortion Generators and slipped smoothly into its transluminal journey to New Cambridge, three-and-a-half days away. The Fergusons created a spherical membrane of eleven-dimensional Yao Space, which squirted through the inimical fabric of the universe, carrying within it a bubble of normal space with the Flyer at its center.

Travel between the stars was mainly a question of mass and energy. To save on both, a Flyer consisted of no more than a sealed cylindrical tube, twenty feet long and ten in diameter, with minimal facilities and life support for two passengers. No crew was necessary, so Gloria and Elaine were alone in the Flyer, which was the fastest available form of interstellar transport for human beings.

As soon as they were properly under way, Gloria stripped off her clothing, as she always did on such journeys. There was no point in using up four days' of laundry, especially when you could never be sure if there would be decent laundry facilities available at the other end of the trip. Elaine, making her first interstellar journey, followed Gloria's example.

Beds were built into each side of the cylinder, separated by a narrow aisle. There was a spartan, waterless bathroom aft. Two work consoles, chairs, a table, and galley facilities were crammed into the forward section of the craft. Gloria settled onto her bunk, took out her pad, and resumed reading her history of the war with the Ch'gnth.

Later, Elaine fixed their dinner—microwaved-fish-something, and a concoction that went by the name of DryWine; just add water, and you had a beverage that would have appalled any oenophile in the Empire. But it was palatable as long as you didn't imagine that it had anything to do with real wine, and it packed a considerable kick. By their third packet of the stuff, Gloria and Elaine were pleasantly high and chattering easily and freely.

Elaine's mother was a marine biologist, originally from Fiji, and her father was a Japanese businessman, currently serving a three-year term on a prison colony for fraud and embezzlement. She was philosophical about her family's disgrace, as she was about the fact that it had taken her three tries to pass the Dexta Entrance Examinations. She was Gloria's age, but seemed younger. Gloria knew all of this from Elaine's file, but it was interesting to hear about it from her own lips. Gloria had yet to figure her out to her own satisfaction, and hoped to get to know her better during their trip.

Petra, the Lap Dog, was friendly, smart, loyal, obedient, brave, helpful, efficient, and funny. Elaine, the Tiger-in-the-making, was clever, ambitious, tactful, wary, given to taking shortcuts, and a little too slick for her own good. Gloria liked her, but didn't really trust her, the way she did Petra.

Worse, there was an uncomfortable suggestion of hero-worship in Elaine's attitude toward her, and something more. It was as if Elaine believed that by observing Gloria closely, she might somehow learn and absorb her secret of success and make it part of herself. *Well*, thought Gloria, *she's welcome to try*.

"Another?" Elaine asked, indicating the DryWine.

Gloria hesitated, then said, "Why not?" There were enough packets of the stuff to keep them both blind drunk all the way to New Cambridge, which was probably the way some people preferred to travel. Elaine mixed the brew, poured for them, then lifted her glass in a toast.

"Here's to our first mission together," she said. "May it be successful, and not our last."

Gloria clinked glasses with her and took another gulp of the concoction. The first glass had been dreadful, but the fourth was merely bad. She had an idea about how to improve the fifth even more. Gloria got up, went back to her bunk, found her travel bag, rummaged around in it briefly, then returned forward carrying a small plastic bag.

She swilled down the rest of her glass, then handed it to Elaine. "Here, make another batch. Got an idea."

Elaine did as instructed. Gloria opened the plastic bag, took out a small handful of dried brown leaves, crushed them in her hand, then sprinkled the resulting powder into their glasses. She found a spoon and stirred vigorously until the powder had nearly disappeared.

"Jigli," Gloria explained. "It should improve this stuff, and it has some pleasant side effects."

"What is it?" Elaine asked. "I never heard of it."

"A little souvenir from Mynjhino. Drink up." They did. The tart, astringent taste of the jigli certainly didn't hurt the DryWine—as if anything could have.

Why did I do that? Gloria wondered vacantly. She was getting pretty drunk, she realized, so maybe her judgment was a little cloudy. And maybe she just wanted to shut down her rational mind as completely as possible for the next few hours.

At war with the Quadrant Administrators. Spirit, how had she managed to bungle her way into such a fix? A Fifth Quadrant? Well, it sounded good, but the reality was that OSI was a tiny appendage of Dexta—a little toe, no more—while the Quadrants were the heart and lungs. Did she really believe that OSI could survive and triumph in such an unequal contest? Of course, she could always take the easy way out and go be Empress Gloria . . .

Elaine giggled irrelevantly. Gloria wanted to giggle irrelevantly, too. "What?" she asked.

"I was just thinking how great this is," Elaine answered, and giggled again.

Gloria found no cause for giggles. "If this is your idea of great," she said, waving her arm to encompass the cramped Flyer, "then you have led too sheltered a life."

"Not sheltered," Elaine said. "Definitely not sheltered. Just a little limited, maybe. But that's not what I meant. I meant that it's great, being alone here with you, getting plastered with Gloria VanDeen. You're my ideal, Gloria. I can't begin to tell you how much I admire and respect you."

"Don't, then."

"Really," Elaine persisted, "you've got the Empire by its balls, Gloria. You do what you want, no man owns you, and you have fun on your own terms. You do important work and save a lot of lives and make Dexta look good and . . . oh, just *everything*!"

Gloria sipped some more of the jigli-laced DryWine. The familiar jigli glow was spreading through her, warming her groin, tingling her limbs. And the DryWine was doing a job of its own on her slightly spinning head.

"So you wanna be like me?" Gloria asked Elaine.

"Of course!" Elaine gushed.

"Lemme tell ya, sometimes, *I* don't wanna be like me. It's a full-time job, you know. And sometimes, people try to kill me. Ever smell your own hair being burned? I gotta be Gloria VanDeen allatime, everywhere I go. You think that's easy?"

"No, but it must be a lot of fun."

"Sometimes," Gloria said, "having fun can be a lot of work."

Gloria got unsteadily to her feet, made her way aft, and plopped down on her bunk. A moment later, Elaine sat down on the edge of the bed.

"Are you all right, Gloria?" she asked.

"Fine, just fine," Gloria assured her, then closed her eyes. Suddenly, she became aware of Elaine's lips pressing against her own.

She opened her eyes and tried to focus. "What are you doing?"

"Nothing I haven't done before," Elaine said, giggling again.

Gloria tried to sit up, but the slight weight of Elaine's body pressed her back down. "What the hell do you mean by that?" Gloria demanded.

"Remember that night, a couple of weeks ago, at the Club Twelve Twenty-Nine? I was there, Gloria."

"Spirit," Gloria groaned. She remembered the night, if not all the details. Not Elaine, certainly.

"It took a little doing," Elaine explained, "but I finally managed to squeeze in next to you. I kissed you, like this"—she demonstrated—"and then you kissed my tits. You seemed to enjoy it. Then I kissed yours"—again, she demonstrated—"and you seemed to enjoy that, too."

"Elaine—"

"So then I went on kissing you." Elaine shifted her weight and moved downward, twirling her tongue around inside Gloria's navel. Gloria shuddered.

"Elaine," she said, "maybe this isn't such a good idea."

Elaine looked up at her and said, "I think it is. Here, I have a treat." Elaine held her hand in front of Gloria's face. Two familiar lozenges were in her palm.

"Twenty-nine?" Gloria asked.

Elaine smiled and popped one of the lozenges into her mouth. The other, she placed between Gloria's lips, then continued her journey downward across Gloria's brown belly. She giggled again as Gloria's soft blond thatch tickled her chin.

Not such a good idea at all, Gloria thought. And then she realized, as she shuddered again, that if she really wanted Elaine to stop, she should have said so much sooner. It was far too late for that now.

CLUTCHING PUG'S FOREARM, PETRA PAUSED AT the top of the short flight of polished marble steps that led downward into the vast, glittering ballroom. She took in a breath, took in the scene. Gliding gracefully around an area only slightly smaller than Weehawken, two or three hundred of the Ellisons' closest friends were dancing to the sedate rhythms of a large orchestra playing lush and lugubrious ballads from the twenty-fourth century. Everyone was beautiful or handsome, or both. Gemstones glinted and flashed incessantly as the stalwart men of New Cambridge maneuvered their extravagantly coiffed and garbed women around the dance floor. Liveried servants darted back and forth among the tables that ringed the room, while smiling bartenders kept a steady flow going. The dance number ended, the dancers politely applauded, then, almost as one person, turned to look toward the top of the stairs—at Petra.

It was one of those flash-frozen moments, and Petra knew, even as it was happening, that she would always remember it. The gentry of New Cambridge had come to this party in the expectation of seeing the young woman that the Ellison lad had brought home with him, and here she was—looking as good as she ever had in her life. Makeup just so, hair still brown but artfully highlighted and swirling down to her shoulders, dead on her ideal weight for once, thanks to all that Qatsima, and the dress was one she'd borrowed from Gloria and never given back. It was the dress she'd worn that night at the Governor's Reception on Mynjhino, and it left her mostly naked from her shoulders to far below her navel, with the dark blue smart fabric set at 70 percent transparency. The skirt was slashed in a wide vee almost to the crotch, and there was no back at all, to speak of. Ricky had loved it . . .

Poor Ricky. Dead, just days later. She hadn't worn the dress since then. Ricky had been the first great love of her life, blazing across her sky like a meteor, bright and hot and suddenly gone. Then there had been a brief fling with Bryce Denton, the sexy news weasel, but no one after that until she and Pug had found their way, after much travail, into each other's arms on Sylvania.

She loved Pug, although not quite the way she had loved Ricky; on the other hand, she hadn't loved Ricky the same way she loved Pug. Her love for Ricky had been crazy and fantastic, fierce in its intensity. With Pug the temperature was not quite as high, but she saw in him a love that might last.

So tonight was another necessary ritual, like Meeting the Parents. Now, she had to meet, not Pug's friends, since he scarcely knew most of these people, but his peers—the wealthy, powerful, and arrogant few who ran this planet. The social elite, the very apex of the food chain. She stared at them and they stared back, and for a moment the immense hall fell silent. Pug squeezed her hand, and together they started down the steps. Noise and chatter returned, and Petra had made her entrance. She resumed breathing.

Pug, who looked as if he had been born to wear a white dinner jacket, steered Petra through the throng with his palm on her bare back, smiling and nodding and making quick introductions. Petra felt as if she had been transported into one of those romance novels her mother constantly read, where life was nothing but a series of grand balls and swirling gaiety, punctuated by the occasional kidnapping by dashing rogues. There were even a few authentic Lords and Ladies present, well practiced in their charming condescension.

"Whoops," Pug said abruptly. "Moment of Truth approaching. Here comes one of my old girlfriends."

"Which one?" Petra demanded. "The one who wants to be a nun, or the one who died in the tragic Ferris wheel accident?"

"That one," Pug said, pointing toward a willowy blond with an intricate hairdo and heaving breasts the size of small melons, completely on display in an iridescent confection that had probably been woven together from the tailfeathers of some endangered species of hummingbird. Petra silently gulped, then quickly hit the contact switch in her dress seam, upping the transparency of her own gown to 80 percent. As Petra stepped forward to meet the competition, she found herself wondering how Gloria would have handled a moment like this.

"Pug, dearest!"

"Steff! You look wonderful tonight!" They exchanged quick kisses on their respective cheeks. Pug put his arm back around Petra. "Petra," he said, "I want to introduce you to an old and dear friend, Steffany Fairchild. Steff, this is Petra Nash."

They shook hands and smiled at one another. "Charmed," said Steffany. "We've all been looking forward to meeting you, Petra."

"All?"

"All of Pug's friends, I mean. He's been gone for over a year now, and we've been wondering about this mysterious new woman in his life. I mean, who would have thought that he'd find someone in Dexta?" Steffany laughed at the very mention of such an absurd notion.

"Petra," Pug said proudly, "is Gloria VanDeen's assistant."

"And he's mine," Petra added, possessively clamping an arm around Pug's waist.

"Yes," said Steffany, one eyebrow raised, "so I see."

"And what do you do, Steffany?" Petra asked, gamely trying to make conversation.

"*Do?*"

"Steff doesn't exactly *do* anything, Pet," Pug explained.

"Now that's not true, and you know it. I'm on half a dozen charity committees. Why, just last week your mother and I spent a whole afternoon together, trying to come up with a theme for this year's Founders Day Ball."

"A whole afternoon," said Petra trying to sound impressed. "And what did you settle on?"

"We were torn between 'A Midsummer Night's Dream' and the Sultan's Seraglio. The full committee will have to decide."

An old school chum suddenly appeared and dragged Pug away, leaving the two women staring at each other in brittle silence. Finally, Steffany said, "Charming dress, Petra. But perhaps a little too 'New York,' if you take my meaning. Here on New Cambridge, we keep our pussies covered."

"Yes," said Petra, "I'd bet money on it."

Steffany crossed her arms and tilted her head to one side. "Think you can keep him?"

"I haven't seen any reason yet to think that I can't," Petra replied.

"Really? Then perhaps you should look around you. If you think I'm your only competition for Pug, you're either naïve or foolish. The Ellisons are not about to let their son spend his life as a file clerk—or as a file clerk's assistant. You may think those cute little tits of yours will keep him hooked, but you're dealing with primal forces here, Petra. You might keep that in mind."

A little later, Petra met some of the primal forces, face-to-face. Pug steered Petra over to a knot of distinguished-looking people and made the appropriate introductions. "And this," he concluded, "is my great-uncle Benedict, my mother's uncle." Uncle Benedict had silver hair and piercing blue eyes that took Petra in from head to toe with evident approval.

"Congratulations on the new appointment," Pug said. He turned to Petra and explained, "Uncle Benedict was just named Imperial Governor of Pelham III, out on the Frontier in Sector 23."

"Yes," said Benedict, "a thousand and twelve dreary light-years from Earth, I'm afraid, but an interesting position, nonetheless. My first go at managing indigs."

"Indigs" was Empire-speak for indigenous populations, meaning alien civilizations. Petra nodded and asked, "Have you governed elsewhere?"

"Third time around," Benedict said. "Once for Darius, once for Gregory, and now, Charles has called upon me. Wasn't really eager for the assignment, but I was at loose ends anyway, and one doesn't say no to an Emperor, does one?"

"I never have," Petra agreed.

"As a matter of fact," said Benedict, "I wanted to

have a talk with you about this, Palmer. No time like the present, I suppose. Fact is, I have a few slots to fill in the Dexta portion of my staff. Think you might be interested in taking a crack at being my Undersecretary for Administration?"

Pug's eyes widened. "Are you serious, Uncle Benedict?"

"Entirely. Undersecs are Thirteens, of course. I gather you're still a Fourteen?"

Pug nodded.

"Figures," said Benedict. "Promotion in Dexta is so damnably slow."

"Not really," Pug said. "I mean, I was a Fifteen for less than a year, and I got the bump to Fourteen just last summer."

"Still, for a young man of your quality, it's such a waste to linger in the lower echelons. That's why I want you for this Undersec slot, my boy. My Imperial Secretary will be a carryover, and I'll need her experience for the first year, of course. But after that, I can request her transfer and promote you to fill the position. A year from now, you'll be an Imperial Secretary and a Twelve. What say?"

Pug didn't quite gape or dither, but he was clearly taken aback by the offer. He glanced uncertainly at Petra, then back at his great-uncle. "I don't quite know *what* to say, Uncle Benedict. I thank you for the offer. It sounds like a wonderful opportunity."

"I should think so," said Benedict. "Yet I sense hesitation." He raised an eyebrow and peered expectantly at his young relation.

"Well . . . it's kind of . . . uh, sudden. And, uh, Petra and I . . ."

"Ah, I understand. Ms. Nash, you are, I believe, a Thirteen?"

"That's right."

"Well, I believe I might be able to open up another

Undersec slot on Pelham, come to that. A Dexta position, of course, so I'd have to finagle a bit. They don't seem to appreciate Imperial appointees messing about in their cricket pitch. Might take a few months to clear it, but I see no reason why you couldn't join Palmer in relatively short order."

"Uh . . . that's very considerate and generous of you, sir," Petra said.

"Then it's settled?"

Pug and Petra looked at each other for a moment. Then Pug looked back at his great-uncle and said, "I certainly appreciate your offer, Uncle Benedict. We both do. It's just that we already have a commitment to our present positions in the OSI, and I don't know if we could just walk away from that."

"Don't be silly, lad. This is a Spirit-sent opportunity for a capable youngster such as yourself. I know your parents would be very disappointed if you were to turn your back on this. And as for OSI"—Benedict cleared his throat—"I have it on good authority that Ms. VanDeen's rogue operation is about to be consigned to the ash heap of Dexta's history. You'll do yourself no good, my boy, by clinging to the timbers of a sinking ship."

"Sinking ship?" Petra protested. "Now just a—"

"What Petra means," Pug quickly interjected, "is that there are personal and professional loyalties involved. We can't simply turn our backs on Gloria."

"Do you honestly believe that she wouldn't do the same to you, if it suited her purposes? My sources at Court—and they are very good sources, at that—tell me that Charles has made a very attractive offer to Ms. VanDeen, and that she is seriously considering returning to him."

"What?" cried Petra. "She'd *never* do that. Never!"

Benedict smiled at her indulgently. "I'm sure you

want to believe that, my dear," he said, "but those 'personal and professional loyalties' you seem to value so much are entirely ephemeral, let me assure you. You're still very young, so you believe that everything is eternal. When you're older, you'll realize that nothing lasts, nothing endures—certainly not anything as insubstantial and abstract as 'loyalty.'"

"Gloria is my best friend," Petra insisted.

"Is she, now? Well, then, perhaps she'll take you along when she returns to Charles. Personal secretary, that sort of thing. But if you intend to remain with Dexta, come what may, then I think you should consider the position I've just mentioned. And you, as well, Palmer. I don't require an answer this evening, in any event. I'll be around for the Quadrant Meeting. We'll talk again." With that, Benedict turned away from Pug and Petra and struck up another conversation.

Petra eyed Pug uncertainly as they walked away. "Pug?"

Pug pulled her a little closer. "Don't worry about it," he told her.

But she did.

WORRIES NOTWITHSTANDING, IT WAS AS GLAMorous and enjoyable an evening as Petra could recall. She whirled around the dance floor with Pug, feeling lighter than air and as bubbly as champagne. She knew she was the center of attention and that many eyes were upon her as she spun and twirled to the music. Throwing caution to the wind, she set her gown's transparency at 90 percent and let her shoulder straps fall, flouncing around the room nearly as nude as she had been during her stint as a bar girl in Elba's Emporium back on Sylvania. She was determined to let the nobs and snobs of New Cambridge see that the Ellison lad's new flame was unafraid and unintimidated. She wondered if Gloria felt this way all the time.

In due course, she met two more of Pug's old girlfriends, neither of whom seemed to be a candidate for a convent or a mortuary. She also met, and danced with, a gaggle of his old pals. One of them pawed her breasts, squeezed her mostly bare bottom, and invited her to join him in one of the upstairs bedrooms. She received similar invitations from one of Pug's uncles and a cousin. She politely declined them all, but began to understand why Uncle Benedict thought that loyalty was merely a transitory abstraction.

Late in the evening, Pug led Petra into one of the anterooms and introduced her to a woman he identified as "Aunt Saffron," even though she was not really a relation but, rather, an old and close friend of his mother. She was a tall, thin woman with exquisitely styled blond hair and narrow, aristocratic features that seemed vaguely familiar to Petra.

"You're looking well, Palmer," she said. "And from what I hear, it seems that you've done well in that . . . *place.* You'd do well anywhere, of course, but I still wish that you'd taken my advice."

"Now, now, Aunt Saffron," Pug soothed, "don't get started. I know how you feel about Dexta, but I've made my decision and I have no regrets."

"Everyone starts out with no regrets. They come with age and experience, and I'm confident that you'll collect your share of them. I certainly have." She looked toward Petra. "And you, Ms. Nash, no regrets either, I suppose?"

She snuggled a little closer to Pug and squeezed his hand. "Not tonight," she said.

"I presume you'll be going to Pelham together, then? Well, that's all to the good. The farther away you get from Manhattan, the better off you'll be."

"We haven't made up our minds yet," Pug said. "I

see that Uncle Benedict has already told the family about his offer."

Saffron assayed a rather grim smile. "More the other way around, I think," she said. "I gather that your mother discussed the matter with him."

Pug nodded. "I figured as much," he said. "I wish they'd just stay out of it and let me do things for myself."

"A wise son follows his parents' advice."

"Ain't that the truth?" said a ruddy-faced man who had suddenly appeared at Saffron's side. He wrapped an arm around her and leaned over to give her a kiss on the cheek. "Every word of advice you ever gave me is engraved on my heart. 'Stick around until the old man croaks,' you said, 'and all of this will be yours.' So I did, and it is."

"I never said any such thing."

"You didn't? I could have sworn that was you. Maybe it was Nanny, or the gardener. How's it going, Pug?"

Pug extended an arm and shook hands with the man. "Good to see you, Whit. Petra, this is Saffron's son, Whitney Bartholemew, Jr. Whit, say hello to Petra Nash."

"Hello, Petra Nash," he said, taking Petra's hand and kissing it gently. There was alcohol on his breath, and from the way he swayed back and forth ever so slightly, it was apparent that he'd had a lot of it this evening. He looked to be in his forties, perhaps, and had black hair, a high forehead, and sharp, dark eyes.

"So," Bartholemew said, "are all the women in Dexta as sexy and beautiful as you, or did Pug just get the pick of the litter?"

"Random drawing," Petra explained.

"Ah, it was luck, then. Should have realized. The Ellisons have always been big on luck, you know. While we Bartholemews have always relied on our native cunning and rapacity, Mother's side of the family, on the other hand, ran toward meticulous plotting and cruel calculation. So here I am, the offspring of buccaneers and bureaucrats. I've always pitied young Pugnacious, here, bound as he is by ten generations of stiff-necked rectitude. As a Bartholemew, I have a little more latitude to be a rebel, you see."

"Some rebel," Pug snorted. "He runs a dozen companies and never gets out from behind his desk."

"Not true! I get around more than you think, my boy. I might just surprise you someday." He spun slowly around and pointed toward the glittering throng. "Surprise all of these bastards, just see if I don't."

"Why don't you surprise your mother, then," Saffron said, "and see if you can get through this evening without making yet another scene?"

Bartholemew leaned close to Petra and said in a stage whisper, "My mum doesn't trust me to behave myself."

"Neither does mine," Petra said with a conspiratorial smile.

"Ah! We are kindred spirits, then! Come away with me, Petra Nash, and help me make a scene."

Before Petra could reply, Pug put his arm around her and pulled her away. "I saw her first," he said. "Great to see you, Aunt Saffron. Take care, Whit." Petra waved a weak farewell as Pug hustled her away.

"Whit's a bit loaded, as usual," Pug told her. "A good guy, but he has a tendency to get carried away. Since his father died a couple of years ago, Saffron has been trying to get him to grow up, finally."

"She doesn't appear to have succeeded."

"Oh, Whit's not so bad. He just hasn't found himself yet. His family situation was . . . well, it was difficult."

"I see," said Petra. "What about his mother? What's her story? I mean, what does she have against Dexta?"

"Everything," Pug said.

"Come again?"

"Her full name, in case I didn't mention it, is Saffron Mingus Bartholemew."

"Mingus?" Petra's eyes widened. "Not . . . ?"

Pug nodded. "She is the daughter of Norman Mingus. And," he added, "she hates him."

chapter 13

GLORIA SETTLED INTO HER SUITE IN THE
Imperial Cantabragian, the ritziest hotel on the planet,
feeling drained from the boredom of her trip and the
hassles of securing lodging. With the Quadrant Meeting
about to begin, every hotel room in Central seemed to
have been booked a year or more in advance. Gloria,
with fame and money to spare, had been able to prevail
upon the manager of the Cantabragian to find an appropriate suite, which required a difficult and diplomati-
cally touchy reshuffling of various Dukes, Governors,
and single-digit Dexta nabobs. Being who and what she
was could be a strain at times, but it could also open
doors—literally in this case—that would have remained
closed to anyone else.

Elaine, who had a bedroom of her own in the suite,
was off on a mission to the local Dexta offices to arrange
for security. The impending Quadrant Meeting had
taxed local resources to the limit, but, however reluctantly, IntSec would be forced to provide a round-the-
clock contingent of Bugs to safeguard Gloria VanDeen.

It wouldn't be wise to let harm come to the most famous woman in the Empire on their home turf.

"I just got here," Gloria said to herself, "and I've already inconvenienced scores of people. No wonder everybody hates me." Well, not everybody—just the Quad Admins and everyone who valued their future at Dexta. Spirit, life was complicated!

It had become more complicated than necessary during the Flyer voyage to New Cambridge. After that first night, Gloria had explained to Elaine that she never had sex with anyone who worked for her at OSI, and that what had happened between them could never happen again. Rather than being disappointed by this news, Elaine had seemed, somehow, to be buoyed by it. She had scored with Gloria VanDeen, after all, and that made her unique within OSI.

It had been a stupid thing to do, Gloria readily conceded. Pleasant and satisfying, but stupid nonetheless. She knew Elaine would crow about her conquest, and that could cause problems with others, whom she had already turned down. She'd probably have to transfer Elaine and get her out of OSI, preferably off Earth. Punish the ambitious little tart for the crime of having had sex with the great and powerful Gloria VanDeen, Avatar of Joy.

Yet Elaine had done nothing that Gloria hadn't done herself—sleeping with a powerful superior to secure her position and advancement at Dexta. The game never changed. Cornell DuBray from above and behind, Elaine Murakami from below; she had been well and truly fucked by both of them, and she could hardly claim that it had been done without her consent. Dexta was becoming indistinguishable from the null-rooms she frequented. She floated at the center of the swarm, seen, desired, and targeted by one and all.

If only Elaine hadn't given her the Twenty-nine, maybe she would have been able to avoid what

"She probably doesn't encounter many young women who *haven't* had a debut," Gloria suggested. "How's the work going? You may recall, this *was* a business trip."

Petra frowned. "Pug and I are being treated like lepers."

"Get used to it," Gloria told her. "We are now more or less at war with the Quad Admins, which means, effectively, the rest of Dexta." Gloria brought Petra up-to-date on recent developments at Dexta HQ. She mentioned that she had dealt with the Manko problem but didn't say how. Petra then treated Gloria to an account of her adventures with the New Cambridge office.

"Anyway," Petra concluded, "we've made some progress, but we still have to do a lot more digging. We haven't even started with Stavros & Sons and B & Q Shipping, but we have managed to find a slew of Dexta material related to that Savoy shipment. We even identified a few Dexta people from that time who are still active, but we haven't been able to meet with them face-to-face yet. But Gloria, we did learn something that's pretty interesting, especially in light of current events. The guy who was the Assistant Quad Admin in 3163, and who signed off on the Savoy shipment? It was Cornell DuBray!"

Gloria nodded. "I knew he was Mingus's assistant at the time, but I didn't realize he had anything to do with the Savoy shipment. I assumed it was all handled routinely at a lower level."

Petra shook her head. "From what I've seen so far, there was nothing routine about that shipment. It seemed to generate more than the usual amount of paperwork, and people at the upper levels were definitely involved with it. I've even seen a couple of memos on the subject that were signed by Norman Mingus."

"When I talked to him about it," Gloria said, "he told me that there was so much going on at the time that he didn't really have any specific memories of that last shipment. But it figures that he would have dealt with it. I just finished reading a history of the war, and apparently the last few weeks before hostilities broke out were a real madhouse, especially on New Cambridge. You know, Savoy is only about seventy-five light-years from here, so this planet was practically on the front lines. Mingus had to make a lot of important decisions on his own, without any direct oversight from Earth. That's one reason why after the war, when he became the Secretary, he pulled all the Quad Admins back to HQ. He thought Quad Admins shouldn't have the kind of independent power that he had when he was here."

"Speaking of Norman Mingus," Petra said, "you'll never guess who I met. His daughter! Saffron Mingus Bartholemew."

"No kidding!" Gloria knew that Mingus had a raft of children from his five marriages; she had even gone to summer camp with one of them when she was eight. But Mingus never discussed his personal past, and Gloria had been unaware of Saffron's existence.

"You can sort of see the resemblance, once you know," Petra said. "She's probably in her eighties and still looks great. Pug says she grew up here on New Cambridge when Mingus was Quad Admin. She was a buddy of Pug's mom in school. These days, she seems to be a wealthy widow with a wayward son. Pug says she hates her father."

"Really? Norman's coming to the Quad Meeting. I wonder if they'll get together? I know he's estranged from some of his family; but it's such a big family, and with five marriages, I suppose something like that is inevitable. Still, it's kind of sad. He's so isolated. I don't think he really has anything in his life now except Dexta."

"And you?" Petra ventured.

Gloria thought about it for a moment, then shook

her head. "I think he views me as a harmless indulgence of his old age, but he won't let it go beyond that. I don't think he's truly very close to anyone, and probably prefers it that way. After the life he's led, I suppose that's not surprising. Petra, until I read that book, I don't think I really appreciated what a great man Norman Mingus is! We might not have won that war if it hadn't been for his leadership in this Quadrant. He's probably one of the four or five most important men in the history of the Empire."

"And his daughter hates him," Petra added.

"I suppose," said Gloria, "that it's hard to pay the proper amount of attention to your family when you've got an empire to run."

"Yeah," said Petra. "Family and career." She looked pensive for a moment, then turned and stared Gloria in the eye. "Gloria? Are you going back to Charles?"

"Spirit! Does *everyone* know about that?"

"Pug's great-uncle Benedict knew. He's an Imperial Governor out on the Frontier, and he wants Pug to come work for him. First as an Undersec and a Thirteen, and then within a year he'll move up to ImpSec and a Twelve. He also said that he might be able to find another Undersec slot for me."

"I see."

"Pug hasn't decided. I mean, I think he wants to stay with OSI, but I know there will be a lot of pressure on him from his family. And, well . . . if you're going back to Charles . . ."

"Petra, I honestly don't know what I'm going to do. He offered me real power as Empress, and with everything that's happening with the Quad Admins, I admit it's tempting. But for now, I intend to fight it out at OSI. I hope you and Pug will want to stay. But I understand the situation. Whatever you decide, you know you have my blessing."

"And you have mine, Gloria," Petra said.

• • •

THE SKIMMER TAXI DEPOSITED PETRA AT THE specified address in the Old City, near the harbor. After her visit to Gloria, she had decided to spend the rest of the afternoon checking out B & Q Shipping. But now that she was here, she wondered if maybe she should have waited until Pug was available. The neighborhood was seedy, the buildings were in disrepair, and the people watched her with avaricious interest.

Gusty winds from the harbor did dangerous things with her brief miniskirt and her unbuttoned shirt. Being nearly naked at the ball or at Elba's was one thing, but it felt risky to be parading her bare breasts and bottom in a place like this. And yet . . . there was something oddly delicious about it, too, and she realized that risk was part of what made it fun. Anyway, she knew some Qatsima now. She had even thrown Gloria! Petra smiled at the dangerous-looking denizens of the street as she passed them, and made no attempt to cover herself.

A faded sign on the exterior of the brick building told Petra that she was at the right location. She entered the front door and found herself in a dusty, mostly deserted complex of glassed-in office space. Glancing at a sign, she learned that B & Q Shipping was on the top floor; another sign informed her that the elevator was not in service. With a weary sigh, Petra assaulted the five flights of stairs. The surface gravity of New Cambridge was 1.06 G, and the difference was enough to give her sore feet.

Panting slightly, she arrived at the top floor and saw that here, most of the office space was unlit, and the only sign of life was an old man with ragged gray hair sitting at a console, staring at images of nearly naked women. Petra discreetly cleared her throat, and the old man looked up abruptly. His alarm quickly turned to delight as he focused on the living, breathing, nearly naked woman standing before him.

"Well, hello there, cutie," he said, breaking into a grin. He was a centenarian, at least, Petra figured, maybe even 120. It was hard to tell because at around the century mark, the effectiveness of the antigerontologicals began to decline, at rates that varied from individual to individual.

"Good afternoon," Petra said, smiling. "Is this B & Q Shipping?"

"You're lookin' at it, sweetie pie. I'm the 'Q.' Jamie Quincannon." He pushed himself up to his feet and held out his hand. Petra took it in hers.

"I'm Petra Nash, from Dexta, and I'd like to talk to you, Mr. Quincannon."

Quincannon's left eyebrow rose slightly. "Dexta, you say? Yeah, I heard they were havin' their big convention here. You lookin' for a room, sweetie? Do a little real estate on the side, y'see, and I just happen to know where I could get you a furnished apartment for the length of the convention. Prime location, just up the coast in Overlook. Only fifteen minutes from the Transit."

"Uh, thank you, Mr. Quincannon, but I already have accommodations." She suppressed an urge to point out the window at the Ellison compound looming high on the cliffside above Central. "What I need is to talk with you, or someone, about a shipment B & Q made about fifty years ago. I'd also like to look at your records."

"My records? Y'got a warrant?"

"No. I could get one," Petra told him, "but you don't want to make me go get a warrant, do you?" She smiled again and leaned forward a bit to give Quincannon a better view of her small, round breasts.

Quincannon noticed and smiled back at her. "Naw," he said. "Say, you bein' from Dexta, would you know if that Gloria VanDeen is comin' to the convention?"

"She's already here," Petra said, her smile taking on

a slightly rueful complexion. Even here, in the midst of vamping a dirty old man, she was overshadowed by Gloria. Quincannon proceeded to emphasize the point by turning back to his console and tapping a few keys to bring up an image of a very naked and stunningly beautiful Gloria.

"Damn, she sure is somethin'! Hope I get to see her while she's in town. You wouldn't happen to know her, would you, sweetie?"

"Would you believe me if I told you I was her assistant?"

Quincannon's eyes widened. "You wouldn't be pullin' an old man's leg, would you, cupcake?"

"Not a bit of it. In fact, I'm here to work on an assignment for Gloria. We need to learn all we can about a B & Q shipment in September 3163. It was the last shipment to Savoy before the start of the war. Were you here then, Mr. Quincannon?"

"Told you I was the 'Q,' didn't I? Sure, I was here. Remember the shipment, too. Why do you want to know about it all of a sudden?"

"Mr. Quincannon, weapons from that shipment have turned up in the hands of terrorists. We need to find out what really happened to that shipment. We don't think it ever reached Savoy."

Quincannon took a heavy, rasping breath, almost a sigh. "Terrorists, you say?" He shook his head slowly, like a judge confirming a sentence. "Told Bart. Told him. Knew it would come back to bite us. But did that stiff-necked son of a bitch listen? Did he ever?"

"Bart?"

"My late partner. The 'B.' Died three years ago. Now there's only me here, give or take his son. Junior's got other fish to fry, but he keeps the office open. When he needs a special shipment for one of his other businesses, he leases a freighter through B & Q, which means that I lease one and pass it on to Junior at twenty percent under cost. Tax deal. Junior makes more money when B & Q takes a loss, y'see. But it gives me somethin' to do once in a while. Y'know, cutie, we used to own— *own*!—twenty-three freighters. Whole building used to be B & Q offices. Now, we got one office, one employee, and no freighters. Anyway, that whole shipment was Bart's deal. Didn't want to touch it, myself."

"The insurance company paid you for your missing freighter, though," Petra reminded him.

Quincannon grinned suddenly at the memory, then resumed his usual slightly suspicious countenance. "Yeah," he said, "they did. Bart's deal again. Knew how to play both ends against the middle, my partner did."

"And what actually happened to that freighter, Mr. Quincannon? It didn't go to Savoy. Where *did* it go?"

Quincannon shook his head with a bit of vigor for emphasis. "Told ya, it was Bart's deal. Far as I know, that freighter got blown to shit by the Ch'gnth."

"I see," said Petra, frowning. "In any case, I'm going to have to look at your records. We're particularly interested in getting a cargo manifest."

Quincannon pointed to another console on the other side of the room. "Help yourself, honeybunch. Bart's dead, and I don't give a rat's ass, so go ahead. Download any damn thing ya want. Just don't tell the kid I let you do it, okay?"

"The kid?"

"Bart's son. Whitney Bartholemew, Junior."

"Oh," said Petra. "*That* kid."

chapter 14

GLORIA, PETRA, JILL CLYMER, ALTHEA DANTE,
Elaine Murakami, and Brent Rostov and Darren
Mogulu, two of OSI's bright young men, huddled in a
corner of the immense room where the reception was
being held following the opening session of the
Quadrant Meeting. More than five thousand Dexta representatives and interested onlookers from throughout
the Quadrant, having endured three hours of speeches
and platitudes at the famed Central Opera House, were
now jammed onto the floor of the city's main sports
arena, where food, drink, and important people were
freely available. Norman Mingus had not yet arrived on
New Cambridge, but Cornell DuBray was somewhere
in the room, accepting the obsequies of the toiling
Dexta masses who worked for him.

"Try to avoid DuBray," Gloria instructed. "I don't
want any big, ugly scenes—at least, not this early in the
conference. Plenty of time for that. Meanwhile, keep
circulating around your assigned area and schmooze
every breathing soul, except the waiters. I don't want

anyone to leave this conference without having had face time with someone from OSI. I want us to be *noticed*!"

There was little doubt that they would be, since among them, the five women wore enough fabric to decently clothe no more than two or three of them. Althea Dante, the petite, alabaster-skinned, raven-haired Imperial Coordinator, whose reputation within Dexta was even more notorious than Gloria's, wore nothing at all except for some oversized gems depending from golden chains around her neck and hips. The other women were at least partially covered, if not exactly concealed. For her part, Gloria wore a swooping, deep purple toga-dress, held together by diamond brooches at her right shoulder and left hipbone, leaving her left breast, leg, and buttock entirely bare. Brent and Darren, meanwhile, were decked out in their Imperial finest, as handsome as the women were beautiful.

"And remember our message," Gloria said. "OSI is here to help one and all, to be an advocate for the bureaucratically disadvantaged. Our one and only goal in life is to make Dexta function like a well-oiled machine for the benefit of all concerned. We are a threat to no one and a friend to all."

"And if that doesn't work," Althea added, "I've staked out a utility room over there where you can screw their brains out."

"Purely optional," Gloria assured the others. "Everyone got their pin-pads?" Pin-pads were tiny receivers linked to their personal computer pads, and each woman was equipped with one. "Make plenty of notes—in fact, do it after every conversation, if you can. We are going to follow up each personal contact with a letter that will make reference to your conversation, so be sure to record some specifics. The personal touch is vital. Okay, ladies and gentlemen, go do your stuff."

Petra, Jill, Elaine, Brent, and Darren turned and walked off to their designated quadrants of the

Quadrant, while Althea lingered to discuss some details concerning the OSI reception. She had already handed out a small fortune in bribes to cooks, caterers, musicians, staff, and managers in order to secure a workforce for the date she had chosen. But finding a suitable venue not already booked proved to be a problem that resisted her largesse.

"Gloria," she said, "it's hopeless, unless you want to rent an alfalfa field and put up a circus tent. Aside from the six Sector receptions and all the Big Twelve receptions, you've got a hundred and twenty-odd Divisions, and each of *them* is throwing a reception. Every theater, auditorium, museum, hockey rink, and barn has already been booked."

"I may have a solution," Gloria told her. "Pug Ellison's family owns that neo-Gothic monstrosity up on the cliff. The Ellisons are here tonight, and Pug's going to introduce me to them. Maybe I can arrange something."

"Gloria, darling, that would be marvelous. I'm off, then."

"Althea?"

"Yes?"

"You were kidding about that utility room, weren't you?"

Althea's violet eyes widened in innocent surprise. "No," she said, "I wasn't."

JILL CLYMER CAUGHT SIGHT OF ALTHEA DANTE emerging from an unmarked doorway on one side of the hall, a languid smile on her face. Jill laughed to herself, amused by her OSI colleague's dedication to the cause. She saw no need for such extreme measures, but didn't mind putting on a bit of a show for the sake of OSI. Considering the public image Gloria had imparted to the OSI, she could hardly have done less.

She could hardly have worn less, at any rate. Her microns-thick smart-fabric dress, featuring random starbursts of silver and gold flashing against an inky backdrop, was cut low to reveal impressive cleavage, both fore and aft. She had never been shy about her physical endowments, but since joining OSI she had come to feel downright dowdy next to Gloria and Althea and, lately, even Petra. Jill had always considered herself to be in the Lion category, but she had to admit that there were advantages to Tiger stripes.

Schmoozing, in any case, was an art she had been practicing since she was six. Her father had been in Parliament for a while, and Jill had grown up at gatherings like this one, where the most important and self-important people in the Quadrant stood around with drinks in their hands and sneers on their faces as they sized up the competition. Jill chatted them up with skill and confidence and made, she felt, a good case for OSI.

She was glad she had accepted Gloria's offer to join OSI permanently following the Sylvania mission. She liked and respected Gloria and believed that OSI could play an important role in Dexta and the Empire. Like her father before her, she believed in good, clean, and efficient government; Dean Clymer had been hounded from office and into an early grave because of that belief, and Jill had entered Dexta in an attempt to carry on the good fight.

She had just finished dictating some notes to her pin-pad when she was approached by a tall, strikingly handsome man decked out in his "Imperials"—black knee boots, tight white trousers, and deep blue tunic, the standard garb for men at formal affairs like this one. Jill had never met him before, but recognized him immediately—Eli Opatnu, the Sector 19 Administrator. He was, she knew, that rarest of animals in the Dexta menagerie, a male Tiger. Rumor had it that he possessed genetic enhancements that allowed him to pump out pheromones on demand, although his confident good looks, trim body, and tighter-than-necessary trousers all suggested that he didn't really need them. He smiled at her, and Jill had to catch her breath.

"Ms. Clymer, I presume?" he asked, extending his hand. Jill nodded and shook it.

"Good evening, Mr. Opatnu," she said. "A pleasure to meet you."

"Likewise. I hear very good things about you, Ms. Clymer."

"It's Jill, and I've heard good things about you, too. And I know you've met with Gloria about the double-flagging problem. That's my project-of-the-moment."

"Yes, I know. Can you tell me if you've made any progress? Naturally, I'm curious, although Gloria has been somewhat reticent about sharing all of OSI's secrets."

"We have a Financial team on Staghorn," Jill told him, "but they haven't really reported much yet. When they do, we'll be sure to keep you informed."

"I'd very much appreciate that, Jill." Opatnu grinned and gleamed, his green eyes all but boring holes into hers. She held his gaze and felt a hot flush creeping into her cheeks and an urgent ache in her stiffening nipples. *Spirit, the man is fast!* Jill tried to get a grip on herself.

"As you know," she said with what she hoped sounded like professional detachment, "the investigation is centering on Wendover Freight and Storage, which is based in Sector 19. But they have offices here, as well, so as long as I'm here anyway, I plan to pay them a visit."

"Mind if I tag along?"

"If you'd like. Say, the day after tomorrow?"

"Splendid. And in the meantime, perhaps I can lure you away from this den of iniquity and show you some of Central's more intimate and intriguing nightspots?"

Jill shook her head. "Sorry, I'm on duty at the moment. I have hundreds of hands to shake and asses to kiss tonight, I'm afraid."

"As long as mine is one of them," he said, grinning again with full intensity, "I'd be happy to wait until you've fulfilled your duty to Gloria. Perhaps we can even induce her to join us."

A twofer, Jill wondered. Or was she getting ahead of herself? Was she simply reacting to the man's reputation, the way men reacted to Gloria's, or was she responding to Opatnu himself, pheromones and all?

"At the moment, however," Opatnu said, "I need to kiss a few backsides, myself. How about if I look you up later this evening?" He took Jill's left hand, raised it to his mouth, and kissed it gently.

"I'll be here," Jill said noncommittally. Opatnu released his hold on her, smiled again, then turned and strolled off into the glittering throng.

"Steady, girl," Jill told herself.

PETRA WONDERED WHERE THE HELL PUG WAS. He was supposed to be shepherding his parents around the reception, but she had seen him from a distance, and that wasn't his mother he'd had his arm around. It was Steffany Fairchild.

Old friends. Entirely innocent.

You bet.

Her feet hurt in the high gravity and high heels, and she'd had more champagne than was consistent with ladylike deportment. Perhaps that accounted for her growing desire to plant one of those spiked heels in the shapely derriere of Ms. Fairchild, the Spirit's gift to the overbred men of New Cambridge.

But, she reminded herself, she had a pretty shapely derriere of her own, as men had been telling her, one way or another, all evening. And her tits weren't bad, either—small but enticing and entirely uncovered in the low-slung, gold-leafed black pareu Pug had bought for her on a shopping spree the day before. He liked to see her undressed this way, as if she were Gloria's alter ego instead of merely her assistant, and Petra was willing to play along. She had no intention of losing Pug to that bouncy blond airhead or any other rich bitch from his old stomping ground.

A passing waiter paused near her, and Petra took the opportunity to trade her empty glass for a full one. Half-drunk and about 97 percent naked, she was feeling combative and defiant tonight. How had Gloria put it that time, when she tried to explain what it meant to be a Dexta Tiger? Tits, tush, and twat fully mobilized for the sake of Dexta? Fine—and if not for Dexta, then for her rich and handsome boyfriend. And also, perhaps, for herself, the glamorous and sexy new Tiger on the block, no longer the mousy and unsure Lap Dog. And maybe, just maybe, it was also a way of saying, "Fuck you, New Cambridge!"

She wasn't sure, but she thought she might actually hate this goddamn planet. Snobby, disapproving Ellisons by the score; interfering uncles; wayward offspring of the rich and powerful; undead girlfriends; hostile and brain-dead bureaucrats . . . So far, the only person on the whole planet she had actually liked had been lecherous old Jamie Quincannon. On the fifth floor, with the elevator broken.

And maybe Whitney Bartholemew, Junior, too, who, it had turned out, was not only the grandson of Norman Mingus but also the heir of the man who had run B & Q Shipping fifty-five years ago, and the man who ran it today. She had liked his insolent air and whatthe-hell attitude and the hint of contempt for the High Society of New Cambridge. He didn't seem to be here tonight. She needed to talk to him, so maybe she could get Pug to arrange a meeting later in the week. Assuming Pug could be persuaded to neglect his family and friends for an hour or two.

Petra noticed a distinguished-looking silver-haired man staring at her bare breasts. One more Dexta functionary to charm. One more anonymous cog in the vast wheels of Empire. She maneuvered toward him and plastered yet another grin on her face. "Hi," she said brightly, "I'm Petra Nash from OSI."

"How nice for you," said the distinguished-looking man. "I'm Edwin Ogburn, and I'm the President of the Republic of New Cambridge. How are you enjoying our planet, Ms. Nash?"

Not anonymous, then. Not even Dexta. Still, he was just the man she wanted to see. She reached out with her free hand and clutched his upper arm.

"Mr. President," she said, "I wanna file a complaint! It's about your damned gravity . . ."

GLORIA HID BEHIND SOME OVERSIZED POTTED plants as she spoke into the pin-pad that was part of her jewelry. "Jerome Devers-MacDowell, hyphenated, I think, Level Nine, Assistant Quadrant Coordinator, based on Alhambra Four in Sector 22, has been in Dexta forty-two years, married, wife Ethel, two children, five grandchildren and he has images of them. Nice, unassuming guy, seemed a little starstruck. Send him a signed picture, the usual. Seemed sympathetic to OSI. Myra Chow, Level Eleven, Assistant Sector Supe, Sector 20, Norska Two, divorced, has thirteen-year-old daughter Joanne, who is a big fan, send her the glam package. Myra says she has arguments with her coworkers about me, and about OSI. I seem to be a subject of much watercooler controversy. Myra sees me as an empowering role model, whatever the hell that is. Anyway, she's on my side and should be cultivated."

How many did that make? She had lost track. And here came another one . . .

This one walked right up to her, stuck out his hand, and introduced himself. He was probably in his fifties, medium height, with a sharp nose, slicked-back black hair, and an unidentifiable accent, probably from somewhere off in Sector 3 or 4, where they spoke an increasingly strange brand of Empire English, when they spoke it at all. "I'm Anton Grosz," he told her. "I'm the Assistant Admin of the ETR."

ETR—the Office of Exo-Technology Review—was one of those small, specialized ecological niches that proliferated within Dexta, whose purview included bits of bureaucratic flotsam that didn't fall under the aegis of the Quadrants. The Empire was expanding in every direction, and regularly absorbed alien civilizations—nearly three hundred of them so far. Such acquisitions inevitably brought with them an array of alien technologies. The Empire needed some way of organizing and controlling the influx of exo-technology, and that job belonged to ETR.

The ETR identified, cataloged, and classified the technological achievements (as opposed to purely scientific ones, which were the responsibility of another Office) of the new civilizations that had joined the Empire, willingly or otherwise. The task sounded larger and more interesting than it really was. Fully 94 percent of all alien technologies proved to be nothing but idiosyncratic elaborations of existing Terran processes or devices. Technological evolution followed much the same pattern among different civilizations, just as biological evolution tended to reproduce optimal design features for similar environments on different worlds. Fish, for example, looked pretty much the same on most planets; so did can openers. So the ETR identified, cataloged, and classified a lot of can openers.

The Big Twelve corporates looked over the ETR's

shoulder as it checked the new technologies to see if they overlapped with existing Terran patents. If they did, they were denied Export Permits, effectively restricting the technology to its homeworld. If something genuinely new or useful turned up, the Big Twelve were free to strike whatever deals they could with the new worlds. Soon, the new technologies would become available throughout the Empire, to the considerable profit of the corporates who landed the contracts. Meanwhile, new markets opened up for the export of Terran technologies.

ETR also tested the new technologies for safety, environmental compliance, and what was known in the trade as "weirdness." Perhaps once or twice a century, some truly weird and unexpected alien technology would turn up and suddenly revolutionize the way Terrans did things. The mass-repulsion devices that made skimmers and null-rooms possible had arrived that way, the fruit of a victory over a race of intelligent insects in the twenty-fourth century, back in pre-Imperial days.

Gloria had already targeted ETR as a potential ally, so she was pleased to meet Grosz. But she was more than a little surprised when Grosz said, "Ed Smith says hello."

"Ed Smith? You mean . . . ?"

Grosz nodded solemnly. "I'm your contact inside Dexta," he said. "Obviously, you can't go on having public meetings with Mr. Smith, although he hopes to meet with you privately after your return to Earth. When you have a message for him, or he has one for you, I'll be the go-between."

"I see," said Gloria. She stared at Grosz and tried to imagine him as a daring undercover agent, but couldn't quite manage it. "So, the zamitat has its hooks in ETR, huh?"

"We have an understanding," Grosz said modestly.

Gloria was well aware that the zamitat had people inside Dexta, but it felt odd to be meeting one of them. This, after all, was precisely the sort of thing the OSI was supposed to be in business to correct.

"The Big Twelve have a formal presence," Grosz went on, "but the zamitat has its own place at the table. Every so often we find a piece of exo-tech that could be of interest to them."

"And they pay you to tip them off?"

"They pay me to represent them at ETR. If you disapprove, you should have thought of that before now."

"No, no," Gloria said, anxious not to offend Grosz. "It's not that I disapprove, exactly. It's just that I'm a little new to this sort of thing."

"It will grow on you," Grosz assured her. "Anyway, I have a message from Mr. Smith. He says that there was definite zamitat involvement in the historical matter you inquired about. He hasn't been able to ascertain any details yet, but he's pursuing the matter and will keep you apprised."

"Thank him for me. And thank you, too, Mr. Grosz."

"You're very welcome, Ms. VanDeen. And now, I shall slink off into the night, intent upon my dark errands." Grosz gave her a modest bow, then darted away to the other side of the potted plants.

Well, well. The zamies had something to do with the Savoy shipment. Details to follow. Based on what Petra had told her, it was beginning to seem likely that the zamitat had either diverted or in some manner controlled that final B & Q shipment to Savoy. If that were the case, then perhaps Ed Smith or his minions could track down the shipment and provide some indication of how those weapons had wound up in the hands of PAIN. Petra had yet to go through all the data she had downloaded from the B & Q files, so perhaps additional information would turn up from that source.

Gloria felt a sense of relief at their measured

progress. There had been no new reports of terrorist attacks, and no one else had taken a shot at her, but the thought of all those weapons in the hands of enraged anarchists continued to be troubling. The Quadrant Meeting was an obvious target, and despite the heightened security on New Cambridge, a determined PAIN attack might do serious damage—not only to Dexta, but to the reputation of the Empire itself.

But it was the reputation of OSI that was her prime concern tonight. Althea, Elaine, Jill, Petra, and the two guys were busily spreading the word, and Gloria was grateful for their presence. They took some of the pressure off her and reinforced OSI's image as the sexiest and most appealing branch of Dexta. Just now, she caught sight of a very nearly naked Petra chatting with a group of three men. And over in another corner, Elaine Murakami, in her hardly there black minidress, seemed to have captured the complete attention of three more men. Women generally seemed to be responding favorably, too, if Gloria's own contacts so far were a reliable indicator; Brent and Darren seemed to be making quite an impression. OSI was something new under the Dexta sun, and despite the opposition of the Quad Admins and other entrenched powers, it was clearly attracting a lot of interest, if not active support.

Gloria took a deep breath, fixed a smile on her face, and stepped out from behind the potted plants. Back to work.

PETRA'S PAREU HAD FINALLY FALLEN OFF AND she had simply draped it over her shoulders like a shawl, leaving the rest of her body uncovered. Just like being back at Elba's, she thought, or at the Ellisons' party. The center of attention again—or *a* center of attention, anyway. Gloria was here, of course, so no other woman really had a chance. Except maybe the lovely Steffany Fairchild.

She spied Pug, along with his parents and Uncle Benedict, his arm around Steffany, off in a corner with Gloria, Althea, Elaine, Jill, and Eli Opatnu. It was late, and the party was emptying out, so Petra was able to chart a fairly direct course to them. She arrived at the corner, swaying slightly on her high heels and aching feet. Pug grasped her arm and pulled her away from his family; his father looked pleased to see her but his mother wore a disapproving frown.

"Are you drunk?" Pug demanded in a harsh whisper.

"What if I am? And what is *she* doing here?"

"She came with her father."

"Then where is *he*?"

Before Pug could answer, Steffany joined them. She cast her eyes over Petra's body and offered a supercilious smile. "Good evening, Petra," she said. "Still showing off your dowry, I see."

"Dowry?" Petra replied blearily. "What? Is that some kind of crack? Oh, wait, I get it. Dowry. Cute. Is that what you call it? Perfect. I bet if I pulled on your arm, hundred-crown coins would drop out of *yours*."

"*Really,*" Steffany sniffed, and turned away.

"Come on, I'm taking you home," Pug told her.

"No, you're not," Petra responded. She slipped away from him and sidled up next to Jill Clymer. "I'm staying here with my friends!"

"Uh . . . actually, Petra," Jill said, "Eli was just going to take us all out to a club."

"Great. I need more champagne."

"Don't you think you've had enough?"

"Not yet," Petra declared, glaring at Pug.

JILL ASSIGNED HERSELF TO TAKE CHARGE OF
Petra as they made the rounds of Central's nightspots.

Opatnu was their knowing guide, evidently familiar with all the more intriguing hideaways in the city. He somehow managed to pay equal attention to all five women, and Jill found herself wishing that the other four were somewhere else. When she danced with him, his charm, grace, and outlandishly good looks all but melted her resistance, and she snuggled up close to him while he rhythmically stroked her nearly bare bottom. But all too soon, the dance ended, and Jill was back at their table keeping Petra company while Eli whirled around the dance floor with Elaine Murakami, who had doffed her minidress and was as naked as Petra.

Then it was on to another club, and another, this one darker and more intimate than the others. Opatnu excused himself for a few moments, leaving the women from OSI to themselves. Gloria was smiling happily. "Thanks, ladies," she said. "You did a great job tonight."

"It was all due to your inspiring leadership, Gloria, dear," Althea replied. "And getting the Ellisons to agree to host our reception was nothing less than a coup."

Petra looked up at the mention of the Ellisons. "Yeah," she said, "you'll love it there, Althea. Did I tell you, Pug has a bed the size of Weehawken? O' course, if you wanna use it, you'll probably have to kick Steffany Fairchild out of it." Petra took another gulp of champagne, then nearly toppled out of her chair. Jill caught her by the arm and propped her back up.

Opatnu returned, took a seat, and grinned like a cat who had swallowed a medium-sized canary. "Got something special," he said, and held out his hand. Resting in his palm were six purple lozenges.

"Twenty-nine!" Elaine cried.

Opatnu shook his head. "Better," he said. "It's Forty-eight."

Gloria's eyes widened. "Forty-eight? How did you . . . ?"

He smiled modestly. "I know some people," he explained. "Works the same way as Twenty-nine. Just make sure that you don't crunch down on it. And I've booked a null-room, for those who are interested."

Opatnu extended his hand. Gloria, Elaine, and Althea didn't hesitate. Petra looked at the lozenges briefly, but didn't show much interest, so Opatnu moved on to Jill. She stared at his offering for a long moment. She'd tried Twenty-nine a few times, and was no stranger to null-rooms. But something about it all did not feel quite right to her. Perhaps she just didn't want to have to share Opatnu.

"I think I'll just stay here and keep an eye on Petra," Jill said at last.

"Are you sure?" Opatnu asked. He looked at her with an expression of profound disappointment on his handsome features.

"You go ahead. We'll be fine."

"Some other time, then," Opatnu said.

"We'll see," Jill replied.

Opatnu nodded, then got to his feet. Gloria, Elaine, and Althea followed him across the floor to the null-room. Jill watched them go with decidedly mixed emotions.

Petra looked up, looked around, and asked, "Where'd everybody go?" Before Jill could answer, Petra quietly passed out, slumping forward onto the table.

Jill appropriated Petra's champagne glass and offered a toast. "Here's to OSI," she said. "The Fifth Quadrant." Softly, she added, "Spirit save us."

chapter **15**

PETRA AWOKE THE NEXT MORNING TO THE
sound of her beeping wristcom. "Yeah?" she mumbled.

"Petra Nash?"

"I think so."

"Good morning, Petra Nash. This is Whit
Bartholemew. How are you today?"

That was a question Petra was not prepared to answer just yet. She felt too awful to be able to calibrate
precisely how awful. The only response she could manage was a weak groan.

"Sorry I missed you at the reception last night, but I
was called away on business," Bartholemew said. "I was
truly looking forward to seeing you. I hear you were the
toast of the Quadrant."

"I was?"

"So they say. But I would prefer not to rely on mere
gossip. I'd much rather see for myself. Would you consider having lunch with me today?"

"Uh . . ."

"Wonderful. I'll send a limo for you, say, about noon?"

"Uh . . ." Petra looked around for the first time and realized that she was not at the Ellisons'. She seemed to be in a bed in Gloria's suite at the hotel. "I'm at the Imperial Cantabragian," she said.

"Yes, I know. Noon, then?"

"Uh . . . yes, noon is fine."

"See you then, Petra Nash."

Petra tried to get up, didn't quite make it, but managed to swing her legs around and sit on the edge of the bed while the room gradually stopped whirling around her. She took a few deep breaths and noticed her pad on the bedside table, glowing orange to announce a message. She reached out and keyed it.

"First things first," Gloria said brightly. "There are some No-Regret tabs in the bathroom. Elaine and I are off to the committee venues. I got a call from Pug, who says he hopes you're feeling better and that he'll be checking out Stavros & Sons today. He says he'll see you tonight at the Ellisons'. I don't know what you had planned for today, but if you need to take the day off, go ahead. Oh, and Elaine says you're welcome to borrow some of her clothes. Have a great day, and I'll talk to you later."

Petra made her unsteady way into the bathroom, found the pills, and swallowed two of them. Then she stepped into the shower, hoping she would be lucky enough to drown. She didn't, and by the time she turned the shower off, the pills had taken effect and she was feeling marginally human, if not exactly chipper. She remembered most of what had happened last night and gave the bottle of pills a skeptical look. "No regrets, huh?"

She supposed that she had not completely disgraced herself, but she had probably come pretty close. Prancing around in the nude in front of all the Dexta bigwigs of Quadrant 4 might not have been a prudent career move, now that she considered it. On the other hand, with Gloria there, it was possible that no one had even noticed. Gloria was like a black hole, sucking in light and energy from the minor bodies that orbited her, and sometimes it was impossible for Petra not to resent her. Still, Gloria couldn't help being what she was, any more than Steffany Fairchild could help being a tall, blond, big-titted bitch. Petra, fated to be cute and little, felt that she had to resort to extreme measures in the presence of such overpowering competition.

If Pug thought he could take her for granted and cuddle up to Steffany while Petra labored away for Dexta and OSI, maybe he needed a little reminder that Petra Nash was nobody's doormat. Whit Bartholemew seemed to think highly of her, at least, even if nobody else on this fucking planet did. He'd missed the show she put on last night? Okay, she would put on the same show for him today. She didn't bother with borrowing something from Elaine, but found her black-and-gold pareu and knotted it recklessly low on her hips. Just the thing for a casual lunch.

Petra ordered coffee from room service, and while waiting for it to arrive, she rummaged around in Gloria's room until she found the inevitable package of jigli. She lit up one of the potent cigarettes and settled comfortably in a chair to smoke and stew. By the time the coffee arrived, she was tingling all over with sexual arousal and righteous indignation.

THE LIMO DRIVER EXPLAINED TO PETRA THAT she would be having lunch in Bartholemew's office rather than a restaurant. That was probably just as well, Petra reflected, as she got out of the limo in front of the Bartholemew Building in downtown Central. The provincials of this two-crown world didn't seem to be used to the sight of sophisticated Manhattan ladies striding past them at high noon, bare-breasted and practically nude. Come to think of it, this would have been pretty extreme even for Gloria. So be it; Petra Nash, Dexta Tiger, didn't care.

She arrived at the top floor (the elevators in this building, thank the Spirit, were working) and was quickly ushered into Bartholemew's private office by a secretary who kept giving her disapproving sidelong glances. Whit Bartholemew greeted her with a wide smile and wider eyes.

"I didn't have a chance to change after last night," Petra explained as Bartholemew kissed her extended hand.

"Why change perfection?" Bartholemew said as he focused his gaze on her pert breasts and sensuously bared belly. Petra felt a surge of jigli-fired tingles.

Bartholemew took her hand and led her on a short tour of his palatial, fiftieth-floor office as he explained that Bartholemew Enterprises, of which he was president, was really a holding company that managed fourteen different concerns. They ranged from the moribund but occasionally useful B & Q Shipping to a financial company that underwrote construction projects throughout the Quadrant. "My father, of course, is the one who built this overweening enterprise," he said. "And through no fault or merit of my own, I now sit in his big chair and crack the various whips that keep the serfs busy and productive."

"You sound as if you regret it."

"Endlessly. I tell you, Petra Nash, if not for the disadvantages of my birth, I might have amounted to something in life." He led her to a small table, where wine and a salad course were waiting for them.

"Well," Petra said as she sat down, "it's not too late. I mean, you could still just chuck it all and go . . . do what? What would you have done with your life if you hadn't been burdened with wealth and position?"

"Interesting question, that," Bartholemew said as he poured the wine. "Poet? Politician? Proctologist? In a way, I've had to be all of those things anyway. Especially the last one. You wouldn't believe how many assholes I have to deal with."

Petra smiled. "Me too," she said.

"I shouldn't doubt it. Tell me, whatever possessed you to join that gang of fascist file clerks?"

"Oh, it's not that bad. Dexta's just another bureau-cracy, with all the faults of any bureaucracy. I joined because I wanted to make something of myself and help run the Empire. Maybe do a little good in the galaxy. Why are you and your mother so down on Dexta, anyway?"

Bartholemew sipped a little wine and leaned back in his chair. "You've met my grandfather?"

Petra shrugged. "Not really. But Gloria knows him well and thinks he's a wonderful man."

"Gloria, no doubt, would. Actually, I barely know the man. I've only met him three times in my life, and the last time was over twenty years ago. But I know what he is, what he's done. He's a tyrant, nothing less. He ab-solutely controls our pathetic self-indulgent, milksop Emperor, and has the goods on everyone in Parliament. I tell you, Petra Nash, *no one* can be trusted with power, let alone *absolute* power. Least of all, Norman Mingus."

"His power is hardly absolute," Petra pointed out. "He has plenty of trouble just controlling Dexta, from what I hear. As for the Emperor and Parliament . . . well, we do have an *Imperial Code*, don't we? Dexta is just one part of the balance of powers."

"Right out of the textbook. Is that what they taught you back at dear old Alexander Hamilton High School in lovely Weehawken? Odd that they should name the place for a man who was killed there, don't you think? Why not Aaron Burr High School?"

"You've been checking up on me," Petra said with some annoyance.

"From the moment I met you," Bartholemew agreed. "You intrigue me, Petra Nash. You are intelligent, witty, charming, and beautiful in a way that your famous boss could never be. You're a real person. I like real people. I've met so few of them in this charade I call my life."

"Why are you so bitter?"

"Better to ask why *everyone* isn't that bitter," Bartholemew said. He drank some more wine. "Everyone certainly has cause to be in this benighted Empire of ours. Why aren't *you* bitter, Petra Nash? You certainly have cause to be, after all the miserable cards you've been dealt. Absentee father, shrew of a mother, egotistical, self-absorbed boss, weak-kneed, two-timing boyfriend . . ."

"Now, wait a minute!" Petra felt a hot flush of anger burning her cheeks. "Ever since I got here, you've been going out of your way to insult me, my job, and all the important people in my life. What the hell gives you the right to set yourself up as the Universal Judge?"

"Nothing," Bartholemew admitted. "You're quite right. I'm no more qualified for that job than anyone else. And that's my whole point. My contempt, I assure you, is not directed at you, or Gloria VanDeen, or Pug, or even Norman Mingus. It's a purely impartial contempt, aimed at one and all—Whitney Bartholemew, Junior, not excepted. Forgive me, I didn't mean to upset you."

"I'm not upset."

"Yes, you are. There's some color in your cheeks. And your exquisite nipples are so stiff, they look like gun barrels aimed straight at my heart." Bartholemew clasped his hands over his chest in mock agony.

Petra laughed, in spite of herself. She took a sip of wine and stared at the man across the table from her. She didn't think she'd ever met anyone quite like him. If he was obnoxious and hurtful, he was also brutally honest. There was something to be said for that. Bartholemew seemed to be a man who was determined to live without illusions—or maybe he just preferred the illusions he created for himself.

Bartholemew hit a button on his wristcom, and an instant later a wheeled robot dumbwaiter came in and served the main course of fish, rice, and vegetables. The robot departed, and Bartholemew poured more wine.

"As long as I've already provoked your pique," he said, "allow me to annoy you even more. I must confess that I didn't invite you here simply so I could insult you and stare at your lovely face and that splendid little body—which, by the way, I am extravagantly grateful to you for revealing so completely. No, I have another motive, entirely. I understand that you paid a little visit to that old fart Quincannon."

"Yes. I needed some information about B & Q Shipping for an investigation I'm doing. I didn't know that you owned the company."

"But now you do know it. And much more. You downloaded all of the company's files, sixty years of them."

Petra nodded. "I needed to find out about a B & Q shipment in 3163. I didn't want to spend hours looking for exactly what I needed, so I just downloaded everything."

"So I gather. That nitwit Quincannon apparently didn't realize that something like that would immediately show up in our master computer. I would never have approved letting you do that, had I known."

"It wouldn't have mattered whether you approved it or not," Petra told him. "I'm investigating a possible link to terrorist activity. I didn't have a warrant, but I could have gotten one easily enough."

"Possibly. That's neither here nor there. If you are investigating something that happened in 3163, you hardly need *all* of B & Q's records, do you?" Bartholemew offered her a friendly smile.

"I told you, I didn't have the time to do a specific search. But once I've downloaded everything from my pad to the office computer, I'll be able to find the stuff I need."

"Fine. And what of the stuff you *don't* need?"

Petra shook her head. "I have no interest in that."

"In that case, before you dump all of that information into the maw of Dexta's computers, would you be kind enough to separate the wheat from the chaff, then permanently dispose of the chaff?"

"Why? I told you—"

"Yes, I know, you have no interest in that. But someone else might. That's my problem. You see, some of the material that is of no interest to you contains information that could be, shall we say, *embarrassing,* to B & Q Shipping and Bartholemew Enterprises and to me, personally."

"Look, if you have some skeletons in your corporate closet, don't worry about it. I couldn't care less. The only thing I'm concerned with is that shipment to Savoy in 3163, and Pug and I are the only ones who are going to be using that data. Your secrets, whatever they may be, are perfectly safe."

"I wish I could be certain of that. But the ugly truth is that it's not simply a matter of a few skeletons in a closet. Apparently no one has told you about my father."

Petra frowned. "What about him?"

Bartholemew drank some more wine, then sighed. "You see," he said, "the fact is that my sainted father, Whitney Bartholemew, Senior, spent his entire adult life working in and for the zamitat. Those records, Petra Nash, do not constitute a few skeletons in a closet. They constitute an entire fucking boneyard."

"Oh," said Petra.

"Indeed. So you can understand my reluctance to let you drop the whole sordid mess into the hopper. It's not simply that *I* would be embarrassed. I'm not even in their damned cartel. But if the zamies ever got wind of it, there could be some unpleasant consequences for everyone concerned. Me, Quincannon . . . possibly even you and Pug. You unwittingly downloaded a time bomb into your little pad. For my sake, and for your own, it would be wise of you to get rid of all that information as quickly and quietly as possible."

"I see," Petra said.

"You'll do it, then?"

"I'll have to think about it. What you're asking is, in itself, illegal. I mean, just *asking* me to do that is a felony. Actually doing it . . . Spirit, I just don't know." And she didn't. Petra had never been confronted with anything like this and didn't have a clue how to deal with it. The zamitat? What had she gotten herself into? She felt a sudden chill up and down her bare back.

They finished their lunch in relative silence. Bartholemew opened another bottle of wine, poured some more, then led Petra to a corner of the vast office that appeared to be a small library. He put his arm around her back and gently massaged her right shoulder.

"You needn't be afraid of me," he said.

"I'm not. But I am curious. Your mother married a man in the zamitat. Mingus must have known. Is that what went wrong between them? Did he object to her marriage?"

To her surprise, Bartholemew erupted in a genuine laugh. "Object? Hardly! He arranged it. Or more precisely, he forced her into it. More precisely still, he sold her to that fucking thug I am pleased to call my father."

Petra looked up into his eyes. "But why?" she asked him.

Bartholemew shrugged. "It suited his needs. My grandpa needed something from my daddy, so he gave him my mommy, and everyone lived happily ever after. Heartwarming, isn't it?"

"I don't understand. Why would she go along with a thing like that?"

"I can see that you don't understand power. I mean serious, enduring, political, economic, and societal power. Stay with Pug a while, and maybe you will."

Petra thought about it for a moment and nodded. "I think I see what you mean," she said. "I've seen the kind of power the Ellisons have. I mean, I don't think Pug really wants to take that job on Pelham, but . . ."

"But he will," Bartholemew said with flat confidence. "Just as my mother married old Bart. She was in love with another man at the time—and that, too, had been arranged by my kindly old grandfather. But then his needs changed, so he redirected his daughter's life. If he hadn't, I wouldn't have been Whitney Bartholemew, Junior. I'd have been Cornell DuBray, Junior."

"DuBray?"

"None other. He was Mingus's assistant at the time, and it must have seemed an obvious and convenient match. But then, events intervened. Mingus made DuBray break off the engagement, then delivered his innocent young daughter into the waiting and eager arms of the biggest bastard in the Quardrant. And Mother went along with it, because what choice did she have? None, really; no more than those ancient princesses who were bartered off to unholy wedlock with foreign kings and potentates because it suited someone's needs. The needs of power."

"I can understand the marriage, I guess," Petra said. "But why did she stay with him all those years?"

"You don't divorce a man like Whitney Bartholemew, Senior. And, in time, a bond developed between them.

Call it love, if you like. My mother was beautiful, glamorous, and well connected; my father was handsome, powerful, and domineering. She made him look respectable, and he made her feel needed. But she never forgave her father for what he did to her."

Petra looked up at Bartholemew. "It must have been difficult for you," she said.

"Compared with what?" Bartholemew shrugged. "It was the only life I knew. I suspect that it was actually pretty easy compared with, say, growing up in poverty in a broken home in Weehawken, New Jersey."

"Oh, that wasn't so bad, either. Not really. It was the only life *I* knew."

"And yet now, you seem to be prepared to embark on an entirely different sort of life. Consort, or perhaps wife, to the scion of one of the wealthiest and most powerful families in the Empire. Are you sure that's what you want, Petra Nash?" Bartholemew raised his right hand and stroked her gently under her chin with his index finger. She looked up into his dark eyes.

"I . . . I'm not sure," she said. "I love Pug, but . . ."

"And I'm reasonably sure that Pug loves you, as well, as far as he is able. And yet, at this very moment, he's with Steffany Fairchild."

Petra pulled away from him. "No, he's not," she insisted. "He's busy with Dexta work."

"He was, this morning. Now, he's with Steffany."

"I don't believe you. How could you know that?"

"Because he told me. I called him this morning when I was trying to find your commcode. If you don't believe me, why don't you call him yourself?"

Petra almost did, but thought better of it.

"Pug is with Steffany," Bartholemew said, "and you are here, with me. Don't try to tell me, Petra Nash, that you came here dressed like that just to have a social luncheon."

Bartholemew gently ran his hand over Petra's bare

breasts, toying with her nipples. Petra's breath came in short, tense gasps as her jigli-enhanced nerves tingled in spasms of intense pleasure. His hand moved downward, probed her belly button, then slid on across her belly and down to where her pubic hairs curled over the top of the knot in her pareu. He paused there for a moment, then deftly unknotted the pareu and cupped her groin with his palm.

Petra tilted her head back as he stroked her and finally breathed, "You're right. I didn't." She reached for him, pulled him down to her, and kissed him.

GLORIA'S FEET HURT. SHE DIDN'T LIKE HIGH-gravity worlds; humans weren't designed for them. But humans were nothing if not adaptable, and they lived on Empire planets with gravitational forces ranging from .1 G to 1.7 G. In time, evolution would sort things out, but that thought was no comfort to her as she roamed the corridors of the Convention Center on her high heels and aching feet. She had sat in, briefly, on a few of the many committee meetings, but most of the day had been spent schmoozing in the corridors, selling the delegates on the benefits and potential of the OSI.

A gaggle of media reps had trailed her, off and on, but she mainly ignored them and concentrated on buttonholing Dexta people and chatting them up. She wore a sheer-to-the-point-of-invisibility white blouse with a wide, deep neckline, a matching skirt slit to the hipbone, and a businesslike dark blue blazer. Everyone could see everything she had, but she still managed to look brisk and efficient. It was a combination she knew worked well for her and somehow symbolized the image she was trying to promote for OSI. We're open and friendly, we have nothing to hide, and we get the job done.

Last night, she knew, had been a triumph. Jill, Althea, Elaine, Petra, and the guys had put a personal, smiling face on OSI for hundreds of Dexta delegates who would otherwise have known it only from rumor and reputation. Oh, Althea may have overdone it a bit, as usual, and Petra had been too drunk to function by the end of the evening, but overall, they had accomplished everything she had hoped for. And she hadn't done badly herself.

And afterward . . . Eli Opatnu and Forty-eight! The new drug was everything it was said to be, and more. Gloria closed her eyes for a second and shivered at the memory of the fantastic sensations that had coursed through her for what seemed like hours. Spirit, that was powerful stuff! And Eli was pretty powerful stuff, too; he had more than satisfied Gloria, Elaine, and Althea in the null-room. It was a shame that Jill had declined the opportunity and Petra was too far gone to participate. They might have learned something from the experience.

Eli, Gloria realized, was her opposite number, her mirror image. He was concentrated sexual energy in a package of stunning beauty. Perhaps her reaction to him was the female equivalent of what men felt with her. She felt no desire to form a lasting relationship with him; that, she was certain, would destroy them both. Like Forty-eight, Eli Opatnu was a transcendental treat, but not something you'd want to take with breakfast every morning. But there was no reason they couldn't continue to see each other from time to time and delight in each other's gifts.

"Ms. VanDeen?" Gloria was roused from her reveries by a trim-looking, dark-haired woman standing in front of her.

"Yes?" she said, smiling pleasantly.

"I'm Harriet Graves, Level Eleven, Sector 24 Social Services Coordinator."

"Pleased to meet you, Harriet."

"Ms. VanDeen, I just wanted to tell you that I think you're a disgrace!"

Gloria raised an eyebrow. "Oh?"

"You've cheapened and degraded yourself and Dexta. You've harmed every woman in the organization with your narcissistic display and self-indulgent theatrics. As if women had nothing to offer but sex!"

"Well," said Gloria, "you're entitled to your opinion. But I think the record shows that I've offered a lot more than just sex. I'm sorry if my personal style offends you, but, you know, the OSI has a great deal to offer Dexta. We've been able to solve problems that the traditional Dexta structure was incapable of dealing with, and as the Office expands, we'll provide new opportunities for creative and flexible resolution of—"

"Oh, don't give me any of your OSI garbage, Ms. VanDeen! I don't care a fig about your Office of Strategic Intervention, and the truth is, neither do you! All you care about is making a spectacle of yourself and getting every man in the Empire to lust after you!"

"And what would be wrong with that?" Gloria asked with a bemused smile. "Do not deny yourself joy, Ms. Graves, it's the wellspring of—"

"And don't give me any of your Spiritist crap! I'm a decent, God-fearing Christian woman! Avatar of Joy, huh? Hmmpf!" Ms. Graves whirled around and stomped away in high dudgeon.

A small crowd had gathered during the confrontation. Gloria turned to the onlookers and said, "Well, you can't please everyone, but I think—"

She was interrupted by a loud, sharp *crack-boom!* The unmistakable signature of a plasma discharge came from somewhere down the corridor. Gloria turned to look, but before she could see anything, two of Arkady Volkonski's Bugs lifted her off her feet and whisked her away. Volkonski himself was suddenly there, directing them through an unmarked door and into what appeared to be a supply closet crammed with janitorial robots, jugs of cleaning fluid, and an array of mops. Volkonski dashed off, slamming the door behind him.

Before Gloria could say anything to the two Internal Security men sharing the closet with her, the door opened again. Two more Bugs herded their charge into the tiny room. Gloria suddenly found herself face-to-face with Cornell DuBray.

They stared at each other in awkward silence for a few moments, then DuBray turned to his security men and gave a subtle nod. They opened the door and departed. Gloria gave a similar nod to her own Bugs, and they left the room and closed the door behind them.

"I hear you've been busy, VanDeen," DuBray said.

"Just showing the flag for OSI," Gloria replied.

"Showing a lot more than that," DuBray said. "I heard your little exchange with that Graves woman. She's not alone, you know. For every slavering man you win over with your charms, you probably alienate two women."

"Not by my count. Most of the women I've met here seem to think I'm a positive influence. They like to see a woman succeed on her own terms and not have to kowtow to anyone who happens to have a Y chromosome."

"Perhaps. In the end, it won't make any difference. The Quadrant Administrators and most of the Sector Administrators are still adamantly opposed to the whole concept of the OSI."

Gloria nodded. "I'm sure that's true. But the thing is, DuBray, Dexta consists of tens of thousands of men and women who are not Quadrant or Sector Administrators. I know you think you run the organization, and maybe you do in a formal sense. But the reality is that Dexta couldn't function without all those lowly Nines and Twelves and Fourteens that you think don't matter. They *are* Dexta."

"That's a romantic and unsophisticated view, VanDeen. The fact is, when I give an order, those Nines and Twelves and Fourteens obey it. Even glamorous, self-important Tens will obey it, if they know what's good for them."

Gloria shook her head and smiled grimly. "You know what your problem is, DuBray?" she asked him. "You've been so high for so long that you've forgotten what it's like to breathe air that isn't rarefied. You never come in contact with anyone who isn't intimidated by you. But all those faceless Dexta drones are *people,* with their own hopes and aspirations and agendas. Their own *lives.* They aren't just names in organizational charts. They respond to forces that have nothing to do with bureaucratic imperatives raining down upon them from the heavens above. They *like* me, DuBray—and they don't like *you.*"

"Perhaps not," DuBray conceded. "But they fear me."

Gloria crossed her arms and cocked her head at a defiant angle. "I don't," she said.

"Then you're foolish."

"Oh? Why, is Erik Manko out of the hospital?"

"This has nothing to do with Manko. That was just a little warning shot across your bow, VanDeen. You should have taken heed. Much worse things can happen to you."

"Well here's a little warning shot of my own, DuBray. My people have established that you signed off on that missing shipment to Savoy in 3163. And I also know that there was zamitat involvement. If I can establish a connection . . ."

DuBray's bodily reaction was so sudden and sharp that Gloria was certain that her warning shot had, in fact, scored a direct hit. He stiffened, arched his back, and scowled at her.

"You have no idea what you're dealing with here, VanDeen. None! Take my advice, and—"

Gloria never found out what DuBray's advice would have been because Arkady Volkonski abruptly opened the closet door. "You can come out now," he said. "Excitement's over."

Giving DuBray a frosty parting glance, Gloria stepped out into the corridor. "What happened?" she asked Volkonski.

Volkonski shook his head in disgust. "Two undercover Security men," he said. "Each thought the other looked suspicious. So they shot each other. The surprising thing is that it doesn't happen more often."

"Were they seriously hurt?"

"They'll recover. One of them will need a new arm, the other a new ear. Fortunately, their incompetence extended to their marksmanship."

DuBray and his two Security men brushed past them and started down the hallway. Gloria watched him go, feeling a subdued thrill in her gut. She knew now, as surely as she was standing there, that she was going to bring that son of a bitch down.

chapter 16

PETRA SULLENLY SOAKED IN THE TUB IN HER rooms at the Ellison mansion, staring at the ceiling. A mural here, too: water sprites and mermaids. Did the Ellisons control the aquatic mammal franchise on this planet, too, she wondered?

They seemed to control practically everything else. Mainly, they controlled their son. She was certain now that Pug would take the Pelham job. How could he not? Whit Bartholemew might be a cynic, but he was perceptive. Like Saffron Mingus long before him, and countless others, Palmer Ellison would wind up doing what was expected of him. Enduring dynasties like that of the Ellisons did not permit their substance to be frittered away by independent offspring. Even Whit, for all his contempt and bitterness, had wound up running the family business.

She could see the future as clearly as she could see the water sprites on the ceiling. Pug would become Imperial Secretary under Uncle Benedict, spend a few years on Pelham, then move onward and upward in

Dexta until he was, probably, about thirty. He'd have stalled at about an Eleven or Ten by then, or at least, failed to advance to the higher levels as quickly as his family would prefer. They wouldn't let him waste more than a few years in Dexta before they pressured him back into the family orbit. By the time he was thirty-five, Pug would be a senior vice president in the Ellison empire, and eventually, he'd take the reins from his father, just as Whit Bartholemew had.

And she could be right there beside him. If that was what she wanted.

Unless Pug decided that Steffany Fairchild would make a more appropriate companion on such a journey.

Not for the first time, she wished they had never come to this goddamn planet. Ever since Sylvania, it had been just the two of them, and it had been wonderful. Now, Steffany Fairchild and Whit Bartholemew had materialized in the midst of their lives, complicating and confusing everything.

She wasn't sure if she had simply been getting even with Pug or whether she felt something deeper for Bartholemew. He was a fascinating but frightening man. Petra was flattered by his attentions and couldn't deny that she had enjoyed making love with him—more than she ever had with Pug, frankly. Maybe it was just the jigli, or the delicious tang of naughtiness, but there was something about Bartholemew that reached a part of her that Pug had never touched. Nor had any other man.

Petra got out of the bath, stepped in and out of the stato-dryer, then paused in front of a full-length mirror. She spent a long time standing there, staring at her naked reflection, wondering just who that person was.

A rap at the door roused her from her meditations. She threw on a robe, went to the door, and found Standish, one of the Ellisons' omnipresent butlers, waiting there. "Dinner in ten minutes, Miss Petra," he said.

"Would you make my apologies to the Ellisons, please? I'm not feeling well. Do you suppose I could be served here in my room?"

"Certainly, Miss Petra." Standish departed, Petra closed the door, and slumped down on the immense bed. She didn't feel like having to deal with the Ellisons this evening. Let them think she was still hungover. Let them think whatever the hell they wanted.

PUG CAME IN MUCH LATER AND FOUND PETRA staring at vid coverage of the Quadrant Meeting. He watched over her shoulder as their boss gazed into the imagers, smiling and sexy, and gave her standard OSI spiel. Gloria seemed to be getting more than her fair share of vid time, but the coverage eventually moved on to other matters. "Makes you proud to be in OSI, doesn't it?" Petra said without looking up from the screen.

Pug didn't rise to the bait. "I checked out Stavros & Sons today," he said. "No Stavros, no sons. They were absorbed years ago by a division of Trans-Empire. Apparently they purged all the old files. I didn't get anything because there was nothing left to get."

"Took you all day, did it?" Petra turned her head and looked up at him.

Pug looked back at her. "Some of it," he said at last. "And how was your lunch with Whit?"

"We had fish," Petra told him. "What did you and Steffany have?"

"Make you a deal," Pug said. "You don't ask me about Steffany, I won't ask you about Whit."

"Sounds reasonable to me." Petra got to her feet and stared at Pug. "Why didn't you tell me Whit's father was in the zamitat?"

"I didn't see that it was relevant."

"I was investigating B & Q Shipping, and you didn't think it was *relevant*?"

"I didn't realize B & Q was a Bartholemew company. If I had, I would have told you. But speaking of B & Q, have you deleted those files yet?"

Petra opened her mouth, then closed it again without having said anything. She turned sharply and marched over to a dresser, seized her pad, and held it up for Pug to see.

"It's all in here," she told him. "I haven't deleted anything, and I'm not going to."

"Petra, you have to—"

"Don't tell me what I *have* to do! First Whit, now you! What the hell is this, anyway?"

"Look, Petra, be reasonable. All you need is the files from 3163."

"I don't know *what* I need because I haven't looked at it yet. Spirit, Pug, how can you ask me to delete information from an official Dexta investigation? Don't you realize what you're asking?"

"What I realize," he said evenly, "is that you inadvertently downloaded information that could be very damaging—and dangerous. Do you have any idea what could happen if the zamies ever found out what you've got?"

"Why would the zamies find out? Whit certainly isn't going to tell them. Or is there something I don't know? Maybe something else you didn't think was relevant? Is *your* father in the zamitat, too?"

"Of course he's not!" Pug glared at her from across the room. "My family's business is entirely legitimate. Or as legitimate as any business ever is."

"Then why are you so upset about this? What difference does it make to you if I accidentally stumbled across something about the Bartholemews?"

Pug walked toward her, stopped halfway there, then turned and sat down on the edge of the bed. "Petra," he said, "you know my mother is very close to Saffron Bartholemew. Our two families are . . . well, *close*. Over the years, my father and Whit's father have had converging interests in a number of matters. It could hardly have been otherwise. There have been times when the Ellisons were able to do favors for the Bartholemews, and vice versa. For Spirit's sake, Petra, that's how things *work* in this galaxy! There's nothing underhanded or illicit about it; it's simply the way things get done."

"One hand washes the other?" Petra smirked.

"*Yes!*" Pug ran his hand through his hair and breathed heavily. "Look, Petra," he said, "I don't expect you to understand this, because you haven't had the . . . the *background*. Among families like mine and Whit's, there are certain mutual relationships, certain understandings . . ."

"Which I couldn't possibly comprehend because of my . . . *background*?"

"I didn't mean it that way," Pug said. "Honestly, Petra, I'm just trying to explain why you should delete those files. Don't try to turn this into class warfare, all right? I know what you think of my family and my friends, but I'd appreciate it if you'd try to be a little more understanding. I mean, I put up with your mother, didn't I?"

Petra had no answer for that. She put the pad back on the dresser and went to sit down next to Pug.

"You're taking the Pelham job, aren't you?" It was more a statement of fact than an accusation.

"I haven't decided yet," he said.

"But your parents have. And that's all that matters, isn't it? Just another one of those understandings that families like yours have, right?"

Pug abruptly rose to his feet. "Give me a break, would you?" He turned and looked down at her. "You think this is easy for me? You think there aren't times when I want to tell my father to take his fucking empire and shove it?"

"You sound just like Whit Bartholemew," Petra observed. "And look what he wound up doing."

"If I wanted to run my father's business, would I have joined Dexta?"

"You might have," Petra replied. "Just a little youthful, pro forma rebellion, before returning to the fold. Isn't that the sort of thing that usually happens in families like yours?"

"You know, you're as big a snob as your mother. I don't hold it against you that you were born poor, Petra. Why must you hold it against me that I was born rich?"

Petra considered that for a moment and decided that it was a fair question. "Sorry," she said. "It's just that I need to know where we're going, Pug." She stood up, closed the distance between them, and put her arms around his neck. "I still want this to work."

"So do I." Pug drew her closer and kissed her softly on the neck. "And as for where we're going . . . yes, we're probably going to Pelham. Would that be so awful?"

Petra pulled back a little so she could look at his face. "I made a commitment to Gloria," she said. "We both did."

"And what if Gloria decides she'd rather be Empress? Where would that leave us?"

"I talked to her about it. She says she hasn't made up her mind. But if she did leave Dexta, I think she'd want me to come with her. Personal secretary, maybe."

"And I could be your assistant?" Pug released his hold on her. "Look, I really don't mind being your assistant now. But I don't want to spend my whole life doing that. This Pelham job could put me on the fast track at Dexta. If I rise high enough, soon enough . . ."

"Then you wouldn't have to come back here to the family business?"

Pug nodded. "That's right," he said. "In any case, if Gloria leaves, or OSI collapses, I wouldn't be hurt. And neither would you if you came along. There's nothing wrong with an Undersec slot on Pelham, you know."

"And in a year, when you make ImpeSec, I could be *your* assistant."

"That bothers you?"

Petra sighed. "I guess not," she said. "Unlike you, it looks like I *am* going to spend my whole life being *someone's* assistant. I suppose that's the most I can expect, given the tragic limitations of my background." She offered Pug a weak smile, which he returned.

"Right now," he said, reaching into her robe and fondling her breasts, "I'd rather concentrate on your *fore*ground."

"Which is also tragically limited."

"That's all right," he said. "I don't mind slumming."

CORNELL DUBRAY STARED AT GLORIA VANDEEN, chattering away about OSI on the far side of the room. If he was honest with himself—and he usually was, because he could afford to be—he had to admit that he admired her, and not simply for that magnificent ass, which was currently on full display in a bizarre bit of sartorial architecture that left her front mostly covered in swirling silver tinsel. VanDeen was smart and ambitious and, in her own way, as ruthless as DuBray himself. She was easily the most formidable woman he had encountered since Elsinore Chandra in her prime.

The Sector 21 Reception was well attended because it was the host Sector, and it was no surprise to find VanDeen here. Inevitably, he was going to keep tripping over her at these affairs throughout the length of the Quadrant Meeting. That could prove to be inconvenient; he didn't want any public scenes with her because there was no way he could come out on top in such an encounter. She had public support that he could never hope to muster. And, as she had pointed out in that broom closet this afternoon, Dexta people liked her. DuBray resolved to keep to the far side of the room from her and avoid confrontations.

That was ridiculous, of course, but there was no help for it. This was *his* Quadrant, and—at least until Norman Mingus arrived—he was the senior Dexta official on New Cambridge. Yet that twenty-five-year-old harridan had somehow put him on the defensive.

DuBray helped himself to a fresh glass of champagne from a passing waiter and munched on a caviar-covered cracker. If he didn't watch it, he'd probably put on ten pounds in the next two weeks. Long ago, when he'd lived on this planet, he'd been lithe and athletic and didn't have to worry about such things. In bed, Saffron had called him "Slim."

Saffron was here tonight, too. They'd made their peace years ago—or an armistice, at any rate—but there were unexpected moments when he still felt a pang. It had all worked out for the best, in the long run, he supposed; fifty-five years certainly qualified as the long run. They had each prospered, the Empire survived, and history had buried all their tawdry little secrets.

Until now.

He was certain that he was correct in what he had said in the closet that afternoon. VanDeen truly had no idea what she was dealing with. She was like a dog tugging on the corner of some half-buried shroud because, just maybe, there was a bone somewhere down there. If he told her the truth, would she stop tugging, stop digging?

She might. But he simply couldn't risk it. Truth was like a plasma bomb; you only used it when there was no other choice. Truth, like unleashed plasma, was indiscriminate and unyielding and devoured everything in its path. Lies were safer because lies could be controlled.

He had learned that, if nothing else, in seventy years at Dexta.

One of his aides caught his eye and signaled to him. DuBray nodded, set down his champagne, and followed the aide out of the mansion's ballroom, down a long corridor, and into a small, opulent private office. The aide retreated, closing the door behind him, leaving DuBray alone with the girl.

She stood before him, clearly frightened, but with her widely set dark eyes gleaming in anticipation. Something big was about to happen to her, and DuBray gained the impression that she might possibly welcome it.

"Ms. Murakami," he said, "thank you for coming. You know who I am?"

The girl nodded. "Yessir. Cornell DuBray, Quadrant 4 Administrator." Then she added, unnecessarily, "Level Four."

DuBray smiled. "That's right," he said. "And you are Level Fourteen, currently assigned to the Office of Strategic Intervention."

"Yessir."

She was very attractive, another one of OSI's young Tigers. She was wearing nothing on her small, slim body but a tiny scrap of black mesh band skirt and a matching shawl carelessly draped over her shoulders. Her face, Asian-Pacific, was carefully made up to emphasize her hypnotic dark eyes. She looked as if she might have been about twelve, but DuBray knew she was twenty-five. And he knew much more than that.

"Ms. Murakami," he said, "your father is currently incarcerated at the prison colony on Hingson III. He has two years left to serve on a three-year term for fraud and embezzlement. Would you like to get him out next month?"

Her eyes widened even more. "You could do that?"

"Of course I can. And I will, if you cooperate."

DuBray could tell from the way she hesitated that

Murakami was not the innocent young waif she appeared to be. She was already calculating the angles, measuring the moment for maximum advantage, like a pool shark plotting a three-cushion shot. So much the better.

"I'll cooperate in any way I can, sir," she said at last.

"I know you will."

"What do you want me to do?"

"You are presently working as Gloria VanDeen's assistant, correct?"

She nodded. "Petra Nash is her regular assistant, but she's busy on another assignment, so I'm filling in for her."

"And just how close are you to Ms. VanDeen?"

The girl hesitated, then smiled slyly. "We've made love," she said.

"Have you, now?" DuBray found that intriguing, but not entirely relevant. "Does she confide in you? Tell you her plans? Share information?"

Murakami shrugged. "In general. I don't think she tells me everything that's going on, but I think I have a pretty good idea of what she's up to, most of the time."

"And how would you feel about sharing that knowledge with me?"

"You want me to spy on Gloria?"

"That's what I want. Will you do it?"

The hesitation again. The girl would not have been a good poker player.

"I . . . I'm not sure. I need to think about it."

"Think about *this*, Ms. Murakami. Your father is in prison on Hingson III. I can have him released, or I can send you there to join him."

A look of sudden doubt flickered across the girl's features.

"On an irregular basis for the past two years," DuBray said, "you have been involved in the sale and distribution of illegal substances—Orgastria-29, to be precise."

"How did you know that?"

"How I know is of no moment. What matters is that I *do* know. Well, Ms. Murakami, can I count on your cooperation?"

"I'll do it," she said.

"Of course you will. After we're through here, my aide will instruct you in your duties and communication procedures."

"How do I know I can trust you?" Murakami asked. She had some nerve, DuBray was pleased to see.

"If you do as I ask, your father will be released. Frankly, I don't care a farthing whether your father is released or rots in prison. I have no interest in the matter, so I have no reason to lie to you."

"And what about me?"

"What about you?"

"Naturally, I want to see my father released. But I could be risking my Dexta career by doing this for you, Mr. DuBray. I mean, what's in this for *me*?" She gave him that sly smile again.

DuBray smiled back at her. "I'm glad you asked me that," he said. "Selflessness makes me suspicious. Very well, then, what's in it for you is a promotion to Thirteen when we return to Earth and a transfer to an appropriate position on Quadrant staff. Does that meet with your approval, Ms. Murakami?"

"Yes . . . but wouldn't that let Gloria know what I've been doing?"

"By then," DuBray assured her, "it won't matter."

EDWIN OGBURN, PRESIDENT OF THE REPUBLIC of New Cambridge, made the introduction. "Ms. Gloria VanDeen of Dexta, allow me to present Ms. Saffron

Bartholemew, one of our world's most beautiful and respected citizens."

They shook hands politely and took each other's measure. Saffron's resemblance to her father was unmistakable; something in the aristocratic slope of her nose and the high, unlined forehead. Her fine, cornsilk hair was artfully arranged, and her V-shaped jaw jutted out just a little. Her eyes were the same color as her father's, a watery blue-gray.

Both women simultaneously turned their heads to look at the man who had introduced them. Ogburn, no fool, quickly made his apologies and departed, leaving the two women alone.

"So," Saffron said at last, "you're my father's latest popsy."

Gloria ignored the verbal sally and smiled pleasantly. "I'm hardly that," she said, "but I do work closely with him."

"All the stories and rumors aren't true, then?"

"I doubt if one percent of them are true. But we aren't intimate, if that's what you're getting at."

"No?" Saffron frowned, as if disappointed at this news. "Well, he is a hundred and thirty-one. Finally slowing down, I guess."

"I wouldn't know about that. But the fact is, his health has not been good of late. He just had a new pancreas put in. He'll be here next week, Ms. Bartholemew. Perhaps you should take the opportunity to find out for yourself how he is, instead of relying on rumors and secondhand reports."

Saffron raised an eyebrow. "I'll take it under advisement," she said.

"He's a lonely old man," Gloria said. "It would do him good to see his family."

"Ah, but would it do his family any good?"

"I don't see how it could do you any harm."

"Then, Ms. VanDeen, you don't know my father as well as you think you do."

"Look, Ms. Bartholemew," Gloria said, feeling a growing sense of exasperation, "I don't know anything at all about Norman's personal life. I don't know why the two of you are estranged, and I don't want to know. But I think he's a good man, and I care very much about him."

Saffron gave her a lingering, appraising stare, like a jeweler considering a gem. Then she said, "You really do care about him, don't you?"

Gloria nodded. "I do."

"No reason you shouldn't, I suppose," Saffron said. "He does have . . . qualities. You know, I was just about your age when we became, as you say, estranged. Until that point, I worshipped him. Thought the galaxy revolved around him. And I suppose it does, now. Even then, you could sense greatness in him. But greatness is not necessarily an endearing trait, Ms. VanDeen."

"Is that why you resent him? Was he too busy being great to be a good father?"

"Not at all. I wasn't neglected—far from it. My mother died in an accident when I was only twelve, you know. And my father was very devoted to me. Credit where credit is due—I can't deny him that. He positively doted on me, and took great pains to see to it that I grew up with every advantage. He was also demanding, but not oppressively so. I think he simply wanted me to be perfect so that I could have a perfect life."

"And now you blame him because you didn't?"

Saffron didn't quite laugh at that. "That's one way of looking at it," she said. "Ms. VanDeen, you are obviously unaware of what transpired between my father and me. Perhaps my father will see fit to enlighten you someday, but I have no intention of dredging up painful memories just for your sake. I'm glad that I had the chance to meet you, Ms. VanDeen. Allow me to give you some advice.

Whatever affection or esteem you feel for my father, and whatever his emotional attachment to you may be, don't for one minute imagine that you are anything more to him than what I was—what everyone is."

"And what is that?"

"A tool, Ms. VanDeen. A tool."

chapter **17**

PETRA AND PUG RETURNED TO THE OLD ANNEX
the next morning to continue their research. They had
said no more about the files in her pad, but when Petra
connected the pad to the main console, Pug gave her a
hard look.

"You're going to do this in spite of everything?"

"It's my job," she told him. "Yours, too, or had you
forgotten?"

Pug snorted wordlessly and got to his feet. "I'll be
over in Gibraltar," he said. "I'm going to see if I can find
some of those people who were here in 3163."

"Good idea. Maybe they'll even talk to you."

Pug left, and Petra finished downloading the files
from her pad. After all the talk, she was eager to get
down to cases and see what was in them. The main thing
she was after was a bill of lading for that final shipment
to Savoy. Aside from the 24,000 Mark IV plasma rifles,
they still didn't know what else was in that shipment.
Whatever it was, it was now probably in the possession
of PAIN.

She quickly zeroed in on August and September of 3163. Before she found the bill of lading, she happened upon the log and registration information for the freighter that had been used for the shipment. She made note of the names of the captain and crew of twelve, thinking that some of them might very well still be alive and willing to talk, assuming they could be found. Officially, at least, they had all disappeared, along with their freighter, when the Ch'gnth attacked. The freighter itself, a LoadStar, was rated at sixty thousand tons capacity and was seven years old in 3163. B & Q had bought it new, for 73 million crowns, with a loan from the Bank of New Cambridge. Before its final voyage, the vessel had logged just over thirty-nine thousand hours in Yao Space and 42,154 light-years traveled. There was nothing interesting or unusual about it, as far as Petra could tell.

Next, she studied the contracts that had been negotiated between Dexta and B & Q. Whitney Bartholemew had signed for B & Q; as Quincannon said, it had been "Bart's deal." There were a number of signatures for Dexta, as required by a web of regulations: everyone from Port Masters to the Export Decontamination Control Authority to Assistant Quadrant Administrator Cornell DuBray had been required to sign it, and did. Petra stared at the contracts for quite some time. She had already seen the Dexta copies of the same documents. Out of curiosity, she called them up and did a side-by-side comparison.

There were differences between them. Nothing dramatic, or even meaningful, as far as she could tell. The standard wording in the contract text was nearly the same, but the fill-in sections of the documents contained minor variations in style and language, almost as if they had been completed at different times by different people. That, in itself, was not particular cause for concern. It was not unreasonable to assume that in the back-and-forth of the transaction, different people at Dexta and B & Q might have gotten their hands on the contracts. Still, now that she knew the truth about Whitney Bartholemew, Senior, Petra couldn't help wondering.

She got to her feet and paced around the tiny office space they had been granted. For today, she had shed her Tiger stripes and was wearing jeans, a loose gray shirt, and, praise the Spirit, comfortable shoes.

If something was wrong with the contracts, how could she tell? How could she recognize something for what it was, even if it was staring her in the face? Answer: she couldn't, because she had no idea what contracts like this were supposed to look like in 3163. But there was a cure for that gap in her knowledge.

With a sigh of resignation, Petra sat down again and called up a random assortment of B & Q and Dexta shipping contracts from 3163. She studied them for a full hour before returning to the Savoy contract. This time around, the truth leaped off the pages at her. She double-checked, and there was no doubt.

The Savoy contract in the B & Q records had been written, not in late August 3163, but no earlier than late October of that year. With the coming of war, in early September, the basic shipping contract text had been altered to include war-related issues. In the newer version of the contracts, there were additional lines and boxes, and some tacked-on paragraphs related to wartime liability, insurance riders, military escort regulations, and the like. None of that new material appeared verbatim in the Savoy contract, and yet Petra had the feeling that it had been there, then deleted. The result was that the spacing and some of the phrasing in the Savoy contract was subtly different from other prewar contracts.

But what did it mean?

The Savoy contract had been written—or rewritten—

after the fact, and imperfectly altered to make it appear as if it had been written in August. Why?

No answer occurred to her.

Finally, she put the contracts aside and resumed her search for the bill of lading. When she found it, she gave it a once-over, without really registering any of the information it contained. She moved it to a corner of her screen and called up another random assortment of bills of lading from the relevant period. After another hour of study, it was clear to her that the same thing that had been done to the contracts had been done to the bill of lading. Again, why?

She returned to the Savoy shipment bill of lading and examined the specific contents. As expected, it listed the 24,000 Mark IV plasma rifles, gross weight, 264 metric tons. A Mark IV, she calculated, weighed—with packing material—about eleven kilos. No wonder they phased them out.

Along with the rifles, there had been 2.4 million plasma cylinders—extra ammo, in other words. Gross weight, 2400 tons.

Ten thousand cases of plasma grenades. Gross weight, 1200 tons.

What else? Three point six million Imperial Marine Corps Field Ration packets. Gross weight, 2160 tons.

Two hundred and eighty-six orbital plasma mines. Another 5148 tons.

And—holy shit!—eighteen 200-quadrijoule plasma bombs. Ninety-five lethal tons. PAIN had plasma bombs!

Petra had to sit and think about that one for a while. So far, PAIN had been content to shoot up Dexta offices. They could have been blowing up entire cities!

She was shocked and frightened by the discovery. But there was nothing she could do about it, so she returned to the bill of lading and continued adding up the monstrous inventory.

Except that it *didn't* add up.

• • •

JILL CLYMER, WAITING OUTSIDE THE DOORS TO
Wendover Freight and Storage in downtown Central,
saw Eli Opatnu approaching and felt her heart skip a
beat. Did his pheromones work at a distance, she wondered, or was she just reacting to the man himself? She
had always thought of herself as a pretty cool customer
when it came to the male of the species. She enjoyed sex
and had never been shy about it, but until now she had
always felt able to keep a rein on her emotions. Her ex-
husband had even complained about it. She never let
herself go, he said, never abandoned herself to the raw
realities of sex. "You think you can wade across a raging
river and never get your feet wet," he had said.

And yet, here she was today, doing her best Gloria
VanDeen impression in a nearly transparent shirtdress,
unbuttoned and flapping open to reveal her breasts and
thighs, not a stitch on underneath, damn near as naked
as Petra had been the other night. And all for Eli
Opatnu, a man who collected women the way some people collected butterflies.

And here he was, damn him, smiling to beat the
band, eyes gleaming, supple hips and broad shoulders
moving rhythmically as he walked toward her. So utterly
sure of himself, so full of life, so insidious. Jill took a
deep breath and returned his smile.

"Sorry I'm late," he said as he clasped both of her
hands in his. "Hard to get a cab this week." *His hands
are warm; or maybe mine are just cold,* she thought.

They went inside and introduced themselves to the
woman at the main desk. Jill flashed her Dexta ID, but
the woman scarcely noticed; her attention was focused
on Eli. He gave her his best smile, and within a minute,
they were ushered into the office of Wendover's regional
manager, a Ms. Sophie Darceau. *Swell,* Jill thought.

Ms. Darceau didn't quite ignore Jill, but seemed to

regard her as a distraction from the main business of the moment, which was making small talk with Eli Opatnu. Finally, Jill simply interrupted them and held up her pad. "Ms. Darceau," she said, "I have here a list of nine freighters owned or operated by Wendover in this Sector. Some discrepancies concerning their records have turned up, and we would like to clear up the confusion. I'll transmit the list to your console, and I would appreciate it if you could give us a full accounting of the whereabouts of those freighters for the last two years."

Ms. Darceau looked up, as if noticing Jill for the first time. "What? Oh, yes, I see. Now that I think about it, we did receive a memo concerning this from the home office on Staghorn."

"Then you know that Dexta is conducting a formal investigation."

"Yes, that's what they said. But they also said that I was not to give out any proprietary information without first consulting Staghorn."

"That would take weeks," Jill pointed out.

"Yes," said Ms. Darceau, "I suppose it would."

"Ms. Darceau," Jill said with more patience than she felt, "if you make it necessary, I can go see an Imperial Judge and be back here this afternoon with a warrant."

"I'll consult with our legal department, in that case. My understanding is that we can challenge the warrant."

"But why go to all that trouble?" Opatnu broke in, smiling ingratiatingly. "Look, Ms. Darceau, Jim Takahashi—your boss on Staghorn—is an old friend of mine. I know he'd want you to cooperate. In fact, as soon as I return to Staghorn, I'll tell him exactly what happened here and that you made every effort to comply with the memo from the home office. I know he wouldn't want a lot of unnecessary legal entanglements . . . warrants, suits, countersuits, that sort of thing. And *you* wouldn't want that, would you?" He turned up the smile to maximum wattage.

"Well . . ." said Ms. Darceau, "I'd still have to consult with Legal."

"Of course. We understand that. Why don't you do that, then, and we'll be back this afternoon to see where we stand. I'm sure we can work this out without dragging the courts into it." He got to his feet and held out his hand to Ms. Darceau. "A very real pleasure meeting you, Sophie. Have a pleasant day, and I'll see you this afternoon."

Jill followed him out of the office. On the sidewalk, Opatnu turned to her and grinned. "There! Now we have two or three hours for a leisurely lunch."

"But we don't have the data on those freighters."

"We'll have it this afternoon. If we get a warrant, we'll just wind up in a legal hassle that might take weeks. Trust me, we'll get what we need. Now, what about lunch? There are some lovely restaurants down on the waterfront overlooking the strait. Shall we?"

They settled in at an outdoor table on a terrace two hundred feet above the choppy blue waters of the strait. Jill noted that Opatnu was careful to sit upwind from her. Was that so she would get a full dose of his pheromones, or merely to get a better view of the breeze flapping around her unbuttoned shirt and baring her breasts? Both, probably; Jill had already noticed that nearly everything Opatnu did or said was carefully calculated.

The man annoyed her and fascinated her in equal measure. That, in itself, was annoying. Why couldn't she get a handle on the situation? Why did he make her feel so unsure of herself, so helpless and foolish? Like some damned adolescent.

Opatnu asked her about her past and her homeworld. She told him that she was from Minnetonka, an agricultural planet in Sector 2, five hundred light-years from Earth. It was something of a backwater, rural in its economy and attitudes, and Jill had grown up longing for bright lights and big cities. She had gotten a taste of that early on when she accompanied her father to sessions of Parliament on Luna. Jill found herself telling Opatnu about those trips, and about her father, a man she had loved and admired without limit.

"Yes," Opatnu said, "I vaguely remember the story. He caused a bit of a stir in Parliament ten or fifteen years back, didn't he?"

Jill smiled, then pointed to a swirling eddy just offshore in the strait. "See those waves?" she asked. "That was my father. A tiny ripple in a big, blue sea. In about a million years, that ripple will probably carve out a bit of the shoreline, just through sheer persistence. My father thought that if he persisted, he might get a few worthwhile things done, eventually. But they didn't give him the time he needed."

"There was some sort of scandal, wasn't there?"

Jill nodded. "He found some corruption and tried to expose it. Oh, it wasn't anything major, just some illegal loans that a Parliament committee was dishing out to some cronies back in Sector 2. The kind of thing that goes on all the time, I suppose, but it offended my father. He thought that the money going to those big shots should have been going to people who actually needed it—his constituents, the people who voted for him and sent him to Parliament to represent them and protect their interests. Dean Clymer was a man who took his responsibilities seriously."

"And what happened?"

"The big shots back home didn't appreciate what he was doing. So they dug up something from his past and used it to smear him. Again, it was nothing major. But the thing was, it was true. My father made a mistake thirty years ago, but thought that he had made up for it by being an honest and dedicated public servant. When the mistake was dredged up, people began to wonder if Dean Clymer was really the honest man he seemed to be. And my father couldn't bear the shame of it. So he killed himself."

Jill finished the story and turned to look out to sea, so she wouldn't have to look at Opatnu. So he wouldn't see the tears welling in her eyes.

Opatnu reached across the table and clasped his hand around hers. "I'm glad you told me," he said. "I wondered why a measly little double-flagging scam seemed to be so important to you. Now, I think I understand. It isn't about Wendover, is it? It's about your father."

Jill blinked back her tears and nodded. "I think of him all the time," she said. "I imagine him looking over my shoulder, asking me if I'm sure I'm doing the right thing. That was one reason why I was glad when Gloria asked me to join OSI. It seemed like a way to make a career out of doing the right thing." She smiled self-consciously. "Silly, huh?"

"Not at all. It's admirable. But I get the impression that you have some doubts."

"Not doubts, really. Gloria wants to do the right thing, too. Her style is a little overwhelming at times, but she gets the job done. But this whole business of turning OSI into the Fifth Quadrant . . . I don't know. I'm afraid she's getting too caught up in bureaucratic rivalries and internal Dexta politics."

"How could she avoid it?" Opatnu wondered.

"I know, I know. That's the game at Dexta, and she has to play it. But I can't help worrying that she's making the same kinds of mistakes that my father made, and that eventually she'll have to pay for it. You start out making little compromises to serve some higher purpose, and you wind up making bigger and bigger compromises, because, hey, you've *already* compromised yourself, right?"

Opatnu frowned. "It sounds like you're saying that

any compromise at all is fatal. That's not a very realistic attitude."

Jill gave Opatnu a rueful smile. "That's us Clymers," she said. "Pure but stupid."

"I admire you for your purity, Jill, as well as for your stupidity. Maybe we could all benefit by a little more of that kind of stupidity."

"My father used to say, 'When you sup with the Devil, you need a long spoon.'"

Opatnu released his hold on Jill's hand and picked up one of her spoons from the table setting. He examined it carefully and said, "Looks about the right size to me."

"We'll see," she said.

WHEN PUG DIDN'T RETURN, PETRA WORKED straight through the lunch hour and into the afternoon. Finally, hunger and curiosity drove her out of the Old Annex and into the bustling streets of Central. It was only a mile or so to the Old City and the office of B & Q Shipping, so she decided to walk. She undid a couple more buttons on her shirt, figuring she would give lecherous old Jamie Quincannon a thrill. And herself, too. She couldn't deny it—this Tiger business was getting to her. Whit Bartholemew had said she was the sexiest woman he'd ever met, and even if he had been lying, it was still nice to hear.

She stopped in a small shop for a sandwich and coffee. Cream, but no sugar; she had noticed that her jeans seemed a little tight. Too much high living, not enough Qatsima lately. The walk would do her good and give her a chance to think.

Contracts, bills of lading, and gross weights swirled through her mind as she walked. She wondered if she was making too much out of what she had seen. In her ignorance and suspicion, could she be tilting at a windmill of her own construction? If she hadn't known that Whit Bartholemew's father was a zamie, would she have made anything at all out of the minor anomalies she had uncovered? Did they even mean anything, or were they just the routine slips of harried bureaucrats and flawed human beings? She remembered a history professor in college who had said, "If you hear hoofbeats, don't go looking for zebras." He had also said, "Incompetence explains more of history than conspiracies."

And yet, this conspiracy was real. Weapons from the Savoy shipment had undeniably turned up in the hands of PAIN terrorists. But how far did the conspiracy go, and what did it all mean? The records she had downloaded were sterile, lifeless. They listed facts—or someone's preferred version of the facts—but they didn't tell her what had really been going on fifty-five years ago. Maybe Jamie Quincannon could tell her.

Maybe he could tell her why 27,542 metric tons of cargo had been shipped to Savoy on a freighter that could hold 60,000 tons.

It made no sense. Why send a valuable, half-empty freighter off on a risky errand to a place where war might erupt at any moment? Even if the freighter had never gone to Savoy, why send it *anywhere* half-empty? Petra knew that the economics of interstellar trade were exacting and unforgiving. The expense of traveling between the stars was simply too great to waste cargo space. She and Gloria usually traveled via a Flyer, which was nothing but a tiny tin can with an engine attached, yet even a Flyer trip was expensive. Sending a sixty-thousand-ton freighter on a seventy-five-light-year hop to Savoy without a full hold would be not only stupid, but unprofitable. Why not send the shipment in a smaller freighter? That would be cheaper and faster.

Maybe no smaller freighter had been available. That was something she could check in the B & Q records. But then, why use B & Q? Why not let the contract to a big outfit, like Trans-Empire, that would certainly have an appropriate ship available? Or would Trans-Empire have been reluctant to send a ship into a potential war zone?

And what was Bartholemew's angle? An insurance scam? Possibly . . . Quincannon had said that his partner knew how to play both ends against the middle, so maybe that was it. B & Q had collected on the insurance a few years later; why collect for a small ship when you could collect for a big one?

Meanwhile . . . what had happened to the shipment itself? However it was shipped, and whatever angles people were playing, it had gone *somewhere*. And wherever that place was, PAIN had found it.

If anyone knew the answers, it would be Jamie Quincannon. And Petra had a feeling that, with the proper inducement, he just might tell her what she needed to know. She undid one more button, then entered the building, and, with a game smile fixed on her face, assaulted the five flights of stairs.

It was dark at the top of the stairs, no light at all except for what filtered in through a couple of grimy windows. Petra walked slowly over the creaking wooden floor and waited for her eyes to adjust to the gloom. Her left foot suddenly skidded ahead, and she nearly fell. Gathering herself, she stooped down to see what had caused the skid and noticed a dark liquid staining the floor.

Rising, she looked into an open room on her left and saw the source of the dark liquid. It was the body of Jamie Quincannon.

chapter 18

GLORIA GATHERED HER TROOPS IN THE SUITE at her hotel the next morning. "I thought it would be a good idea to bring everyone up to date on recent developments," she said. "First off, I want to thank you again for the great job you've been doing. From the feedback I've been getting, I think we've done ourselves a lot of good here this week. Everyone's talking about OSI, and most of the comments I've heard have been very positive."

"I should *hope* so," Althea Dante cackled. "I've devoted body and soul to the cause."

"I won't ask in what proportion," Gloria said. "Now, I'd like to announce that our very own Elaine Murakami will be promoted to Thirteen when we return to Manhattan. In the meantime, she will be spying on us for Cornell DuBray, so if there's anything you don't want the Quad Admin to know, don't say it around Elaine."

Elaine grinned happily. "He asked me just the way you said he would," she said. "How did you know?"

"Lucky guess," Gloria replied. She didn't add that it

was what she would have done in DuBray's place. "We'll feed him just enough information to keep him happy and make him think he knows what we're doing. Now, Jill, I understand that we've run into a snag on the double-flagging investigation."

"I'm afraid so," Jill said, frowning. "Eli Opatnu and I went to the local Wendover office yesterday morning. I thought we were going to get what we needed from them without any hassles. But when we returned in the afternoon, we found that while we were at lunch, Wendover had gone to court and gotten a restraining order against us. We can't file any subpoenas or get any warrants until a lawyer from their home office arrives here to file a brief. That will be at least a month." Jill looked disgusted.

"Is there any chance that we can overturn that ruling?"

"Possibly," Jill said. "But that would mean bringing in the local Dexta office for Sector 21, and since one of the things we're investigating is whether there is any Dexta involvement, that could defeat our purpose. Of course, by now, they've heard about the restraining order, so if anyone here is involved in the double-flagging, they've already been alerted."

"I see," said Gloria. "So what are our options?"

"I can stay here for a month and try to see this through on my own. Or, when we get back to Earth, we can send one of OSI's lawyers here to deal with it. Either way, we're stalled for at least a month. No recent word from the Financial team we sent to Staghorn, so I don't know where we stand at that end."

"Well," Gloria said, "let me contact the Sector 21 Administrator and see what I can do. In the meantime, you might as well join Althea and the boys on the committee circuit and start schmoozing."

Gloria turned to Petra, who was sitting on a sofa next to Pug, glumly staring off into space. Petra had spent most of yesterday afternoon dealing with the Central Police. She had called them when she found Quincannon's body, not knowing what else to do. When the initial shock had worn off, she had called Gloria, who dispatched Arkady Volkonski to the scene. The Central Police, who had had their fill of Dexta Internal Security in the past week, tried to keep him out of the way while they interrogated Petra, but he had simply run roughshod over them and rescued Petra from a grim ordeal. Volkonski, citing the superior mandate of Dexta and Imperial Security, had told the cops as little as possible about Petra's interest in Quincannon and B & Q Shipping, then marched out of the building with Petra in his grip.

"Petra," Gloria said, "I know you had a rough day. But is there anything you can tell the rest of us about your investigation?"

Petra looked around the room. She was among friends, but she seemed reluctant to talk about what had happened. "I've turned up a few things," she said. "I'm not really sure what to make of it all. But, Arkady, there is something that you should know. The bill of lading for that Savoy shipment mentioned eighteen two-hundred-quadrijoule plasma bombs."

Volkonski nodded. "Internal Security suspected as much, but it's good to have confirmation. I'll inform Quadrant Security immediately."

Gloria stared at Petra for another moment, then moved on to Pug. "How about you, Pug? Anything?"

He shook his head. "I found a couple of people yesterday who were here in 3163, but they didn't know anything about that shipment. There are three others that I couldn't find, but they are supposed to be around here, somewhere. I'll keep trying."

"Okay." Gloria got to her feet and the others did the same. "I want all of you to stay alert. Arkady's Bugs will be assigned to cover each of us, just in case, although I doubt that what happened yesterday has any direct connection to OSI. So let's all just do our jobs and be happy in our work. Have a good day, people."

Jill, Althea, Brent, Darren, and Arkady left the suite. "Petra," Gloria said to her, "would you stay for a few minutes? Pug, she'll catch up to you later." Pug nodded and left.

"Do you want me to stay, too, Gloria?" Elaine asked.

"That won't be necessary," Gloria told her. "I want to have a few words alone with Petra."

"Are you sure?" Elaine asked again. "It's no trouble, really."

"Don't take this spying business too seriously, okay? I'll see you in a while at the Convention Center," Gloria said. Elaine walked slowly from the room. When she was gone, Gloria went to Petra and hugged her. "I'm awfully sorry about what happened. It must have been a terrible thing for you."

Petra shook her head. "I was just stunned," she said. "I don't think it really got to me until this morning. I woke up and it suddenly hit me that Jamie Quincannon *wouldn't* be getting up this morning. Nice old man, must have been a hundred and twenty, and suddenly, it's all just . . . *over.* Spirit, Gloria, I feel awful! I mean, what if something I did . . . ?"

"None of that," Gloria insisted. "You can't let yourself think that way. You have a job to do, and a lot of lives might depend on your doing it right. Quincannon's death doesn't change anything, Petra. You can't start second-guessing yourself."

They sat down on the sofa and Gloria poured coffee for them. Petra took a small sip of hers, then put her cup down on the coffee table. "Gloria?" she said. "There are some things . . . things I didn't tell the police."

"Don't worry about it. You did the right thing. Quincannon's murder may have had nothing to do with our investigation. Let the police handle their end of it, and if anything turns up to connect it to what we're doing. I'll inform them when I think it's appropriate."

"But there are other things, too. Spirit, Gloria, this is turning into something that I didn't . . . didn't expect. Did you know that Whitney Bartholemew, Senior—"

"Was in the zamitat?"

Petra's mouth fell open. "How did . . . ?"

"I have some additional sources of information," Gloria told her. The additional source had been Anton Grosz, who had delivered a one-time-only message from Ed Smith the previous evening. Gloria had played it on her pad; then the message destroyed itself and any traces of its presence.

Smith had told her that he had talked with some "senior people" in his organization. He had learned that Bartholemew had "scammed the insurance" on the missing freighter, making a handsome profit, while selling off the freighter that had presumably been lost at Savoy. Meanwhile, Smith said, the original Savoy consignment had been spirited away from New Cambridge on three separate shiploads. His sources didn't know where it had all gone.

Petra seemed annoyed that Gloria was ahead of her. "You mean I've been digging through all those old files, and you already knew everything?"

"Not at all," Gloria assured her. "My source has only very sketchy knowledge of what happened. But he did say that the shipment that was supposed to have gone to Savoy was broken up into three different shipments and sent somewhere from New Cambridge. He didn't know where."

"Three?"

"That's right. Why?"

"That doesn't make sense. I mean, one of the weird things I discovered was that the Savoy shipment only came to about 27,000 tons, and the freighter had a capacity of 60,000 tons. It would have been flying half-empty. But now, you say those 27,000 tons were divided in three, then sent away in other freighters."

"Maybe they were smaller freighters," Gloria suggested. "Three ten-thousand-tonners."

"Yeah," Petra agreed, "that would explain it. But that really complicates things."

"How so?"

"Well, a 60,000-ton freighter is strictly space-to-space. They can't land. But a ten-thousand-ton freighter can make planetfall."

"So?"

"I was thinking that we might have been able to trace where that original freighter went instead of Savoy. There are only so many planets that have orbital storage facilities. We could have checked every appropriate planet within, say, two hundred light-years of New Cambridge to see what 60,000-ton freighters docked at their orbital stations during, say, the last four months of 3163. It would have been a huge job, but eventually we might have turned up something. But now, if they used three smaller, planet-capable freighters . . ."

"I see what you mean," Gloria said. "They could have gone practically anywhere. But still, that was a good idea, Petra. And something else occurs to me. Did the B & Q records say anything about what *other* freighters B & Q had available? Like, say, some ten-thousand-ton jobs?"

Petra's face lit up. "I didn't check for that, but I will. Wow, Gloria, that's a great idea! I'll get right on it."

"That's why we pay you the big bucks, Petra. Sounds like you've been making a lot of progress."

Petra shook her head. "I'm not sure if I have or not. It's all pretty confusing. One thing, I think that the Dexta contracts with B & Q were altered, or written after the fact." Petra explained in detail the reason for her suspicions.

"Interesting," Gloria said. "And you say that Cornell DuBray signed the contracts?"

"DuBray and a lot of other people. Don't make too much out of that, Gloria. It would have been odd if DuBray or someone in his office *hadn't* signed those contracts."

"I suppose so." Gloria sighed. "Damn, if we could just tie him into all of this, somehow . . ."

Petra looked down at her coffee cup. "We can," she said.

"What?" Gloria stared, wide-eyed, at her assistant. "Out with it, Petra! What have you got?"

Petra sighed heavily, then looked at Gloria. "I had lunch . . . I mean, I met with Whitney Bartholemew, Junior two days ago. I learned some things . . . personal things . . . that sort of connect DuBray with Whit's father. I'm not sure exactly how, but . . . well, it seems that DuBray was engaged to Saffron Mingus at about the same time we're investigating. And then, Whit says that Norman Mingus forced them to break off the engagement and sort of delivered Saffron into the arms of his father. I don't know what it all means, but if you're looking for a connection . . ."

"That certainly qualifies," Gloria said, leaning back against the sofa. "Spirit . . . you say *Norman* did all of this?"

"That's what Whit says. Of course, he hates his grandfather, so who knows what the real story is? Except that I think he was telling me the truth."

"I think so, too," Gloria said. "I met his mother the other night. Did Whit say why he did it?"

"Just that it suited his needs. It was all about power, according to Whit. He's kind of hung up on that subject. Gloria? There's something else you need to know about all of this. I didn't just have lunch with Whit. I made love with him."

Gloria looked at her. Petra didn't exactly look guilty, but she didn't look very happy, either.

"I see," Gloria said slowly. "And do you think that Whit could have been saying all these things just to get you to go to bed with him?"

"I suppose it's possible. That's why I thought I should mention it. I *think* he was telling the truth, and I don't think he had any reason to lie. I mean, it was pretty obvious from the moment I walked in the door that we were going to wind up in the sack." Petra practically blushed, not in guilt but in embarrassment, it seemed to Gloria.

Petra sighed. "Maybe I'm just not cut out to be a Tiger," she said.

"Petra, you don't have to be *me,* you know. I don't need a clone for an assistant. I need *you* . . . Petra Nash. That cute little girl from Weehawken . . . remember her?"

"Vaguely," Petra said. "But she's been running with some pretty fast company lately."

"You think she got lost?"

"Maybe. Dammit, Gloria, I just don't know anymore. I mean, I enjoy all the outrageous things I've been doing, and wearing these ridiculous outfits and, yes, I enjoyed being with Whit. Pug's been cheating on me with Steffany Fairchild—at least, I *think* he has—and I just figured . . . well, you know. But so much has been happening, with Pug, and the Ellisons, and Whit, and this whole investigation, I just don't think I'm sure who I am anymore, or where I'm going." She looked at her boss. "And speaking of where I'm going, I think Pug's going to take that job on Pelham."

"I see. And are you going to go with him?"

Petra started to answer, stopped, started again, then simply threw her hands into the air. "Who knows?" she said with a forlorn laugh.

"Well, I'm in the same boat, kiddo. I don't know

what the hell I'm going to do about Charles. He's coming here, by the way. Going to make some major address at the end of the Meeting. I just hope he's not planning to announce that we're getting married again."

"Whit said something to me about those ancient princesses that used to get married off to royalty because of power politics. He says that's pretty much what happened to his mother. Gloria? Don't let it happen to you."

Gloria chuckled, then squeezed Petra's knee. "Thanks for the advice. But it's not my family that's putting the pressure on. It's me. Oh, my mom would love it if I became Empress, but the main thing is that I think *I* might love it, horrible as that sounds." Gloria got to her feet and struck a regal pose. "The Empress Gloria, Mistress of All She Surveys. Got a ring to it, don't you think?"

"You'd be great at it, Your Highness—if that's what you really want."

Gloria flopped down on the sofa again. "That's the kicker, isn't it? Petra, how does *anybody* know what they really want? I want to run Dexta someday, but I also sort of want to be Empress."

"And I want to stay with Pug—but I also want to stay with *you*, whether it's in Dexta or Rio or wherever. It's not always easy being your assistant, Gloria, but it's never been boring."

Petra's brow suddenly furrowed, and she looked very serious. Gloria looked at her and said, "What?"

"Gloria? They beat him to death. I mean, someone pounded on his face until it looked like strawberry jam. At first, I wasn't even sure it was him. I had to take a good, long look. I don't think I'll ever forget that. I want to ask, who would do a thing like that? But I already *know* who would do it, and what's more, I know why. The zamitat."

"We can't be sure of that," Gloria said.

"It was them," Petra insisted. "Gloria, there are some things I haven't mentioned because . . . well, because it might get both Pug and Whit in trouble. If I tell you, you have to promise me you won't do anything about it."

Gloria was silent for several moments. "That's a lot to promise," she said at last.

"I know. But you have to promise."

"All right," Gloria said. "You have my word."

Petra took a deep breath. "Jamie Quincannon let me download all of B & Q's records the minute I asked. He didn't really care. But he made me promise not to tell Whit Junior. But Whit found out anyway. Apparently it showed up on his master computer. Anyway, because of his father's zamitat connection—and Whit says that *he* isn't connected with them—well, he said that the stuff in those files could be embarrassing and damaging. And, well, he asked me to destroy them. I told him it was a felony just to ask me to do that, but he kept on asking."

"A natural enough thing for him to ask, under the circumstances," Gloria said.

"But that's not all. That night, Pug asked me the same thing. He said his family and the Bartholemews had always been close and had done a lot of favors for each other. And so he asked me to destroy those files. And both of them, Whit and Pug, said that it could be dangerous if the zamitat ever found out what I had. What Quincannon had done."

"But how could they have found out?" Gloria wondered.

"Maybe the same way Whit found out. Maybe they've got a monitor on all of Bartholemew's old computers. Who knows? But Gloria, who else could have done it? And why? It *had* to have been the zamies."

"Maybe," Gloria said. "In any case, I'm going to order extra security for you."

"But you won't do anything about Whit and Pug, will you?"

"I said I wouldn't. I can understand Bartholemew. But I'm disappointed that Pug would ask that. He knows better."

"I think he felt it was something he owed his family, and Whit's. You're rich, Gloria. You must understand these things better than I do."

Gloria shrugged. "I suppose so," she said. "But Petra, I'll tell you this. I'm proud of you for not destroying those files."

Petra gave her a wan smile and stood up. "Then I suppose I should get back to them, shouldn't I? Who knows *what* might turn up?"

chapter 19

THE FIRST TERRORIST ATTACK HAPPENED THAT night.

It was a hit-and-run raid, featuring plasma pistols and chemical bombs that made a lot of noise but didn't do a great deal of damage. The target was a reception at the K'Spanci consulate. The K'Spanci were a race of flightless, owl-like creatures who had been members of the Empire for more than two centuries. Like other nonhuman species, they felt left out and neglected at affairs like the Quadrant Meeting. They complained—and not without good reason—that extraterrestrial species were underrepresented in Dexta, and that the Empire unfairly discriminated against them in favor of *Homo sapiens*. The K'Spanci reception attracted a fair number of alien representatives, but only a smattering of humans. That made it an attractive target for the terrorists—not PAIN, but PHAP, the Pan-Human Alliance for Purity.

The attack was a failure, in that no aliens, but two humans, were killed. So were two of the three terrorists.

The third was captured by Internal Security, who quickly extracted enough information from him to be able to stage a raid on the PHAP command post, such as it was, where two more terrorists were taken into custody.

It was a relatively minor event, but it served to put everyone's nerves on edge and caused security to be ratcheted up another notch. Gloria noticed the heightened tension as she made the rounds of committee meetings the next day, and receptions the following night. She was feeling it, herself, and decided to do something about it. The next morning, she rounded up her troops and declared that Sunday would be a mandatory day off for everyone in OSI. Just to be certain that her orders were carried out, she organized a group excursion to a beach resort on the south coast of the continent, and attendance was definitely *not* optional. Her people were going to relax if it killed them.

Gloria herself was late arriving from the Transit. She had accepted an invitation from the Central Spiritists to speak before their congregation that morning in their six-hundred-year-old church in the Old City. She figured that it wouldn't hurt to shore up her support among the Spiritists and, at the same time, remind the Dexta delegates of her special status in the largest religious organization in the Empire.

She had recited a few passages from the Book of the Spirit, then elaborated on her particular province, Joy. Gloria made it clear that she was in favor of sex, as everyone should be. "I have been reminded lately," she said, "that not everyone agrees with the wisdom of the Spirit, and that many of our fellow beings embrace other systems of belief. The other day, a woman told me that she thought I was a disgrace and that my behavior somehow degraded women." The parishioners hooted and jeered at that, but Gloria quickly quieted them.

"As you may expect, I disagreed with her. But I

believe that she did have a point, and it is one that I have pondered, and that all Spiritists would do well to keep in mind. We are a diverse Empire, with many species, many beliefs, many points of view. Even though we Spiritists constitute some seventy percent of the population, we cannot simply ignore the deeply held beliefs and attitudes of the other thirty percent. Just as we may consider many of *their* beliefs to be silly or oppressive or simply wrong, many of them find *our* beliefs and behavior to be profoundly offensive. What are we to do about this?

"Well, we could exterminate them. Wipe out the infidel minority who disagree with us. Throughout the course of history, many groups have tried to do just that, when confronted with nonbelievers. But the Spirit counseled not only Joy, but Peace, so that option is closed to us, as it obviously should be.

"Nor can we forcibly convert those who disagree, for the Spirit also taught us Compassion, Tolerance, and Generosity. So I believe that the answer must lie in the remaining two Seeds of Wisdom—Love and Knowledge. Long before the Spirit's Visitations, other religious leaders told us that we must love our fellow beings—even our enemies—and the Spirit reminded us that we must know them. In other words, we must learn to love them. How are we to do that?"

Gloria had paused at that point and grinned at the vast congregation. "Beats the hell out of me," she said.

"My point, of course, is that we all have much to learn—about life and love and our fellow beings. Even Avatars of the Spirit don't have all the answers. *I* certainly don't. But in my role as a Dexta official, I have tried to learn as much as I could about the many ways of life in our Empire. Indeed, it was that desire to learn about our fellow citizens that first drew me into Dexta. Now, as I exercise my various powers and responsibilities within Dexta, I try—always—to keep in mind the fact that my knowledge and wisdom are limited, and that I can only strive to be wiser tomorrow than I am today. I believe that is the most—and the least—that any of us can do. It is what the Spirit asks of us, and what our humanity requires. Thank you for inviting me here today, and may you keep the Spirit with you always."

As Arkady Volkonski escorted her out of the church, she shook her head and said, "God, the bullshit that comes out of my mouth sometimes!"

"It wasn't bullshit, Gloria," Volkonski replied.

"Wasn't it?"

"I didn't think so."

"Really?"

"Really."

Gloria smiled in bemusement. "Maybe there's hope for us all, then," she said.

JILL NOTED GLORIA'S ARRIVAL. LIKE MOST OF the people on the beach, including Jill, Gloria was nude, but she was flanked by Arkady Volkonski and three of his Bugs, all of whom were clothed and looking uncomfortable about it. Of course, they needed clothing to conceal their weapons, for Bugs were *never* off duty.

Jill squirmed and sighed as Eli applied some more suntan lotion to her breasts and belly. Pheromones aside, the man had an almost instinctive feel for what a woman wanted, and how she wanted it. Sex with him had proved to be an astonishing experience for her; she had reached physical and emotional highs that were beyond anything she had known. She couldn't help wondering if sex was like that for Gloria all the time. It would explain a lot.

At the same time, a quiet voice of caution somewhere deep inside her was never still. Jill was well aware that a man like Eli Opatnu would never limit himself to a single woman. There was no reason he should, when he could have literally any woman he wanted. She was grateful that—for the moment, at least—he wanted her, but she knew it wouldn't last. Eli was based in Manhattan, so there would undoubtedly be other opportunities even after they returned to Earth, but there was no prospect for the kind of relationship that she had always wanted. Her marriage hadn't worked, and she freely admitted that it had been mostly her fault; but that didn't mean she had given up on finding a lasting and devoted partnership. But Eli wasn't the man for that.

In love, as in her life, Jill resisted compromise. As Eli had pointed out, that was not a realistic attitude, but it seemed to be the one she was stuck with.

Gloria greeted them, then ran across the beach and plunged into the surf. Jill watched her, then watched Eli watching her. "What's it like for you and Gloria?" she asked him.

Eli looked at her with a quizzical smile. "Comparisons are invidious," he said.

"No, I didn't mean that. I just wondered what it was like for you genetically enhanced types. Is it just more of the same, or is it something different?"

Eli shrugged. "I have no basis to make such a comparison, since I don't know what it's like not to have my enhancements. It's all subjective, you know, for everyone. When I make love with you, it's a sublime experience. When I make love with Gloria, it's a sublime experience."

"But is it sublimer?"

" 'Sublimer'?"

Jill punched him in the ribs. "You know what I mean. I'm going to start calling you Eli the Eel because you're so damn slippery. You wiggle out of everything."

"A useful survival trait," he said. "If eels weren't slippery, there wouldn't be any eels."

"So you won't talk, huh? Well, maybe I can *make* you talk." Jill grabbed him and pulled him down to her.

"I DON'T LIKE THAT GUY," PUG SAID TO PETRA

on another blanket not far away.

"Why?" Petra asked. "Is it because he gives you an inferiority complex?"

Pug reflexively looked down at himself, then quickly looked back at Petra, who couldn't help smirking. She leaned over and kissed him on the cheek. "Don't worry about it, Cowboy, it ain't the size o' the shootin' iron that counts, it's the aim."

"I just don't like the way he thinks he can always get anything—or any*one*—he wants," Pug said.

"I feel that way about Gloria, sometimes," Petra admitted. "I don't think normal standards work for people like that. I think you just have to accept them as they are."

"Maybe," Pug said. "But I still don't like him."

"Oh, stop being so . . . so *male*. You just resent him because he's invaded your little hunter-gatherer group and upset what you thought of as a set of stable relationships."

"What?"

"You heard me. And you needn't act so dumb—you went to college, same as I did. OSI is like a little family group. Gloria's the mother, Jill's your big sister, and I'm your mate. So Eli shows up and scores with Mom and Sis, and now you're afraid that he'll bag me, too. Don't worry, he's not my type." Petra took a closer look at what was going on next door and added, "*Although* . . ."

"Very funny," Pug sniffed. "Anyway, Eli would have to wait in line behind Whit, wouldn't he?"

Petra looked away from him and concentrated on picking some sand out of her belly button. "I thought we weren't going to talk about that," she said.

"What should we talk about, then? Maybe we could talk about the way you totally ignored my wishes and went ahead and downloaded all of that Bartholemew data into the Dexta computer? Or how about the way you carried on at the opening night reception?"

"Carried on? What do you mean, carried on?"

"You know what I mean. Practically naked like that, in front of everybody."

"Well, *you* bought me that pareu, you know. You're the one who keeps telling me I should be more like Gloria."

"Well, I didn't mean you should do it at a place like that. You embarrassed me in front of my family."

"And how do you think I felt, seeing you with your arm around Steffany?"

"You were so drunk, I'm surprised you noticed."

"Fuck you, rich boy!"

"WHAT IS WRONG WITH THIS PICTURE?" GLORIA said to Althea as they stood together in the surf. Strategically scattered around the OSI group, Volkonski and his Bugs kept a stoic watch. To their right, Elaine was industriously screwing a man she had just picked up. Directly in front of them, Jill and Eli were writhing like two devout Spiritists in Central Park on a Visitation Day. To their left, Pug was angrily stomping away from the blanket where Petra lay with her back to him.

"Trouble in Paradise?" Althea wondered.

"Could be," Gloria said. "I think we're going to lose Pug. Maybe Petra, too, although from the look of things at the moment, I'd say probably not."

"And what about you? Are we going to lose you, too, Gloria?"

Gloria sighed. "I honestly don't know, Althea. Maybe I should just flip a coin and get it over with, one way or the other."

"You'd make a marvelous Empress, Gloria, you truly would. But I'd hate to lose you."

Gloria smiled at her. "Don't get carried away, Althea," she said.

"I know we've had our differences in the past," Althea said, "but I don't think I've ever told you how grateful I am to you. There I was, stalled at Thirteen for years and years, and then you plucked me out of my little cul-de-sac and brought me into OSI as a Twelve and gave me all these wonderful assignments. Did I ever tell you how much I *adored* running the Emporium on Sylvania?"

"I thought you might."

"And it's been ever so much fun arranging for the reception. Oh, did I tell you? I found a band that plays those little twentieth-century blues numbers you like so much. I don't understand it, myself—all that caterwauling and wailing about lost dogs and lost women and such—but I knew you'd love it, so I signed them up as soon as I heard them."

"That's great, Althea. Thanks."

"The very least I could do."

They turned and watched the scene on the beach for a few moments.

"Do you think I could seduce Arkady?" Althea asked.

"Althea"—Gloria chuckled—"I think you could seduce anything with warm blood."

"That's why I asked about Arkady. I'm not sure his blood *is* warm. I'm not even sure he's got any."

Gloria thought about what Volkonski had said to her coming out of church that morning and said, "He does."

"Oh?" Althea asked in surprise.

"It's not what you think, Althea. But I learned something about him today. He's deeper than I thought he was. And you know what?" Gloria grinned self-consciously. "So am I."

• • •

NORMAN MINGUS ARRIVED ON NEW CAMBRIDGE the next day. He occupied an entire floor at the Imperial Cantabragian, and late that evening, following a round of receptions, Gloria went up to see him. She made her way through a phalanx of security and a half dozen aides and finally found him in his bedroom, clad in pajamas, a robe, and slippers, sitting in a comfortable chair with a glass of warm milk and some cookies on a table next to him. Gloria sat down in a chair next to his.

"Are those chocolate chip?"

Mingus looked up from some papers he had been reading and noticed Gloria for the first time. He took in the sight of her, resplendent in a low-cut black micro-dress. He smiled, then handed her one of his cookies. "For an Avatar of Joy," he said, "I believe I have a few chips to spare. But don't get greedy."

Gloria munched the cookie. "Just one," she assured him. "I'm getting fat." She slapped her mostly bare left hip.

"Not from where I'm sitting."

"Mind if I take off my shoes?" Without waiting for a response, Gloria slipped off her high heels and started massaging her aching feet. "I tell you, Norman, late nights and high gravity can be hard on a girl."

"I hear you've been keeping very busy."

"Maintaining a high profile, showing the flag for OSI."

"Quite effectively, I gather. What's all this I hear about a 'Fifth Quadrant'?"

"Oh, it's just a sales pitch. The idea is that OSI will serve as a nucleus for all the Dexta offices that aren't ef-fectively represented by the Sectors or Quadrants."

Mingus nodded thoughtfully. "It's not such a bad idea," he said. "Although, from my point of view, four Quadrants are more than enough. But it's a valid point you make, and it strikes me as a useful ploy in your squabble with the Quad Admins."

"It's not just some little squabble, Norman," Gloria said. "They mean to eviscerate the OSI."

"Well, you'll just have to keep them from doing that, won't you?"

"I may need your help."

Mingus shook his head. "I can't openly oppose the Quad Admins, Gloria. And you know why. I'll referee and keep the fight fair, if I can, but don't expect me to intervene on your behalf. In any event, you seem to be doing pretty well without me."

"You think so?"

"I'm not as isolated up there in my ivory tower as you think. My sources tell me you've won a lot of support here this week. If the Quad Admins try to slap you down too blatantly, they'll only be making trouble for themselves. Grigsby and Chandra certainly understand that, and Algeciras will keep his finger to the wind, as always."

Gloria looked at him. "And DuBray?"

Mingus leaned back in his chair and crossed his right leg over his left knee. "I've known Cornell a long time," he said. "I don't always approve of his methods, but I can't argue with the results he gets. He's the most effective administrator I've ever known. He can be remarkably pigheaded, but he's not a fool. You can't beat him, but if he can be made to see that defeating you is not necessarily in his best interests, you may be able to live with him. More importantly, he may decide that he can live with you."

"Maybe I *can* beat him," Gloria said. "Norman? I think DuBray was involved in the diversion of that Savoy shipment. I don't have the proof I need yet, but—"

Mingus abruptly uncrossed his legs, leaned forward, and took Gloria's wrist in his hand. His watery eyes locked with hers.

"Gloria," he said evenly, "whatever Cornell DuBray may or may not have done fifty-five years ago is of absolutely no moment. I will not have you dredging up the dead past just to gain an advantage in your little turf war. Do you understand me?"

"It may not be so dead," Gloria protested. "We're tracking down that missing Savoy shipment, and I really think we're going to find it. And when we do, I think we'll see Cornell DuBray's fingerprints all over it. He was mixed up in it with Whitney Bartholemew and the zamitat, and they couldn't have gotten their hands on that shipment without DuBray's active cooperation. DuBray's rich, isn't he? Well, where did his money come from? I think if we start digging into his finances—"

"You'll do no such thing!" Mingus released his hold on Gloria's wrist, glared at her for a moment, then collected himself, took a sip of milk, and bit into a cookie. Gloria waited for him to say something, shocked that he had raised his voice with her.

Mingus swallowed the cookie and took another sip of milk. Finally, he said, "Fifty-five years. I can't expect you to understand what that means. It was another time, another age. The things we did then seemed necessary, and so we did them without worrying about what history might say. If Cornell DuBray had anything to do with diverting that Savoy shipment, you can be sure that he had good reasons for it, and lining his pockets was not one of them. You will not investigate his finances, or anything else that does not directly contribute to locating those missing arms. Is that understood?"

"But, Norman—"

"Is that understood?" Mingus repeated more emphatically.

Gloria looked at him in silence for a few moments and saw an intensity in his eyes that she had never seen before. At last, she said, "Yessir. I understand." After a pause, she added, "I mean, I really think I do understand. I met Saffron. I know she was going to marry DuBray, and then something happened and she wound up marrying Bartholemew. I never meant to dig around in your personal affairs, Norman."

"But you must wonder about them."

"That's none of my business. It just happened to come up in the course of the investigation. When I realized there was a link between DuBray and Bartholemew and the zamitat, I automatically figured it was something I could use against him. It didn't occur to me that I might be hurting you in the process. It should have, but it didn't. I'm sorry, Norman."

Mingus was silent for a long time. Gloria could hear the slight rasp in his breathing.

"Gloria," he said, "if I knew anything at all that might help you find those missing arms, I would tell you. Precisely how and why they went astray is another matter. Leave it be. As for hurting me, I doubt that there is anything you could do that would add or subtract a single atom from the pain I have felt for fifty-five years."

"I understand," Gloria said softly. "Norman? Are you going to see her?"

Mingus thought about it for a few moments, then said, "Perhaps."

"I think you should."

"It must be nice to be so sure you know what other people should do."

"I'm sorry, I didn't mean to presume."

"That's quite all right. Ignorant presumption is one of the privileges of youth. Enjoy it while you can." Mingus smiled at her. "Here," he said, "have another cookie."

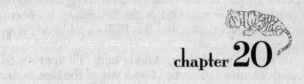

chapter 20

GLORIA WAS FINISHING HER COFFEE AND A light breakfast with Elaine the next morning when Petra and Pug arrived at her suite. Gloria offered them coffee, which they declined, then rose and joined them in the living room area.

"I asked you to stop by this morning because I met with Mingus last night. By his order, we will no longer be investigating Cornell DuBray and his links to the Savoy shipment. Our one and only objective is to find where those weapons are now. If you were doing any digging about DuBray that is not directly relevant to that goal, stop doing it. Is that perfectly clear?"

"No problem," Petra said. "I've been working on another angle anyway."

"Pug?" Gloria looked at him. Pug shuffled his feet and cleared his throat.

"Uh, Gloria?" he said. "There's something I have to tell you." He looked at Petra and said, "I'm sorry, Petra, I meant to tell you first, but as long as we're here, I think

I should just get it over with. I've made a decision, and I'm going to accept that job offer on Pelham."

Petra stared at him and said nothing, but it was clear from her face that Pug's announcement did not come as a complete surprise to her. Pug looked away from her, pulled his pad from a pocket, and tapped a key on it.

"I've just transmitted my formal transfer request to your pad, Gloria. This wasn't an easy decision for me, and I want you to know that I'll always be grateful to you for bringing me into OSI in the first place. It's been a wonderful experience, but this Pelham job is an opportunity I can't ignore."

"I understand, Pug," Gloria said. "I'll approve the transfer immediately. And I wish you all the best in your new position."

Both Gloria and Pug turned to look at Petra.

"Petra?" Pug said after an awkward pause. "That offer of an Undersec position on Pelham is still open. Uncle Benedict says it should take three or four months to free up the spot, and if you still want it then, you can come to Pelham. But . . . there's something else you should know. Steffany is going to be coming to Pelham."

Petra's eyes widened, but before she could say anything, Pug raced ahead. "Uncle Benedict invited her for a visit. You see, he's *her* great-uncle, too. Benedict is my mother's father's brother, but he's also married to Steffany's father's mother's sister, so . . ."

"So you expect me to wait around for three months on Earth while you and Steffany have a high old time on Pelham?"

"Well, I didn't . . ."

"That tears it!" Petra's eyes flashed with righteous anger. "Gloria, can I bunk in here with you?"

"No problem," Gloria said. "I'll have them put another bed in Elaine's room."

"Great. As soon as I pack up my things . . ."

"There's no need for you to do that," Pug said. "I'll

have the staff collect your things and deliver them here. Petra, I'm sorry I didn't tell you this earlier, but I only came to the decision last night and I—"

"Oh, spare me! Just get out of my sight!"

Pug looked around uncertainly. "Uh, Gloria, I can continue working for you as long as you're here on New Cambridge. I mean, I never intended to leave you short-handed."

"Under the circumstances," Gloria said, "I think it's best if we terminate your connection with OSI immediately."

"I understand. Well . . . uh . . . look, this doesn't affect the OSI reception at my parents' house, of course, so I'll be seeing you there. We can . . . well, we can say our farewells then." Pug looked once more at Petra, then turned and quickly left the room.

Gloria said, "I'm sorry, Petra."

"Well, I'm not!" Petra insisted. She looked at Gloria and gave a wan smile. "I don't think I would have been very happy in the Ellison family. Too damn many mother's father's uncle's sisters."

GLORIA FOUND CORNELL DUBRAY AT THE Convention Center later that morning. He was surrounded by his usual retinue of security guards and aides, but they cleared a path for her as she approached. "Could I have a word with you in private?" she said.

DuBray nodded, and they soon found themselves alone in an empty conference room. "I spoke with Norman last night," she told him. "He ordered me to discontinue any investigations into your links to the Savoy shipment. Of course, I'll respect his wishes, but I do have one question for you, and I expect an honest answer. Do you know anything—anything at all—about where those weapons went or where they are now?"

The Quadrant Administrator stared at her for a moment, then offered a bemused smile. "You must have a remarkably low opinion of me, VanDeen."

Gloria didn't say anything to that.

"You see me as a villain," DuBray said. "Understandably so, I suppose. So you assume that I must therefore be villainous in all things, at all times. I'm the Evil Cornell DuBray, so I must be capable of any imaginable form of treachery, treason, or betrayal. I might even know where the missing arms are and remain silent merely to protect myself. PAIN terrorists run riot and slaughter people who work for me, yet I just smile and twirl my mustache like the villainous character in a melodrama that you imagine me to be. Really, that's quite insulting."

"So you're saying that you don't know anything?"

"What I'm saying, VanDeen, is that I was serving Dexta and the Empire long before you were born. Who are you to question my loyalty?"

"It's a question that must be raised," Gloria said. "I know you were linked to that shipment, somehow. Bartholemew couldn't have gotten it without your help. You must know something about it."

DuBray turned his back on her, walked a few paces away, then turned around. "You say you spoke to Norman about this? And what did he tell you?"

"Not much. Only that I should let the past remain buried. But those weapons—"

"Are Spirit knows where! If I knew where they were, don't you think I'd have done something about it by now? Or would that be inconsistent with your image of me as an archvillain?"

Gloria thought about it in silence for several moments and realized that DuBray had a point. She had been so eager to bring him down that she hadn't considered the possibility that he might be innocent—or, at least, not entirely guilty.

"All right," Gloria said, "I may have made some unwarranted assumptions about you. But it's still possible that you could know something that would help us find the weapons, maybe without realizing it. Didn't Bartholemew say anything about what he was going to do with them?"

DuBray chuckled mirthlessly. "You don't understand the situation."

"Then help me to understand it."

"If Norman didn't explain it to you, I certainly won't. All you need to know, VanDeen, is that from my point of view, those weapons vanished as completely as if they had fallen into a black hole. When they started turning up again, I was more surprised than anyone."

"But they never went to Savoy, did they?"

"Apparently not."

"They desperately needed those weapons on Savoy," Gloria said. "They might have made all the difference. I've been doing some reading, and—"

"*Reading?*" DuBray bellowed in evident contempt. "You've read a book or two, and now you think you're an authority on what happened half a century ago? The ignorant arrogance of youth never ceases to amaze me."

"Are the books wrong?"

"The books are . . . *books*! Spirit, VanDeen, *I was there*! You and the authors of those books were *not*. You cannot possibly know or understand what happened then. Don't speak to me about Savoy. You haven't the right."

"But I do have a responsibility to find those weapons. They took a shot at *me* with one of them, you know. That gives me the right to ask you about them."

"Perhaps it does," DuBray conceded. "Investigate to your heart's content. Strategically intervene till the cows come home. But don't waste your time asking about Savoy. It simply isn't relevant to your inquiry."

Gloria nodded. "I'll accept your word on that, then."

She started to turn to go, but DuBray stopped her with a look. "I know it may be hard for you to imagine, but we really are on the same side. I want those weapons found even more than you do. Those bastards have been using them in *my* Quadrant, and they will undoubtedly use them again unless they are stopped. Internal Security is already looking high and low for them, and perhaps your historical inquiries will bear some fruit. I welcome any contribution you can make to the investigation, and I will help you in any way I can. If you have any *relevant* questions you need to ask me, don't hesitate."

Gloria nodded. "Thank you, Administrator DuBray," she said.

DuBray returned the nod. "You are very welcome, Ms. VanDeen."

THE UTILITY CLOSET SEEMED SPACIOUS NOW. IT was amazing how much difference a 50 percent reduction in the population could make. Petra even had an extra console, which came in handy for the work she was doing.

She had pored over the B & Q records and found that the company had owned no fewer than seven ten-thousand-ton freighters in August of 3163. She meticulously checked the logs and cargo manifests of each of them, but found nothing out of the ordinary. Still, the apparent falsification of the records of the sixty-thousand-ton freighter made her suspicious of anything she saw in the records from that period.

She attempted to be logical and systematic. Fact: The weapons existed and had been shipped to New Cambridge—assuming the *other* records could be trusted. That was a necessary assumption, because if the shipment had never arrived at New Cambridge, then she was wasting her time anyway. Fact: They had been stored, initially at least, in the orbital warehouse of Stavros & Sons. But the relevant records of the defunct Stavros & Sons no longer existed, so it was impossible to tell precisely how long the shipment had remained at New Cambridge. So she made the reasonable assumption that the weapons had been removed no later than the end of 3163. Fact: The weapons had officially been transferred to the custody of B & Q Shipping for transshipment to Savoy. Fact: Gloria's source said that the weapons had been removed in three shipments.

Therefore: Only B & Q could have removed the weapons from the Stavros warehouse during the specified time frame, and it made sense that they would have used their own ships to do it. So one or more of those ten-thousand-ton freighters owned by B & Q must have done the job. One freighter in three trips, or three freighters in one trip, or some combination that added up to three.

But trips to *where*?

They had to have gone somewhere. Bartholemew hadn't simply dumped them in space, because the weapons had shown up again, fifty-five years later. There was a large but finite number of places Bartholemew could have taken them. Using freighters capable of making planetfall, virtually any world in the Empire could have been the destination. But the logs of the seven freighters in question placed a limit on how far away the shipments could have been sent.

Petra made another necessary assumption: that the logs of the freighters could be trusted. Contracts might be falsified, but a vessel's logs were sacrosanct, or should have been. The information contained in them—hours in Yao Space, light-years traveled—needed to be accurate. Ferguson Distortion Generators and fusion reactors had to be inspected and overhauled at regular intervals. Someone might fudge the destinations and

dates that appeared in a log, but it would be foolish—
perhaps even suicidal—to tamper with time and distance figures. So hidden in those figures lay the answer
to where the weapons had gone.

One more assumption was necessary. She couldn't
prove it, but Petra operated on the assumption that all
three shipments had gone to the same place. It seemed
unlikely that Bartholemew would have broken up the
weapons cache and stored it on three different worlds.
If he had, then her investigative strategy wouldn't work.

But if they had all gone to the same place, and more
than one freighter had been used, then a careful exami-
nation of the logs of each of the seven freighters could
lead to . . .

Headaches, Petra thought. It all made sense to her,
but finding the needles in this particular haystack was
going to take a lot of work. If the freighters had gone directly to their secret destination, then immediately returned to New Cambridge, it would have been easy. But
she realized that Bartholemew would have covered his
tracks. Almost certainly, each freighter would have proceeded from Destination X to one or more additional
ports of call before returning to New Cambridge. If they
had simply gone to the secret hideaway, then returned,
they would have been flying either with empty holds or
with cargoes that had originated at Destination X. So
they would have gone elsewhere before returning.

Still, the time and distance figures in the logs put
limits on how far the freighters could have gone. Petra
calculated that the mystery world could have been no
more than eighty-five light-years from New Cambridge.

On the second console, Petra called up galactography charts, and was dismayed to discover just how many
planets there were in a sphere of space 170 light-years in
diameter. There were, it seemed, no less than 146
Empire worlds encompassed by the sphere. But it was
worse than that, because that figure included only estab-

lished, inhabited colonies. The total number of known *planets* in that volume of space exceeded ten thousand. Conceivably, Bartholemew could have stashed the weapons on some barren rock or methane-shrouded moon.

But, between the ship logs and the galactic atlas, she had a place to start. Slowly but systematically, she fed assumptions into the computer involving journeys from New Cambridge to any two planets—inhabited or otherwise—within the target sphere. The computer quickly kicked out time and distance figures, which she then compared with the numbers in the logs. Any two-legged itineraries that were numerically feasible, she stored in another file for further analysis.

This could take a while, she realized. On the other hand, what else did she have to do with her time?

"AH. MY TAX CROWNS AT WORK."

Petra looked up and saw Whit Bartholemew at the door of her utility room, grinning.

"What are you doing here? How did you get in?"

Bartholemew shrugged. "I'm not unknown in this city. Getting in was easy enough, but finding you once I was inside took some doing. My word, didn't they even give you a real office?"

"OSI is not universally popular," Petra said.

"Figures. The only thing worse than being outside a fascist bureaucracy is being inside one. They eat their young, you know."

"Look, Whit, I have a ton of work to do, and I don't really have the time to sit here and listen to you insult Dexta. Why are you here?"

"I thought I might take you to dinner."

"I've already eaten." Petra glanced at the crusts of the pizza she'd had delivered.

"If you call that eating," said Bartholemew. "Very

well, then, what about a drink? I imagine you could use one after the day you've had."

"You heard, huh?"

Bartholemew nodded solemnly. "Exit Palmer Ellison," he said. "I like the lad well enough, but nevertheless, I say good riddance—for both of us. You really are better off without him, you know."

Petra sighed heavily. "Whit, I really don't want to talk about it."

"Nonsense. Of course you do. You've spent all day staring at these consoles, diligently doing your job, and all the while you've been thinking of all the things you wish you had said to Pug. Well, you can't say them to him, but I stand ready to listen in his stead. What kind of friend would I be if I weren't willing to do that? And as your friend, I insist that you come with me for a drink. I'm much bigger than you are, Petra Nash, and if you won't come voluntarily, I'm perfectly capable of carrying you out over my shoulder."

So Petra went out with Bartholemew. He waved away his limo and they strolled along the busy sidewalks of nighttime Central. As they approached the Dexta complex known as Gibraltar, they were herded across the street by harried police and Security personnel.

"I imagine everyone in Central will be happy to see the Quadrant Meeting end," Petra observed.

"On the contrary. They'll miss all the money your people have been spending. People will put up with almost any amount of official harassment as long as there's something in it for them. In any case, blind obeisance to arbitrary authority is the lot of most of humanity. You'll find more independence and freedom in the average herd of sheep than you will on a city street."

They came to a sidewalk café that looked good to Petra, but Bartholemew had another destination in mind. He pointed upward toward a lofty skyscraper.

"There's a restaurant up there with a spectacular view of the city."

"I'm not dressed for a place like that," Petra protested. She was wearing jeans and a clinging white pullover top.

"That won't be a problem," Bartholemew said, "since I happen to own the restaurant. You know, this is the first time I've seen you wearing actual clothes. Very sexy. Makes me want to rip them off."

"Not tonight, Whit."

"The night is still young. At least give me a chance to ply you with soft words and strong drink."

The view from the fortieth-floor restaurant proved to be as spectacular as Bartholemew had promised. From their table, they could see the dark mass of Gibraltar a few blocks away, the variegated architecture of the nearby Old City, and the brightly illuminated vessels plying the harbor. "Central is quite a city," Petra said as she sipped her white wine.

"So were Sodom and Gomorrah," Bartholemew said. "And you know what God did to them."

"Is there anything you don't hate?" Petra wondered.

Bartholemew thought about it for a moment. "I'm rather fond of my mother," he said at last. "And I've taken quite a shine to you. Beyond that . . ." He shrugged inconclusively.

"Why?"

"Why do I detest that which is detestable? Why do I loathe the loathsome? I was born and reared in the belly of the beast. Is it so surprising that I would grow to hate it?"

"That's too easy, Whit," Petra said. "I was born and reared in a slum, but I don't hate the Empire that created that slum."

"You should. But instead of rising up against your oppressors, you joined them. That's all too common a story. Perhaps if someone had shown you a different path, you might have followed it, instead of the well-worn trail you chose."

"I'm not sure which bothers me more," Petra said, "your cynicism or your hypocrisy. If you really believed half the things you say, you'd have gone off somewhere and joined PAIN."

Bartholemew laughed.

He raised his glass in a toast. "Up the rebels," he said.

Petra shook her head. "I will never understand rich people. Gloria was the only one I knew, and she always seemed pretty well adjusted. Then I met the Ellisons and discovered what ten generations of inbred arrogance can do to people. And now you, with your ridiculous posing and prosing, damning the establishment while you sip expensive wine in your own restaurant."

Bartholemew reached across the table and cupped Petra's cheek in his right hand. "You know what your problem is, Petra Nash? You expect the world to make sense. Trust me, it doesn't."

"Tell me about your father," she said.

"Now, why would you want to know about such an odious subject as that?" Bartholemew leaned back in his chair and drank some more wine.

"I've been trying to get into his head," Petra told him. "Didn't he ever say anything to you about that Savoy shipment?"

"The old man and I weren't much for father-to-son heart-to-hearts. When I was a boy, we mainly ignored each other. By the time I was an adolescent, our relationship had blossomed into mutual contempt, which lasted as long as he did. I'm not sure when I first realized that he was a zamie, but somewhere along the line it became clear to me that the Bartholemews were not quite as respectable as my mother wanted everyone to think we were. In any event, he rarely talked about his work."

"What kind of man was he?"

"Self-contained. Short-tempered. Dictatorial."

"I suppose that accounts for your attitude toward authority."

"I suppose it does. A reasonable response to my situation, wouldn't you say? I never had the luxury of—"

Bartholemew stopped short as a dazzling, blue-green flash illuminated the city. It seemed to emanate from beyond Gibraltar, and was followed an instant later by a second brilliant eruption from the Old City. There was a third flash, coming from somewhere off to the left, then three deafening thunderclaps in rapid succession.

Central was under attack.

chapter 21

PETRA HAD NEVER BEEN IN SUCH A HIGH-LEVEL
conclave, and felt even smaller than usual. She had
never seen so many single-digit Dexta brass gathered
in one place. The conference room in Gibraltar was
packed with interested parties, of whom she was the
lowliest. She sat between Gloria and Arkady Volkonski
at the big conference table, trying not to gape.

At the head of the table sat Norman Mingus him-
self, whom Petra had seen but never met, looking craggy
and imperturbable. At the far end sat Cornell DuBray, a
study in icy composure. Arrayed between them were
Dexta's Internal Security Administrator, Gavin Chang
(Level V), the Quadrant 4 IntSec chief, Elizabeth Irons
(Level VI), and a flock of Level VII's. An aide to
President Edwin Ogburn of the Republic of New
Cambridge was in attendance. Also present was General
Nelson Alvarez, deputy chief of Imperial Security, who
was not in Dexta but effectively outranked everyone
there except Mingus.

One of the Sevens was reciting a summary of the

damage from last night's attack. "The Imperial Museum in the Old City sustained major damage, including the collapse of the roof of the East Wing. Damage to the collections has not yet been determined, but it is likely to be considerable. The New Cambridge Department of Revenue Building is gutted, a total loss. And Dexta's Old Annex is about seventy percent destroyed, with heavy damage to the parts of the structure that are still standing. Casualties, as of ten o'clock this morning, are put at 173 dead, 543 injured, and at least 100 missing."

And one of them could have been me, Petra thought. If Whit hadn't lured her away when he did, she would have been in the Old Annex when the terrorists' bombs destroyed it. The thought somehow resisted analysis. Maybe it was one of those things that you couldn't think about very much without going crazy. Petra suppressed a shudder and tried to concentrate on the meeting.

No one said anything for a moment after the Seven had finished. Then Elizabeth Irons cleared her throat. "It's still very early in our investigation," she said, "but the three detonations seem to have been of approximately equal force, so presumably similar devices were used in each attack. My technical people say that the energy expended was equivalent to what you would get if you simultaneously detonated a cluster of perhaps six or seven plasma grenades. Thanks to the OSI report"— Irons glanced quickly at Gloria and Petra—"we know that such grenades were included in that missing Savoy shipment. So it seems likely that they were used in the attack."

Mingus looked at the presidential aide. He straightened up in his chair and said, "As you know, President Ogburn has declared a state of emergency, planetwide, and called up several militia units. We were going to declare martial law in Central, but I gather that would be superseded by the Imperial declaration."

"Correct," said General Alvarez. "The city of Central

and everything within a hundred kilometers of it has been under a decree of Emergency Imperial Rule since six this morning. All Imperial Marine units on the planet are on full alert, and the Navy has increased orbital patrols to the limit of their capability. We've sent out couriers asking for additional ships from other commands, but it will be several days before any of them get here."

"Thank you, General," said Mingus. He turned to look at Gavin Chang, who was known around Dexta as the Boss Bug. "Gavin, I understand you have some late news."

"Yes, Mr. Secretary. Just before we convened this morning, I was informed that PAIN has released a communiqué claiming credit for the attacks. The usual ideological claptrap, but they promise more and bigger attacks. It's significant that they struck Imperial, Dexta, and planetary targets, meaning that we will have to increase security for all three categories. I would point out, Mr. Secretary, that last night, they hit only soft targets. That implies a limited capability."

"Or maybe they're just building up to the big one," suggested Elizabeth Irons. "We have to assume that they have the quadrijoule plasma bombs from that Savoy shipment."

"If they do," asked the presidential aide, "why didn't they use one last night? They could have destroyed the whole city at one time instead of doing it piecemeal."

"Maybe they're waiting for a bigger target," said General Alvarez. "The Emperor is due here at the end of the week. I've sent a courier recommending the cancellation of his trip, but, of course, the Household would never agree to that. The Emperor can't be seen to be intimidated by terrorist threats, so they'll go ahead with the trip no matter how risky it is. If PAIN sets off a big one while he's here, they could effectively decapitate the Empire. Secretary Mingus, if we can't keep the Emperor out, maybe I can persuade you to leave."

Mingus smiled grimly. "Not possible," he said. "I have to stay, for the same reason that Charles cannot stay away. I assume that Imperial is taking all necessary measures to assure the Emperor's safety while he's here?"

"We're doing everything we can," said Alvarez. "We got one break, though, in that the Emperor won't be staying in or near the city. He'll be staying at the estate of Lord Brockinbrough, about sixty kilometers north of Central. So even if the city goes up, he should be safe there."

"Well, what about the people of this city?" asked the presidential aide. "I'd like to recommend to President Ogburn that we begin an immediate evacuation of non-essential personnel. There are a hundred million people within fifty kilometers of where we sit, and every one of them would be killed by a two-hundred-quadrijoule bomb."

"Where are you planning to send them, Bill?" DuBray asked dryly.

"Well . . ."

"That would never do," Mingus said, shaking his head. "If PAIN ever got the notion that they could force mass evacuations of major cities just by setting off a few grenades, we'd never see the end of it. I realize that for political reasons, President Ogburn must be seen to be doing something about all of this, but we can't countenance an evacuation. Certainly not at this point."

"Our best bet," said Chang, "is to locate PAIN's base of operations and put the kibosh on the bastards before they can spring their next move. If they have those plasma bombs, they've got to be storing them somewhere."

"Agreed," said Mingus. "And in that connection, I believe OSI has something relevant. Ms. VanDeen?"

"Yessir," Gloria said. "My assistant, Petra Nash, has

been investigating what happened to that Savoy shipment in 3163. Petra?"

Petra hadn't realized that she would be required to say anything. She swallowed hard and cleared her throat a couple of times. "Uh . . . well . . . I think I may be able to trace what became of that arms shipment after it was removed from New Cambridge. We have some old records that should allow us to narrow down the possibilities, at least. The thing is, I was working in the Old Annex, and, well . . ."

"Petra still has the original data she was using, stored in her pad," Gloria said. "Ms. Irons, if you could get her some office space here in Gibraltar, she could continue her investigation."

Irons nodded. "I'll see to it," she said. "Ms. Nash, you can resume your work immediately after we're through here."

"Thank you, ma'am," Petra said politely.

"That's all very interesting," said Alvarez, "but I don't see what it does for our present situation. Just because the weapons were stashed somewhere fifty-five years ago doesn't mean that they're still in the same place."

"Maybe not," Gloria agreed, "but finding their initial destination may give us a lead to where they are now."

"We'll let OSI concentrate on that possibility," said Mingus. "In the meantime, Internal Security and Imperial will continue their ongoing investigation. Gavin, you mentioned that they hit soft targets last night. I assume we are going to harden any other such targets."

"To the extent that we can," said Chang. "But IntSec is already stretched thin. Local law enforcement is also fully committed. The unpleasant fact is that there are a lot of potential targets that are only minimally protected."

Petra knew what Chang meant. She thought of how

easy it had been for Whit to gain access to the Old Annex last night. Not to mention the pizza delivery guy.

"And if they have a big bomb," Irons added, "they could put it anywhere and still destroy the city. I'd like to do a full sweep of Central and the surrounding region, but we just don't have the personnel to do something like that in a reasonable amount of time."

"We can do a random sweep," said Chang, "and maybe we'll get lucky."

Mingus frowned at his Security chief. "It always distresses me," he said, "when I hear my Security people use the word 'luck.'" He continued staring at Chang for another moment, then said, "All right, you know what needs to be done, so let's all get busy doing it. We'll meet again tomorrow morning."

Mingus got to his feet, then everyone else did. Gloria turned to Petra and said, "I'm going to give Jill a call and tell her to get over here and help you. Schmoozing will have to wait."

FASTER THAN SHE WOULD HAVE BELIEVED POSsible, Petra had her own office in the Internal Security section of Gibraltar. Whatever prejudice the locals might have had against OSI had been put in abeyance for the duration of the crisis. The Bugs helped her get settled and even brought her coffee.

All the work she had done yesterday was lost when the Old Annex was destroyed, but Petra still had the B & Q files in her pad. She downloaded the data into her console in the new office and got to work. It occurred to her that she had been doing things the long way around yesterday, and came up with a more streamlined search strategy. She set things up the way she wanted and had just begun work when Jill arrived.

Jill sat down next to her and stared at the console screen while Petra explained what she was doing.

"These are the seven freighters I'm interested in," Petra said, indicating a list on the console screen. "In the last four months of 3163, they made a total of thirty-one trips. My assumption is that three of those trips involved hauling the arms shipment to what I'm calling Destination X. There are logs and cargo manifests for each freighter and each trip, but they can't be trusted."

"That's for sure," Jill agreed. "One thing I've learned in looking into this double-flagging business is how easy it is for documents like that to be altered. And that would be business as usual for someone like Bartholemew if he was in the zamitat."

"Nevertheless," Petra said, "I'm assuming that the records for total light-years and Yao Space hours for each vessel are accurate. I'm also making the assumption that the records for the final, homeward leg of each trip are correct. If Bartholemew was using these trips to transport the arms, he wouldn't want any questions raised about the voyage when the freighters returned to New Cambridge."

"Makes sense," said Jill.

"Okay, then, here's what I'm doing with each trip for each freighter. We'll start with this one, for Freighter Number One. It departed New Cambridge on August 30, returned on September 19, having traveled a total of 141 light-years. The final leg, according to the records, was 52 light-years, from Halcyon to New Cambridge. The logs list two previous ports, but we'll ignore those. What we have to look at is the other 89 light-years of that journey. I'm assuming it made at least one stop—at Destination X—and maybe one other stop to pick up cargo to take to Halcyon. The computer is going to look for any combination of either one or two ports or planetary systems that would add up to 89 light-years, beginning on New Cambridge and ending at Halcyon."

Petra tapped a key and the computer processed the problem and displayed its results a second later.

"Yikes!" Petra exclaimed. The computer had kicked out forty-seven possible routes for Freighter Number One. "I didn't think there would be that many."

"It's a bunch," Jill agreed. "Now what?"

"Now we go through the same routine for each of the other thirty trips. Then we'll compare the results and look for three trips to the same place. But I'm afraid we'll get a hell of a lot more than three. Might as well get started. I'll take Freighters One through Four, you take Five through Seven."

"Gotcha," said Jill.

GLORIA STOOD IN A QUIET CORNER OF THE South Central High School gymnasium, dictating notes into her pin-pad. The reception for Sector 19, Division Gamma-Five, was a sparsely attended, low-key gathering, with second-rate eats and a band that played a dismal selection of popular songs from the thirtieth century. Ahhh, the glamour!

She had met an assortment of lower-level Dexta folk, resolutely giving each of them her standard OSI-is-wonderful spiel. She had danced with many of the men, posed for scores of handshake-and-a-smile pictures, and generally provided a touch of sophistication and glitter to what was, by any standard, a tedious affair. But the job had to be done, even if the Empire was going up in flames all around her.

People were jittery tonight, and the forced gaiety was a strain. There was solace only in drinking—or so it seemed from the heavier-than-usual consumption of alcohol—and the knowledge that the very obscurity of the reception probably provided them with an additional measure of security. PAIN wouldn't waste its weapons on a two-crown affair like this one.

Gloria wasn't so sure of that. This certainly qualified as a "soft" target, and another well-placed cluster of grenades could wipe out a couple of hundred Dexta people—including, not incidentally, the most famous of all. Volkonski and three of his OSI Bugs were there with her, in addition to the normal Dexta and local security, but Gloria was acutely conscious of her special status as a high-priority target. The smell of burned hair was something she was not likely to forget. And you never knew when another Eloise Howell might turn up.

Still, there was some odd comfort in the knowledge that PAIN wasn't simply trying to kill *her*. They were trying to kill *everybody*. And if they had one of those plasma bombs secreted somewhere in the city, they might very well succeed.

But they would wait, she knew. They wouldn't detonate the big one until Charles was in the city.

She hadn't realized that the Brockinbroughs had an estate on New Cambridge. That no doubt meant that Cousin Larry would be accompanying Charles on the trip—an unappealing prospect for Gloria. She had hoped to find some time alone with Charles, but she could hardly avoid Larry if Chuckles was going to be rooming with him.

She had been far too busy to give much thought to the whole question of becoming Empress. It was just too big to deal with. She would prefer to continue delaying and deferring it, but Charles would not wait forever. He needed an heir, so he needed an answer, and Gloria could not avoid making a decision. Just what that decision would be eluded her completely. The appeal of becoming Empress was undeniable, but things seemed to be looking up for OSI. At the meeting this morning, OSI had a place at the table right alongside all the high Dexta and Imperial muckety-mucks, and even Cornell DuBray had not objected to her presence. And most of the people she had met here this evening seemed to be in favor of OSI.

"Durward Inglesby," she said into her pin-pad,

"Sector 19, Assistant Deputy Sector Admin, Level Eleven. Happily married, he says, with three kids. Mentioned that two of the people in his office have applied for transfer to OSI. Got the impression that he wouldn't mind losing one of them, but didn't say which one. Check into it."

"And what about me?" Eli Opatnu said over her shoulder. "Would you accept *my* application for transfer into OSI?"

"In a heartbeat," Gloria said, spinning around to face him. "Unfortunately, we aren't rated for a Seven. You'd have to accept a demotion to say, Thirteen. That would involve making coffee and picking up my dry cleaning. Think you're up to it?"

"For you, anything!" Opatnu gave her a kiss that singed her lips.

Gloria took a deep breath, sucking in pheromones by the billions. She'd been too busy even for sex, and hadn't been with anyone since that night with Eli and the others in the null-room. But that old urge to merge had been building up within her, and Opatnu, in his natty Imperials, was looking better than ever. On the other hand, there were potential complications.

"How are you and Jill getting along?" Gloria asked him.

"Lovely lady, Jill," Opatnu said. "Not the equal of her even lovelier boss, of course." Opatnu stepped back a pace to take a better look at Gloria, who was wearing nothing but a silver-and-blue pareu, fastened with a turquoise brooch.

"Her lovely boss," Gloria said, "wouldn't want to get in the way of anything."

"I think Jill understands the situation."

"Nevertheless, I don't want people who work for me to think I'm interfering in their love life."

"Laudable of you. Still, allow me to point out that

Jill is not here tonight and doesn't need to know anything about this."

"True," Gloria agreed. "You know, I think I've done my quota of schmoozing for this evening."

"Strangely enough," said Opatnu, "so have I."

GLORIA AND ELI SAT NEXT TO EACH OTHER ON a sofa in her suite, sipping expensive brandy, following an explosive interlude in her bedroom. Sex with Eli, augmented by a little jigli and Forty-eight, was a searing, incandescent experience, like nothing she had ever done before. Even Charles had never matched Eli's volcanic sexuality, although she wondered what Charles might achieve with the aid of Forty-eight. She might have a chance to find out, she discovered, when Eli offered her a present.

He pulled a handful of lozenges from his pocket and carefully deposited them on the coffee table—half a dozen purple pills, and as many green ones.

"Forty-eight," Gloria cried in delight.

"Purple's the Forty-eight," he explained, "and green is the neutralizer. Just in case. Enjoy."

Gloria gave him a kiss, then picked up one of the purple lozenges and examined it. "Back on Earth," she said, "I was told that it wouldn't be ready for full distribution for at least another six months. Do you know if they've been having problems with it?"

"Some, from what I hear. In spite of the warnings, some people get carried away and crunch down on it. There have been some deaths reported. I gather that there's some debate about whether they should routinely give out the neutralizer along with the Forty-eight. That might just encourage people to go ahead and crunch down. Anyway, I expect they'll get it all sorted out before long, and you'll be able to get Forty-eight on

Earth and throughout the Empire. In the meantime, just be careful with it."

"I'll think of you every time I use it," Gloria told him.

"I can't imagine a greater compliment," he said. Opatnu pulled her closer and kissed her.

Before they had broken, the outer door of the suite opened, and in walked Petra and Jill. Gloria saw the sudden look of hurt on Jill's face, but was immediately distracted by the look of triumph on Petra's.

"We got it!" Petra declared. "We know where they took the weapons!"

chapter 22

THE SAME HIGH-POWERED GROUP AS THE PRE-
vious morning had assembled in the conference room at
Gibraltar, and Gloria watched with a feeling of pride and
accomplishment as Petra stood and delivered a summary of her findings. Her assistant looked smart, sexy,
and confident in her gray skirt, blue blazer, and half-
unbuttoned white silk shirt. After the way things had
worked out with Pug Ellison, Gloria was glad to see
Petra rebound so quickly. Not many Thirteens ever got
the chance to brief Norman Mingus.

Petra stood next to a large display screen and explained her search strategy quickly and efficiently, then
turned to describe what was on the screen. "This is a
representation of the local region of space, centered on
New Cambridge," she said. "After the first stage of our
search for possible routes for the thirty-one trips by
those seven freighters in the final four months of 3163,
this is what we wound up with." The screen suddenly
blossomed in a profusion of arcing red lines that looked

like the tracks of subatomic particles in the beam of a high-speed collider.

"Three hundred and fourteen possible routes," Petra said. "Then we looked for planetary systems that could have been visited at least three times." Petra clicked a key in her palm pad, and most of the red lines on the screen disappeared. "That brought us down to thirty-seven possible destinations. However, if you look at each individual route, you find that eighteen of them don't make sense, practically speaking. This one, for example, goes out ninety-six light-years, then doubles back on itself fifty-three light-years, then out again twenty-seven light-years. It seemed unlikely that anyone would plot such a path, so we discarded such cases."

The screen responded to Petra's command, and nearly half of the remaining traces vanished. "That left us with nineteen possibilities. But eleven of them plot courses in the direction of Ch'gnth territory. It's highly unlikely that anyone would have gone in that direction in the fall of 3163. Even after the Empire victory at Savoy in September, the Ch'gnth still had plenty of power in the region. It would make no sense to transport the weapons to a place where they might fall into the hands of the enemy. In addition, I doubt that Bartholemew would have risked his ships that way. So now, we were left with just eight possible destinations."

Gloria noticed that the people around the table were beginning to lean forward slightly. Petra had their complete attention.

"Of the remaining eight," Petra continued, "I eliminated Halcyon. It seemed unlikely that they would transport the weapons from one big, busy, well-regulated port to another. And although it's smaller than Halcyon, I eliminated Ifni for the same reason. Two more, I eliminated because they were too small. Parker's Planet has nothing on it except a minor Imperium mining operation. And St. Regis is just a tiny

Catholic utopian community, centered around a monastery. Bringing the weapons to either place would have attracted too much attention. So now, we're down to just four.

"Each of the four is an uninhabited planetary system. They don't even have names, just Imperial Survey numbers. This one," Petra said, tapping a spot on the screen, "has no terrestrial planets, just gas giants and some very small moons. And this one is a variable star that flares up every sixteen months. It didn't strike me as a likely destination, so I eliminated that one, as well."

Petra paused, glanced quickly at Gloria, then continued. "Of the remaining two, this one, GAC 4361, has two terrestrial planets. But one of them is a Venus-clone, and the other is smaller than Mars, very cold, and has almost no atmosphere. Which brings us to GAC 4367."

A single red dot remained on the screen. "The third planet from this star was first surveyed by the Terrestrial Union nearly nine hundred years ago. It's a scumworld."

As humans advanced into the galaxy, they had discovered that life was quite common, but usually not very interesting. On most planets where life had evolved, it was similar to the sort of life that had dominated Earth for more than three billion years: pole-to-pole mats of one-celled, blue-green algae. They came to be known as scumworlds.

"As you know," Petra said, "in the early era of human expansion, prime real estate was hard to find, and the old Terrestrial Union embarked on an ambitious program of terraforming. Scumworlds were considered candidates because the algae had created an oxygen-rich atmosphere. Anyway, the Union established a small, preliminary base on GAC 4367-III in 2297. Not much was accomplished, terraforming went out of vogue, and the base was abandoned in 2349. As far as we know, that base is still there. It's just forty-three light-years from

New Cambridge, and I think that's where Bartholemew took those weapons."

There was a long moment of silence around the conference table. Finally, Norman Mingus said, "An excellent piece of work, Ms. Nash. Thank you very much." Petra tried but failed to suppress a grin as she returned to her chair. Gloria reached over and gave her hand a squeeze.

Mingus looked around the table. "Well?" he asked. "Any comments?"

General Alvarez scowled and said, "Pretty damn thin, if you ask me."

"You do make a lot of assumptions, Ms. Nash," said Elizabeth Irons.

"How do you know they didn't stash them in the basement of that monastery on St. Regis?" asked Gavin Chang. "Or at the bottom of a mine on Parker's Planet?"

"For that matter," said Alvarez, "I don't see how you can justify eliminating Halcyon or Ifni."

"Well," Petra said, with obvious uncertainty in her voice, "it was necessary to make some assumptions, but I tried to put myself in Bartholemew's head and look at things the way he would have. I just think that GAC 4367 is the most likely possibility."

"We're not claiming certainty," Gloria quickly put in. "Maybe those weapons *are* hidden in that monastery. But the most reasonable assumptions all lead us to that scumworld Petra found. From Bartholemew's point of view, it would have been perfect. An uninhabited world with an oxygen atmosphere, and storage facilities already available at the old Terrestrial Union base."

"A base that was built over eight hundred years ago," Alvarez objected. "For all we know, it collapsed centuries ago."

"Maybe," Gloria conceded, "but those old terraforming projects were supposed to take a couple of thousand years. They probably would have built that base to last."

"I question the entire basis for this line of investigation," said Chang. "Wherever those weapons went originally, is it reasonable to assume that this Bartholemew character absconded with them simply for the purpose of leaving them on some deserted hunk of rock for half a century? Seems to me, he would have sold them off at some point. Even if Ms. Nash's assumptions are correct, those weapons were probably removed from that scumworld decades ago."

Gloria noticed Mingus and DuBray staring at each other from opposite ends of the table. Mingus nodded fractionally, then looked at Chang. "Your point is well taken, Gavin," he said, "but we can only work with the information now available to us. For our immediate purposes, I believe we should discount any speculation about what might have become of those weapons in later years. I think Ms. Nash has given us, at a minimum, a reasonable place to start. The question becomes, what do we do about it?"

"Isn't that obvious?" Gloria asked. "I think we should send a LASS and a company of Marines to GAC 4367 immediately."

If it was obvious to Gloria, it was anything but to General Alvarez. "Ms. VanDeen," he said, "do you think Land-Air-Sea-Space vehicles grow on trees? Do you think Marines grow like weeds? Our resources here are already stretched to the breaking point. The Navy is now searching every last vessel that enters the New Cambridge system, and it has to be done *before* they reach port because the Orbital Station itself could be a target. We simply don't have any ships available for fishing expeditions."

Gloria turned to Chang. "Well, what about Dexta? Internal Security has its own ships."

"All of which are engaged in the interdiction operation," Chang responded. "Nor do we have personnel available to be diverted from their present responsibilities."

Gloria could see where this was headed, and she didn't like it. She turned to Petra. "Are there port facilities or landing strips on that planet?"

"According to the old Terrestrial Union charts we found, there's no landing strip, but the base was built on the shore of a big bay. They must have had a dock."

"Good. Then we can take a Cruiser." She looked at Mingus. "Mr. Secretary," she said, "unless you have any objections, on my authority as head of OSI, I intend to take a Cruiser and half a dozen of our Bugs and go check out that planet. Forty-three light-years is only about thirteen or fourteen hours in a Cruiser. We can leave this afternoon and probably be back by tomorrow evening."

"And just what would you expect to accomplish with so small a force?" Alvarez asked. "Suppose you are right, and you find not only the weapons, but an active base crawling with PAIN terrorists? What then, Ms. VanDeen?"

"Then we'll *know*, General Alvarez. This isn't a military expedition, it's simply a scouting party. And if we don't come back by tomorrow evening, you'll know that we ran into trouble. If we do come back, we'll be able to tell you if the weapons are still there."

"It still strikes me as a waste of resources," said Alvarez. "But they aren't *my* resources." He looked at Mingus.

"Gloria," Mingus said, "do I understand you correctly? You are planning to make this journey *personally*?"

"It's my job," she replied. "I mean, isn't this the kind of thing that you created OSI to do in the first place?"

"Broadly speaking, I suppose so," said Mingus.

"Nevertheless, I never intended for you to go charging off like Custer looking for Indians. If you want to send your Internal Security people on this mission, I have no objection. But I think you should stay here."

"Stay here doing *what*?" Gloria demanded. "Looking pretty at parties?"

"Let her go," Cornell DuBray said from the other end of the table. Gloria looked at him in shocked surprise. He gave her a thin smile and said, "One thing I have learned recently is that it is never wise to underestimate Ms. VanDeen."

Mingus's eyebrows rose for a second, then he sighed and said, "Very well, then. Good luck, Gloria."

JILL AND ELI OPATNU TRUDGED DOWN THE LONG flight of marble steps leading from the Imperial Court. "You weren't much help," Jill said to him.

Opatnu spread his arms in wounded innocence. "What would you have had me do?"

"You might have backed me up when I said that it was critical to get the Wendover records immediately."

"What's so critical about it? Jill, this investigation is likely to take months, if not years. The judge isn't going to let us stampede him."

"But the longer it takes us to get those records, the more chance they'll have to alter them."

"They could do that in fifteen minutes," Opatnu pointed out.

"Well, we'd already have them if you hadn't lured me to lunch, then back to your hotel, that first day. If I had been alone, I'd have gone straight to court and I'd have gotten them before Wendover could have filed for a restraining order."

Opatnu stopped at the base of the steps and looked at her. "Are you telling me that you regret the hours we spent together in my hotel room?"

Jill gave him a crooked smile. "Well, no, I'm not saying *that*."

"So if you're not complaining about that, what *are* you complaining about? Last night?"

Jill looked down at her toes for a moment. "I just wasn't expecting to see you there. It caught me off guard."

Opatnu put his arm around her, drew her close, and gave her a kiss on the cheek. "I would never do anything to hurt you," he said. "Gloria and I weren't expecting to see you there, either."

She pushed away from him. "What you and Gloria do is none of my business. I'm sorry, Eli, I know I'm being foolish."

"What do you say we spend the rest of the afternoon being foolish together?"

"Well," Jill said after a pause, "I can't do anything more about Wendover. And I'm finished helping Petra. I suppose I really ought to spend the afternoon back at the Convention Center, schmoozing."

Opatnu seized her hand, brought it up to his mouth, and kissed it. "Schmooze *me*," he whispered.

And so she did.

PETRA ALLOWED HERSELF TO BE TAKEN TO lunch by Elizabeth Irons and some of her Internal Security people. It was a short lunch, since everyone but Petra had something to do, but Irons had been effusive in her praise. It was nice to be appreciated, and not just for her work; one of the young men on Irons's staff had spent a lot of time looking down her unbuttoned shirt and asked if she was free for dinner. Petra was flattered, but was just too worn-out by her labors to accept. After lunch, she returned to the Imperial Cantabragian and collapsed on her bed.

An hour later, she was awakened by the arrival of

two detectives from the Central Police. Blearily, she led them into the main room of the suite and offered them coffee. They accepted, so she called room service.

She tried to stay focused as the detectives explained that they were here for a routine follow-up in their investigation of the murder of Jamie Quincannon. They mainly seemed interested in whether she had anything new she might share with them. They asked the same questions several times in slightly different ways, and Petra managed to answer them without saying much of anything. The coffee arrived and she perked up a bit.

"Dexta's investigation of the information we received from Mr. Quincannon is essentially complete," she told the detectives. "I really don't think we have anything relevant to add to what we've already told you. We already mentioned the possible zamitat connection. Didn't that lead anywhere?"

"No, ma'am," said one of the detectives, a man named Connors. "We haven't turned up anything that would point in that direction. Oh, we know Quincannon was a partner of Whitney Bartholemew, and if the old man were still alive, maybe the zamitat would make sense. But his kid isn't connected, as far as anybody knows. And it didn't look like a zamitat hit. They'd have shot him, neat and clean."

"So you don't have any leads in the case?"

"Didn't say that," said Connors. "Quincannon was mixed up in some shady real estate deals, and we're looking into that angle."

Petra nodded. "He tried to rent me a room," she said.

"He's got some property here and there around the city. We've checked up on some of his partners in the real estate deals, but haven't really developed anything. It's possible that it was just some low-level street crime kind of thing. That's a tough neighborhood, you know, and we didn't find any cash on Quincannon's body."

"He was a nice old man," Petra said. "I liked him."

The cops finally got up to leave, but Connors stopped. "Ms. Nash? I know this isn't any of my business, but half the people in the department are out looking for terrorists. I just wondered if you could tell me anything about how *your* investigation is going. My wife is real worried and wants to send the kids to stay with her sister in Brattle."

"We think we're making some progress," Petra said, glad to be able to say that honestly.

"Like we're making progress on the Quincannon case? Or *real* progress?"

"Real progress, we hope." She offered him an encouraging smile.

"Nice to hear that," said Connors. "I'll tell my wife to keep the kids here."

The detectives left and Petra sat down to pour another cup of coffee. It occurred to her that the two cops were about the only *real* residents of Central that she'd met. And maybe Jamie Quincannon. Everyone else was some rich snob from up on the cliffside, or Dexta people. It was odd how you could spend weeks in a city and never really connect with anyone.

Her wristcom beeped. "Petra Nash," said Whit Bartholemew, "are you hungry? Or do you expect to be hungry at some point in the day? *I'm* hungry. I hunger for the sight of your sweet face and flashing green eyes. I hunger for your wit and charm and intelligence. For your soft white flesh."

"Are you asking me to dinner, or have you taken up cannibalism?"

"The former, I assure you. I know your time here is limited, and the fireworks the other night prevented me from completing my wily seduction. In all fairness, you owe me another chance."

"Whit, I'm awfully tired. I was up half the night working."

"We'll make it an early evening, then. I'll pick you up at seven."

Petra shrugged. She was a single woman again, after all. Maybe an actual date was in order. And Whit Bartholemew was a man who intrigued her, although probably for all the wrong reasons. She decided abruptly that for one night, at least, the wrong reasons could be precisely the right reasons.

"I'll see you at seven," she said.

chapter 23

GLORIA, ARKADY VOLKONSKI, FIVE OF HIS
Bugs, and a pilot accelerated away from New
Cambridge. Within an hour of their departure, they
would reach 92 percent of the speed of light, turn on the
Cruiser's Ferguson Distortion Generators, and enter
the strange realm of Yao Space. Interstellar flight was
not very exciting, and the Bugs all tried to get some
sack time.

The Cruiser could carry as many as twelve passengers in something approximating comfort. Two rows of
bunks flanked a central passageway that connected the
cockpit and a tiny galley with a small bathroom and the
even smaller engine room. There was really not much
need for an engine room at all, since in-flight repairs
would have been virtually impossible if anything went
wrong, but pilots found it comforting to think that they
could control their own fate with a screwdriver and
some elbow grease.

Gloria sat with Volkonski in the galley, sipping coffee and munching sandwiches. Volkonski had expressed

his skepticism about this entire venture and, particularly, Gloria's participation in it. "If anything happens on that scumworld," he said, "you'll just be in the way."

"No, I won't!" Gloria protested. "You're forgetting, I commanded an entire army back on Mynjhino. I know how to handle myself."

"You commanded a bunch of half-assed volunteers, and nobody ever fired a shot," Volkonski said. "You've never been in actual combat. You haven't had any training in small-unit tactics. And you've probably never even fired a plasma rifle."

Gloria couldn't deny any of that. "So train me," she said. "We've got about thirteen hours. Tell me what I need to know."

Volkonski sighed. "It doesn't work that way, Gloria. We're not exactly set up to put you through boot camp here. It's not something you can learn from lectures or books. Anyway, if I tried to give you some instruction, you'd immediately decide that you were an expert and insist on running the show."

"No, I wouldn't."

"Of course you would. You couldn't help yourself."

Gloria scowled and propped her chin up on her fist. "You know me too damn well," she said petulantly.

"Keeping you alive requires a close study of my subject," Volkonski said. "I wasn't on Mynjhino, but I know what happened there and I know you tried to handle everything personally. And I saw you in action on Sylvania. Sooner or later, Gloria, you are going to have to learn that an executive simply issues orders and lets other people carry them out. I mean, why are you even *here*?"

"It's my responsibility to—"

"The hell it is. It's *my* responsibility to carry out this mission. It's your responsibility to define the mission and see to it that I have all the resources necessary to complete it successfully."

"I think it's part of my responsibility to be with my people when I send them into a potentially dangerous situation."

"That's a very romantic notion," Volkonski said, "but it's also total nonsense. I mean, just look at yourself! Who the hell goes into a combat situation dressed like that?"

Gloria glanced down at herself. She was wearing a molecules-thick white bodysuit, set at 70 percent transparency, with the pressure seam in front opened from her neck to her navel. "I wore this on Mynjhino," Gloria said. "No one seemed to mind."

"I'm sure they didn't," Volkonski said, "because nobody on Mynjhino knew what the hell they were doing. But if we get into a fight on this scumworld, you'll just be a distraction to my men."

"I'll also be a distraction to the enemy."

"Or a target."

Gloria pursed her lips, then decided she might as well give in. She hit a contact switch and reduced the transparency of her bodysuit to 30 percent, then closed the pressure seam up to the base of her sternum. "There. Is that better?"

"Not really," Volkonski said, shaking his head. "But I suppose it's the best I can expect. Why must you always be the center of attention?"

Gloria reached across the table and put her hand on Volkonski's. "Arkady," she said, "I *like* being the center of attention. And I don't really have any choice, do I?"

Volkonski looked at his beautiful boss for a few seconds and broke into a grin. "I suppose not," he said.

"I know how I look," Gloria said. "I realized early on that I could either fight it, and try to be drab and plain even though I wasn't, or just accept it, enjoy it, and try to get maximum mileage out of it. Dressing the way I do gives me a kind of power that isn't available to all you big, strong, tough guys. And I use that power to get the job done."

"You certainly do that," Volkonski agreed.

"And as for why I'm here, well, that sort of goes with the territory. Gloria VanDeen can't be just another bureaucrat. She's got to be out there where people can see her, sexy and glamorous to the end, even if it kills her. Spirit, do you know how I spent the last two weeks? I put myself on display and let myself be ogled and groped by half the bureaucrats in the Quadrant. And do you know what the result of all that was? OSI is going to make it, Arkady! We really are going to become the Fifth Quadrant! You saw it for yourself at the meeting this morning. OSI was right there at the same table with all the grown-ups. The public is crazy about me, I've gotten the support of the Dexta rank and file, and even people like DuBray have to accept the fact that OSI is here to stay."

"Unless," Volkonski pointed out, "Gloria VanDeen gets her beautiful head blown off on that scumworld."

"Well, yes," Gloria conceded. "There's always that, isn't there?"

WHIT BARTHOLEMEW FOUND HIS MOTHER SIT-ting on a sofa in the library of the Bartholemew family mansion on the cliff north of Central. Sitting with her, to his considerable surprise, was his grandfather, Norman Mingus.

Whit stopped short a few feet away from them and stared at Mingus. "What are *you* doing here?" he demanded.

Mingus got to his feet, walked toward his grandson, and held out his hand. "Good to see you again, Whit. You're looking well." When Whit made no move to offer his own hand, Mingus withdrew his. "Still the same as I remember you, I see."

"Believe it." Whit turned to look at his mother. "What is this bastard doing here?"

Saffron Mingus Bartholemew waved her hand dismissively. "Oh, relax, Whit," she said. "It won't kill either one of us to spend a few minutes with him. Of course, a few minutes is all he has."

"Ah, the doting grandparent! Managed to find ten minutes for us after twenty years, did you?"

"Fifteen, actually," said Mingus. "But perhaps I was being overly optimistic."

"You can drag your ancient ass out of here right now, for all I care."

"Oh, now both of you, just sit down and stop acting like babies. Father, right here where you were. Whit, plant yourself in that chair and try not to suck your thumb and pout." Saffron stared at both of them, and the force of her gaze finally drove them to do as she had ordered.

"Father was just explaining why he couldn't come and visit us while Bart was still alive," Saffron said.

"And I was hoping that you might explain why you and Whit never came to visit me in Manhattan," said Mingus. "It was never my desire or intention to be alienated from you."

"Your desire and your intention," echoed Saffron. "You never really managed to sort those out, did you, Father?"

"You know why I did what I did," Mingus answered softly. "And it wasn't such a bad life, was it? Bart took care of you and tried to do right by you. He was not a bad man, was he?"

Saffron took her father's hand and squeezed it gently for a moment. "No," she said, "he wasn't."

"He was an even bigger bastard than his father-in-law," Whit interjected. "You ran your big noble Empire, while he ran his greasy little empire. And Mother and I were caught in between, and nobody ever gave a damn about that."

"That's not true, son," Mingus said. "I cared very much about you and your mother, and I'm sure that Bart did too, in his way. But life is never as simple as we would wish."

"Spare me the grandfatherly philosophy about life, old man. You want to know what life is? I'll tell you what it is. It's an eternal struggle between the fat cats like you and dear old Dad, and all the rest of the poor, stupid, swarming mass of humanity. Only they don't have a chance, do they? Because the fix is in. The game is rigged and always has been. People like you get what they want, and everyone else has to settle for wanting what little they get."

"You sound just like you did the last time I saw you," Mingus said. "You were just out of college then, with your long hair and your beard, spouting leftist drivel as if you were the first one ever to think of it. The boy's hardly grown up at all, has he?"

"Oh, that's not true," Saffron protested. "He's done a fine job of running the family businesses, and without any help from—from *those people*. You realize, don't you, that by the time he died, Bart had made his enterprises almost entirely legitimate?"

"Which is more than anyone can say for you," Whit said accusingly. "The Empire is the most corrupt enterprise in the history of humanity."

"The Empire"—Mingus sighed—"is what it is." He got to his feet, and Saffron and Whit did, as well. "I'm sorry, but I didn't come here to debate political theory. I have to be going, but I expect to see you—both of you—at the OSI reception Saturday night. You'll be there, won't you?"

"I don't know," Saffron said. "Of course, the Ellisons will expect us, but I just don't know."

"Come," said Mingus. "I'll introduce you to the

Emperor. Whit too, if he'll promise to behave himself." Mingus kissed his daughter lightly on her cheek, paused to gaze for a moment at his grandson, then strode briskly from the room.

"He'll introduce us to the Emperor," Whit said with bitter sarcasm. "I have a much better idea. I've been planning a little working vacation, and I want you to join me. We'll leave Saturday afternoon and go to the mountain lodge on Belairus. You always liked it there, and the mountain air will be just the thing to clear the stench of all these bureaucrats."

"Belairus is lovely," his mother agreed. "But I honestly don't see how we can avoid that reception. The Ellisons would be disappointed and despite your disapproval, I suppose I *would* like to meet the Emperor."

"I'll make you a deal, then," Whit said. "We'll go to that reception Saturday night, and I'll behave myself. Then we'll leave Sunday morning."

"That's still rather sudden. Couldn't we make it next week?"

"No," Whit said flatly. "Sunday morning. I told you, it's a working vacation, and I already have meetings scheduled. We can't leave any later than Sunday morning. If you don't agree, I'll make an ugly scene with the Emperor."

Saffron looked at her son. "You'd do that, wouldn't you?"

"Damn right I would. Sunday morning?"

"Very well, then. Sunday morning." Saffron pursed her lips and shook her head as she looked into her son's eyes. "I never could say 'No' to you and make it stick."

"Really? I always thought it was more the other way around. I remember one time when—"

Saffron pressed her fingers against Whit's lips. "Hush," she whispered. "We'll speak no more about it. Now, as for this evening, I had hoped we could have a—"

"Sorry, Mom," Whit said. "Got a date."

Saffron raised an eyebrow. "A date? Anyone I know?"

"You met her at the Ellisons' party. Petra Nash."

"That cute little girl who was with young Palmer Ellison? Yes, I gather they've broken up. Only to be expected, of course. Steffany is a much more suitable match for the boy. The Ellisons would never have consented to his staying with someone so . . . common."

"She's not common. In fact, she's delightfully uncommon."

"Oh? What's this? Honest attraction, dare I hope?"

"Decide for yourself. I'm going to ask her to join us on our trip."

"Will wonders never cease?" Saffron asked. "You aren't finally falling in love, are you?"

Whit had no answer for that. His mother thought he even looked a little embarrassed.

PETRA FELT EVERY EYE ON HER AS SHE WALKED into the fancy restaurant on Whit's arm, wearing only a filmy green band skirt, adjusted shockingly low on her hips, and a matching halter top that didn't quite conceal her nipples. Pug had gotten the outfit for her on their shopping spree, and while she doubted that it was something she would wear back home in Manhattan, it somehow seemed just right for this staid, heavy planet. One more way of thumbing her nose at them all.

They were seated at the same table they'd had two nights earlier, with its sweeping, panoramic view of the city. Wine was served, Whit approved it, and they raised their glasses in a toast. "Here's to two people in a trillion, finding each other in the midst of all this rot and decay," Whit said.

"You're cynical even when you're being sentimental," Petra noted.

"It's the Hegelian dialectic," Whit explained, "the

eternal clash of opposing forces, out of which the future is forged."

"That's a little better," Petra said, and sipped her wine.

"With the right motivation, I could do *much* better. You bring out the poet in me, Petra Nash. The other day in my office, we were simply two rutting animals. Under the proper circumstances, in the right setting, you might find that I can be quite human."

"I think you're more human than you realize, Whit. You're a very attractive man. Maybe I was just getting back at Pug the other day in your office, but that doesn't mean that I don't feel something for you."

" 'Something,' " Whit said. "Could you be more specific?"

Petra smiled. "Not just now," she said.

"Well, I feel 'something' for you, as well. I can't give a name to it, and I won't insult us both by pretending that it's love, but whatever it is, it's real and deeply felt."

Petra's smile turned into a grin. "Took the words right out of my mouth," she said.

Whit returned her grin. "We understand each other, then."

"Not as well as I'd like to. I wish I knew where all your anger comes from. It can be a little frightening."

He drank some more wine. "My anger," he said, "is my oldest companion. A friend of my youth."

"Have you ever tried living without it?"

"No," he said, "I haven't, and I have no wish to. My anger is my magnetic north. It provides orientation and direction in my life. It tells me what I must do, and why. Don't you ever feel it?"

"Not the way you do," Petra replied. "Sure, I get angry sometimes. But I don't let it control my life."

"What does control your life, then? What do you *want*, Petra Nash?"

Petra sipped some wine. "That's not an easy question to answer," she said as Whit poured more wine for both of them.

"It never is," Whit said. "That's why we so seldom ask it of ourselves. Confronting our deepest desires is a risky business. We might learn something about ourselves that we'd rather not know. Take you, for example. You've just traded in an upright, respectable young boy for a ne'er-do-well, middle-aged rascal. Have you considered just why you did that?"

"It wasn't exactly something I planned, you know."

"Plans have nothing to do with it. The fact is, you did it. Here we sit, Petra Nash, together and, to all appearances, enjoying it. That is the reality of the moment."

"If it's reality, does it have to have an explanation?"

For a moment, Whit had no response. They watched in silence as a brightly lit vessel in the harbor rose into the dark sky on a plume of blue fire.

"I'm taking my mother away to our lodge on Belairus," Whit said, looking Petra in the eyes. "We leave Sunday morning. Come with us."

"What?" Petra asked, taken aback.

"You heard me. It's only a two-day journey in my yacht."

"Whit, I have a job. I can't just take off at the drop of a hat."

"Why not? The Quadrant Meeting will be concluded by then. You don't need to stick around just to watch the Emperor blab to the masses in the soccer stadium on Sunday. Don't you have some time off coming?"

"Well, as a matter of fact, I do," Petra said. "But—"

"Then take it now—with me! We have a beautiful lodge in the mountains. Have you ever seen Belairus? The most beautiful little world you can imagine. And low-gravity, too—only .82 G. You'll feel as if you were inflated with helium."

"Now *that* sounds good!" Petra had already kicked off her high heels beneath the table.

"Then you'll come?"

"Spirit, Whit, I don't know what to say! There's so much going on, and even with the Quadrant Meeting ending, Gloria may need me to help wrap up some loose ends. I just don't see how I could leave Sunday. But I could talk to Gloria, and maybe next week, when she goes back to Earth, I could get away for a week or so."

Whit shook his head. "No, it must be Sunday."

"Why can't you just delay it a few days?"

"I'm sorry, but I can't. It must be Sunday. Talk to Gloria about it tomorrow."

"Can't. Gloria's not here and won't be back until tomorrow night."

"Not here? Where else would she be?"

"I can't tell you that," Petra said. "But it's important. Whit? I did something good today. Maybe something very good. You asked me what I want? I think what I want is the chance to do something like that every now and then. The chance to make a little difference in the galaxy."

"A little difference in the galaxy?" Whit smothered a chuckle in some more wine. "Why not a *big* difference?"

Feeling slightly offended by Whit's reaction, Petra replied, "And what difference have *you* made? What difference will you *ever* make?"

"You never know, Petra Nash," Whit said, "you never know."

Later, Whit took Petra back to his big mansion, up a lavish staircase, and into his bedroom and bed. Petra wriggled out of her minimal clothing, lay back, and shuddered happily as Whit made his way down the length of her body, from the ticklish hollow of her throat to her straining pink nipples, her smooth, slim belly, and the warm, tingling wetness of her groin. He was confident and thorough, and left her gasping in urgent fulfillment.

Pug had been an ardent and playful lover, and she'd had no complaints, but there had always been something about him that made her think of a boy who thought he was getting away with something—or maybe, not quite getting away with it. It was as if, she thought, he could never really get out from under those murals staring down on him from the ceiling above. But Whit was sure of himself, selfish and, yes, angry. She could feel his anger as he entered her, plunging and pounding himself against her like a wave beating against a shore it desperately desired. A meeting of opposites.

And when he was finished at last, and lay next to her, panting and drained, he said, "Sunday morning. You'll come away with me. You must, Petra Nash; you *must*!"

chapter 24

GAC 4367-III WAS AN UGLY WORLD. FROM PO-lar orbit in the Cruiser, Gloria and her Bugs watched the pea-green landscape slide by beneath them and she felt no desire to descend into that miasma. Here and there, a crenellated range of stunted mountains provided lit-eral relief from the featureless continental masses, and ocean currents had cleared narrow, open arcs of the bio-logical infestation, but all else was algae.

The terraformers of the old Terrestrial Union had believed that with the proper encouragement, a scum-world such as this might be turned into a garden. A billion years' worth of decayed algae would provide or-ganic nourishment for muscular, better-evolved terres-trial plants, which would simply take over the planet. Sow some wheat, then step back and watch it grow, free of pests and competition. It had actually worked that way on a few worlds, but more often, the unexpected complications of alien ecosystems frustrated the hopes of the terraformers. GAC 4367-III occupied the atten-tion of Earthbuilders for half a century, until better and easier worlds became available, and the experiment was abandoned. The triumphant algae reclaimed their world from the alien invaders.

"There's the terraforming station," said Volkonski as he and Gloria examined a display screen in the cockpit of the Cruiser. He fiddled with some controls and magnified the image until the sloping rooftop of what seemed to be an immense warehouse stood out against the background slime. The structure seemed to be covered with the algae mats, and only the long shadows of early morning defined its shape and size.

"I don't see any sign of people," Gloria said.

"I don't know," said Volkonski. "We're getting a faint infrared signature. That building is leaking some heat."

"Could it be from an old reactor?" Gloria wondered.

"Possible. They used uranium reactors in those days. It might still be generating a little heat. We should check for radiation before we enter that building."

"That looks like a dock on the shore of the bay."

"Right." Volkonski turned to the pilot, a sandy-haired young man named Erskine. "What do you think?"

Erskine shrugged inconclusively. "Spirit knows how deep that water is. There's no channel marked out that I can see. We'd have to land well offshore and hope for the best."

"And if anyone is down there," Volkonski said, "they'd have plenty of time to see us coming. I'd prefer to wait and make a night landing, but it's early morning at this location. Planetary rotation period is twenty-eight hours, so we'd have to wait fourteen or fifteen hours before we tried it."

Gloria shook her head. "We can't do that. We'd be half a day late getting back to New Cambridge. They might get worried and send another ship. Anyway, our main priority is to find out if the weapons are there and, if they are, to see if any of the big plasma bombs are missing. If they've taken one of them to New Cambridge, they could use it as soon as the Emperor arrives, tomorrow night. We have to get down there now, Arkady."

"Agreed. You heard the lady, Erskine. Set us down."

"Yessir," said Erskine. "But before I do, there's one more thing you should be aware of. According to these readings, the atmospheric oxygen content is 29 percent."

"Spirit!" Volkonski exclaimed.

"What's the problem?" Gloria asked. "We can breathe that, can't we?"

"We'll probably get drunk on it," said Volkonski, "but yes, we can breathe it. That's not the problem."

"Then what is?"

"Begging your pardon, ma'am," said Erskine, "but with 29 percent oxygen in the air, that planet is a fucking tinderbox."

"Oh?"

"Yes, ma'am. See these brown, splotchy areas scattered around? I think those are burned-out areas, probably from lightning strikes. Any sort of flame would immediately set off a conflagration. Anything that could burn—like the algae mats—*would* burn, until rains put it out."

"What does that mean for us?" Gloria asked.

"For one thing," said Volkonski, "it means this entire planet is most definitely a no-smoking area."

"Yessir," said Erskine. "And it also means that our exhaust could start a fire."

"But other ships have obviously landed without burning down the planet," Gloria pointed out.

"Yes, ma'am. I think we'll be okay if we come down in the water just offshore. You can see that the wave action has pretty well broken up the algae mats. I don't think we'd touch off any big conflagration. We'll use thermoelectric propulsion once we're in the water, so that should be okay. But we need to be aware that there's a potential problem."

"Thank you for mentioning it, Erskine," Gloria said. "Anything else we should be worried about?"

"Rocks just under the water, ma'am. Once we're down, we'll be able to spot them with our sonar. But the actual touchdown will be a crapshoot. Come down in the wrong place and we could rip the bottom out of our hull."

Gloria sighed in frustration. "If only they'd given us a LASS. It never occurred to me that there could be so many complications in just landing on the damned planet."

"That's the problem with ordering these romantic little excursions," Volkonski said. "They're never quite as easy as they sound when you're giving the orders."

" 'Ready, fire, aim,' huh? Sorry, Arkady, I guess I should have thought this through a little better."

"If you had," he said, "we'd be here anyway, doing exactly the same thing. You were right, Gloria. This is a job that has to be done."

"Then let's do it," she said. "Erskine, let's shoot some craps."

ERSKINE BROUGHT THE CRUISER IN FOR A feather-soft touchdown a mile offshore. As he carefully puttered the craft in toward the dock, Volkonski focused the image-intensifiers on the area and warily scanned the screen.

"Someone has cleaned off that dock and the area around it," he said. "People have definitely been here, and more recently than eight centuries ago."

"If anyone's here now, they would have seen or heard us coming in," said Gloria. "But I don't see anyone near the dock."

"They could be hiding behind those rocks, or farther inland. If I had my druthers, I'd send in a boat with a few men to cover our landing."

"Why don't you?"

"We don't have enough men to divide our force that way."

"So I should have sent a bigger team?"

Volkonski shook his head. "*I* should have. Tactical considerations are my job, not yours. Speaking of which, I should go aft and get the squad ready. Keep a watch and sing out if you see anything."

Gloria stared intently at the image screen but saw no movement of any kind. There were no birds or insects, no creepers or crawlers. It was a one-celled world.

"How are we doing, Erskine?"

"So far, so good, ma'am. Water depth is okay, and the bottom is sandy with a gentle slope. Those Terrestrial Union guys probably surveyed the area and built their dock in a good spot. We should be fine."

They were. Erskine expertly guided the vessel toward shore and brought it in snug against the dock. Gloria patted him on the shoulder, then went aft to join Volkonski and his Bugs.

The five IntSec men and Volkonski wore their standard gray uniforms, pantlegs tucked into black boots, with bulky, glossy helmets packed with electronic gear. Each of them hefted a Mark VI plasma rifle, except for Volkonski, who carried a holstered plasma pistol.

"Minimum beam setting on all weapons," Volkonski instructed. "No one fires at anything, for any reason, without my specific order. And if you do have to use your weapons, try to hit the person you're aiming at and nothing else. And under no circumstances does anyone fire in the direction of that building. Is that clearly understood? We don't know what's in there, but if you put a hole in the containment of a plasma bomb, your mothers, wives, and/or sweethearts would be very upset. Any questions?"

"Where do you want me?" Gloria asked. "Right behind you?"

"I want you exactly where you are now. In the ship, buttoned up."

Gloria started to protest, but one look from Volkonski closed her mouth. "I'm sorry, Arkady," she said. "You're in charge. I'll do as you say. But I want you to keep an open comm link at all times."

"Will do. And Gloria? If things go wrong out there, you and Erskine get the hell out of here immediately, understand? Someone can come back for us later, but the vital thing is to get word back to New Cambridge."

Gloria nodded. Volkonski gave her a stern look, as if to reinforce the message, then, without another word, turned and hit the control that opened the sliding hatch panel. An airlock was not necessary, since a mass-repulsion field kept the interior and exterior atmospheres separate—at least in theory. But somehow, a pungent waft of the scumworld managed to penetrate into the Cruiser.

"Phew!" Gloria cried.

"Hydrogen sulfide from rotting algae," Volkonski said. "Okay, take a deep breath and let's go!"

The Bugs charged out onto the dock, each of them running to a specific spot, as if the whole operation had been choreographed in advance. They knelt and scanned the horizon as Volkonski went out at a dogtrot to the landward end of the dock. Then the first men out ran past Volkonski and stationed themselves in the jumble of rocks onshore. One of them immediately slipped on the slimy algae mats and took a header. He picked himself up, looking chagrined, and Volkonski called out, "Watch where you step!" He looked back at the Cruiser and motioned for Gloria to close the hatch. She watched the Bugs advance for another moment, then reluctantly hit the control to seal up the ship.

Gloria went forward, where Erskine had already established the comm link with Volkonski. The image on the screen bobbed up and down and from side to side as Volkonski's helmet moved, and she could hear his heavy breathing. The land sloped upward from the water, and the big building, less than half a mile away, could not be seen from Volkonski's current location. The Bugs fanned out, slipping and sliding on the algae as they moved. It was not a graceful-looking operation, but the team made steady progress inland.

"Iglesias! Reynolds!" Volkonski shouted, and the screen showed his arm extended, pointing to locations on either side of what seemed to be a pathway leading upward. The two men hustled to the spots at the top of the rise and threw themselves onto their bellies. Erskine hit a control button, and suddenly Gloria was looking at the scene from Reynolds's viewpoint. Ahead, the massive structure built by the terraformers of long ago loomed on the horizon. It seemed to have been constructed from sheets of corrugated metal, and there was a large central doorway, currently closed. The entire building was coated with the omnipresent gray-green slime.

"I got movement!" shouted Iglesias. Erskine switched to his camera, but Gloria saw nothing amiss.

"Here, too!" called Reynolds. Now, Erskine called up a split-screen image, and they could see the view from the positions of both Bugs. Gloria thought she could see a flicker of motion near some rocks in the mid distance.

"I make it three . . . check that, four unknowns, at three hundred meters," Reynolds reported. "They've got some kind of camo on, hard to see."

"Visors," Volkonski ordered. Immediately, the view on the screen switched to the ghostly, green glow of infrared imaging. Now Gloria could plainly make out at least three human forms crouching near some boulders scattered to the front. Volkonski advanced and took a position next to Reynolds. Gloria saw his hand at the edge of Reynolds's screen, his index finger pointing toward a little swale ten meters ahead. As Reynolds scrambled forward, there was a muffled bang from somewhere, and the image from the Bug's camera suddenly showed nothing but algae and mud.

"Shit! I'm hit!"

"Stay down!" Volkonski shouted. "Byerly, Mitsui, go get him! Gordon, Iglesias, covering fire! Over their heads! I don't want to start any fires, but let's show 'em we've got some teeth!"

The dazzling bursts of plasma overloaded the imagers for a moment. To the sound of grunts, heavy breathing, and a pained moan, Byerly and Mitsui dragged Reynolds back to the near side of the rise. Volkonski knelt over his man, and the screen showed Reynolds's anguished face and then the ripped fabric of his uniform and the dark stain spreading from his right shoulder.

"Flèchettes," Volkonski muttered. "Figures—they don't want to start any fires, either. Relax, Reynolds, it probably hurts like a son of a bitch, but it's not that bad. You're going to be fine." Volkonski looked around. "Gordon, Iglesias! What do you see?"

"Still just the four of 'em, sir! Not moving."

"Okay, keep watching, and if they try to move, fire more warning bursts. Gloria?"

"Right here, Arkady."

"I think we've got an answer to our main question."

"I think you're right. What do you recommend?"

"Under the circumstances, our plasma weapons are useless, but they can use their flèchettes. I think we should pull back to the Cruiser and get the hell out of here."

"Understood," Gloria replied. She still wanted to get into that building and see if any plasma bombs were missing, but that no longer seemed possible. Arkady was right: Their only mission now was to get back to New Cambridge and report what had happened.

Volkonski issued the necessary orders, and Byerly and Mitsui carried Reynolds back to the dock, while Gordon and Iglesias remained at the top of the rise to provide covering fire if necessary. Then he ordered Gordon and Iglesias to fall back. Gloria opened the hatch and stood to one side as Byerly and Mitsui came in with Reynolds and gently placed him on one of the bunks. The young man was alternately gritting his teeth and gasping for breath, but when he saw Gloria, he tried to smile. She returned the smile and squeezed his hand. It was covered with slime.

"Sorry 'bout that, ma'am," he said. Gloria blinked back tears and said nothing.

A moment later, Volkonski, Gordon, and Iglesias came tumbling into the Cruiser. Volkonski smacked the hatch control with his palm and shouted to the pilot, "Get us out of here, Erskine!"

The bass rumble of the engines vibrated through the ship, and the vessel gently lurched into motion. Then Erskine cried, "We're under fire!" Volkonski and Gloria dashed forward.

"Plasma burst into the water," Erskine said. "Damn, another one!"

Volkonski checked the external imagers. "And one behind us, too. Hold where we are, Erskine."

"Yessir!"

"Two of them," said Volkonski as he examined the screen, "up there at the top of the rise."

"What can we do?" Gloria asked.

"Not one damn thing," Volkonski said between his clenched teeth. "They want the ship. They could put a hole through the hull anytime they want and prevent us from taking off, but they haven't done that. They want us to stay here and they want the ship intact."

"Can't we fire back?"

"No external weaponry on this tub. We could open the hatch and start a fire out there with a plasma burst, but they'd still have time to burn us. What we seem to have here is an old-fashioned Mexican standoff."

"Can we talk to them?" Gloria wondered.

"My thought exactly," said Volkonski. "Erskine?"

"External mikes and speakers on, sir. Just use your throat mike."

Volkonski took a couple of breaths, then said in an authoritative voice, "This is Dexta Internal Security. Cease fire at once!"

"Fuck you, Bug!" came the reply, followed by another blue-green plasma discharge into the water just ahead of the Cruiser.

"Who are you?" Volkonski demanded.

"We are the People's Anti-Imperialist Nexus, and we've got you in our crosshairs, lickspittle!"

"I guess you boys don't get many newstexts out this way," Volkonski said in a more conversational tone. "PAIN's leadership group has been captured, and the whole operation is disbanding. The war's already over, and your side lost. Give it up now and you'll get off easy."

"You must think we're idiots!"

"As a matter of fact, I do. Who else but idiots would let themselves get stranded on this stinkhole fighting for a cause that's already lost? How long have you guys been stuck here, anyway?"

There was no immediate response. Then a different voice called out, "None of your business, Bug!"

Volkonski put his hand over his throat mike and said to Gloria, "I thought so. They've been here a while. The main thing they want is to get off this planet. I don't think they'll do anything to damage the ship."

The first voice from outside called, "Hey, Bug! We'll make you a deal. Come out with your hands up, and we won't kill you."

"We'll make *you* a deal," Volkonski replied. "Put your weapons down and we won't set fire to your planet. Twenty-nine percent oxygen out there—you'd go up like torches."

"Then we'll all burn together, Bug," came the response.

"He means it," Volkonski said to Gloria.

"This could go on all day," Gloria said.

"Unless you have a better idea."

"Just one," she said. "I think this may be the time for a distraction." She hit the contact switch that quickly rendered her bodysuit 90 percent transparent, then opened the pressure seam in front as low as it could go.

"Just remember the mission, Arkady. If you get a chance to get away, take it. You can always come back for me later."

Volkonski nodded. "Good luck, Gloria."

Gloria leaned toward Volkonski's throat mike and announced, "This is Gloria VanDeen of Dexta. I'm coming out."

WHIT BARTHOLEMEW'S LIMO RETURNED PETRA to the Imperial Cantabragian that morning, and she walked through the crowded lobby, still nearly nude in her flimsy nighttime togs. She immediately encountered Althea Dante, who gave her a friendly kiss on the cheek and gushed, "Petra, darling! We're all so proud of you! A marvelous piece of detective work."

"They made a public announcement?" Petra asked.

"Of course not. But Dexta people know. And don't you look glamorous!" Althea gave her a wicked grin. "I trust you had a fulfilling evening?"

"It was interesting," Petra said.

"I'll just bet it was. You're getting to be quite the Tiger, aren't you? Maybe I could teach you a few things sometime."

"C'mon, Althea, you know I don't do that."

"Variety is the spice of life," Althea countered.

"I think I've got enough spice in my life for now," Petra said. "But tell me something. What do you know about Whitney Bartholemew, Junior?"

"Not much," Althea replied. "I get the impression that you must know a lot more than I do. Why do you ask?"

"Just wondering. He's a strange man, in some ways."

"So I gather. I never really knew him, but as it happens, we went to the same college. He was a few years ahead of me, of course. At the time, he was one of those hairy campus radicals—you know the type. Always hogging the microphone at demonstrations and droning on and on about the evil pigs and the Hagoolian dialectic."

"Hegelian," Petra corrected.

"Whatever. He was never exactly my type." Althea eyed her inquisitively. "Is he yours, Petra, dear?"

"I'm not sure," Petra answered. "Althea, what do you do when you're attracted to a man you know is bad for you?"

"I usually give in to my own low urges and let the chips fall where they may. But that's just me. I'm not sure it's *you*, though. Petra, would you mind some gratuitous advice?"

"Please."

"You're a delightful and charming young woman, and very sexy when you want to be. But you have an unfortunate streak of innate goodness in you. That can be very inconvenient when it comes to sex. When you get right down to it, women like Gloria and I are—to be coarse about it—cunts. The difference between us is that Gloria wants people to think that she's a *nice* cunt, and I don't give a shit *what* they think. But you really *are* nice, in some fundamental way. Don't lose that, Petra. Just because things didn't work out with Peter Pan, don't throw yourself at Captain Hook. You're better than that. And now," Althea said, giving Petra another peck on her cheek, "I must be off. *Ciao,* darling!"

Petra made her way to the elevators, deep in thought, pausing briefly to accept congratulations from two Dexta people she didn't even know. Once in the suite, she stretched out on a sofa and contemplated her navel, which she had heard was a good way to achieve enlightenment. She thought she needed some of that.

Whit wanted her to fly away with him on Sunday. With his mother. Just what she needed, another disapproving matron to impress. She wanted to go, wanted to spend a week or so on a far-off world—with low gravity!—and just forget about everything that had happened on New Cambridge. Lose herself in the angry passion of Whit Bartholemew.

But why did it have to be Sunday? Why couldn't he just wait a few days? What was so important about Sunday?

Abruptly, unexpectedly, Petra achieved the enlightenment she had sought. It had a physical force to it, and it almost made her ill.

She grabbed her purse and pad and all but ran out of the suite to the elevators. She had to get back to her office in Gibraltar. Enlightenment was one thing, but she needed facts.

chapter 25

GLORIA STEPPED OUT ONTO THE DOCK AND IM-
mediately wrinkled her nose at the pungent scent of the
scumworld. The oxygen-rich air seemed to burn her
lungs, but after a couple of deep breaths, she felt better.
The air was cool and the sky was a faded blue-green. She
saw two men flanking the path at the top of the rise, aiming their rifles at her. One of them carried a flèchette
gun, the other an old Mark IV plasma rifle. She walked
slowly to the end of the dock and waited. One of the
men waved her on, and she made her way up the path; it
looked as if someone had sprayed it with an herbicide
that kept the surrounding algae mats in check.

Reaching the top of the rise, she paused again. Two
more men appeared, one with a flèchette rifle and the
other holding a plasma pistol. They were all dressed in
pea-green jumpsuits, mottled with random patterns of
brown and tan.

"Who's in charge here?" Gloria asked.

"No one," said the man with the pistol. "We are not
hierarchical. We are an affinity group and we make col-

lective decisions." Yet it was clear to Gloria that, anarchist ideology aside, the man with the pistol was effectively in charge. He was about thirty, brown hair, brown eyes, and like the others, wore a scraggly growth of beard.

"You mean I have to negotiate with all four of you at once?"

"Who said anything about negotiations?" said the man with the pistol. All four men were staring at her with what seemed to Gloria to be hungry appreciation.

"We didn't invite you to come out here," said the man with the plasma rifle.

Gloria slowly turned to look at each of them. "Come on, guys," she said, "we've got a situation here, and we need to discuss it. You obviously want our ship, or you'd have holed the hull by now."

"We can do more than that, Ms. VanDeen," said one of the men with a flèchette rifle. "We've got plasma RPGs, and we can blow that ship straight to hell."

"And probably yourselves, too," Gloria pointed out. "But even if you lived, you'd still be stuck here. How long have you been here?"

"Long enough," said the man with the pistol. "But our relief could arrive at any time. Maybe even today."

Gloria shook her head. "I wouldn't count on it. Didn't you hear what we said? PAIN is out of business."

"Why should we believe you?"

"What choice do you have? Look, we've got something you want, and maybe you've got something we want. Let's walk over to your building so I can get a look at those weapons—if you have them."

"We've got 'em, Ms. VanDeen," said the man with the plasma rifle.

"Then let's see them. I'm not going to negotiate until I see what we're negotiating about."

The man with the plasma pistol frowned, then turned to one of the men with a flèchette rifle and said,

"Take her down the path a little way and watch her."
Then he walked past Gloria and huddled with the other
two men. Her guard motioned for her to move, and she
did, but she noticed that the other three men were engaged in what seemed to be a heated discussion behind
her. Apparently it was difficult for anarchists to give orders to each other.

The man guarding her was tall and thin, with dirty
blond hair and hazel eyes. From the look of his beard,
she guessed that they had been here at least three
months. And they probably hadn't seen a woman in all
that time.

Gloria smiled at him. "I'm Gloria," she said. "What's
your name?"

The man hesitated, then answered. "Doug," he said.
"And that's Marty, and the other two are Alex and Rick."
Doug was trying to look Gloria in the eye, but his gaze
kept darting down to her mostly uncovered breasts and
her torso, which was not at all concealed beneath the
clinging, nearly transparent bodysuit.

"Is it just you four?" Gloria asked. "Must get lonely
around here."

Doug started to answer, stopped himself, then said,
grinning self-consciously, "We got a whole army just
over that hill."

Marty, the man with the pistol, returned, having
completed his parley with the rest of the affinity group.
His comrades looked back over their shoulders at
Gloria, then turned to concentrate their attention on the
Cruiser.

"Okay," Marty said, "walk. And if you try anything
funny, we'll shoot you where you stand. We mean it."

"I know you do," Gloria said. "One of your comrades parted my hair with a plasma rifle a few weeks
back."

"Yeah," Doug said, "we heard they were going to try
for you. Kind of glad they missed."

"Shut up and walk," Marty said, and so they did. Gloria kept ahead of the two men, putting a little extra hip waggle into her stride. Anarchists, Gloria assumed, had the same hormones as other men.

After a few minutes, they reached the building. The main door, about twenty feet on a side, was closed. Marty indicated that she should go through a smaller door to the right. That led into a small pressure chamber, and when the outer door was closed behind them, there was a brief hissing sound and the inner door popped open. Inside, the stench was less noticeable, and the air seemed more Earth-like.

"Just so you'll know, we can use a plasma weapon in here," Marty told her.

"I'm sure there won't be any need for that," Gloria replied. Marty led her down a short corridor, opened a door, and gestured for her to go ahead. She stepped out onto the concrete floor of the main room. Ahead of her sat a medium-sized freight skimmer with a closed cab and a flatbed, parked immediately in front of the large pressure door at the entrance. Beyond it, she saw a variety of unfamiliar machinery and equipment, apparently left behind by the terraforming crew. To the right, and extending two hundred feet to the rear of the building, were stacks of shipping containers and crates of various sizes. Overhead panel lighting cast a diffuse, yellowish glow.

Gloria walked ahead of the men, toward the containers. She glanced around, like a potential housebuyer idly checking out the premises. When she reached the first of the containers, she paused and read the stenciled notations on their sides. Deciphered, the string of letters and numbers seemed to announce that the containers each held two orbital plasma mines. The date read 06-23-63.

"This what you came to see?" Marty asked, a hint of a sneer in his voice.

"Some of it," Gloria said, trying to sound unimpressed. "Where are the big plasma bombs?"

"Back there," Marty said, pointing with his pistol.

"How many?"

"Enough."

"Come on, Marty," Gloria said. "Don't play cute. We know there were eighteen of them in the original shipment. You sent one of them to New Cambridge, and we already have that one, so you should have seventeen left here. Unless you sent some of them elsewhere. We need to know. Seventeen?"

Marty pursed his lips for a moment, then nodded. "Seventeen," he said. "Back there on the left."

"Let's see them. I want to count."

They walked on. Marty said, "How do we know you really got the one on New Cambridge?"

"I told you, we broke up your whole New Cambridge operation. Think about it. How else could we have found you here?"

"She's telling the truth, Marty," Doug said.

"Maybe. So why'd they send you here, Ms. VanDeen?"

Gloria turned and smiled at the two men. "Oh, you know. Glamour. Publicity. 'Beautiful Dexta Agent Finds Missing Arms Cache.' That sort of thing."

"Figures," Marty snorted.

"You boys are just a loose end," Gloria told them. "Nobody from PAIN is coming to pick up you and the weapons. We're your only ticket out, guys. Or do you want to spend the rest of your lives here?"

"Shit, I knew it!" Doug said in disgust. "They said it would just be two months, and it's already been three."

"Shut up," Marty told him.

"Shut up, yourself! I'm sick of listening to your crap, Marty. First among equals, my ass!"

"Are these the plasma bombs?" Gloria asked, pausing in front of some big black containers.

"That's them. Go ahead and count, if you want. There are seventeen of them, like I said." Marty waved his pistol in her direction. "But don't get any stupid ideas."

Gloria made a show of counting and inspecting the containers, crouching and bending as needed to give Doug and Marty a good view of her assets. Her bluff was working, so far, and sex was providing the necessary distraction. It was simply a question of waiting for the right moment.

"Okay," she said at last, "seventeen. Maybe we can do some business, but I need to see the other stuff, too. Where are the plasma rifles and grenades?"

"Over here, on the right," Marty said.

Gloria walked over to the crates. "I don't want to have to count all 24,000 rifles," she said. "Help me out here, guys. How many of them have been distributed so far?"

"Couple hundred," Doug said, "give or take. About the same with the grenades."

Gloria looked at Marty. "That right, Marty?"

"Yeah," he said with some apparent reluctance. "That's about right."

"Good," Gloria said. "Now we can negotiate."

"What did you have in mind?" Marty asked her.

"We'll trade you. Our Cruiser for the weapons. You can leave and go anywhere you want. We'll stay here, and when we don't show up on time at New Cambridge, they'll send another ship for us." Gloria gave him a satisfied smile.

"We don't have a pilot," Marty said.

"You can have ours, as long as you promise not to hurt him."

She could tell from Doug's face that he was eager to accept the deal. But Marty looked as if he needed a little more persuasion.

"And I'll throw in a bonus, just for you two. The others don't need to know a thing about it."

"What bonus?" Marty demanded.

"How long since you guys have had a woman?" Gloria stood in front of them, grinning.

Doug's eyes bulged out, but Marty remained skeptical. "You expect us to believe you're going to put out for us?"

Gloria allowed herself to look wounded by this show of doubt. "Hey, Marty," she said, "I'm Gloria VanDeen! You've heard all about me, right? Sexually voracious. Wantonly uninhibited. The best fuck in the galaxy. And it's all true. But don't take my word for it—find out for yourselves! You must have some beds in this dump."

"Over there in the crew quarters," Doug said, trying to be helpful.

"Shut up. It's some kind of trick."

"Oh, fuck you, Marty! Three months in this fucking place, and for what? You heard her—it's over! This is our only chance to get out of here!"

"Maybe. But I don't like this sex business. Use your head, Doug. She's just trying to split us up."

"One of you can fuck me, and the other one can watch, with a gun in his hand," Gloria said. "I don't mind. Unless you think you wouldn't be able to . . . you know . . . do it. I mean, that happens with some guys. I think I must intimidate them or something. And, of course, if it's just been you four guys here together for three months, well, maybe you've worked out some other arrangement for yourselves. And that's okay, really. There's nothing wrong with same-sex sex. I mean, I've done it with plenty of other women, and if you guys are like that—"

"Hey!" Doug interjected. "It's not like that at all. You just let me show you!"

"You moron! Can't you see what she's trying to do?"

"What are you worried about?" Doug turned and

got in Marty's face. "We've still got the guns! What can she do?"

At that precise instant, Gloria showed them what she could do. A flying Qatsima kick caught Marty square in the face and sent him reeling backwards, his plasma pistol clattering along the concrete. Doug reacted, but not quickly enough, and as he fumbled with the awkward flèchette rifle, Gloria bounded up in another kick that put a heel in Doug's groin. He doubled over, and Gloria finished him off with a knee to the chin.

Gloria picked up the plasma pistol and raised her left wrist near her mouth. "You hear all that, Arkady?"

"Every bit of it," Volkonski said over the wristcom. "Is everything secure there?"

"No sweat," Gloria assured him. "I've got the pistol, and Doug and Marty are in dreamland."

"Nice work, Gloria."

"Thank you, thank you. There's a freight skimmer, and I think I can use that. Just give me a few minutes to tie up the affinity group here."

"Roger. Nothing new happening here."

Gloria bent over and checked the anarchists' pulses, relieved to find that she hadn't killed either one. She looked around, and after a brief search found some bungee cords wrapped around the cartons of grenades. At summer camp, when she was eight, she had learned how to tie a variety of knots, and she used that knowledge now to secure Doug's and Marty's arms behind their backs and tie their feet together. Then, one at a time, she dragged them over the concrete floor to the front of the building next to the freight skimmer. Maneuvering them into the cab of the lorry took some doing, and she had to pause and catch her breath after the job was done.

She inspected the cab of the skimmer and found that she could operate it. Then she checked out the mechanism controlling the big pressure door and found that it involved no insoluble mysteries.

"Arkady? I'm all set here, but we need to coordinate."

"What are you planning?" Volkonski asked.

"I thought I could just barrel on out of here in the skimmer and down to the dock. If you can give me some covering fire . . ."

"It won't work, Gloria," Volkonski said. "Even if you got past the two guys on the rise, they'd still have plenty of time to put a hole through our hull. What's your range from the building to the rise?"

"Maybe five hundred meters," Gloria said. "Why?"

"Too long for accuracy with a flèchette. You'll have to use a plasma rifle."

"To do what?"

"To pick off the last two from behind."

"But wouldn't that start a fire?"

"Not if you're careful."

"Hey, Arkady, I've never even fired a plasma rifle. Anyway, I really don't want to have to kill anyone."

"Gloria," Volkonski said patiently, "this is no time to get softhearted."

"Give me a couple of minutes, Arkady. Let me think."

Gloria wandered around the vast shed, almost at random, pondering the possibilities. She came to an opened crate of plasma grenades, reached into it, and lifted one out to inspect it. It felt heavy in her hand, not the kind of thing you could throw very far. She knew there were slinglike launchers that were used to fling them a fair distance, but didn't see one. On the underside of the grenade, there was what appeared to be a timing mechanism. She studied it for a few moments, then went back to the skimmer.

She contacted Volkonski and told him what she had in mind. He didn't sound very enthusiastic about it, but didn't have a better idea. Reluctantly, he gave her the go-ahead.

Gloria got into the cab of the freight skimmer and fired up the engine. The skimmer rose a couple of feet off the concrete and hovered patiently. After checking to see that Doug and Marty were still unconscious, she got out of the cab and walked to the controls of the pressure door. She hit a couple of buttons and the inner door rose. Two more buttons, a harsh warning *blat!* from a Klaxon, and, with a loud sigh, the outer pressure door lifted. Cool, putrid air rushed into the warehouse. Gloria dashed back to the cab of the skimmer and started it moving.

She paused just outside the building. After setting the timer on the grenade, she opened the door and tossed it out into the vast mat of algae. Then she shut the door and floated forward along the path. Ahead, she could see Alex and Rick, in apparent confusion, watching as the freight skimmer closed the distance between them. A hundred meters short of them, she paused and spoke into her wristcom. Volkonski had linked it to the external speakers on the Cruiser.

"Alex! Rick! Listen to me! This is Gloria, and I've got Marty and Doug here with me in the cab. They're still alive, and you guys can stay alive, too, but only if you do exactly what I tell you."

Gloria waited. The two men had pointed their weapons at the skimmer, but they looked back and forth at each other for a few moments before one of them shouted, "You'll never make it to the dock, lady!"

"Neither will you, if you don't shut up and listen," Gloria responded. "In about thirty seconds, a plasma grenade I left back there is going to explode. The door is open, and the fire will spread inside. The munitions in there will start cooking off, and pretty soon something's going to put a hole through the containment of one of those plasma bombs. You know what that would mean."

She paused for a few seconds to let them think about it. "All seventeen of them will go off, but one will be more than enough. In the meantime, that fire will be spreading in this direction. There's only one way off this planet, so if you want to live, drop your weapons and get down to the dock as fast as you can."

Before either man could reply, the grenade detonated. Gloria saw a green flash in her rearview mirror, then twisted around in her seat to get a direct view. She was amazed by what she saw.

In the oxygen-rich atmosphere, the plasma released by the grenade had touched off an instant inferno. Flames fifty feet high engulfed the warehouse. The mat of algae flared into brilliance and, as Gloria watched, the blaze moved rapidly in her direction. Too rapidly.

Gloria wasted no more time watching. She gunned the skimmer and dashed forward. Ahead, Rick and Alex had flung their weapons aside and were running toward the dock. A quick glance in the mirror told her that they would never make it, so as the skimmer reached the top of the rise, she slowed just enough for the two men to leap onto the flatbed. Gloria charged down the slope, turned sharply, and glided onto the dock. Before she could get out of the door on her side, two of the Bugs had opened the other door and were extracting Marty and Doug from the vehicle. As she darted around the front of the skimmer and headed for the hatch of the Cruiser, she took a last look over her shoulder and saw the blazing algae at the top of the rise. She dived into the Cruiser, the hatch closed, and Erskine maneuvered them away from the dock.

Gloria looked up and saw Volkonski standing above her, a half smile of admiration and amazement on his features.

"Whew!" she said.

"We're not out of the woods yet," he told her. He

extended a hand, pulled her to her feet, then turned and went forward into the cockpit. Gloria followed.

"Erskine?" Volkonski asked.

"Workin' on it, sir!" Erskine replied breathlessly.

"Forget about rocks," Volkonski commanded. "Just get us *up!*"

"Yessir!" Erskine worked the controls so rapidly that even the sensitive mass-repulsion units that softened acceleration and provided ersatz gravity inside the Cruiser couldn't react fast enough. Gloria felt a lurch and almost lost her feet as the Cruiser clawed its way into the sky.

On the image screen, she saw the dock far below, quickly receding into invisibility. Beyond it, a flaming landscape and the warehouse, smoking and blazing. Then, even the warehouse was gone, and there was nothing left to see but the curving shoreline of the big bay—

And a flash that overloaded the imaging system for a moment. When vision was restored, she saw a billow of green fire rising from the receding landscape, and a concentric shock wave racing outward in every direction. She felt a slight bump as it caught up with the Cruiser.

Erskine looked around with a wan, weary grin on his face. "Made it!" he said.

"With six or seven seconds to spare," Volkonski said. "That was cutting it a little fine, Gloria."

Gloria put her fists on her hips and glared at Volkonski. "You're just never satisfied, are you?"

PETRA DOUBLE-CHECKED THE FINAL RESULT. Not because she wasn't sure—she had been sure ever since her moment of enlightenment back in the hotel—but because she needed to steel herself to do what had to be done next. She stared at the console for a long moment, then slid her chair back and got to her feet.

She walked out of her small office and down a corridor to the office of Elizabeth Irons, chief of Internal

Security for Quadrant 4. Petra gave a nod to the assistant at the outer desk, but didn't pause, and barged straight into Iron's office.

Irons's mouth fell open slightly when she saw Petra in her scandalously revealing night-on-the town garb. "Ms. Nash," she said, "I don't know what they wear to work back in Manhattan, but here on New Cambridge—"

Petra interrupted her. "Ms. Irons," she said, "you have to arrest Whitney Bartholemew, Junior—immediately!"

chapter 26

PETRA STOOD ON THE SIDEWALK WITH Elizabeth Irons, a block from the Bartholemew Building in downtown Central, as Dexta, Imperial, and local security forces swarmed around the area. The immediate neighborhood had been evacuated, not that it would make any difference if a quadrijoule plasma bomb detonated. Somewhere high in the building, Whit Bartholemew was surrounded, with no way out, and Spirit knew what he might do.

She wondered how long she had known the truth and refused to recognize it. That moment of enlightenment in the hotel had not come out of nowhere. No one else had seen the truth, either, but no one else had been as close to the investigation or as close to Whit. She could hardly have been closer; just hours ago, he had been inside her, a welcome presence in her body and her life. Even now, she regretted that there would be no trip to Belairus, no more nights of angry lovemaking.

People stared at her, as if they knew what she had been doing; she felt their eyes on her all-but-naked body. She wished that she had taken the time to change her clothes in the suite, but her internal mood somehow matched her external appearance. She was emotionally naked, too, with no fig leaves of rationalization left to hide the truth: She had been passionately involved with a man who was a mass murderer. Something to put on her résumé.

"He wants to see you."

Petra noticed that Irons was staring at her. "What?" she asked.

"I just got word on the comm that Bartholemew wants to see you," Irons said. "He's holed up in his office, and apparently has a detonator switch that he says will set off the plasma bomb. You need to go up there."

"Yes, ma'am," Petra said. "I guess I do."

"A hundred million people could die if he sets off that bomb. We can't evacuate the city—it would be foolish to try. I'd give you a weapon of some kind, except that you have nowhere to hide it, and he'd probably insist on a strip search anyway. But if you get the chance to disarm or disable him . . ."

"I know a little Qatsima," Petra said. Very little, she silently added.

Irons nodded. "Don't take any unnecessary risks. Keep him talking as long as you can. We have teams searching his properties around the city, and every other likely location. With luck, we'll find the bomb before he can detonate it."

"Yes, ma'am. And if I could suggest something, maybe you should try to find his mother."

"Already in the works, Ms. Nash. But you're the one he wants to see. Good luck." Irons offered her hand, and Petra shook it.

All was silent, except for the click of her high heels on the pavement, as she walked the block to the Bartholemew Building. The light breeze felt cold on her exposed flesh, and she fought off a shudder. Uniformed

Bugs and cops stared at her as she passed, and the high gravity of this world had never seemed higher. The entire planet pulled at her.

She entered the building and was shepherded to the elevator. A Bug she didn't know joined her on the ascent. "He has a little switch in his right hand," he said. "If he puts it down for any reason, just hit your wristcom's transmit button, and we'll be in the office a second later. But whatever you do, don't try to take the switch away from him."

They reached the floor of Bartholemew's office, and the Bug guided her out of the elevator, past dozens of tense security people. He pointed toward the door to the inner office and said, "We're all counting on you, Ms. Nash."

"Yes," she said. "I know."

Bartholemew was waiting for her, seated behind his big desk. In his neat, dark business suit, he didn't look much like an anarchist. He smiled at her, and Petra couldn't help returning it. She stopped a few feet in front of his desk and waited.

"So, you figured it out, did you, Petra Nash?"

"Isn't that what you wanted?" Petra asked him.

Bartholemew made a little head motion. "Perhaps," he said.

"I should have realized sooner. All that radical rhetoric. And dragging me out of the Old Annex just before you blew it up. And then insisting that we leave on the trip Sunday morning, just before the Emperor's speech. You couldn't have been more obvious if you'd left a trail of bread crumbs, but I was too dumb to see it."

"Not so dumb. I mean, here we are, aren't we? The fate of millions riding on our every word, perhaps the very future of the Empire itself hanging in the balance."

"I think the Empire will survive, no matter what happens."

"Your precious Empire will collapse of its own

weight," Bartholemew said, letting his familiar anger show. "If not now, then later. I'm merely giving it a timely shove. Even if I don't get the Emperor himself—thanks to you—I'll still get my saintly old grandfather and half the bureaucratic offal in the Quadrant. People will see that there is nothing inevitable about Imperial rule."

"And they'll rise up and spontaneously overthrow their oppressors?" Petra asked.

"With a little help and guidance," Bartholemew replied. "Operatives from PAIN are on half the planets in the Quadrant, ready and fully capable of providing a revolutionary vanguard to lead the uprising."

"Maybe," Petra said, "but they'll have to do it without all those weapons you've got on GAC 4367. I found them, Whit. That's where Gloria is right now."

Bartholemew frowned. He seemed genuinely and unpleasantly surprised. Then he nodded and said, "That B & Q data?"

"That's right. It took some work, but eventually I figured out where that Savoy shipment had to have gone. And then I used the same process to track that freighter you leased in November. That's when you brought the bomb and the other weapons to New Cambridge."

"Right again," Bartholemew acknowledged. "That idiot Quincannon gave you everything you needed."

"And that's why you killed him?"

"One of the reasons," Bartholemew said.

Petra closed her eyes for a moment and saw, again, the battered corpse in the dark, old office. "You did it yourself?" she asked him.

"With my own two hands," he said, a note of satisfaction in his voice. "What's more, I personally set the grenades in the Old Annex building. I had some help for the others, of course, but I'm not one of those delegate-everything leaders. I wasn't afraid to get blood on my hands—literally, in the case of Quincannon. I did my share of the killing. A necessary overture to the symphony of destruction to follow. Anticipation is an essential element of terror, you see. Spreading fear and a sense of helplessness, underlining the authorities' impotence—it all contributes to the final result."

"More than two hundred people died that night, Whit," Petra said.

"And a hundred million more will die if—when—I flick this switch," he said, holding up the tiny device between his right thumb and forefinger.

"And you'll be one of them. So will I. So will your mother."

"An unfortunate but necessary sacrifice. We might have avoided that if you hadn't been such a dedicated little bureaucrat."

"Do you really want to kill them, Whit? Do you want to kill your mother? Do you want to kill me?"

"No," he said, "truthfully, I don't. Not you, not Mother, nor any of those faceless millions. Quincannon's another story. But I honestly have no desire to kill all those people."

"Then why do it?"

"Historical necessity. We anarchists understand that destruction is really the most profound act of creation. Did you know that a hundred million sperm cells die in order to fertilize a single egg? Today, a hundred million people will die to fertilize the egg of revolution."

"Bullshit!"

Bartholemew tilted his head to one side. "Yes," he said, "I suppose that one was a bit of a reach, wasn't it? They can't all be gems. But the point remains, and it is not merely bullshit. From the collision of opposing forces, new worlds are born. Better worlds. That is the inevitable result of the historical dialectic."

"If it's inevitable," Petra said, "then why do this? Why not let history work things out for itself?"

"Fabian heresy!" Bartholemew cried out in mock

horror. "Like the benighted masses themselves, you lack the ideological underpinnings necessary to appreciate the beauty and necessity of revolutionary acts. History requires human agents to work its will. A few people among trillions understand that and have the courage and selflessness to make themselves into such agents. We offer ourselves as necessary sacrifices upon the altar of history."

"Oh, brother." Petra sighed. "Courage! Self-sacrifice! My goodness, I never knew you were such a great man, Whit. Here I thought you were just a bitter, resentful, angry, and confused guy who was pissed off at his father."

"Well . . . that, too," Bartholemew conceded, offering Petra a crooked smile. "Individuals have histories, no less than empires. I admit, if I'd had a happy home life, I probably wouldn't have spent twenty years working to build up PAIN, diverting funds, providing safe houses, and so on. It was the dialectic applied to the Bartholemew family, I suppose. The father works to build an empire, of sorts, and the son devotes himself to destroying it. Tell me, is that Hegelian, or merely Oedipal?"

"It's just sick, if you ask me. All this bullshit about historical forces—Spirit, Whit, do you really believe any of that stuff? Or is it just something you tell yourself to justify your fantasies?"

Bartholemew was silent a moment. Then he said, "Sometimes I believe it."

"And sometimes you don't?"

"Sometimes it's historical, sometimes it's personal. I admit the possibility that I'm wrong about the history. It's a big subject, after all, and it's possible that no one really understands it. But I believe that history requires us to act, in spite of our doubts and reservations."

"Did history require you to beat Jamie Quincannon to death with your bare hands?" Petra asked him. "He was a nice old man, Whit. I saw what you did to him."

"But you never saw what he did to me," Bartholemew said. His ruddy face darkened, and he looked down at his desk for a moment.

"What do you mean?"

"About forty years ago," he said, lifting his gaze to meet hers, "I was entrusted to the care of that nice old man. And he took me up to that office—the very same office where I killed him—and . . . and he did things. Hateful things."

"He molested you?"

"He did. Even then, I knew it was wrong, somehow. And I desperately wanted to tell someone. But my mother . . . somehow, I knew she wouldn't have understood. Or wouldn't have been able to do anything about it. I knew I needed to tell my father, but I couldn't. Quincannon was my father's partner, you see, and I was only his son. I didn't want to force him to choose between the two of us, because I knew what his choice would have been. So I never told anyone . . . until this very moment, Petra Nash. Since we are both about to die, it seems appropriate. Anyway, I grew up feeling as if *I* had done something shameful and unforgivable. Eventually I realized how foolish I had been, but by then, it was too late to change anything. The child I was had grown to be the man I am."

"I'm sorry, Whit," Petra said. "That must have been awful for you. But do a hundred million people have to die just because you had a terrible childhood?"

"You think it's infantile revenge?"

"Isn't it?"

"If it were no more than that, you'd have a point." Bartholemew spent a moment staring at the device in his hand, then looked back at Petra. "I told you once that my father and I never really talked. But when he knew he was dying, he wrote me a letter that I received after his death. It was mostly just an exercise in self-justification, a litany of excuses for all his parental failures. Exactly the sort of thing you'd expect a man like that to say under the circumstances. But it also contained a few revelations that gave me a new resolve. You might say it was that letter that put this switch in my hand."

"What do you mean?"

"Dear old Dad tried to explain to me how it came to pass that he married my mother. It seems that my grandfather had made a big mistake. Details were not specified, but I gather that it was one of those grand, history-altering mistakes. Anyway, Norman Mingus, being intelligent, resourceful, and altogether unscrupulous, called upon Whitney Bartholemew to help him cover up that mistake. My father, you see, had the means available to help my grandfather dispose of the evidence."

"The Savoy shipment?"

"Precisely. Father's letter was unclear about exactly what happened and why, but he was explicit about the price he demanded in return for his help. The price was my mother, the lovely young Saffron Mingus. She was the belle of the Quadrant in those days, and she was engaged to Cornell DuBray, my grandfather's faithful assistant. But young Whitney Bartholemew had desired her from afar, and now he seized his opportunity to have her for his own. And my grandfather obliged him, gave him what he wanted. Again, details were lacking, but he promptly delivered my mother to my father as if she were . . . a shipment of arms."

Bartholemew smiled—to himself, it seemed to Petra. She realized that his words were for himself, as well. He had wanted her here merely as a sounding board, an audience for his final soliloquy.

"In the process of all this self-revelation," Bartholemew went on, "my father revealed to me the whereabouts of that Savoy shipment. He said that he had kept his part of the deal with my grandfather and had never attempted to move or sell those weapons. Mingus had apparently hoped that he would simply destroy them, but never really inquired. But old Bart was no fool, and knew that those weapons might give him considerable leverage if it ever became necessary to strike another deal with Mingus, who soon became Secretary of Dexta. I gather that he never had to use them for that purpose, but the potential was always there. Anyway, as a final gesture of filial affection, dear old Dad passed the secret on to me, his only begotten son. He figured that I could use that knowledge to extort Mingus for any favors that *I* might need in the future. A wonderful gesture, don't you think? Except that Father never realized that I might think of another use for those weapons. I doubt that he even thought of them as weapons, per se, merely as potential blackmail material. But to me, they were precisely what they were intended to be—weapons that might be used against a powerful enemy. Like the greasy little criminal he was, Dad always thought too small. He thought he might use those weapons to blackmail Mingus and figuratively destroy him. I'll use them to destroy him physically, and much else. Perhaps even the Empire itself."

"And me," Petra added quietly. "And your mother."

"I'm truly sorry about that, Petra Nash."

"I don't want to die, Whit," she said. But she was certain now that she would. Her chin trembled and her eyes filled with tears.

"You're not going to cry, are you? I hate it when women do that. It's so terribly unfair."

"What were you going to do with me if I'd gone to Belairus? Keep me captive? Hold me hostage?"

Bartholemew shook his head. "I'd simply have loved you, as well and as truly as I could," he said. "I'd have run my various enterprises from there, of course, and continued helping PAIN as the revolution unfolded around us. But you would have been safe. And happy, I'd like to think."

"I don't think so," Petra said.

"Who can say?" Bartholemew asked. "But I wanted you to be happy, if that means anything. You made *me* happy, at least. No one had ever really done that before. Oh, now, stop that crying! I told you, it isn't fair."

"But it's fair for you to kill me? Forget about the other hundred million people, Whit. You're killing *me*!"

"I'm sorry. But I no longer have any choice."

"Of course you do, Whit! The choice has *always* been yours! Put it down, Whit! Put down your anger— and for Spirit's sake, put down that damned switch!"

"You heard her, dear. Put it down. I'm not ready to die yet, either."

Bartholemew looked up and Petra looked behind her. Saffron Mingus Bartholemew had entered the office, looking solemn and gravely beautiful. She stared at her son with loving, disappointed eyes.

"Put it down, Sonny," she said softly. "Put it down now. Make your mother happy."

Bartholemew looked at her, his eyes bright and shining. At last, he said, "Yes, Mother."

And he put it down.

chapter 27

GLORIA STOOD IN THE RECEIVING LINE AT THE
entrance to the Ellisons' ballroom and watched as the
Emperor approached. Black-clad Imperial Security
forces were everywhere, but the mood was festive and
relieved. The greatest threat to the Empire since the
Fifth of October Plot had been overcome—at least, that
was what the media said—and Gloria and the OSI had
played a vital role in that triumph. It was a night to crow,
and she felt proud and happy.

Charles, resplendent in his gaudiest Imperials, was
accompanied by his cousin, Lord Brockinbrough, and
Larry's son, Gareth, as well as a flock of aides, equerries,
and ranking flotsam. First in the reception line was
President Ogburn; he and Charles exchanged minutely
calculated bows. The legal fiction maintained that the
Emperor could not set foot on a planet without the invitation of the local government, and all the necessary rit-
uals were observed.

Following Ogburn came the Ellisons and their son,
hosts for the affair, then Quadrant Administrator

Cornell DuBray, the Parliament Minister from New Cambridge, a collection of local and Dexta bigwigs, and finally, Gloria VanDeen, Director of the Office of Strategic Intervention, whose reception this was. Conspicuous by his absence was Dexta Secretary Norman Mingus. His daughter, Saffron Mingus Bartholemew, was also absent. And his grandson was in prison.

Gloria's satisfaction over the resolution of the PAIN threat was tempered by her awareness of the very personal pain it had caused Norman Mingus. Publicly, details about the Savoy shipment remained hidden, but it was impossible to hide the fact that Mingus's grandson had been deeply involved in terrorism. Unflattering facts about Whitney Bartholemew, Senior, had also been dredged up, and an unwelcome spotlight had been aimed at Saffron Mingus Bartholemew. The media were already speculating about whether Norman Mingus might be forced to resign over the affair.

Gloria could not bring herself to believe that it would come to that. Mingus had told her once that he would never resign, and, after forty-two years in office, he was far too wise in the ways of power to allow himself to be forced out.

The Emperor made his way down the line, seemingly relaxed and unhurried. Gloria marveled at Charles's ability to put commoners at ease and give them the impression that there was nothing more important in all the Empire than making small talk with his subjects. After two weeks of nearly nonstop schmoozing, Gloria thought she was beginning to get the hang of it, herself, and the experience would come in handy if she decided to become Empress. *If.*

She still didn't know and hadn't had time to give the matter much thought. But the sudden reversal of OSI's fortunes made a future in Dexta seem more viable than it had a few weeks ago, when Erik Manko loomed large on her horizon. And, as Empress, would she be permitted the fun of dashing off to putrid scumworlds and risking her life in hand-to-hand combat with dangerous terrorists? Unlikely.

And then Charles was standing before her, handsome and grinning. Gloria gave him a little bow and let him clasp her hands. "A splendid reception, Ms. VanDeen," said the Emperor in a formal and audible voice. "We thank you for inviting us."

"And you honor OSI by your presence, Highness."

Formalities out of the way, Charles ran his eyes over Gloria's almost entirely naked body. She was wearing nothing but two strands of alternating diamonds and lapis lazuli, one low around her hips and the other hanging down from it to provide strategic, if symbolic, coverage, along with matching bracelets and earrings. She had last worn the gems on Mynjhino, on an evening that had ended in gunfire. No such excitement seemed likely tonight.

"Those diamonds look vaguely familiar," Charles said in a quieter, more private voice.

"They should," Gloria said. "You gave them to me for our second anniversary. You said the lapis lazuli matched my eyes."

"Ah, yes. I did, and it does. You look marvelous, as always, Glory."

Gloria leaned close to him and whispered in his ear. "You got my message?"

"I did."

"And you brought the . . . uh . . . item?"

"Right here in my pocket."

"Thanks, Chuckles. I owe you one."

"No, I think it is I who owe you. A nice piece of work, Glory, by all concerned. We'll talk later. For the moment, I still have some Imperializing to do." Charles kissed Gloria's hand, gazed into her eyes for a few long seconds, then moved on to mingle with the local gentry.

Larry and Gareth were next. Gloria shook hands with them and said, "Lord Brockinbrough, Gareth, thank you for coming tonight."

"The pleasure's all ours, Gloria," Larry said expansively. "I trust you'll be coming to visit my humble residence?"

"Not tonight, Larry," Gloria said. "Maybe tomorrow, after Charles's speech. I didn't realize that you had an estate here."

"One big one in each Quadrant, and a scattering of lesser hovels. My forebears liked to feel at home wherever they went. By the way, congratulations on your latest coup."

"Yeah," Gareth added, "that was pretty cool stuff, Gloria."

"Thank you, gentlemen."

The Brockinbroughs moved on, replaced by a Duke and Duchess, then a smattering of lesser Lords and Ladies. Gloria smiled her way through the rest of the formal presentations, then finally broke free to do some mingling of her own. She wandered out onto the dance floor and drank in the ambience.

Althea's little blues band had turned out to be a twenty-piece orchestra that specialized in twentieth-century music of all kinds. They played a few blues numbers, but also everything from Irving Berlin to the Beatles. When they struck up "In the Mood," Gloria found a partner and assayed an acceptable thirty-third-century version of the jitterbug. Three more men took turns cutting in on each other as they danced with her to the plaintive melody of "Yesterday." Then Gloria saw something that provoked a laugh and inspired her to do some cutting in of her own.

Elaine Murakami was dancing with Cornell DuBray to a Gershwin tune. Smiling, she tapped Elaine on the shoulder and said, "Pardon me, Elaine, but I'm pulling rank on you." Elaine giggled and got out of the way.

"Administrator DuBray," Gloria said, "I hope you're not planning to steal Elaine from me. OSI is very jealous of its personnel."

"Fear not, Ms. VanDeen," DuBray said. "Elaine is a delicious little treat in bed, but she wasn't much of a spy."

"You knew that I knew?"

"I figured it out quickly enough. You do have a way of inspiring loyalty in your people. In any event, I'll see to it that her father is released from prison."

"Thank you. You're very gracious in defeat."

DuBray raised an eyebrow. "I wasn't aware that I had been defeated."

"Well," Gloria said, "you certainly haven't won. In case you hadn't noticed, OSI is here to stay."

"Yes, I suppose it is. Very nicely played, I must admit. You won the hearts and minds of the Dexta masses, then capped it off with a dazzling bit of personal bravado. The Quad Admins can hardly dispatch you to bureaucratic limbo after such a performance."

"We're the Fifth Quadrant now," Gloria said. "Get used to it."

DuBray actually laughed at that. "As I told you, Gloria, we really are on the same side. OSI's triumph is Dexta's triumph, and Dexta's triumph is my own. However, we still have our differences, and don't imagine that the Quad Admins will simply bow before your brilliance. We won't, you know."

"I'd be disappointed if you did," she said. "I look forward to a long and lively rivalry."

"As a matter of fact," said DuBray, "so do I."

PETRA WISHED SHE WERE SOMEWHERE ELSE.
Anywhere. Weehawken, even.

After what had happened the day before, she was not really in the mood for festivities and gaiety, least of all at the Ellisons' bemuraled mansion. Barely a month ago, she had enjoyed her triumphant entry into New Cambridge society in this same ballroom, but she could take no pleasure in the memory. She had lost Pug, she had lost Whit, and somehow, she felt that she had lost herself.

She didn't feel like being a Tiger tonight—maybe not on any night, ever again—but she had discovered that she had little choice. She'd had no time to run out and buy something conservative, so she found herself wearing a violet gown with a wide, deep neckline and a plunging back. Just the thing for a woman who romanced mass murderers.

On a night when she wanted to attract as little attention as possible, she found herself being asked to dance and offered drinks by a seemingly endless succession of smiling Dexta men. They offered their congratulations and expressed their admiration while staring at her daring cleavage, and Petra simply smiled grimly and tried to get through the evening without a complete emotional meltdown.

And there were the Ellisons to be endured. The haughty parents and their upward-bound son, with Steffany Fairchild at his side. She had exchanged formal and frosty greetings, then tried to avoid them. But she could feel them, staring down their noses at her, disapproving of her very existence.

She had also tried to avoid the media riot that followed the capture of Whit Bartholemew and the subsequent recovery of the missing plasma bomb. Dexta Internal Security had clamped a tight lid on the precise facts, but the Public Affairs Office could not resist exploiting such a triumph, and very much against her will, Petra had been trotted out at a press conference that afternoon. She had made a brief statement, then offered terse answers to a flurry of questions. When someone asked her about the nature of her relationship with

Whitney Bartholemew, Junior, she had said only, "We were friends," then quickly exited the meeting.

Her friend had tried to blow up the city, and she had tried to put him in jail. Friends, indeed. They hadn't really been friends, at all. They had been hot, passionate, angry lovers, each seeking something indefinable from the other. Perhaps Whit had sought something normal in her, some link to an everyday existence that he despised; and perhaps she had yearned for something abnormal in him, an expression of defiance and rebellion against a world that had rejected her. Whit's father ignored him, but hers had walked out on her. Pug's parents pushed him upward; her mother seemed to want to pull her downward. One lover killed, another yanked away from her by his family, and a third who was nothing less than a monster. Some life.

There was a sudden regal fanfare from the orchestra, and the Emperor appeared on the bandstand. Petra watched from the far end of the ballroom and wondered what was going on.

"One of the nice things about being Emperor," Charles said as a hush fell over the crowd, "is that occasionally it is my lot to recognize and reward the accomplishments of certain of my subjects. While it is something I enjoy, it is not something I do lightly. Imperial honors are not easily earned, nor carelessly handed out. They signify that the person designated has served the Empire in a way that goes beyond the norm and is worthy of our highest recognition and gratitude. Tonight, it gives me great personal pleasure to honor one such individual. Would you please come forward and be recognized . . . Petra Nash!"

It took a moment to register. *Me?*

All around her, people were applauding. They opened a path for her, and Petra found herself walking dazedly forward, then up the steps to the bandstand, where the smiling Emperor awaited her. He put a hand on her shoulder and maneuvered her around till she stood next to him. Petra looked around, still not certain there hadn't been some mistake.

Charles raised an arm, quieted the crowd, then dipped his hand into a pocket of his tunic and withdrew a blue-and-gold ribbon with a large gold medallion dangling from it. "Petra Nash," he said, gazing directly into her eyes, "in recognition of your outstanding and meritorious service to the people of the Empire, and with deep personal gratitude for a job well and bravely done, I am pleased to present you, on behalf of three trillion grateful and admiring subjects, the Imperial Distinguished Service Medal." With that, he draped the ribbon around her neck. The golden ornament, with a profile of Hazar the Great etched on it, felt cold and heavy as it nestled between her breasts. She found it hard to breathe.

As the applause swelled, the Emperor bent down and said, "Congratulations, Ms. Nash. Would you do me the honor of the next dance?"

Petra gulped and nodded. Charles took her by the hand and led her down to the dance floor. The orchestra began to play "Moonlight Serenade" as the Emperor put his arm around her and guided her around the floor.

"I'm glad we finally had the chance to meet," Charles said. "Gloria often speaks of you."

"She mentions you, too, sometimes, Your Highness," Petra managed to reply.

"Favorably, I trust?"

"Uh . . . mostly, sire."

"Yes, well, I'm hoping I can enlist your aid in a most important matter, Ms. Nash. As you must be aware, I've asked her to marry me again and become Empress. I fear she's reluctant to leave Dexta, however, and I know she would not want to be separated from her dearest friend. So you must promise me that if Gloria agrees to become Empress, you will accompany her to Rio and serve as her personal assistant."

"Uh . . ."

"And, of course, if you do, you won't simply be Petra Nash."

"I won't?"

"No, you'll be Lady Petra of Weehawken. Sounds rather nice, doesn't it? You know, I don't believe I've ever ennobled anyone from New Jersey before."

Petra nearly tripped over her own feet, but the Emperor smoothly rescued her and smiled down at her. At six feet four inches, he towered over her.

"Your . . . Your . . . uh, Highness," Petra stammered, "I . . . I . . ."

"You will help me persuade Gloria, won't you? As Emperor, I know the importance of having strategic allies."

"I . . . uh . . ."

Charles laughed indulgently. "Say no more, Ms. Nash. Just keep my request in mind, if you would."

"I certainly will, Your Highness."

"Splendid." As the song ended with the familiar swirl of Miller reeds and muted horns, the Emperor leaned over and gave Petra a kiss on her lips. Then he stepped back and led the crowd in applauding her once again. Amid the kaleidoscope of color and noise, Petra saw the Ellisons standing at one side of the room. Mr. and Mrs. Ellison were clapping politely, Steffany Fairchild looked supremely miffed, but Pug was staring right at her, grinning, and slapping his hands together with enthusiasm. Petra grinned back at him.

Maybe she was glad to be here, after all, she thought.

AMONG HIS OTHER ACCOMPLISHMENTS, ELI Opatnu proved to be an excellent dancer. To the strains of "I've Got You Under My Skin," he whirled Gloria around the dance floor with grace and aplomb.

"I'm so happy for Petra," she told him. "She's had a tough time of it lately."

"Honors well deserved," Opatnu agreed. "And you didn't do so badly, yourself. But then, you already got a medal for Mynjhino, didn't you?"

"You'll get one of your own someday, Eli."

"I doubt it," he said. "Certainly, I won't get one for what I have to do now. Gloria, you have to shut down the investigation of Wendover and the double-flagging operation."

"What do you mean, I *have* to?" she demanded angrily. "Where do you get off telling me to do a thing like that? I realize it might be an embarrassment for your Sector, but—"

"You don't understand, Gloria. I'm not telling you this for myself. I'm speaking on behalf of Ed Smith."

Gloria looked up at Opatnu in openmouthed shock. In return, he gave her a guilty shrug.

"Did you imagine you were the only one in Dexta who had a debt to the zamitat?"

"Spirit!" Gloria breathed.

"I'm just thirty-seven," Opatnu said, "and I'm already a Level Seven and a Sector Administrator. I'd like to think that my native abilities had something to do with that, but the truth is, I've had some help. Of course, that kind of help isn't free. You should realize that by now, Gloria."

Gloria took a deep breath and let the air out very slowly. "I guess I did realize it," she said. "I just didn't think I'd be making a payment so soon. It won't be easy to tell Jill."

"Jill will get over it," Opatnu assured her. "And what does it matter? This Wendover thing is just routine. The zamies aren't asking you to sell your soul to Beelzebub. They just want a little help. They turn a few extra crowns on the double-flagging, a couple of minor Dexta officials get some kickbacks, and the Empire loses a little tax money that it will never miss. As I said, it's routine."

"And what's in it for you, Eli?"

"The continuing gratitude and cooperation of Ed Smith and people like him. I get to look good, appear to be clean, and go on doing what I think has been pretty good work for the people of the Empire. The same goes for you, Gloria."

"I suppose so," she said. Ever since that meeting in the restaurant with Ed Smith, she had known this day would come. She had accepted it then, and she had to accept it now. It was just quid pro quo, after all. Routine.

OPATNU CAUGHT DUBRAY'S EYE, THEN FOL-lowed him into an unoccupied sitting room just off the ballroom. "You told her?" DuBray asked him.

Opatnu nodded. "The deed is done," he said.

"And how did she take it?"

"She accepted the necessity. You know, this whole thing would have been much easier if you'd told me in the beginning that she has a debt to our friends."

DuBray shrugged. "If I had known, I would have. That's one of the problems in dealing with our friends. Half the time, one of their hands doesn't know what the other hand is up to. Fortunately, I got to wondering how she dealt with Manko and made some inquiries. It surprised me a bit, I can tell you. Pure and high-minded Gloria VanDeen!"

"She's as human as the rest of us."

"And as flawed, it would seem. In any case, our friends will be pleased that the investigation has been buried. With the new product ready to hit market, this was no time for complications."

"I just wonder how Jill will take it," Opatnu said.

"Jill?"

"Clymer. The one who was running the investigation."

"Of course. Why, will she be a problem?"

"Probably not. But she won't be happy about it."

DuBray clapped a hand on Opatnu's shoulder. "Take some advice, Eli," he said. "Stop worrying about other people's happiness. We don't do these things to be liked, you know."

"Why do we do them?"

The two men stared into each other's eyes for a long, silent moment. Finally, DuBray said, "What else is there?"

"WHY DO I HAVE TO DISCONTINUE THE INVESTIgation?" Jill Clymer demanded. "I've worked hard on this, Gloria, and I don't see why we should just stop in midstream."

Jill had raised her voice a little when Gloria gave her the news, so Gloria took her by the arm and led her off to one side of the ballroom. The band was playing "With a Little Help from My Friends."

"Jill," Gloria said, "I appreciate all the work you've done. But the way things are shaping up, with the restraining order and everything, it looks as if this could drag on for months or years. I just don't think this is the kind of thing that OSI should be getting involved with. Send me all the files you've put together, and I'll see to it that the Comptroller's Office gets them. It's more their sort of thing, and maybe they'll want to pursue it. But as of now, OSI is out of it."

"Is this your decision," Jill asked, "or are you getting pressure from higher up?"

"Nothing from higher up," Gloria replied, accurately, if not with complete honesty. "It's my decision."

"Well, I don't like it."

"You don't have to like it, Jill. You just have to do it."

"I see." Jill stared at her for another moment, then turned and walked away.

It hadn't been so difficult, after all. In fact, Gloria was mildly surprised by how easy it was.

Routine.

chapter 28

HAPPY BUT EXHAUSTED, GLORIA AND PETRA returned to the suite at the Imperial Cantabragian sometime after two in the morning. During the limo ride, Petra had alternately stared off into space with a distracted half smile on her face and babbled almost incoherently. The prospect of becoming Lady Petra of Weehawken had all but unhinged her. At the same time, she was well aware that Gloria had not made up her mind about becoming Empress.

"Maybe you could do both," Petra had suggested. "Be Empress Tuesdays, Thursdays, and weekends, and Director of OSI Mondays, Wednesdays, and Fridays."

"I don't think that would work very well."

"Then alternate weeks? Or months?"

"You really want that title, don't you?"

"Well . . . yeah, I guess so. Spirit, Gloria, I don't know. I mean, I'd hate to leave Dexta, but . . . well, you know . . ."

"Yes," Gloria said, "I do."

"And the Emperor!" Petra gushed. "I mean, he's

just so handsome and tall and dreamy. How can you resist him, Gloria?"

"I've had plenty of practice."

"Oh. Yeah, I see what you mean." Petra had lapsed into silence for a while and stared out the window of the limo. Then a goofy smile crept over her face and she said, "I danced with the Emperor!"

They walked into the suite, with Petra humming "Moonlight Serenade," and Gloria noticed the message light on the pad she had left on the coffee table. It proved to be a message from Norman Mingus, asking her to come upstairs to see him when she got in, no matter how late.

After a moment's indecision, Gloria reluctantly removed her diamonds and slipped into some jeans and a tee shirt. She knew Mingus liked to see her in full flower, but she had a feeling that this was not the right time. She said good night to Petra and went to the elevator.

There was still a gaggle of Bugs upstairs, but she breezed through them, was met by an aide, and directed into Mingus's bedroom. She found him there, in pajamas, robe, and slippers, sitting quietly in a comfortable chair. On the table next to him stood a bottle of what appeared to be Belgravian whisky, reputedly the best in the Empire. No milk and cookies on this night. Gloria walked over to him, gave him a kiss on the cheek, then sat down in a chair next to his.

"You missed a good party, Norman," she said. "I'm sorry you weren't there, but I understand."

"I saw some of it on the vid," he said. "You looked very enticing. And I'm pleased for Ms. Nash. She deserved that medal."

"And she gets to be Lady Petra of Weehawken if I go back to Charles," Gloria said. "But I think it would be nice if she also got something from Dexta."

"Yes," said Mingus, "I had thoughts along the same

line. She's a Thirteen now? Very well, in the morning, you can tell her she's a Twelve."

"Thank you, Norman. That's very sweet of you."

"Nonsense. She's earned it." Mingus turned a little in his chair to look directly at Gloria. "As for you, young lady, I ought to demote you for that harebrained stunt."

"You gave me the job, Norman," Gloria said placidly, "and harebrained stunts were always a part of it."

"I never meant for you to put yourself at risk like that."

"If I hadn't been there, it would have turned into a stalemate, or worse. I did what I thought was necessary, and it worked."

"I can't deny that," said Mingus. "Nevertheless, I would prefer it if your personal interventions remained strategic rather than tactical."

"Don't get too attached to me Norman," Gloria advised. "You could lose me, one way or another."

Mingus stared at her for a moment. "Charles?"

"I'm still considering it," she said. "I'm going to spend some time with him tomorrow after his speech. Maybe I'll be able to make up my mind."

"I see," he said. "Naturally, Gloria, I hope that you'll decide to remain with Dexta. But you must do what you think is best for yourself. Forgive me, would you care for some whisky? Or anything else?"

Gloria shook her head. "No thank you. I'm fine."

Mingus lifted a tumbler to his lips and took a slow sip of the Belgravian whisky. He held the glass there for a moment, wordlessly staring off into the mid distance.

"Norman? I'm awfully sorry about what's happened."

"As am I," he said as he put the glass back down on the tabletop. "Oh, I'm certain I shall survive the storm, personally. Internal Security has seen to it that those who are aware of what transpired between Ms. Nash and my grandson will keep their mouths shut. What scandal there is will quickly dissipate. My grandson's trial will be a private affair, under Imperial Security, and no one will ever learn the full truth of the matter. Except for you, Gloria. That's why I asked you here tonight. I think you deserve to know."

"Petra told me what Whit said, so I think I have some idea of what actually happened."

Mingus shook his head. "No," he said, "you don't. Only four people ever knew the whole truth of it, and now one of them is dead. Cornell DuBray and my daughter are the others."

"You don't need to tell me, Norman," Gloria said.

"Yes," he said, "I do. I need to tell it, and you need to hear it. If you truly intend to run Dexta someday, you should know what that entails. You should know what it might cost you."

Mingus poured some more whisky, then took a healthy swig of it. "Belgravian," he said. "Are you sure you won't have some?"

"Maybe a little." Mingus reached for a second tumbler and poured a couple of fingers of the amber liquid into it. Gloria took a sip of it and let its silky smoothness caress her tongue for a moment.

"You know that I was Quadrant Administrator here in the summer of 3163," Mingus began. "I already had prospects of rising to the position of Secretary, but that was not yet a certainty. My predecessor, Tom McIntyre, still had a few good years left in him, and I had a potential rival or two. Still, my prospects were good, and I intended to make the most of them. I tell you this because it's important that you keep in mind as you hear what follows the central fact of my personal ambition. Whatever my other motives and justifications for what happened, they cannot be separated from my sense of self-interest, my sense of entitlement. If you are to judge me—and you will—you must keep that in mind."

"I have no intention of judging you, Norman," Gloria protested. "I don't want to do that."

"You must," he said. "And inescapably, you will."

Mingus drank some more whisky and focused his gaze on the darkness in a far corner of the room. "We were going to have a war," he said. "A big one. Everyone knew it. We had been fencing with the Ch'gnth for hundreds of years, and by the middle of the last century, conflict had become all but inevitable. The Emperor, Edward III, had been on the throne for more than thirty years and had just a few more years to live. He was not a bad Emperor, and he had some competent people around him. And Tom McIntyre was, at his best, quite capable. Yet there was a pervading sense of drift in those final years before the war, a lack of focus. We were not truly prepared for the war we knew was coming. I suppose no one quite believed that it would really happen. The Empire hadn't fought a major war in nearly a century, and the prospect of one seemed unreal, somehow. We stood on the brink of a precipice, idly playing lawn croquet as the ground crumbled beneath our feet, and wondered only how that would affect our next shot. It's one of those things that historians and posterity can never truly understand because they weren't there and didn't breathe the same air as we did.

"So there I was, Administrator of a Quadrant that was about to explode. And I knew, to a near certainty, that when the Ch'gnth attack came, it would be focused on Savoy, just seventy-five light-years from where we sit. Just three days away for a battle fleet. Ch'gnth space was closed to us, of course, but we had some scattered intelligence reports from neutral traders, and we knew that the Ch'gnth were assembling a powerful strike force in the region. And, of course, galactography virtually dictated that they would attack Savoy. It was a salient, intruding into space that was rightfully theirs. Once they had it, the entire Empire position in this Quadrant would be at risk. Their next target would surely have been New Cambridge, and from there, they would have had a clear path leading to Earth itself. Thus, the strategic position."

Mingus took some more whisky, then continued.

"We weren't blind to it, of course. I had been sending warnings to Earth for years. I was rather strident about it, in fact, and I suppose that contributed to their tendency to discount my recommendations. In any event, little was done to strengthen materially our position here. Oh, there were plans aplenty, the occasional Fleet Exercise and what have you, but somehow the essential gravity of the situation never truly penetrated. It wasn't until negotiations finally broke down in June of 3163 that anyone in authority on Earth fully appreciated the urgency of the situation. So they quickly threw together a shipment of arms and sent it to New Cambridge, for transshipment to Savoy. It arrived here in August. But by then, it was too late." Mingus looked at Gloria and added, "Or so I believed."

"The history books say that you were the only leader at the time with the vision to see what was coming," Gloria said.

Mingus allowed himself a marginal smile. "The history books," he said, "are wrong. As usual. There were others. Even as I sat here dithering on New Cambridge, Admiral Bryant was already pulling together the pieces of what would become the Second Fleet. That's important for you to understand. For all my presumed vision and foresight, I was only viewing things from my own limited perspective. Here in Quadrant 4, things looked truly desperate. But there were three other Quadrants, you see. The Empire was never quite as fragile and vulnerable as it appeared to me. Others, with a broader vision—like Admiral Bryant—had a more comprehensive and realistic understanding of our position. But I could see no farther than Savoy. And what I saw was that Savoy was doomed."

Mingus shook his head sadly and sighed. He took another sip of whisky.

"I couldn't see it then, of course, but from the distance of half a century, it's clear to me now that in August of 3163, I was in an advanced state of panic. I envisioned the swift and final destruction of Savoy, followed by an inexorable, irresistible attack on New Cambridge. In my mind, Savoy was already lost. Gone. All that mattered was to preserve New Cambridge. Savoy could not be saved, but New Cambridge might be, if we could husband what strength we had and do what was necessary for our defense."

Mingus looked at Gloria. His blue-gray eyes were misted and shining.

"And so," he said, "I didn't send that final shipment of arms on to Savoy. I kept it here, for the defense of New Cambridge. I knowingly decided to sacrifice a hundred million lives on Savoy in order to save my own skin."

"No," Gloria insisted. "You're being too hard on yourself. You already said that you didn't think Savoy could be saved, no matter what you did. Given what you knew and believed at the time, you did the right thing. The only thing possible."

"Wouldn't it be nice to think so?" Mingus said. He poured himself some more whisky. He took another sip and so did Gloria.

"Norman, you can't—"

Mingus raised his hand. "Hear me out, Gloria."

"All right, but I refuse to believe you panicked."

"Call it what you will. If you prefer, say simply that I tragically misjudged the situation. For when the Ch'gnth attack came, on September 8, those weapons were stored in an orbital warehouse above New Cambridge, when they should have been deployed on and around Savoy, where they might have done some good. We heard about the attack from a courier that got through a day later. I fully expected that Savoy would fall within a few days, a week at most. And if it had, I suppose my decision would have been fully justified. That single shipment of arms would not have changed the outcome of the battle. The Ch'gnth force was overwhelming, and would surely have prevailed in time. But time"—he shook his head sadly—"time was what mattered above all.

"Savoy did not fall within a few days. Nor within a week, or even two. It held out for nearly three weeks. Three desperate, bloody, heroic weeks." Mingus shook his head again. For a moment he seemed too overcome with emotion to continue. Gloria made a point of looking away as Mingus dabbed at his eyes.

"Afterward," Mingus went on, "we were able to reconstruct what had happened. To truly understand it, you need to know something about the tactics and weaponry that were employed at the time. In the initial wave of the attack, the Ch'gnth engaged and defeated Savoy's orbital defenses. That was inevitable and nothing could have prevented it. They were just too strong, and Savoy was too weak—in space. But on the surface of the planet, Savoy possessed formidable defenses—and a will to fight that, even now, makes the hairs on the back of my neck stand on end when I think of it."

"Mine too," said Gloria. "I remember learning about it in school when I was a little girl. My teacher cried when she told us about the defense of Savoy. We all did."

Mingus cleared his throat. "Savoy," he said, "has a single major continent, and most of the population was concentrated around Savoy City, on the northern coast. The city was impervious to attack from orbit. The point defenses against space-borne or ballistic projectiles were simply too strong. The only way to get at the city was from the surface. The task facing the Ch'gnth was to establish a bridgehead on the surface, then launch terrain-following missiles aimed, ultimately, at the city. They made three landings. The first was repulsed. So was the second, after a pitched battle that lasted six days. But the third landing succeeded, and the Ch'gnth established a defensible perimeter in a weakly defended desert region, about two thousand kilometers southeast of the city.

"From there, they were able to unleash their terrain-following missiles and literally blast their way forward, toward the city. I saw it from orbit a few months later, and you could see each crater, each blast zone, marching straight as an arrow aimed at the heart of the city. They'd launch a missile and detonate a plasma bomb perhaps twenty kilometers beyond their lines. There simply wasn't time to defend against such an attack; by the time the defenders spotted the launch, the warhead had already exploded. One after another, day after day, more than a hundred of them. Until finally, nineteen days after their initial attack, they reached the city. And annihilated it."

Mingus closed his eyes, leaned back in his chair, and took a deep, slow breath. Then he went on. "By then, of course, they had already exterminated the outlying settlements. And on the nineteenth day, they killed every remaining human being on the planet."

"A hundred million of them," Gloria said softly.

"One hundred and three million, two hundred and seventy-nine thousand, four hundred and ninety-one," Mingus said, "according to the 3160 census. Of course, by September of 3163, it would have been more. But for a round figure, I suppose one hundred million will do."

Mingus poured himself some more whisky and took a big swallow. Gloria sipped some more of her own drink.

"Nineteen days to kill a planet," Mingus said. "And on the twenty-first day, Admiral Bryant and the Second Fleet popped out of Yao Space, suicidally close to the planet, and blasted the Ch'gnth fleet to perdition. They speak of Salamis and Lepanto, Midway and Caliban Four, but really, there had never been anything quite like it. If the navigation had been off by a thousandth of one percent, they'd have smashed into the planet or missed it entirely. If the timing had been off by a tenth of a second, they could not have hit the Ch'gnth fleet. The Spirit must have been with us." Mingus shook his head.

He looked at Gloria. Tears were running down his cheeks. "Do you see now what I had done?" he asked her. "Do you understand the enormity of my crime?"

"Norman—"

"Two days!" Mingus shouted. "Two Spirit-forsaken days! That last shipment of arms, which I, in my vast wisdom, withheld because Savoy was already doomed and could not have been saved—can you tell me that it would not have made a difference? Can you tell me that it would not have given those poor, brave souls the time they needed? A hundred million people, who might have lived, died because of what I did! No, that's wrong. A hundred and three million, two hundred and seventy-nine thousand, four hundred and ninety-one. I mustn't shortchange them. They all counted. Every man, woman, and child. They all counted."

Mingus put a hand over his face and sat there, quietly sobbing. Gloria wiped tears from her own cheeks.

"Norman," she said, reaching for his hand, "you couldn't have known."

"Well, I damned well *should* have known, shouldn't I?" Mingus took a handkerchief out of the pocket of his robe and wiped his face. He cleared his throat and helped himself to more whisky.

"Anyway," he said, "the outcome of the Battle of Savoy left me in a rather embarrassing position. The weapons that might have saved Savoy, the weapons I had withheld, were sitting up there in those orbital warehouses. What was I to do with them? If what I had done ever came to light, I'd have been pilloried . . . lynched. As I should have been. I couldn't just hand them over to Admiral Bryant and say, 'Here, old boy, you might need these,' now, could I? The survival of Savoy had become a moot issue, and all that mattered was the survival of Norman Mingus."

Mingus drank some more whisky. Gloria thought he was getting a little drunk; his words were slightly slurred and his face looked unnaturally red and puffy.

"If I was to avoid disgrace, or worse, I had to dispose of those weapons. Fortunately, I happened to know a man who had the means to do that. His name was Whitney Bartholemew, and he was the neighborhood distributor for organized crime. The zamitat. I'd had dealings with him, of course—it's unavoidable."

"I know what you mean," Gloria said quietly. Mingus ignored her.

"So I approached him and explained my situation. He was not unsympathetic, and offered to help me in my hour of need. I asked him what he desired in return. Money? Official protection? His for the asking! Only he didn't ask for that. He wanted only one small, inconsequential thing in return for his assistance. He wanted my daughter."

Mingus turned to Gloria and offered her a self-deprecating smile. "Poetic, don't you think? Downright Shakespearean. I was like Shylock, crying, 'Oh, my daughter! Oh, my ducats!' Only I was the borrower, not the lender, and life was extracting its pound of flesh from my very heart. I was properly shocked and offended, of course, like the good father I pretended to be. But I knew as soon as he asked what my answer would be.

"Saffron was betrothed, at the time, to my friend and assistant, Cornell DuBray. I knew that Saffron would never understand, but that DuBray would, so I went to him. And like the master politician and bureaucrat I was, I proposed a plan that I knew would be acceptable to him. In return for my protection and patronage throughout his career at Dexta, he would break off his engagement to my daughter. And it would be done in such a way—as finely calculated as Admiral Bryant's attack at Savoy—that Saffron would, with my subtle encouragement, be thrown directly into the waiting arms of Whitney Bartholemew. And that is precisely the way it happened. A masterpiece of creative plotting, if I do say so myself—some of my finest work. Saffron was never to know, of course. And in the meantime, Bartholemew disposed of the weapons. I never knew just how or where until you and Ms. Nash unraveled the mystery this past week."

Mingus allowed himself some more whisky. "All very neat and tidy, you must admit. Except for one thing. After they were married, for some petty reason or another, Bartholemew told Saffron what had happened. You can imagine how she reacted. No, I suppose you don't have to imagine it. You already know. She hated me. And, whether intentionally or not, she passed that hatred on to her son, my grandson . . . with the tragic results you have seen. So you can add a few more to my score of one hundred and three million, two hundred and seventy-nine thousand, four hundred and ninety-one blighted lives—another two hundred from the terrorist attacks on Central. Plus two more."

Gloria squeezed his hand. She badly wanted to help him, to ease his pain, but she could think of nothing to say.

"I tried to speak to Saffron after my grandson was arrested," Mingus said. "But she wouldn't speak to me. She probably never will again. As for Whitney, there is little I can do for him. It's an Imperial matter, and the outcome of his trial is a foregone conclusion. They'll execute him for what he did and tried to do. Perhaps, in his perversity, that will even make him happy. He'll get to be a martyr."

Mingus sniffed and wiped away some more tears. "There is, perhaps, one thing I could do for him, and I briefly considered doing it. I could make a clean breast of it. Confess. Tell the Empire the truth about Savoy and my crimes."

"Norman, you can't do that!"

"Of course not. And I won't. Just an idle fantasy. No, I shall continue as before, but with the additional burden of knowing the irreparable harm I have done to my own family."

He looked into Gloria's eyes. "For fifty-four-and-a-half years, Gloria, not a single day has gone by when I have not thought of Savoy, when I have not felt the pain and guilt and remorse. I shall feel them to the end of my days."

"I'm so sorry, Norman," she whispered.

"Do you still want to run Dexta?" Mingus asked her. "Spirit willing, nothing like Savoy will ever happen to you. But if you truly seek that power, then it is all but guaranteed that something else will happen. Something uniquely yours, heartbreaking and inescapable. Having power means making decisions, Gloria, and because you are human, some of those decisions will be wrong—perhaps fatally so. And you will have to live with the consequences, with the responsibility for whatever tragedies are unleashed by your mistakes and frailties. With the best of intentions, I condemned a hundred million people, and because I was clever and selfish, I managed to evade the direct consequences of my actions. They fell, instead, on my family, and on total strangers. And yet, I know. *I know.* And you will, too."

"Oh, Norman," Gloria said softly.

Mingus managed to smile at her. "Thank you for listening to an old man's lachrymose confession, Gloria. I needed to tell someone. I'm sorry to have burdened you with this knowledge, and yet, perhaps it will help you to make the decision that you face. I love you, Gloria . . . like a daughter. And if you truly were my daughter, I think I would tell you to forget about power and responsibility and simply to live a happy and carefree life. Go be a smiling, glamorous Empress, and avoid the kind of pain I have known. That is what I would wish for you."

"You want me to leave Dexta?"

"I want you to be happy. And now, I find that I am very tired. Sweet dreams, Gloria."

"And to you, Norman."

He shook his head. "My dreams are never sweet," he said.

chapter 29

THE EMPEROR'S PERSONAL LASS ROSE FROM the grounds of the soccer stadium and into the air above Central. Gloria looked out of the windows, down at the sprawling city, and wondered what it would have looked like if Petra hadn't saved it. It would have looked, she realized, like Savoy.

Charles's speech had closed out, at long last, the Quadrant Meeting. Bureaucrats by the hundreds would soon be crowding the port and Orbital Station, bound for their distant domains, where they would carry on the endless work of empire. And the ordinary people of New Cambridge would get on with their lives, secure in the embrace of a government that had protected them from the unsleeping evils of the galaxy. Under a handsome young Emperor who loved his subjects.

"I hate making speeches like that," Charles said. "I don't mind the smaller, formal affairs so much, but these big, outdoor extravaganzas give me delusions of grandeur. I feel like Hitler at Nuremberg or Hazar at Golconda. I raise my arm and thousands cheer. I clear my throat, and thousands cheer. I could fart, and thousands would cheer."

"As long as it's cheers and not jeers," his cousin Larry said, "what are you complaining about?"

"Point well-taken," said the Emperor. "Still, the unreality and absurdity of it all bothers me. The Caesars used to have slaves who stood behind them, whispering, 'Thou art mortal,' or some such thing, just to keep their feet on the ground." He turned to look at Gloria and added, "But I'll have you to do that for me, won't I?"

Gloria smiled at him. "Maybe," she said.

"You've looked over the agreement my people prepared?"

"Glanced at it," Gloria said. "It looks pretty good, but I have some questions about a few of the specifics. We'll talk about it later."

"As you wish." Charles gave her a probing stare. "Is something wrong?" he asked.

Gloria shook her head. "I'm just tired," she said. "And I have a lot on my mind."

"I'll not press you, then." Charles went forward to chat with the pilot, while Gloria gazed out the window at the glowering cliff face and the churning waters below.

She had not slept at all last night following her meeting with Mingus. It had drained her emotionally and left her feeling adrift. To see Norman Mingus sobbing in grief and remorse was almost more than she could handle. And his final words of advice confused and unsettled her.

Even though the agreement Charles had offered promised her real power, she knew that the accomplishments of an Empress could never measure up to what she might do—had already done—at Dexta. The real power, the life-and-death power, would remain with Charles, as it had to. The weight of responsibility would fall only lightly on the shoulders of an Empress, and perhaps she might be vouchsafed the happy and care-free life that Mingus wished for her.

Poor Norman! She ached for him and wished that there were something she could do for him. She wondered how he had endured so much pain, for so long. Could she endure such a burden, or would it crush her?

Back on Mynjhino, less than two years earlier, she had saved, perhaps, millions of lives. The pride and satisfaction she felt were beyond description. Yet, how would she have felt if it had gone the other way? What if she had made some fateful, fatal mistake, and instead of saving millions, had killed them? Could she have lived with the knowledge, the guilt, the way Mingus had?

It hadn't happened that way. But someday, it might. According to Mingus, it almost certainly would, because she was human, and because Dexta offered the kind of power that few humans had ever possessed. Perhaps humans *shouldn't* have that much power. Maybe they should just turn the whole thing over to computers. The computers would probably make mistakes, too, but would they feel pain and guilt over it?

The anguish of Norman Mingus frightened Gloria. If a strong and good man like Mingus could be so tragically wrong, and so haunted by it, who was she to think she could do better, or as well? Did she really even want to try?

Dexta! Empress! She smiled to herself and thought, *Do I want to be a Lady or a Tiger? Which door should I open, which should I close?*

THE BROCKINBROUGH ESTATE SPRAWLED ALONG the cliff top north of Central, overlooking the narrow straits. The main building looked like a medium-sized museum, with columns and arches and domes, while the many outbuildings made Gloria think of a feudal village surrounding a castle. The LASS settled onto a vast greensward in front of the main building, and the occupants debarked amid much bowing, scraping, and fussing by the Brockinbroughs' liveried attendants. Black-clad Imperial Security personnel were much in evidence, but they didn't seem to have a lot to do. The Emperor's arrival was routine in every respect.

Larry and Gareth led Charles and Gloria into the building, playing at being tour guides. Larry explained that the original building had been constructed five hundred years earlier, with various new additions and appendages added as the centuries passed. Some artwork and sculptures by renowned artists were worthy of particular note, especially a life-size rendering of the Spirit that had been done in the early 2900s by Komari. "The Imperial Museum in Central has been begging us to let them have it," Larry said. "Good thing we didn't."

Charles nodded distractedly. Larry noticed the Emperor's lack of interest.

"Perhaps we should save the grand tour for another time," Larry said. "I can see that you and Gloria have other things in mind."

"Can't slip anything by you, can we?" said Charles, who had his arm around Gloria's waist.

"Allow me to conduct you to your quarters, then." It took nearly five minutes to reach them, but it was worth the wait. The bedroom was huge, with high, ornate windows overlooking the strait, and furnishings that would have done Louis XIV proud. The adjoining bathroom gleamed with late-Roman-era decadence.

"And then," Larry said, conducting them through another door, "there's this." He ushered them into a smallish room that was covered—floor, walls, and ceiling—in a deep blue plush fabric that was soft and bouncy. There were no windows or furniture, and only the single door. "A null-room built for two," Larry explained. "Enjoy. Gareth, let us leave our distinguished guests to their own devices—I'm sure they'll manage without us."

"The null controls are voice-activated," Gareth said as he and Larry left the room and closed the door behind them.

Charles turned to Gloria. "There, now," he said. "And you always say that Larry is a thoughtless and selfish jerk."

"He's probably got peepholes hidden somewhere around here," Gloria said.

"Then we should give him something to peep *at*, shouldn't we?" Charles pulled her close and pressed his lips against hers. When he began pulling at the thin fabric of her dress, Gloria backed away.

"One second," she said. She opened her handbag and spoke into her pad. "No messages or calls for the next three—make that four—hours. No exceptions." Then she put the bag down on the soft floor and looked at Charles. "I'm all yours, Chuckles."

"For four whole hours. I'd much prefer to measure our time together in years, Glory. Or decades."

"We're both too young to understand what decades mean," Gloria said, thinking of Mingus's five decades of anguish. "Maybe we should just concentrate on the present."

"I'm willing," Charles said. "But I need an answer, Glory. If not now, then soon."

"I know," she said. "And I'm sorry it's taken me so long. It's just that there's so much to think about." She grinned at him. "For what it's worth, I think you got Petra's vote last night."

"Charming young woman," he said. "I can see why you like her so much. But if I have the Petra Precinct locked up, perhaps I should do some more campaigning in *your* district."

"What did you have in mind? An Imperial Poll?"

"Interest is already rising," Charles said, "and I predict an imminent eruption of popular support. I intend to stuff your ballot box, my dear."

"Vote early and often," Gloria urged him.

Their garments were soon scattered around the room. They wrestled and writhed on the soft floor for a few minutes. Then Charles said, "Computer. We'd like to float about four or five feet off the floor."

There was a sudden soft hum, coming from all around them, and they clutched each other's bodies as the null field engaged and gently lifted them into the air. The field stabilized, and Gloria felt the soft pressure from above and below, caressing her like a warm bath. Charles skillfully orbited her, his fingers, tongue, and lips precisely mapping her prominences, bays, and declivities until, his circumnavigation complete, he made his final approach and accomplished his landing with confidence and finesse. They spun and twirled together, locked in a celestial embrace, like ancient gods or randy avian creatures. Gloria raked her fingernails across his back, inspiring redoubled Imperial ardor, until, at last, Charles grunted, growled, and gasped in the ecstasy of release, and Gloria followed him a moment later.

They clung to each other as the tide receded, content to float on the aimless currents like driftwood after a hurricane. Gloria sighed happily and wondered why it couldn't always be like this with Charles. Maybe, she thought, it could. Maybe . . .

She abruptly became aware that the door had opened, and Larry and Gareth were standing there, staring and grinning at them. Charles raised his head and snarled, "Just what the hell do you think you're doing, Larry?"

"What do I think I'm doing, good cousin?" Larry asked. "Why, I think I'm assassinating you!"

Before Charles or Gloria could respond, Larry manipulated some controls on a small electronic device in his hands, and suddenly the air pressed down on them. They fell to the floor with a heavy, jarring impact, but the pressure from above never relented. Gloria felt it crushing her downward against the soft blue of the floor, squeezing the very air out of her lungs. She fought against it, but she was immobilized by the tyrannical, invisible weight. Beside her, she could sense but not see Charles fighting his own futile battle against the enveloping force. She gasped for air but could find none.

"You're smothering them, Dad," said Gareth. "Here, let me." A moment later, Gloria felt the pressure lessening around her head, and she was able to open her mouth and gulp a hard-won breath. But the pressure on her chest and limbs never relented.

"Sorry," said Larry. "Gareth is much more adept with these gizmos than I am." Gloria managed to tilt her head upward enough to see that Gareth now had the control device in his own hands. Father and son continued standing just beyond their feet, smiling at them.

"Are you out of your mind?" Charles demanded in a labored gasp.

"Not in the least," Larry assured him. "I'm in complete possession of all my faculties, and I'm about to accomplish something that has never been done before. In the long and bloody history of our glorious Empire, many have assassinated *one* Emperor, but I shall be the first to have dispatched a second." He shook his head. "A pity the history books will never give me the credit I deserve."

Gloria was able to look toward Charles. "What is he talking about?"

Charles gritted his teeth and said nothing.

"He never told you?" Larry asked. "Not surprising, I suppose. Still, I think you should know the truth before you die. Do you want to tell her, Charles, or shall I?"

"You bastard!" Charles growled.

"Calling me names will get you nothing," Larry said.

He looked at Gloria. "Haven't you ever wondered about the Fifth of October?" he asked her. "Haven't you ever asked yourself why Charles was fortuitously away on Luna when the conspirators were doing their bloody work in Rio? Didn't it ever seem a trifle too convenient? No? Well, no matter. It never occurred to anyone else, either, thankfully."

"I don't believe it," Gloria said flatly.

"You should . . . shouldn't she, Charles?"

"You incredible son of a bitch! Let us go now and I'll forget about this."

"I think not," Larry replied. "Now, where was I? Oh, yes, the Fifth of October. You see, Gloria, I planned the whole thing. And, of course, Charles was in on it."

"I never did a thing, Glory!" Charles protested. "I swear it!"

"That's true," Larry conceded, "in a sense. I told him what I was going to do, and he never lifted a finger to prevent it from happening. He was content to let events take their course, and even cooperated to the extent of arranging to be elsewhere at the crucial moment. No, he never actually *did* anything—and that was his crime. My own crime was much more elaborate. Over the course of more than a year, I carefully set the whole thing in motion. I recruited and coerced my assassins, and gave them a vision of the glorious destiny that awaited them once they disposed of the dour and despicable Gregory. The coup would elevate them to power and end the corrupt dynasty of the Hazars, once and for all. I planned it out for them to the finest detail, and convinced them that they would be fools not to play the roles I had assigned them. Ah, it was a true thing of beauty!"

Gloria couldn't believe what she was hearing. Her fear multiplied as she realized that Larry was entirely serious.

"And," Larry continued, "once my cast of conspirators was in place, I assembled a second band of plotters whose task it would be to betray the first. Then—and here is the true genius of the thing—still a third group, to dispatch the second once their work was done. That third group, small and tightly organized, professional killers all, knew only what little I told them and vanished into the depths of the galaxy once their own job was concluded. The result of it all, of course, was a dead Emperor, with two dead sons and three dead nephews, and a stage full of dead and eternally silent conspirators, plus some living but embarrassed Imperial Security men who imagined that it was their own efforts that had aborted the coup. All of which left the throne to none other than the callow youth who now lies beside you, awaiting his own demise. Clever, don't you think?"

Gloria wanted to believe it was a lie, but couldn't. She could just glimpse Charles out of the corner of her eye, his face furrowed in impotent rage.

"Now," said Larry, "you might well ask yourself why I did all of this for the benefit of a young cousin whose company I enjoyed but whose rise to the throne would do me little good. That's a question you might have asked, as well, Charles. If you had any sense, you would have had me killed, but I was reasonably certain that you wouldn't. You're really a little too softhearted for your job. But you were convenient.

"I, of course, could never be Emperor, given my scarlet past. The Council of Lords would never have approved of it, nor would Parliament have confirmed my accession. Gareth was too young, then, so the throne would have passed to Cousin Andrew. He would have made far too clever and competent an Emperor—for my purposes—so it had to be you, Charles. You would serve as a competent placeholder until the time drew nigh for the second act of my little drama. Which it has."

"I almost did have you killed," Charles breathed. "Spirit help me, I should have."

"But you didn't, and now it's too late. We had some fun, cousin, but now it's time for you to die. Gareth, you see, is now of age. I'll step aside, and the Council of Lords will be so relieved to have me out of the way that they'll anoint my son without a second thought. Parliament will go along with it, and the people of the Empire will happily accept Gareth the First as their new Emperor, then get on with their lives."

"You'll never get away with it," Charles said.

Larry shook his head dismissively. "Of course I will," he said. "I did before, and this time it will be much simpler, much cleaner. No messy bodies lying about, no inconvenient doubts about what happened. Oh, I would have preferred not to have done it in my own home, but the opportunity was just too good to let pass. You see, the deaths of Emperor Charles V and his once and future wife will not be the result of assassination. No, it will be the tragic outcome of their well-known propensity for self-indulgence and sexual excess. Show them, Gareth."

Gareth held up a small, flexible bulb with a long tube extending from it.

"You know of Orgastria-29, of course," said Larry. "Well, this dispenser contains a new drug called Orgastria-48. Perhaps you've heard of it. It's not generally available yet because it can have some unfortunate side effects—death being one of them. When people crunch down on a dose of it, the sudden shock to their system, the sudden overload of sensory input, can be fatal. Some sort of neurological spasm, I gather, resulting in the shutdown of the autonomic nervous system. The brain stops functioning, the heart stops beating, breathing ceases, and death results within a few minutes."

Gloria managed not to cry out in joy and relief. She already had the neutralizer! It was right there in her handbag, just a few inches away from her left hip. But her relief died stillborn when she realized that it might as well have been on Earth. She was completely immobilized, and could not possibly reach the lifesaving antidote.

"Just to be sure, what we have here is a concentrated saline solution with what would probably be three or four times the ordinary dose, for each of you. I'm assured that this will be more than sufficient to terminate the vital processes. You see how it will look, don't you? When your bodies are found and examined, it will seem that our randy young Emperor and his famously lascivious ex-wife overindulged themselves, and tragically fucked each other to death. Lovely, don't you think?"

Charles seemed to strain against his invisible bonds but could make no headway. Finally, he relaxed and whispered, "I'm sorry, Glory."

Sorry didn't seem to cover it. Gloria said nothing and concentrated on trying to move her left hand. She managed to flex her fingers slightly, but true motion was still impossible.

"What else?" Larry absently asked himself. "Oh, yes. This room is soundproofed, so it will do you no good to yell or scream—but feel free. It's also shielded against electromagnetic emanations of any sort, so your wristcoms will be entirely useless. About two minutes after the drug is administered to you, the null field will automatically relax, so that your spasmodic death throes will look realistic. By then, of course, you won't even know what's happening. And, naturally, Gareth and I will be elsewhere at the moment of your death, with plenty of respectable witnesses to attest to our innocence and purity. That, I believe, covers just about everything. Any final words?"

Charles said nothing. Gloria strained against the null field to move her hand, but couldn't.

"No? Good, I wasn't looking forward to hearing

them. Well, then, Gareth? Be a good boy and go kill your uncle and his slut."

"Yes, Dad," Gareth said obediently. "Just a second, I gotta adjust the field first." He fiddled with the controls, and Gloria felt a slight contraction of the field. It seemed that the pressure along her left side had lessened, as if she were now on the very edge of the field's restricting influence. With a supreme effort, she managed to move her left hand an inch.

Gareth walked around them, skirting the field, then knelt next to Charles. "You'll never have an easy night's sleep, Gareth," Charles told him.

"Who the fuck cares?" Gareth asked. He reached out and clamped Charles's nostrils together between his left thumb and forefinger. Gloria watched, helplessly, as Charles pursed his lips together and held his breath as long as he could. But eventually, inevitably, he had to gasp for air, and when he did, Gareth quickly stuck the long tube into his mouth and squeezed the bulb.

Charles didn't react for the first few seconds, then suddenly jerked in a convulsive spasm. Only his heels and shoulders made contact with the floor as his body stiffened, arched, and quivered. He gave a strangled cry that sounded like Gloria's name, but then words gave way to mere animal sounds.

Gareth circled around Charles and approached Gloria. She tried to ignore him, ignore the convulsing man at her side, and place herself in a Qatsima mindset. She retreated inward, reaching out for the center of herself, where time and distance, matter and energy were all one. She felt Gareth squeezing her nose and readied herself for the precise sequence of actions she had plotted. There would be no more than a few seconds to act. When she knew she was as ready as she could make herself, she opened her mouth as if to gasp for air, even though she did not yet need to breathe. She felt the warm, salty liquid spraying against the back of

her throat, and at the same instant consciously closed
that passage. Another second went by, and she arched
her body in an imitation of what Charles had done. Her
left hand shot out and thrust into the open handbag. She
continued to jerk and writhe in her fake convulsion as
she frantically fumbled in the bag for the feel, the shape,
of the neutralizing lozenges.

Meanwhile, Gareth had gotten to his feet and made
his way around the null field, back to his father. They
stood together watching for another moment, then
Larry nodded and they left the room, closing the door
behind them.

Gloria had to breathe. Had to. As her fingers closed
around what she hoped was the neutralizer, she tried to
spit the deadly fluid out, but did a poor job of it. She instinctively gasped for air and felt the liquid trickling
down her throat. She focused all her concentration, all
her strength, on bringing her left hand up to her mouth.
It was almost there when the spasm struck. She stiffened and felt a surge of vast, infinite pleasure, far beyond sex or any other sensation she had known or
imagined. It pulled her ever onward into a gaping vortex. Not yet, not yet . . .

Without even seeing what was in her hand, she
managed to force the lozenge between her teeth. It
might have been the neutralizer, it might have been
more Orgastria-48. Whatever it was, she crunched down
on it.

The vortex pulled her in . . . then, just as suddenly,
spat her out. She gasped for air, felt it flowing into her
like life itself. Her body sagged down to the soft floor,
and for a long moment, she simply lay there and
breathed.

Charles! Next to her, he was still convulsing, still
making urgent, animal noises. She reached into her
handbag and came out with another lozenge, but it was
Forty-eight. She dropped the lozenge, tried again, and

saw that she had the neutralizer. With all the energy that remained in her, she tried to pull her hand up and reach toward Charles. But she couldn't make it. In the center of the null field, the force was simply too strong.

And then the field was suddenly gone. Charles's legs and arms flew out in jerking, electric motions, hitting Gloria hard. She ignored it and pressed the neutralizing lozenge between his lips. But in his spasms, his teeth were clamped shut. She could not get it into him. In an instant of inspiration, she squeezed his nostrils shut, as Gareth had done, and a few seconds later Charles's mouth opened in an instinctive gasp. Gloria shoved the neutralizer in, and his jaws closed on it, grinding it to dust.

chapter 30

LATE THAT EVENING, CHARLES TOOK GLORIA BY
the hand and led her out onto the greensward in front of
the main building of the Brockinbrough estate. "There's
something I want you to see," he told her.

He moved stiffly, painfully, like an old man. His
spasms had strained every muscle in his body, and
Gloria was gingerly in her own movements.

After the neutralizer had taken effect, they had lain
there on the floor of the null-room for what seemed a
long time, gradually collecting themselves, slowly coming back from the brink of death. Then they got to their
feet, with Gloria supporting Charles and helping him
to walk.

Larry was in the main drawing room, standing by a
mantel, next to his son. He was holding forth on some
trivial topic for a crowd of sycophants when he saw
them; his eyes bulged out and his lips moved wordlessly.
Charles looked at a black-clad Imperial Security agent,
pointed toward Larry and Gareth, and said, "Arrest
them." Then he collapsed.

They had hustled Charles into a bedroom, where Gloria told the Security men and the Imperial Physician what had happened. Then she, too, collapsed, more from relief than from the trauma she had endured. A few hours later, both of them were on their feet again.

Together, they went into a guarded room and confronted their would-be assassins. Neither Larry nor his son had anything to say, and even Charles didn't say much.

"We don't want a public scandal," Charles had told them. "It will be simple exile for both of you. You'll take your yacht directly to your lodge on Vymar Three. That's eight hundred light-years from Earth and safely out of the way. You'll have no visitors, and your communications will be monitored. You'll spend the rest of your lives there." He had stared at them for another moment, then turned and walked away from them.

Now, he and Gloria slowly made their way to the fence at the edge of the cliff. Charles pointed to the south, toward the glow of Central. "Any moment, now," he said.

Gloria watched and saw a point of light rising from the city, climbing toward the blackness of space above. It rose steadily for a few moments, then flared into sudden brilliance. A dim spray of sparks trailed slowly downward to the sea.

"It seemed the easiest way," Charles said to her.

Gloria nodded silently.

"Don't look at me like that," Charles said. "It seems to me that you did something similar on Sylvania, didn't you?"

"I didn't say anything," she replied. They stood together at the fence and looked out on the darkened strait.

Finally, Gloria said, "I won't be your Empress, Charles. Not now, not ever."

Charles slowly nodded his head. "I figured as

much," he said. "I just hope you can try to understand. I wanted to be Emperor, and I thought I could have it without paying a price."

"There's always a price," Gloria said. She thought of Norman Mingus. She thought of Ed Smith.

"Yes," said Charles. "There always is, isn't there?"

GLORIA SPENT THE NIGHT ALONE IN A BEDROOM at the Brockinbrough estate, then returned to Central the following morning without saying good-bye to Charles. She went up to her suite at the Imperial Cantabragian and found Petra and Jill waiting for her. From their drawn faces and grim expressions, she wondered if they had somehow heard what had happened. No, that was impossible. Then what . . . ?

"Gloria," Petra said softly, "I have some bad news. It's Elaine . . . she's dead."

Gloria stared at her. The words didn't make sense, didn't register.

"It happened last night," Jill said. "She was at a club, a null-room. Apparently she crunched down on some Orgastria-48. They administered a neutralizer, but somehow, it just didn't work. They couldn't revive her."

"Spirit!" Gloria breathed. Her head spun, her knees felt weak. For a moment, she thought she was going to be sick.

"We've taken care of . . . of the details," Petra said. "Her family will be notified, and she'll be sent home."

"Eli Opatnu was with her when it happened," Jill said in a flat tone of voice. "In case you want to ask him about it." Gloria looked at Jill and couldn't read the emotions on her face.

"And that brings up something else," Jill said. "I'm sorry to have to spring this on you at a time like this, but I think it's best if I just tell you now. Gloria, I'm leaving Dexta."

"What? But why? Jill . . ."

"I think I know why you shut down my investigation," she said. "I can add two and two, and I can spell. Eli's strange interest in the case. The way your Erik Manko problem suddenly disappeared. The way Eli kept me from getting a court order immediately, then failed to back me up when I tried to overturn the restraining order. And your sudden turnaround. It all adds up to one thing, Gloria, and you spell it with a Z."

"Jill—"

"Don't try to explain it," Jill said. "I don't want to hear you justifications and rationalizations. I just don't want to hear it. You can't be a little bit corrupt, Gloria, any more than you can be a little bit pregnant. You made your choice, now I've made mine."

"But, Jill—"

"I told you, I don't want to hear it!"

"Dammit, Jill! You're being foolish. Is it worth giving up your Dexta career because of . . . a minor impropriety? Jill, this is trivial!"

Jill pursed her lips. "Is that how you view it?" she asked. "Is that how you justify it?"

"For Spirit's sake, Jill, what are we talking about here? It's just a low-level scam, a little harmless graft. A few shipments evade taxes, a few Dexta people get paid off. Yes, I know it's wrong, but it's the way things work. Where's the harm?"

"How can you say that after what happened to Elaine?" Jill demanded.

"What? What are you talking about?"

Jill fixed her gaze on Gloria. "Harmless? Gloria, what do you think is *in* those shipments?"

Gloria opened her mouth, then closed it without saying anything. She stared at Jill and saw the anger and determination on her features. After a long moment, her face softened slightly. "Gloria, Petra," she said, "I'm sorry, but it's over. Good-bye." Jill turned quickly and stalked out of the room.

Gloria watched the door close behind Jill, then slumped down onto a sofa. She put a hand to her head, as if checking to see if it was still properly attached to the rest of her. She saw Petra standing next to her.

"I'm sorry," Gloria said, "but I'm afraid I have more bad news. You're not going to be Lady Petra."

Petra didn't react for a moment, then slowly nodded and managed a wan smile. "Easy come, easy go," she said. She sat down next to Gloria.

"I can't believe Elaine is gone," Gloria said. "If only I hadn't—"

"You can't blame yourself, Gloria," Petra insisted. "Elaine knew what she was doing."

"Yeah," Gloria said. "We all did."

THEY PACKED THEIR BAGS AND TOOK A TRANSIT up to the New Cambridge Orbital Station. Once there, they discovered that no Flyer or Cruiser was available. The departing Dexta bigwigs had taken them all, and Gloria and Petra were forced to book passage home on a commercial liner. The voyage took a week.

It was a mostly silent week. They shared a small stateroom and couldn't avoid each other, but spent most of their time reading or sleeping, or simply staring silently at the walls. Finally, on the fifth day, they began to talk, hesitantly at first, but then more openly, and finally, they told each other everything.

Petra went first, sharing her pain over what had happened with Pug and his family, and then her guilt and self-doubt over her attraction to and involvement with Whit Bartholemew. She felt cheap and weak and stupid, and yet, even now, she still felt a sense of loss and regret about Whit. She wondered what it said about her that she could fall for such a man.

"I did, too," Gloria said. And then she told Petra about Charles, and the rest of it. She recounted her approach to Ed Smith and explained her debt to the zamitat. Once she had started talking, she found that she couldn't stop, and went on to tell the story of Norman Mingus and his family. And Savoy. And finally, the story of Charles and how he became Emperor. For good measure, she added what Charles had done to the Brockinbroughs and what she had done a year earlier on Sylvania.

"Maybe you want out now, too," Gloria said when she had finished her story. "Maybe Jill had the right idea."

Petra shook her head. "No," she said, "I think I'll stay. OSI has already lost Pug and Jill and Elaine. If OSI is going to be the Fifth Quadrant, you'll need me."

"More than ever," Gloria affirmed.

"Gloria? You realize, don't you, that if you hadn't made your deal with this Ed Smith guy, we would never have known that the Savoy shipment was broken down into three loads? And without knowing that, I would never have been able to figure out where the weapons went. And if I hadn't figured that out, maybe I wouldn't have realized the truth about Whit. So your deal with the zamies probably saved a hundred million lives."

Gloria gave her friend a crooked smile. "You're just determined to see the bright side of everything, aren't you?"

"Oh, you know me—Little Petra Sunshine."

"Well, then, allow me to point out that you are much better off without Pug. He was a nice boy, but a boy is what he'll always be. His family will never let him grow up, or grow out of what they want him to be. And as for Whit—Spirit, Petra, the man spent twenty years fooling everyone! Even his mother. In the end, you were smarter than everyone else, and if anyone saved those hundred million lives, it was you."

Petra shook her head emphatically. "No," she said.

"He was going to press that button, Gloria. He really was. It was his mother who stopped him, not me."

Gloria thought about that, then said, "I should tell Norman. Maybe Saffron's hundred million somehow balances out Norman's on the family ledger. Maybe they can both find some peace now."

"Maybe we all can," Petra said.

THEY RETURNED TO EARTH AND TRANSITED down to Dexta Headquarters in Manhattan. But instead of heading for the street to walk back to their building, Gloria paused at the turnoff to the Transits to Brooklyn. "I'm going to spend a few days at my place on Long Island," she explained.

"Good idea," Petra said.

"Say hi to your mom for me. Tell her for me that she ought to be very proud of her daughter."

Petra grinned at Gloria. "Even if I'm not Lady Petra of Weehawken?"

"Hey, kiddo, you're a Dexta Twelve now! What more could anyone want from life?"

GLORIA QUICKLY MADE THE HOP TO BROOKLYN, picked up her Ferrari skimmer in the Dexta lot, and made her way home. Along the way, Billie Holiday kept her company, singing "God Bless the Child." She pulled into the carport of her house in the dunes, wandered aimlessly through the empty house, then went out to the pool and found, to her surprise, that she had a new tree growing in her yard. An exceptionally ugly tree. A note was pinned to it.

She opened the note. "The Imperial Gardener informed me that a simple cutting wouldn't work, so we brought in a whole tree from Belonna Five," it read, in Charles's flowing handwriting. "I hope it does you some good."

Gloria smiled and looked up at the gnarled, bony limbs, the ungainly proportions, and the bare branches. There were no leaves yet, but the roots looked strong and tenacious.

She walked over the dunes and down to the beach. The tide was low, and she had to walk a long way to reach the water's edge. She stared out to the gray, indeterminate horizon for a long, silent time, thinking no particular thoughts. Then she reached into her pocket and pulled out a handful of purple lozenges. She stared at them for a moment, then threw them as far as she could, into the cold ocean waters. Then she turned and walked back across the dunes and sat down to think and remember, in the comforting shadow of her glashpadoza tree.

About the Author

C.J. Ryan lives and works in Philadelphia.

Gloria Van Deen may have achieved her Fifth
Quadrant, but can she stand up against an alien
civilization which is determined *not* to become
part of humanity's empire?

Don't miss Gloria's next exciting adventure in

BURDENS
OF EMPIRE

by

C. J. RYAN

Coming in Fall 2007 from Bantam Spectra

Here's a special preview:

BURDENS
OF EMPIRE
On Sale Fall 2007

LORD KENARBIN CUT A SPLENDID FIGURE AS he stepped out onto the dock, and he knew it. He was tall and trim, strikingly handsome, with medium-length silver hair curling over the tops of his ears and piercing blue eyes that commanded the attention of all who fell under their gaze. His strong, slightly bony nose suggested Hazar blood, while his smooth, swarthy complexion implied a complex genetic heritage. In his ninety-seventh year, he looked as virile and vigorous as a man half his chronological age.

Kenarbin carried himself with a diplomat's aplomb and a drill-sergeant's precision. His shiny black knee boots, form-fitting white breeches, and gold-trimmed, deep-blue tunic were accented by the diagonal red sash draped across his torso, signifying his Imperial mandate. His features automatically assumed a familiar, well-practiced mien of amiable determination and boundless self-confidence. He paused and stared into the middle distance for a few moments in order to let the swarm of media imagers record his arrival.

Aside from the gaggle of media reps and the cluster of official greeters, both human and native, there was not a lot to see. His Cruiser had splashed down in a broad, sluggish river, brown and oily—the local Mississippi or Amazon, he supposed. The dun-colored landscape offered little in the way of vegetation or relief, and the chill, steady wind sweeping in from the river felt unfriendly and forbidding. The sky was cloudless but yellowed from its cargo of dust and debris, and the single cold star provided a weak, unflattering orange radiance.

In the distance, the dark towers and crenellated walls of the city looked medieval, and the smaller structures dappling the plain could have been the huts and hovels of serfs. A patina of age clung to the place, a reminder of the weary millennia of experience boasted by this civilization, which had achieved star-travel when humans were still scrimmaging with Neanderthals and mammoths. Yet it was this world that had been conquered and occupied by the upstart humans and their burgeoning Empire—an outcome emphasized by the sheltering canopy of military vehicles that patrolled the ugly sky above.

Denastri, he thought. Well, he'd seen worse.

Kenarbin took it all in, then turned to face his welcoming committee and offered them a hearty smile. It was met by unsteady grins from the humans and blank, impassive gazes from the indigs—Empire slang for indigenous species. The Denastri, he had been told, were not a demonstrative race, and the expressions on their alien faces might have meant anything at all, or nothing.

We are not welcome here.

The unavoidable thought did not trouble Kenarbin unduly. Humans weren't really welcome in most places they went. It didn't matter. The Empire was here, and it was here to stay. It was Kenarbin's job to get the locals to accept that immutable fact. *They don't have to like us, and we don't have to like them.*

Lord Kenarbin had been coming to places like this

for more than half a century, representing the Empire with skill and imagination. In the process, he had become something of a legend, having pulled Imperial fat from fires that might have consumed lesser negotiators. His reputation was well and justly earned, and if the job had become familiar from repetition, it remained a point of pride to do it to the best of his considerable ability. These days, Emperors used him sparingly, recognizing that his very presence magnified the significance of any mission on which he embarked: Kenarbin was here because Denastri was important, and Denastri was important because Kenarbin was here.

Three years earlier, in a swift and relatively bloodless little war, the Imperial Navy had smashed the small, antique Denastri fleet, putting an abrupt end to thirty thousand years of conflict within the minor grouping of stars known to Terrans as the McGowan Cluster. While the local tides swept endlessly back and forth between the Denastri and their neighbors, a millennium of relentless human expansion had finally brought the Terran Empire to the doorstep of the McGowan Cluster, 1,053 light-years from Earth, and henceforth the locals would have to behave themselves. The backwater world of Denastri, and everything on it or under it—particularly the latter—now belonged to the Empire. His Imperial Highness Charles V had decreed peace, and peace there would be.

Some of the locals had refused to believe or accept this turn of events, and even the presence of a division of Imperial Marines had failed to convince the holdouts. If anything, the sputtering insurgency had picked up steam in the preceding year, making life uncomfortable and dangerous for the Terrans who had come here for the sake of Imperial power and corporate profits.

The indigs, in any case, were a fractious lot, split three ways and as eager to slaughter one another as their human overlords. Instead of meekly bowing before the overwhelming might of an Empire that spanned two thousand light-years and encompassed 2,673 worlds with a population exceeding three trillion, some of them remained determined to fight on, heedless of the consequences for themselves or their lackluster little world. Kenarbin had come to reason with them.

Sanjit Blagodarski, the Imperial Governor, stepped forward and extended his right hand. Kenarbin clasped it in both of his.

"Welcome to Denastri, Lord Kenarbin," said the Governor.

"Thank you, Governor. Good to see you again, Sandy. You're looking well."

His first lie, less than a minute after setting foot on the planet. In fact, Blagodarski looked awful. Drawn and frazzled, he seemed to have aged twenty years during the ten since they had last met. The Governor shrugged off the obvious falsehood with a weak smile and introduced his Imperial Secretary, a Level XII Dexta functionary named Freya Benitez, and the commanding officer of the Occupation Task Force, General Steven Ohashi. The general gave Kenarbin a crisp military nod along with a firm handshake. "Glad you're here, Milord," said Ohashi. That, in itself, struck Kenarbin as an ominous note. Marines were seldom happy to see diplomats on their turf.

"And now," said Blagodarski, "it is my privilege to present the Premier of Denastri. Honored Premier, may I present Lord Kenarbin?"

The alien stepped forward and extended a four-fingered hand, which Kenarbin took in his. Its flesh felt cold.

"Vilcome to our furled," said the Premier, with obvious effort.

"Thank you, Honored Premier," Kenarbin replied as he stared into the dark vertical slits of the alien's eyes. The creature was vaguely humanoid—two arms, two legs, nearly as tall as Kenarbin. But its face was narrow and noseless, with large, drooping triangular ears, sallow skin, a sharp, pointed chin, and a mouth that would have looked at home on a rainbow trout. The vertical almond-shaped eyes seemed to be all pupil, and looked like the entrances to shadowy, unexplored caverns. From a narrow, bony crest at the top of its head sprouted a long shank of blue-black hair, braided and bound with thin colored threads. The Premier's clothing consisted of a belted saffron-colored robe that fell nearly to the ground.

Kenarbin released the Premier's hand and touched a stud on his tunic, activating the translation software on the computer pad in his pocket. "Honored Premier," he said, "I bring sincere and heartfelt greetings from His Imperial Highness, Emperor Charles V." He paused to let the Premier's own pad translate his words into the fluid, tonal language of the Denastri, then continued. "The Emperor has asked me to convey his deep personal gratitude for your service to the Empire, and to your world. He expresses his confidence that, working together, we shall restore peace and prosperity to his loyal subjects on the rich and beautiful world of Denastri."

He paused again as the Premier absorbed the translation. Kenarbin studied the Premier's face carefully, but could detect no identifiable reaction. After a moment, nictitating membranes closed in from the sides of the Premier's eyes in an approximation of a blink. Then the Premier spoke in a flowing, almost musical passage that was pleasant but incomprehensible to human ears.

The computer rendered the translation in a soft, precise, androgynous voice. "You are mostly kind to be here, generous Lord," it said. "The words of Imperial Highness Fifthborn Charles are registered in deep appreciation by this humble Thirdborn. Peace and prosperity inspire all to high wishfulness. It is a goodness."

Kenarbin frowned and furrowed his brow. He had been warned that the translation software was still a work-in-progress, but he had hoped for something better than this.

"A goodness, indeed, Honored Premier," Kenarbin said. "I look forward to working with you to make it so."

"Yes," the Premier responded. "Work will make good. We will build again that which has fallen and return—*unknown word*—to Denastri and the felicitations of Fifthborn Charles and his grasping Empire. Yes."

Kenarbin glanced at the Governor, who tilted his head a little and offered a wan smile. "You'll get used to it, Milord," he said.

"I think I know what he's saying," Kenarbin said. "I just wish I could be sure that he knows what *I'm* saying."

Blagodarski shrugged. "We manage," he said. "For the most part. We should be on our way now, Milord. We'll have you safely into the Compound in a few minutes. It's not wise to linger too long in an exposed position like this."

"It isn't? Why not?"

"Because we make too good a target, Milord," General Ohashi explained.

"It's not as bad as it sounds," Blagodarski hastily added.

"The hell it isn't," Ohashi mumbled under his breath. The Governor gave him a sharp, reproving glance, but Ohashi looked away, focusing his gaze on the far side of the river, as if searching for snipers.

Kenarbin nodded. "I see," he said. "In that case, gentlemen, ladies, Honored Premier, perhaps we should continue our discussion in the Compound. I look forward to seeing your capital city, Honored Premier. I understand that it is older than any on Earth."

"Earth is young," the Premier agreed. "Denastri is blessed with the continuing wisdom of all our time. Perhaps you will learn—*unknown word*—from us, Lord Kenarbin. A goodness."

"Undoubtedly," said Kenarbin. "A goodness."

The party began moving along the dock. Kenarbin noticed that the dock was flanked by squads of armed, helmeted Marines, who snapped to attention as he passed. Ahead, surrounding a small fleet of limo skimmers, the Marines were accompanied by what appeared to be native Denastri troops, hefting Terran plasma rifles. They were noticeably taller than the Premier and their skin was more orange than yellow.

"Fourth- and Fifthborns," Blagodarski said as they walked. "Warrior caste."

Kenarbin nodded. "Fine-looking troops," he said to the Premier, who seemed momentarily confused by the comment and didn't respond immediately.

After a few moments, the Premier said something that the computer rendered as "Beauty is in the eye of the beholder."

Kenarbin, surprised, looked at Blagodarski. "The software has trouble with clichés," the Governor explained. "Garbage in, garbage out, I suppose. Not that what you said was garbage, Milord."

"Perish the thought," Kenarbin replied with a chuckle.

At that instant, a dazzling burst of intense white light blinded him. A split second later, he was deafened by the thunderous crack of a concussion device. Stunned and all but senseless, Kenarbin felt hands grabbing at him, clutching his arms, and dragging him, then lifting him. He flailed out uselessly and shouted something equally useless, then felt himself being thrown bodily into what must have been the backseat of one of the limo skimmers. Someone shoved him down onto the floor of the vehicle, and he felt it lifting and moving.

Security, he thought. *They're getting me out of here.*

Sound and sight gradually returned. He tried to turn over and push himself up, but found himself being pushed back down against the floor. "What's happening?" he demanded, his own words sounding faint and distant. He could hear no response, and saw nothing but a blurred smudge of maroon carpeting, an inch from his nose.

Kenarbin calmed himself. There had been other attempts on other worlds, and he knew the routine. Security people would treat him like a sack of highly valuable potatoes until they were certain that the threat had passed. Annoying but necessary. He could hear the high-pitched whine of the skimmer now, competing with the ringing in his ears. He wondered if the Governor and the Premier were safe.

Minutes went by, and he felt the lurching, darting progress of the skimmer. It seemed to him that they ought to have reached the Compound by then. He managed to twist around a little and turned his head to look up. He expected to see burly Marines on the seat above him. Instead, he found himself looking into the narrow, orange-tinted face of one of the Denastri warriors.

"What's happening?" he asked again. "Where are you taking me?" The Denastri offered no response. Possibly, he had no translation device and didn't understand.

Kenarbin again tried to push himself up from the floor, but the warrior rudely shoved him back down. The first tickle of fear and suspicion began to dance at the edges of his mind.

"Dammit, what the hell is going on here?"

The Denastri leaned forward a little and stared down at him. The alien eyes looked placid and unsympathetic. "You is ours," it said in Empire English.

"What? What do you mean by that?"

"Vord is 'hostage,' yes?" the warrior asked.

Comprehension flooded into Lord Kenarbin in a cold, unwelcome wave.

"Yes," he said at last, "that's the word."

THE SUN GLARED IN NORMAN MINGUS'S FACE, bright enough to be annoying, even through the polarized panoramic dome. Poised just above the irregular peaks on the north rim of Shackleton Crater, its unrelenting radiance was an imposition on an old man's eyes, and gave Mingus yet another reason to resent the necessity of these semi-annual excursions to the South Pole of Luna. He envied Charles, sitting opposite him on the far side of the three-tiered circular amphitheater where the

Imperial Oversight Committee was pleased to hold court. The solar inferno was comfortably positioned behind the young Emperor's right shoulder, and he had to face only the less constant, if much closer, fires of angry Parliamentarians.

The Empire was in trouble. Mingus had known it for decades, but had hoped—naively, perhaps—that the inevitable reckoning could be postponed beyond his time. Let the next generation deal with it. His own generation had seen enough sorrow and tumult and, Mingus believed, deserved a respite. He had labored to see that they got it, and his efforts had resulted in a half-century of relative peace and prosperity.

But the Terran Empire, like others before it, was a victim of its own success. With the conquest of the Ch'gnth Confederacy in 3174, the last remaining external threat to the Empire had been removed. For a thousand light-years beyond Imperial space, in every direction, no existing power was capable of thwarting the continued expansion of the Terrans. There were, to be sure, a few minor impediments, like the fledgling Gumnaki Hegemony, waiting a couple of hundred light-years beyond the Frontier in Sector 4. The Gumnaki—a race of vast pretensions and minimal subtlety—had carved out a mini-empire of forty or so worlds, but they posed no immediate threat. The Empire would have to fight them someday, Mingus presumed, but probably not on his watch. The outcome, in any case, would be a foregone conclusion. The same applied to the handful of other races that might object to the onward march of *Homo sapiens*.

Paradoxically, it was the very absence of an external threat that now imperiled the Empire. Many historians, Mingus knew, held that it had been the rise of Islam in the seventh century that had forced the consolidation and forged the power of modern Europe. It was not until after the temporary decline of Islam that the Europeans, deprived of a strong external enemy, fell upon themselves in two centuries of fratricidal insanity, polluting the historical record with names like Napoleon and Hitler, Verdun and Auschwitz. The later fall of the Soviet Union had much the same effect on the Americans, who built their doomed empire without ever admitting to themselves what they were doing. The Terran Empire, at least, harbored no illusions about what it was and what it meant to achieve.

But without the balance and focus provided by external powers, the whirling centrifugal forces inherent in so vast an empire were bound to tear it apart someday. Mingus, a lifelong student of history, knew that the larger an empire grew, the harder it was to govern. He also understood mathematics. The old Earthly empires only had to deal with two dimensions, but the Terran Empire was condemned to grapple with three. Thus, the Empire, 2,000 light-years in diameter, comprised some 4.2 *billion* cubic light-years of space, with a surface area on the Frontier of 12 million square light-years—all of which had to be patrolled and policed. If the task was not inherently impossible, it was certainly daunting.

Mingus accepted the implications of the unforgiving math but Charles, alas, did not. Charles was the third Emperor he'd had to deal with during his time in office, and by far the most difficult. Bumbling old Darius had paid little attention to the niggling little details of his realm, which was probably just as well. Gregory hadn't been around long enough to make any difference. But Charles, now in his seventh year as Emperor, was young, arrogant, and ambitious. At thirty, he was finally showing some signs of maturity; perhaps the recent birth of Henry, his son and heir, had something to do with that. Yet his essential character was unlikely to change, and Mingus knew that at his core, Charles was a cold, ruthless son of a bitch. *Takes one to know one,* Mingus wryly conceded. Age might mellow Charles, but it was not likely to improve him.

As the meeting droned onward with the dramatic speed and force of an oncoming glacier, Mingus focused his attention on Charles, who wore an expression of intense and genuine pain on his handsome face. Emperors, like other men, were capable of the most basic of human emotions—even love.

Two years earlier, Charles had attempted and failed to win the return of his ex-wife, the glamorous and popular Dexta official Gloria VanDeen. Mingus didn't know the details of her rejection of his offer of remarriage and elevation to Empress, but he had sensed a profound change in Charles following the episode. He could have any woman in the Empire except for the one he wanted most, and the realization must have seared his soul in some deeply painful way. The private man, Mingus supposed, must have surrendered some essential part of himself to the public figure; Charles had been thwarted, but Charles V could not be. Under pressure to produce an heir, he had wanted Gloria for his Empress and the mother of his son. Denied his desire, he had swiftly turned in another direction and taken Lady Patricia Kenarbin as his Consort. Not Empress, but Consort. Some Emperors never married at all, and were content to sire their successors with a Consort; Charles, it seemed, would be one of them. He didn't need an Empress; he didn't need Gloria; he didn't need love.

And yet, he seemed to have found it anyway. Mingus could not gauge the depth of Charles's feelings for Lady Patricia, but he suspected that it was considerable, and had probably come as a surprise even to Charles. It happened that way sometimes, for some men. And whatever his feelings for Patricia, there was no doubt about his intense attachment to young Henry.

The last time Mingus had seen them together, the Imperial Heir had cutely puked on the shoulder of his Imperial Dad. Charles had merely laughed, and Mingus, a veteran of five marriages and many children, considered it the most human moment he'd ever seen Charles experience. For a moment, Mingus almost liked him.

Now Lady Patricia was in anguish over the fate of

her father, and Charles the man was clearly at odds with Charles the Emperor. What Charles would gladly do for the woman he loved, Charles V could not do. Man and Emperor were trapped together in a golden web that circumscribed his actions as surely as it bound his heart. Charles was no less a hostage than Kenarbin, and no conceivable negotiation could free him.

AS THE MEETING FINALLY BROKE UP AND PEOple drifted off to the buffet, one of the Emperor's aides approached Mingus; Charles wanted to have a word with him. Mingus found him standing alone on the upper tier, staring down into the perpetually shadowed depths of Shackleton Crater. Ice-mining machinery was moving around on the floor of the crater like aimless glowworms.

"How is Lady Patricia holding up?" Mingus asked him.

Charles glanced up. "She tries to put on a brave face, but I know it's killing her. She's not used to this sort of thing. She always led a pretty sheltered life at Court."

"She's Bill Kenarbin's daughter," Mingus pointed out. "She'll be as strong as she has to be."

Charles nodded. "She's only twenty-one," he said. "Sometimes I wonder if I did her a favor by choosing her."

"I'm certain that she thinks you did, Charles. What's more, you did yourself a favor."

The Emperor smiled a little. "Even a blind hog finds the occasional acorn," he said. The smile faded. "Norman? I need to ask you for something. Something difficult."

"I'm at your service, Highness."

"Maybe not this time. I want him back, Norman. I want my son to have a grandfather, and Trish to have a father. This is tearing me up inside. I've never..." He trailed off and shook his head.

"It's different when you have a family," Mingus said.

"Isn't it just? I had no idea, I truly didn't. I never really knew my own parents. Just as well, probably. My father was an idiot, and my mother...well, you knew her."

"It isn't easy, being a Hazar. They meant well, Charles."

"I don't want somebody telling Henry the same thing about me someday, Norman. He was a bastard, but he meant well. Spirit! It's not enough just to *mean* well. I want to *do* well. For both of them."

"What do you want from me, Charles?"

The Emperor looked the Dexta Secretary in the eye and said, "I want you to send Gloria to Denastri and get him back."

Mingus was genuinely shocked by the Emperor's words. He wanted to ask if he was serious, but there was no doubt that he was.

"I know what you're going to say, Norman. You can't do it officially. I understand that. But, dammit, Gloria gets *results*!"

"She does," Mingus agreed.

"I wouldn't ask this if there were any other way. You know that."

"I do." Mingus returned Charles's steady gaze, and for a few moments, neither of them spoke.

Charles ran a hand through his dirty-blond hair and shook his head. "She's infuriating and impossible, but somehow she always gets the job done. She wouldn't do it if I asked her, but maybe you can find some appropriate excuse to send her to Denastri. From what I hear, the Dexta staff there are at one another's throats. Isn't that the kind of thing she's supposed to handle? Strategic interventions, and all that?"

"It is," Mingus said, giving a small nod. "To tell you the truth, I've even considered it myself. She might be able to knock some heads together and at least get everyone on the same page. But as for Kenarbin...I can't ask her to do that, Charles. Not officially, and not even unofficially."

"Well, could you at least *suggest* it?"

"When a Dexta Secretary makes a suggestion, a Level IX can hardly avoid taking it as an order. No, Charles, I can't ask her, and I won't suggest it. There's only one person who can ask her."

Charles nodded and took a deep breath. "Then," he said, "I suppose I must."